NEW 9·99

BOOKWORM READ & RETURN £6·99.

GW00600586

121 DAYS OF URBAN SODOM

JACQUELINE PHILLIPS

DIVA

All characters in this novel are fictitious and any resemblance
to real persons, living or dead, is purely coincidental.

First published 2004 by Diva Books,
an imprint of Millivres Prowler Limited, part of the Millivres Prowler Group,
Spectrum House, Unit M, 32-34 Gordon House Road, London NW5 1LP
www.divamag.co.uk

Copyright © 2004 Jacqueline Phillips

Jacqueline Phillips has asserted her right to be identified as the author of this work
in accordance with the Copyright, Designs and Patents Act 1988

A catalogue record for this book is available from the British Library

ISBN 1-873741-94-4

All rights reserved. No part of this book may be reproduced, stored in
a retrieval system, or transmitted, in any form or by any means, including
mechanical, electronic, photocopying, recording or otherwise, without
the prior written permission of the publishers.

Printed and bound in Finland by WS Bookwell

Distributed in the UK and Europe by Airlift Book Company,
8 The Arena, Mollison Avenue,
Enfield, Middlesex EN3 7NJ
Telephone: 020 8804 0400

Distributed in North America by Consortium,
1045 Westgate Drive, St Paul, MN 55114-1065
Telephone: 1 800 283 3572

Distributed in Australia by Bulldog Books,
PO Box 300, Beaconsfield, NSW 2014

Book One

Day One

I made you a promise and I've never broken my promises to you. I promised you a book. You no longer wanted me, but still you wanted certain sections of my mind. Maybe you can peel me and remove the segments you want and discard the rest. Unfortunately, you don't possess that control over what my mind expresses and I laugh at the irony I possess the same as you. I have a title, a title and a copy of the Marquis de Sade's *One Hundred and Twenty Days of Sodom*.

Like a scientist possessed, I've not seen media nor performed the mediocrity of chores for weeks, my hair permanently tousled, threads committing mutiny from my clothes. Most people deal with lost love affairs with chocolate, hairstyles, diets, mad weeks spent calling clairvoyants, but after seven months and one novel the pain still won't leave me. I will give myself one hundred and twenty-one days and, my love, you must take one hundred and twenty-one days to read your bequest.

Initially I began to read from the beginning. The Arrow version of *One Hundred and Twenty Days of Sodom* begins with a critique by Simone de Beauvoir. From her pretentious waffle I expect *One Hundred and Twenty Days of Sodom* to be a political, philosophical and erotic masterpiece, repulsive but profound. Simone de Beauvoir reveres de Sade as a revolutionary, ahead of his time, with insight to match that of Freud. A fighter for freedom, a philosopher of social mores. My next readings include the beginning of *One Hundred and Twenty Days of Sodom*, followed by random pages in the middle, a break to clear my head, then by the later pages.

Repelled? De Sade doesn't write well enough to arouse repulsion. Sixteen children are kidnapped to partake in orgies by the main characters. The

Bastille begins by containing forty-six people, sixteen people survive. De Sade has written a snuff log, a catalogue of torture, resulting in snuff. His "heroes" are no different from twentieth-century rings who take to the streets luring teenage boys and girls, taking them to another country to rape, bugger, flog and torture in every possible way, before killing. Killing often through sexual acts, being left to bleed to death, asphyxiation, exhaustion, drugs, starvation, dehydration, boys and girls fucked to death and sometimes recorded on film. De Sade didn't have access to a camera, or webcam, so he wrote. His writing is no more eloquent than the present-day acts of snuff. He merely possessed a wider, aristocratic vocabulary. Not an erotic vocabulary or a lulling seductive style: his style was eighteenth-century sleaze, which, were it not so violent and incestuous, might arouse on a primal level. De Sade has succeeded possibly by his breeding in doing what no twenty-first-century person can: he has written and has published and printed a snuff novel, openly available to buy, in the guise of academic interest. Interest in what? De Sade is not original: he writes what turns him on, because presumably no other snuff novels were readily available. His novel consists of sodomy, sodomy inclusive of all. Eight fuckers are brought to bugger the eight boys and the four "heroes". The children, girls and boys, are ritually sodomised. De Sade introduces another favourite theme, all the wives of the heroes are the daughters of another hero and were initially buggered by their fathers before the "marriages". Thus are the constituents of the novel, incest, sodomy, violence, children and snuff.

I rub my temples, agonising over how it began – you, me, the ending, de Sade. I'm trying to make sense, retrace my steps, and now de Sade's steps, we have a *ménage à trois*.

Accidental meeting
My curiosity had awoken to cybersex, not as a lusting, just to satisfy a curiosity at an opportune moment. My body was prepared for fulfilment regardless of the screen flashing into life; pressing against the chair as I loaded www.yahoo.com, then entered sex chat into the search box. My fingers massaged the mouse up and down the screen

and for no apparent reason I clicked www.thesexguide.com. This led me to thesuburbs.com chatrooms and an array of choices. The lounge, the hot tub, the bedroom, the nest, the dungeon, erotic chat and so on, maybe twenty rooms. I settled on the lounge. I am an educated professional woman, but no one was watching, no one was pointing a finger, questioning why I was in a sex site, questioning why I was in a straight room, rather than the lesbian nest. Like de Sade I was free. I had choice. I entered as Fem, wanted to keep the anonymity and this freedom I so liked. Someone clicked on Fem, I don't know who, some guy, and, in the private reserves of a two-way transcript, he typed his hardness out to ejaculation and I typed out multiple.

I used my usual nick, "Girl", when not cybering, which occurred only five times, until I realised reality was preferable and masturbation preferable in its solitude. I'm insular in my pleasure; I have no wish to assist another unless she is real, in front of me and I want her. Girl hung and charmed the nest, until I tired of the monotonous pleasantries and false gestures. People hugged total strangers seemingly oblivious of the fact that they were totally alone with their PCs, not hugging the walls, let alone a person. People "fell in love", had relationships with total strangers, a nom de plume typing from across the other side of the world, who could've been an overweight middle-aged man in Montana pretending to be a cheerleader, or a toothless granny from Carlisle pretending to be a power-dressing lipstick lesbian.

I came to realise that the dungeon and some of the rooms beneath it were domination and submission rooms. My experience of such had been professional dominatrices in some murder drama or other on the television. Osiris and I spent the next couple of weeks analysing and mocking the patrons of the dungeon while on MSN at the same time as being in the room. Our conversations frequently went:

Woman: Ha she called you Sir! Oh hello Sir.
Osiris: Yes slave

Woman: Grrrrrrr I'm no slave!

Osiris: Well, don't call me Sir. Damn subs, they think I'm in denial, they won't believe I'm not a Dom.

I had been working until the early hours, when I logged onto the site for a break; the dungeon was empty apart from you, Colette. I did my usual ironic ice throwing, while you stared drunkenly at the screen, occasionally interjecting with snippets about yourself: you were twenty-eight, a law postgraduate. I was fascinated, didn't know why, just knew I wanted to talk with you more.

The first day of Sodom begins with adulation of leather.

Leather is skin on skin. The overpowering of animal, her carcass, left to dry, then treated, but still the smell of power and death remains. A smell so intoxicating, new leather sucks the oxygen from my mind causing migraine if exposed too long. An aroma that floods every sense, opening the veins to bursting, rushing the life substance to swell every nerve ending at the mere scent. A texture so soft, or hard, depending on preference. Soft curved around your hips so well, thin shards pushing against your swollen rise, evidence of your arousal seeping onto the black. Leather merged with liquid trickling from within you. Black leather adorning your flesh outside, interacting with your want inside, containing it. I could lie for ever, my head on your thigh, just falling into intoxication from the leather and you, your scent, your arousal. Watching you strain against the powerful black material, a fight between your powerful lust and its powerful binds. Watching you cover the thin straps with your delicate potent gloss, turning its matt to shine, a trail of sunlight illuminating your writhing lust. Oh, how I could watch for hours, sit beneath your sensual lily thighs and laze my head against you, but just far enough away, while you read erotica, neither of us touching each other or herself. My swollen nib throbbing against silk, your lips claret against black, pushing the leather out towards me, teasing us both.

When you've finished reading you push me to the other side of the room and caress yourself into the leather, circling around your skin and the black skin covering you, running your finger along the tight binds, nourishing the flesh with your silky dubbing, rubbing in the transparent gel and droplets of white, feeling your pushed-out lips beneath your finger and just a slight escape of your swollen hard bud, pressing desperately to reach your digit, trying to force the black bonds loose. You writhe urgently, your cunt contracting against wisps of leather, trying to consume, take it within you. Your hands drift lower, but you find a wall of leather, rendering your cunt and arse inaccessible, only able to throb and demand against their powerful captive.

The straps could be loosened, but this is an accolade to that sensuous texture and you like teasing yourself for days, bringing to a peak, then stopping, arousing your mind to giddy euphoria, releasing only when lust cascades your body, her waves unrelenting.

Day Two

The fourth time I read *One Hundred and Twenty Days of Sodom* I almost passed out. One of the narrators, an old crone, was describing in the shortest of paragraphs a variety of killing techniques. These ranged from injecting with a venereal disease to frigging a woman to death. Incidentally, de Sade uses frigging to include any kind of masturbation, manipulating a phallus, anus, and, in this case, it refers to a rubbing of the woman's clitoris, not the definition of frigging I am familiar with, which is vaginal fingering. I find de Sade's fascination with death and destruction difficult. There is a certain instinctual excitement in violence and death, but not the same excitement as lust, and de Sade's deaths are neither violent nor passionate, but slow and premeditated. One includes a woman buried from the waist down until she slowly rots to death.

After the giddiness had passed, I put the novel down for a while, and considered the research of Masters and Johnson, who found that women are capable of orgasming until boredom or tiredness overtakes. I wonder how a woman can be orgasmed to death, and conclude that her body would have stopped reacting days before her death, which was probably from loss of blood after the persistent friction burned away her flesh down to her artery. I consider whether she gained any pleasure at all before her death, as men's fingers are not designed or trained for the female form. How absurd that my thoughts give contemplation, thus credence, to a piece of psychotic fiction. Far more valuable are my questions as to how de Sade could gain pleasure from a one-way interaction. The pleasure from sex is the arousal, lust and enjoyment of the other person. Yet the emotion and reactions of de Sade's vessels are rendered impotent. Maybe this is a gender difference or maybe de Sade became so insular after years of incarceration that he trained himself to derive pleasure from immobilised blank objects, human, but dehumanised, and human only in that texture and imagery gave the greater satisfaction.

De Sade wrote fantasies, not realities. His actual experiences consisted of flagellation of and by prostitutes and molestation of innocents. Thought is always more extreme than action, because it can omit boundaries other than those set by the imagination. De Sade's imagination is as wooden as his imagery: all the fuckers have similar penises, thick and long; all anuses are pink and beckoning apart from the dribbling crone with the impossible hanging haemorrhoid. Why didn't he write her as a hermaphrodite, which could have been a scrotum and phallus attached to a vagina, rather than an implausible pile, and far more appeasing to the spectrum of imaginative possibilities?

Getting to know you
My days analysing the behaviour of the dominants and submissives decreased in frequency and intensity as you consumed more of my time and mind. At first we talked a little each day, disclosing our work, lives and eventually fears and desires. You would tease with words,

personality rolling from your linguistics, stamping your idiosyncrasies into every syllable. I love contradictions and you are a perfect specimen. A Geordie lass, a law school graduate, a working-class kid, a styled woman, an English rose, half-Italian, gentle, feisty, vulnerable, strong, open and very, very closed. You would tease and call me yours, then pull away to talk intimately to some American. Your wit surpassed any sublimity during that first phone call.

"Hey, is that Colette?"

"Nah."

"No?"

"Nah."

"That's not Colette?"

"Nah."

Bear in mind I suffer with embarrassing dyscalculia.

"Is that 00654686754?"

"Aha."

"But that's not Colette? OK, sorry to bother you."

"It is me."

"Oh, OK."

We chatted somewhat awkwardly after this and I was left doubting your stability and unsure of much you had said due to an accent barrier. To all intents it could've ended there, yet when you next called a few days later my every cell responded to your soft northern lilt, understand you or not. You had a voice as smooth and husky as velvet espresso dripping down the throat.

The voice is a much underestimated, unutilised tool and corridor to the mind. De Sade pays no homage to sounds. I could lie on my stomach, untouched, just listening to you all day. Your voice is as paradoxical as your personality, swinging from sensual breathy accent, going softer and lower with your arousal, to the fearful, harsher, received pronunciation of your "law school" voice, which always left me feeling like a naughty child, no matter how innocent my actions. Your voice breathed my skin, vibrating the layers between your lips. Your voice caressed my ears, sending me into an oblivion of sensation encased in a bubble containing just you and me. Moans into my mouth, into my shoulder, murmurs that expressed your needs and pleasure, short sharp breaths heralding your explosion into a space where every cell burst open with colour and intensity, each contracting in a harmonic rhythm. Vocals teasing with innuendo and whispered private profanity. Waves of sounds caressing my fears, showing your love, lifting me through exhaustion. I could tune into your arousal immediately from your tone, though your "law" voice tantalised me as much as your soft, low whispers. I wanted your law voice to drive me urgently against you, pinning me, biting me in anger, whereas your gentle lilt I wanted to overpower, take you, consume your voice, your breath, your moans in my mouth. Sometimes our vocals in the lonely nights apart would lead to seduction. It wasn't the same as you by my side; but I would feel you by my side as our breathing communicated the sweet honey lust of previous and future lovemaking.

Day Three

Writing draws me into the early dawn, or maybe it's de Sade, or maybe it's you. I don't recall the last time I chose day over darkness, life over reclusivity, as the world is now my Bastille. A Bastille without you, empty and distorted.

I haven't opened de Sade again; he lies on my desk next to the keyboard, in his favourite position, face down. I'm still chewing over him. He's like liquorice root: you chew until it's dead, but just before you spit or swallow a burst of flavour floods the tongue. I've thought of him all night and morning; he's shared my sleep. I've lolled over why he doesn't enrage me, why he doesn't rip my veins from their sinews and temper my mind with fear and pain, branding my thoughts forever. Why he remains within the realms of intellectual. Here is a man revealing acts of festering, burning, forced fucking, flogging and buggering onto men, women and children. Fresh children, sweet-smelling hymen sealed with no sexual appeal at all. Increasing with fervour to reveal mutilations, disembowelments and foetuses ripped from wombs, and finally murders. Thus, I'm locked in this conundrum. Why do I feel nothing? Am I so depersonalised? Possibly, but, more potent than that, the cause lies in his linguistics. Linguistics that don't build, don't create real people and empathy for them. Children described in three or four sentences outlining their physical attributes. Children silent apart from their use as tools, bodies bent and contorted at the will of the "heroes", but minds and emotions never disclosed to the reader. Maybe he already has them developed in his imagination and his writing is selfish, unconcerned for the reader, or maybe de Sade and his modern-day equivalents never allow their perception to work. They never see the person. Like the scientist, they reduce life, in order to damage and remove life. It may not be the case that they see children as sexual objects, because to see another as sexual requires reaction from his or her responses. De Sade writes of amoral freedom: freedom derived from a pure concern with the egocentric and nothing existing beyond that; a pain that is relative, hurting only the receiver, providing freedom and satisfying the want of the perpetrator, who cannot feel the pain. Thus is it possible that, for de Sade, his "heroes" and contemporaries, they are the centre of the universe? They don't find arousal in the external, but when aroused use people like any other object to relieve themselves as one would dry dishes with a cloth and then discard it? The attraction of children isn't all their attributes, button nose and hormone-free smell of candy that possesses no sexuality, but the ease of usage of this object, compliant, unresponsive, easily overpowered.

The meeting

Our first meeting was the seventh of April, two months after our first exchange of typescript. I waited against the wall of the platform in beige

Gap jeans, a black Gap T-shirt and long, leather trench coat, smoking nervously. A dreamy haze slowed time; people exited the steel cylinder in slow motion, blurring into the background as you slowly stepped out. I stood staring. I didn't know what you looked like, nor you I, we were a mystery to each other; yet, as I laid my eyes upon you, I'd known you for eternity, seen you constantly in my head, in my dreams in my waking moments of solitude.

We melted together, the rest of the world disintegrating, leaving just the ground under our feet. Your shy vulnerable smile drew me to you, stirring the core of my protective instincts. You looked so stylish, black leather gloves protecting your soft white hands, a black cotton jacket, zipped to your neck, blue jeans curving around your sensual hips, widening at the ankles to complement your strong thighs. Wisps of the softest curly dark hair falling before your right eye, lazing on your cheekbone, so soft, so curly, so dark, so tousled, so wild, so real, betraying the Latin against a skin of chalk, striking a contrast, inducing melts of emotion and passion.

The sun shone that first meeting; we walked through the park, climbing the knee-high wall when faced with locked gates, walking without touching yet not a space between us, just the breaths of our nerves. We weren't yet lovers, yet we were no longer strangers held by mouthpieces or screens. I walked slowly, looking straight ahead, scared to look at you, you stirred me so, but every now and then I sneaked a glance, took in your strong Roman nose, your paradoxical, determined, yet vulnerable hazel eyes, your contrasting undefined jaw emphasising small yet full pouting lips.

I can't recite our lovemaking: it's too precious, too sacred, the touch, smell and taste of you still residing with the clarity of yesterday in my mind. I was so totally concentrated and taken with your body, I raised my head from your thighs after taking your tides of pleasure and consuming it within me, raised my head to embrace you, held your quivering body close, stunned by the magnetism between us. I was but a breath away from your thigh, your rise still glistening in my vision, and I meant to say "I love your taste" before kissing you hard, but taste remained silent in my head and I startled, afraid of the three words that actually escaped my mouth, then, realising I really did, I repeated them before kissing you hard and passionately.

Day Four

De Sade has four "heroes", Duc, Curval, Durcet and the Bishop. Each "hero" corresponds to a part of himself. De Sade didn't live the life he wanted to live, be the person he wanted to be. At his father's request he married a wife he neither loved nor wanted. She was rich. The first time he was incarcerated for indecency, he was twenty-three, had visited a brothel, no different from two out of ten twenty-three-year-old men today. His initial crime had been lust, not murder, not paedophilia, not cruelty, but lust, different from random acts of casual sex only by the exchange of money. I wonder if that exchange was more than the cost of a night's worth of alcohol. A drug-needy street-walking prostitute can be bought for less than £20 with a guarantee no less. How different is the man who gives her the cash directly from the man who buys five hours of alcopops and aftershocks? Is the experience different? One woman is numbed by opiate depressants, the other by alcohol depressants. One interaction is socially acceptable, the other publicly condemned. De Sade strips the flesh of hypocrisy away from the bones. He defiles every social construction, reduces humanity to the libidinous id. In doing so he individually creates another construction and neglects the whole, cutting personality, behaviour and society into neat convenient parts, reducing humanity to psychological cells, each dot of vision, syllable of cognition a separate amoeba.

The President de Curval is de Sade's "hero" expressing the archetype of filth. Curval is unclean, unwashed and he finds the unclean arousing. His wife is akin to him in her dirtiness. Neither of them brush their teeth. He loves to kiss her mingling mutual decay. The aroma of her unwashed sex intoxicates him; her slovenly drunken profanities excite him. Curval is the symbol of de Sade's most base lusts. He symbolises total physical freedom, a childlike preoccupation with and acceptance of dirt. That unvoiced pleasure of the film of self, surrounding the body as the result of manual exertion. The total wallowing of the nasal cavity in one's own personal pheromones, bound tightly in inner space, so tightly the body can almost enter itself. The need to be desired so absolutely, early in the morning after the night's perspiration, late afternoon after the day's contamination, to share food from mouth to mouth.

Desired totally without the confabulation of superficial adornment, to be lusted purely, not lusted for the manufactured chemical scent of Chanel or Dior. To have one's true flavour coveted, not the unnatural, cell-stripping, mint of Colgate. Curval lives within us all. Curval is de Sade stripped of clothes, status and refinement, reduced to flesh untouched, undoctored and still accepted, wanted.

Curval is the shadow that finds the market seller, with the earth's soil from the produce she handles grained into the lines upon her face, attractive. Curval is that part of us we have to restrain from licking clean her grime, like wild instinctive beasts. Curval sees past the rotting blankets of the beggar to the person beneath. Curval doesn't smell the influenza germs of the lover, and can wipe the running fluid from the child's nose without recoil. Curval claims personal property with the instincts, writhing scent on freshly laundered sheets, drinking from the same cup all day, inhaling the top removed and put into the linen basket at night for no apparent reason. Curval is our acceptance of ourselves regardless of state or status, our drive towards base instincts, our quest for the animalistic foundations, our leaking expressions of rawness.

Sex is a dirty word

I love you in totality. Your lotions and Chanel Allure are beautiful, little reminders of your refinement, but I truly lust for you in all your purity. The gleam of your unwashed curls, their musky oily aroma, this is the time I sniff your hair more than any other time. When I want to touch and scrunch it tightly through my fingers, pulling your scalp close to my flesh. The power of your morning nudity sealed to mine with our fired hormones painting palettes of colour into my sleepy primal brain, waking me softly with your precious scent, a scent, so closely familiar to my own, residing in my personal domain. Your sex gently exposes her liquid on my thigh, or hips or buttocks. I want more; want to rub you all over my body, all over your body. I want to drink you, to be drenched in you from head to toe and smear you in your fluid, spreading it with my palm and open fingers over your thighs, hips, stomach, so we lie soaked in you. Not a bottle, or a brand, but your own special unique chemicals. The way when your clothes slowly peel away I can smell a bit more of you, teasing me gently. I tease myself more, tease you more, drawing out your scent through your tight silky shorts, clinging like atoms into the folds of your thighs, your rise pouting, pushing against the material, your lips swollen straining for release. Your aroma reigning triumphant, the only escapee, and she dances flirtatiously with the chemicals of my mind, twirling me in tangos of arousal, willing my own scent to join her. Increasing in intensity as I tease my finger between your thigh and the material, running it slowly around. The sweetness filling the air between us, pulling my head down towards its source, transfixing my vision, demanding my sole attention. Bursting molecules of perfume into my every sense as your final layer of material is removed.

When my mouth savours the salt on your thigh and chews the flesh of your hips, your aroma overpowers me, filling my head with you, a heady mixture of sweet skin, strong musky sex and rich earthiness dissolving from your anal bud, each lulling my anticipation of touch and taste. Willing me to immerse myself completely within you and when I must free myself from you consuming my immersed parts deep within my throat, wallowing drunkenly in your flavour.

When gripped by the urgency of my own potent fragrance, I wanted your strong Roman nose to feel my need, to thrust my desire for you in your face, make you understand how urgently, deeply, I needed you. To claim your flesh with my wet, melt my heat all over you, then rub myself into you with my tongue, tasting you, tasting me. When you threw me into oblivion I wanted to spray on your thighs, all of you, soak into your skin, tattooing you with myself and myself with you. Walking around with a permanent invisible mark of you soaked deep into me.

Day Five

I often work well into the night since you are gone. Just de Sade and I. Two corpses, one living, one dead. Though de Sade had a penchant for corpses, fresh ones, albeit he never to my knowledge so far inclined towards necrophilia, though we have another hundred and sixteen days to get further acquainted, de Sade and I.

Duc is the personification of perfection and power, perfection being a relative definition. He is de Sade's perfection, strong, perfectly proportioned, handsome, extremely violent, completely free in body and mind. Duc is the archetype protector. The part of de Sade that is concerned for him alone, his welfare, and will kill any threats to de Sade, and with his strong forearms and astute mind literally throw any obstacles out of the way. At the same time Duc has the charm and glibness to seduce men and women, the wit to make the world laugh with him, the dandy cutting-edge style of an artisan, the refinement to socialise with aristocrats, the sly intelligence to mingle among crooks. Duc is de Sade's confidence to socialise and assert himself with all, to raise his head when feeling inferior. Duc feels inferior to none. Duc interacts easily with groups and individuals, never relenting to emotion, staying objective enough to know a threat before the threat occurs. Duc is the steel barrier de Sade has built around his psyche, not only a barrier that stops de Sade experiencing hurt from the actions of others, but also a barrier from his real self, thus cushioning his ego from the pain of having to confront his inadequacies.

Others or he himself can't judge de Sade. De Sade can do, think or write anything. Duc validates his action; Duc is so perfect. If Duc does it the behaviour can't be wrong, and Duc can justify all. De Sade looks up to Duc, idolises him as everything he isn't, de Sade has created Duc in the image of everything he wants to be. De Sade can be incarcerated, rejected; Curval can be humiliated but none can hurt Duc; and, while they can't hurt Duc, they can't hurt de Sade, of whom Duc is a part.

Duc is not quintessentially more evil or violent than the other "heroes". The root to Duc is his pure self-preservation and concern with de Sade's needs to the sacrifice of all else. De Sade is the centre of Duc's universe. Duc has suffered adversity from a young age, an irrelevance to an apparently "erotic" tale, but not to what Duc symbolises. Duc can resolve anything and the fact that he has done so from a young age expresses this ability as innate. Duc is conqueror, protector, knight in shining armour, not to damsels in distress, but to his creator, to whom he is bound, yet separate from.

The protector

As an unborn foetus, I was protected by my mother's hips and sac of fluid from the punches and kicks of my father. For the child, the sac had to be created. A bubble of cotton wool would suffice for the bite from the elements, but against the fist and phallus of adults there had to be something far stronger. There had to be their equal, an adult woman, tall, strong, invincible and ultimately cold. She felt nothing to cope with everything; no scars touched her psyche, just a single line down her right cheek to identify her cause. Thus, I was born, somewhere, sometime, somehow, but so sorely misunderstood, which bothered me not, as my only concern was the protection of the child. I developed into perfection. The perfection was all that the perpetrators of violence and abuse were not. I grew with integrity and intense calm, patience and eloquence. It wasn't a difficult process: patience is learned through days waiting for psychological, physical and sexual tortures to end, and violence is more easily sidestepped by calm than by reaction. As the child grew into an adult I witnessed beatings by lovers, psychological abuse by others – each tried but they could never break her.

For the first time in my life I experienced the beauty of closeness, warmth and lovemaking; before, I'd always been an onlooker in my head – not even that. People would touch me, yet they weren't touching me; they weren't people; my imagination and I were the benefactors of my pleasure; lovers faded into a distance attenuated by fantasy. Touching them was detached, mechanical, to all intents and purposes absent. Making love with you diminished all but you from my every sense. I held you so close my body merged into yours, kissed you so softly our lips melted together, and sometimes kissed you hard, passionately, wanting you, wanting to take you. You held my attention; you still do with every breath I exhale, mentally, emotionally and sexually. I couldn't reach deep enough within you, nor take you so fully. If I could live an infinity I couldn't caress every cell of your being enough before having new cells to caress. I wanted you so urgently to pull your head back and bite into your neck, look down at your gorgeous curves before me. Moulding your full, firm breasts into your chest, feeling their swell under my palms, the rising of your nipples hardening against my flesh, sealing my mouth tightly around them, controlling with my swift, skilful tongue. Tracing my fingers along the contrast between your pale textured breasts and the silky white scars that ran between and beneath them, watching transfixed, running my lips and tongue over the sensual contrast, exploring you with my most sensitive receptors. When I took you, I wanted to take you all at once, wanted to see you all at once. I wanted your breasts, your clitoris, to be deep into your frontal wall, deeper than possible, pushing myself against you, forcing you wide, until you swelled and writhed inside a smooth larger ball, continually getting larger. I never wanted to return from within you, could have remained there for life, building you up, stopping just before you peaked and building you up again. I wanted to take your breasts, your clitoris, your sweet, wet walls and your tight, contracting orifice all at once. I wanted you to thrash, scream, scratch, and soak me in yourself.

Day Six

I look for de Sade everywhere. I look among rows of young people. I look in the supermarkets. I see plantation owners. I see Aristotle. I see Jung, Van Gogh, but I've yet to find de Sade. I searched for a lifetime, then found it. I found it all, so why am I searching again? Patience, dear reader. We have many days to find the answers. The child begets the man. Generations are not isolated. They are amoebae, each cell splitting, yet it remains identical and part of the whole. The old revile the young, the young the old. They see extremes, look for poles, differences. I see the 1940s pilot in the eighteen-year-old boy. I see the 1920s doctor in the thirty-year-old man. I see the Roman soldier, the Impressionist artist, the thirteenth-century whore. I see reproductions. Generations different only by climate, culture and evolution. The cheekbones, hair, movement, deepest drives transcend time.

Maybe if I search the underground that re-creates his world I can find the re-creation of him. I file such notions away into the trashcan of my psyche, in the knowledge that the seeker never finds because the search becomes the end itself, blinding the substance. De Sade could be one of those rarities, like Colette, of whom there is only one, yet a constant throughout time. A world without any manifestation of de Sade would be the epitome of innocent, serene summer days of perfection. Days I have never seen. A world without Colette would be the fires that torture my soul, but for a brief few months.

As a child I developed a method. Anything that induced fear or pain – all the negative – could be transformed. The idea came to me before I understood my basis. Before that crucial physics lesson. The physics lesson that taught me all things were energy and energy can be transformed but not destroyed. My earlier, more primitive method had been to obliterate anything painful, by refusing to acknowledge its existence. For quite a time reality itself didn't exist. As a small child I created a parallel universe quite by accident. Everything I didn't like became replaced by things I did like – any pain replaced by pleasure, until eventually, by four years of age, reality itself was replaced. I resented the odd flashes disturbing my reality – a reality that was good, warm, safe. I had my own world, which I solely controlled. My own army, police force, school, family. There was nothing left that had not been replaced. Many things – death, pain – ceased to exist at all; anything I feared I simply stopped believing in, developing a different theory for them. This was the protocol for my later method. After the physics lesson, I would write lists and lists. Lists of pain, anything that hurt: some were actions, some emotions. I would pore over each item for hours until I could solve the equation of its transformation to a positive. Anger became dynamics, guilt became awareness, damage became experience and so on. Of course, all these transformations were never-ending and false, so I eventually had a breakdown, and ultimately relived everything I had denied anyway.

I had completed my degree sufficiently tired and deflated. Sat listening at some boring alcohol-awareness course. Scanned the faces around the table, and there was Ellie. A scar gracing her wide strong nose, reams of blonde curls that could put Medusa to shame, strong, pronounced cheekbones and a certain edge to her. The facilitator was discussing Maslow's hierarchy of needs and had set the group a task of writing what each of us would like to change in our lives. The list is endless, but of course one doesn't disclose the important things in such a situation. Ellie tilted her proud chin and defiantly declared she had nothing she wanted to change, thus confirming my fascination. We stood outside leaning against the wall, drawing on cigarettes during the lunch break, and I knew my life and work would never be the same again. The next six months was a whirlwind of craziness. I was insane and Ellie more insane; together we were explosive. She tried to set me up as a saboteur of the council project we were both working on, and all the time I spent every day with her, totally unaware. It began two days before Christmas at the work party. We left our colleagues disappearing to a club, after much flirting and kissing. Ellie suggested going to the Grand Hotel, the biggest and most extravagant in town. I agreed, thinking she was joking. We paid for the room. I went to the bathroom to freshen as Ellie sprawled out on the huge bed. When I returned she had left. Later, she admitted she set me up as a saboteur because I hadn't phoned her. Our days were spent shopping and flirting, our nights in clubs, where we'd work our hips and eyes on men, then Ellie would appear from nowhere, curl her finger, at which I'd go to her and we'd kiss passionately in front of him, pull away and go on to the next. The 13th of February she called at around midnight. She'd taken an overdose; my whole being shook in fear. She survived, just about. Our escapades became worse. We never completely cheated on her lover physically. Nonetheless, I had to get away. Ellie could have prised me from Cline so easily but, the day they came face to face, she walked.

Cline was handsome, short tight curls, deep-blue eyes, a long strong nose and a body so hard and toned that she could lift me with one arm, an arm the size of my thigh. Cline had the stamina of an ox and would take me from dawn till dusk, until I was sore, weak and hungry. Cline also drank a bottle of whisky a day, abused every part of my mind, leaving me shaking on the floor until Cline wanted sex again. I left, sore, weak and hungry, eighteen months too late.

After Cline, I became like de Sade and locked myself in my Bastille, but unlike de Sade I didn't want others, didn't want anything but myself, and that was my method when I met Colette. I wasn't searching, wasn't accepting, the drawbridge was up, the steel doors locked. De Sade I don't need to find. I do need to journey, not to understand de Sade, but, in understanding de Sade, finding the eternal unanswered questions.

Transcendence

I hadn't looked for you, but you were there – a constant. You transcended era and physicality. Our bodies melt as they touch, locking together more than minds, and the destination is frightening. We are making love; I feel every part of you, your heat moving into mine, our eyes held in love, more distinct than the vision and touch of any, yet at the same time we're in a state, locationless, bodiless, just as distinct. I feel my mouth reach yours, our tongues entwine, hear our breathing, the shivers from our skin, knowing you're feeling it as much as I. At another level I feel your thoughts, feel you exploring mine. I don't need the look you give in acknowledgement: I know you're there. Higher still, no thoughts, no words, no visual representations, yet I feel it, know I exist, am there with nothing but the pure essence of our beings. We have reached a core that I don't even know we had alone.

Every single emotion, thought, flash, fantasy was open to you. The fantasies, thoughts I'd pushed away, were again open to me. You explored my every schema and the essence I cannot describe, explored it and opened it to us both, and I yours. I wanted to gradually know you, express myself, over years. I love you so much, I was so afraid of your judgement: judgement of my mind, instinct, primal urges – but fear was futile. We couldn't gradually open; you voiced my most precious thoughts, my grotesque thoughts, private orgasmic flashes. The pain, the hurt, the insecurities, the queue of phalluses stored in some remote dusty file, not a memory, not a thought, just flashes coinciding with deep intense contractions. Old young, beautiful grotesque, one, orgiastic, leather, binds, submission, power, thrusting, pounding, gripping, faceless bodies, fragment parts, feminine screams, ejaculations, robotics, textures, iron, guns, knives, complex stories, snapshots, ancient Greece, 1920s, you saw it all and more. It all cascaded from our lips so fast, so very fast, there could be no fear, no fear of rejection, judgement, no barriers. If we didn't verbalise it would stare at us inside anyway. I tried to slow it, to fear, but you simply took the files and saw it all regardless, and I yours. I didn't want to, don't consciously steal into your mind and essence every moment, nor you mine. It can't be slowed, prevented, controlled, changed. I didn't ask for it, don't want it, there is no choice, without will we transcend barriers of substance and entered a realm without searching, moving, acting, a realm leading us to a state unknown with no return.

Day Seven

Looking for substance follows the demystification, until the substance becomes unimportant, as the knowledge is no longer new. De Sade was demystified as soon my eyes initially scanned his words. You had revered him so. I had expected something phenomenal; duly I was disappointed. If I had been born Simone de Beauvoir instead of myself, maybe I too would have been overwhelmed with intrigue, but my cheap life finds de Sade escaping ordinary only by legend created by others. Is that why I search for him, why I want substance, because I'm still searching for that phenomenal? It isn't a question of patience, a slow leisurely stroll through a dead mind.

When I see de Sade published and today's equivalent incarcerated, nations and individuals defining power by force, a justice system based on storytellers, I don't find my own ideas psychotic. I don't remember my exact age; perhaps I was nineteen, perhaps twenty. It began before, innocently enough, I would introspect through the rooms of my mind, exploring schemas, opening the filing cabinets of my experiences, removing files, inserting files. It was a useful tool for examinations, all the information I had ever been exposed to at my access with a simple turn of a metaphorical key. I needed to go further. It wasn't learning but something within that maintains my disbelief in limits. My initial exploration beyond my schema was through the realms of my imagination. I'd seen my imagination in logical dreams and fantasy many times, but to actually explore its fragmented contents, like scraps on a cutting-room floor... It is so much bigger than the reels of schemata, but of course not enough. I had to travel further and my disbelief in limits had previously invoked the idea that all I am, all everything is, is energy. My energy was not merely chemical and kinetic, but also mental. And is energy necessarily separate units? Either way, my physical energy can interact, influence and be influenced by other physical and mental/emotional energy. For me, this was a dangerous discovery. My obvious deduction and a little inspiration from Émile Durkheim's theory of the "collective conscience" was that if I could figure out how to tap into it, all energy could be interacted with. And we are back at the beginning of this tale. I was nineteen or twenty, the first time I went past the barrier of my imagination. Directions I cannot give. I walked inside myself, through my schemata, past my imagination, very slowly, watching it all disappear behind me, and at some point losing my image of my physicality. For a long time there was apparent barrenness, but I kept going, until eventually I found it. The first time I was afraid, so afraid and drained, very drained. It took me a long time to reach for quite a while.

I consider de Sade's journey to the Bastille, his spindly legs aching under the pressure of his stout frame, eyes protruding out into the world mirroring the forward spill of his head, always a step ahead of his body, not in haste but portraying a false confidence. I wonder if he ever made the mental journey, ever knew himself beyond the gratification of his senses.

The Journey

I'm on the train, my first journey to you. With stops it takes five hours, my torso tense from my stomach to my thighs. I'm scared, and elated at the same time. It's only the second time we've met, the first time I've been to your home. What if I don't like you any more, if you don't like me, if the minds we have opened are crude rather than so complete? The rhythm of the train lulls me; I can't sleep, or pay attention to the salient cues. The other passengers fade into another world, another time, and another reason. My thoughts don't collect. I read a little, force myself to eat a little, not through hunger, but a need to have utmost energy and clarity when I finally see you. The scenery changes as the train draws me closer to you. Less concrete, more small, stone, hobbit-like houses. They remind me of us, not large, chunky, modern boxes, or grand old pretentious dames, just small, organic, delicately featured cottages. An hour away a manic grin spreads across my face. I'm aware of it but cannot stop it and am so utterly conscious, hoping no one is looking at me, about to section me. Your home is the last stop, always the last stop.

The station is huge, I'm overwhelmed, have no bearings. I leave the train, left or right, backwards or forwards; aimlessly I follow the throng. I know not where I am or where I'm going, just follow in faith and hope across a bridge, knowing not what is underneath or at the other side. I step off the bridge into the station terminal, a mass of white tiles and high white walls laced with a few billboards and digital timetables. The ceiling is bricked; in the centre of the floor is a coffee kiosk with Continental-style tables and chairs surrounding. Opposite is a W H Smith. I'm now standing completely still and lost at the end of the bridge, no doubt annoyingly blocking paths. Eventually I see you; you are standing watching my confusion, smiling wryly in amusement. We head to the metro, at which you inform me I can't smoke beyond the imaginary wall separating the station and metro. I'm embarrassed at my haste in lighting a cigarette on the bridge. We walk silently to the escalators, close in a vibe more powerful than words, vocality a necessity during our time apart. Your warmth next to me, the energy surrounding

us defies all my fears. I'm locked in the euphoria I feel only with my
completeness with you, and I don't need to hear your continued words
of affirmation, see your look of love, feel your skin on mine, to know you
feel it too.

Day Eight

I wonder if de Sade ever had an ordinary life, and what an ordinary
life is, anyway, and if I'd know one. My life feels ordinary. It's a
Saturday after a week's work. I woke about noon, checked mail,
showered, wandered around a Continental market with my mum,
took a few calls from friends, walked a while in the afternoon,
before meeting a friend for food and conversation in the evening.
Now let's try that with de Sade. He woke about 10 a.m., read his
mail, ate brunch and spent the afternoon conversing with friends.
Alternatively, I went into town, bumped into a guy my friend and
I had nearly been thrown out of a club for teasing years earlier. I
returned home, sinking myself into my journey with de Sade, his
first day full of food and violence, mixed with buggery and
masturbation, went to my friend's, listened to his commentary on
pornography. De Sade woke up masturbated, ate brunch, without
washing his hands, sat alone in a tavern, until someone joined
him, knowing de Sade would buy the drinks. He left the tavern
after falling prey to several illegitimate deals, couldn't face his
wife, so stopped off at a brothel and considered his fantasies while
being flogged. Maybe the distinction between ordinary and
extraordinary is knowledge.

I've skipped several pages of *One Hundred and Twenty Days of*
Sodom. I find myself at "Part the Third", the 150 criminal passions
narrated by Madame Martine. Although 9 p.m., it is still light
outside; the music is mellow and I'm sitting turning pages of
continual buggery, paedophilia, rape and torture as though
reading recipes in a cookery book. I'm not emotionless, but
reading de Sade is like eating raw ginger: it doesn't burn and

immobilise the throat until swallowed. The 150 passions are split into tiny paragraphs, some only two lines long; each is numbered, removing all humanity. They are like quick-fire snaps: as soon as I start to read one, it has ended and the next begins, blasting my brain with violence before hitting my perception.

After the book is put down, for this can be read only in short bursts, my mouth begins to water in pre-nausea; my senses react to the words. My head turns in avoidance as visualisations of mutilated dead bodies being buggered invade my interior cinema and screams of four-year-old children attenuate the music. De Sade leaves me with a feeling of numbness. His writing is too extreme to react to. If a person slaps another, it is very easy to denounce such behaviour as unacceptable. This is a catalogue of every possible torture, the violation of animals, children, the elderly, the disabled and the dead. De Sade doesn't write about one person buggering another: he writes buggery until that person bleeds to death, buggery of animals whose throats are slit when the perpetrator ejaculates, flogging until a woman's back is covered with blood. Each of these anecdotes is written so succinctly, there is no prose to carry or dilute. De Sade uses text only as a necessary evil to communicate all his fantastical flashes as fast and plentiful as he can. I will read *One Hundred and Twenty Days of Sodom* in its entirety by the hundred and twenty-first day of this journey, but I deny that many have read de Sade, really and completely read de Sade. I have read enough of de Sade now, far more than I can share with you, to know that de Sade is the impetus for insanity. How can a child be born and transform into an adult who has the potential for such schemas? How is that possible? I don't question a killer, a sadist, a psychopath; all of those can induce some kind of explanation. What de Sade writes, for him to have such vast extreme frames, his thoughts must have been constantly little else from infancy. The lack of verbosity between one man being buggered by a serpent, to the next terrorising a pregnant woman until she miscarries, indicates that de Sade can compute little else and that all he writes arouses him, blood, death, ripping skin, vomit, disembowelment, removing limbs. I do not know who de Sade is. I cannot comprehend what drives him. I consider doing a content analysis on his work to discover whether he had acted rather than written the death. Death from fatal injury might surpass that of war. I exaggerate not – that is the extremity of de Sade. He is not one thing to be understood – sadist, killer, necrophiliac, paedophile, masochist, rapist, dominant, submissive, scat and vomit artist, beast, cannibal, psychopath: he is a multiplicity of all and more. I blow out the smoke of my cigarette and ponder whether ordinary is ever a reality.

Lives less ordinary

No amount of fantasy can relate the impact of reality. A hundred of the most twisted films might make a person's life, and we were no different. This tale is but a fragment of our lives, not even a sliver of the cake. The fragment we shared of each other, a nine-month reality, possibly less than one per cent of our whole. The story began, like de Sade, before we met, out of the confines of this novel. Take two beautiful professional women approaching thirty and press rewind. You were born in a northern village to a northern woman and an Italian father you never knew. In her youth she worked several jobs to take care of you and you shared a room at your grandparents'. She died on the operating table during emergency surgery following a fatal undiagnosed illness. At sixteen you ran off to London for two weeks, returned to a large northern city. For eighteen months you lived in a hostel, endured a violent lover, fell into an underworld of drugs and promiscuity, dead-end jobs. You embarked on an eight-year love affair with a social worker from the hostel, completed a law degree and a Master's. That's the story I know; there is so much I don't know. I know you killed your gran's canary by zooming it around her lounge when drunk, then put it back in the cage.

I know you love pretty things, but I don't know the answers to my questions. I don't know what really made you. The next stage in your life was Oxford; this is when we met and where the story apparently begins.

I was born homeless in a Midlands city, watched the violence of my psychopathic father for fourteen years, beating my mother, smashing the house, throttling her, burning her belongings, crashing cars – oh, and sexually abusing me nightly from four. The council house was laced with books, hundreds of books, books on everything, old books, new books, fiction, textbooks. Days of fear, second-hand clothes, horse riding, theatre shows, potato and water, smoked salmon and claret, black damp walls, piano lessons and Mozart, newspaper on the table, I was to keep my elbows off, cotton-wool bread, the Mayfair at eight, market ham hocks, Harrods caviar – and so it went. My mother worked full time; he drank full time. My mother also sold her body; he sold mine. My mother also took a degree. All at once, these contradictions occurred simultaneously. I left home at sixteen, a hostel, then the streets, to damp rooms, had the violent lovers, had a breakdown, worked full time, went to university, brought a tiny house, wrote novels and poetry, all at once, I'm used to all at once, used to contradictions.

Day Nine

The weather has turned, summer heat submitting to cold. De Sade makes no mention of elements or very little outside his Bastille. Since Colette left, the world has become my Bastille. I don't shroud myself like de Sade. I don't entice victims into my walls, like the powerful Comte. What power, de Sade? Did you go outside? Did you seize the world? Did you walk into a room, and still the crowd with a look? Did you gain your will, using no force, or threat of fear, simply because they wanted to?

I hold my head in my hands and look out at the clouds. I'm going crazy. Since Colette left, I see de Sade not just as weak and powerless, but as an irrelevance. I wonder if people pitied and laughed at him when he was alive. I'm pretty sure they would now. What are you, de Sade? You have such mystique, yet you were so terribly afraid. You write of every torture you can imagine while hidden away from the world in self-imposed exile. Your words are an expression of neither wrath nor power. You sat alone, possibly agoraphobic, attempting to catharsise all you fear. Imagining if you just could gain the slightest power. A frightened insecure man. Only the feeble want power; those that really have it don't want it. I wish I had fear, but, since losing Colette, it has lessened even more. De Beauvoir speculates on de Sade's childhood, on his drives. I'm really rather indifferent to de Sade's childhood, but I do know if he'd seen a fraction of the things he wrote, he would not fear. You see the blood, the broken limbs, the knives, the guns, the psychological games, bruises; feel the pain, the hunger, the cold, the lives flashing before you. What is there to fear? The foetus was kicked, punched, the threats, the blows, the broken nose, the hands around the throat, bullet holes in windows, impact of metal on stone wall, kidnappings – yet still I'm alive. Who is there left to fear? What is there left to fear? I'm really rather brave, or dehumanised.

Fears

Evenings were spent talking until the early hours. Sometimes I'd worry it was too powerful, too strong, too intense, too insular. Your knowledge of my head scared me so, but you never seemed afraid. You'd tease and control with your eyes, writhe in all your movements, oozing sensuality and power. Your words emitted certainty. Your voice would switch from gentle Chardonnay to poignant, rich claret. Your whispers breathed sex I'd never heard of. I was in awe of the apparent confident experience you exuded. I assumed you were home so much due to researching your dissertation and the power of not wanting to be far apart that bound us so. It never crossed my mind that, like de Sade, your tidy city flat was so neat because it was your Bastille.

Day Ten

Feeble, enfettered creatures destined solely for our pleasures, I trust you have not deluded yourselves into supposing that the equally absolute ascendancy given you in the outside world would be accorded you in the place; a thousand times more subjugated than would be slaves, you must expect naught but humiliation, and obedience is that one virtue whose use I recommend to you: it and no other befits your present state.

– words of Duc, de Sade's invincible persona.

For de Sade, power is the bully, the big man who commands subservience through force, the little man who commands it through status, but all sharing the same elevated self-importance. De Sade wants to be important, he so wants to be something in the world, so wants people to follow, revere, worship him, and his want leads him to identify with the false power of the Ducs of this world. The irony: in death you now have power, de Sade, you always did marry death and power, but your power is not derived from force. Your power is given by underlived, overeducated, middle-class tabulae rasae who herald you as more than an insecure misogynist.

"... [Y]ou are beyond the borders of France in the depths of an uninhabitable forest, high among naked mountains; the paths that brought you here were destroyed behind you as you advanced along them. You are enclosed in an impregnable citadel; no one on earth knows you are here, you are beyond the reach of your friends, of your kin: insofar as the world is concerned you are already dead, and if yet you breathe 'tis for our pleasure, and for it only." – Duc.

Such power. Do your readers really fall for this, de Sade? The manipulation of the average abuser, first preparation to isolate from the world.

"Tell anyone and I'll kill your mum."

"No one will believe you."

"No one will know if I kill you both."

Then do it, de Sade, and your modern counterparts do it! You might scare the child, might even convince your more naïve readers, and, yes, a few of you really do trade the corpses of children. Such power, manipulating, threatening, torturing and sometimes killing something with not only half your physical strength, not only another of the numerous statistics to go on the missing-persons register, but also void of the world, innocent of the rules of the game. Leave your Bastilles and face the adult.

"... [T]he lives of all women who dwell on earth are as insignificant as a fly... let her adjust bravely to her fate: we are not going to exist for ever in this world, and the most fortunate thing that can befall a woman is to die young." – Duc.

How you betray yourself and your comrades, de Sade. The fear men such as yourself have of the female flesh. Born from a womb, you cannot conceive of, the mystical hidden sex.

"By and large offer your fronts very little to our sight; remember that this loathsome part, which only the alienation of her wits could have permitted Nature to create, is always the one we find most repugnant." – Duc

The power of the adult woman, her scent, her reactions, her muscles, rippling unlike yours not from the groin but through her body. Two seconds and you are spent, a misfortune, and you are eunuchs, but woman can lose herself for days in orgasmic pleasure; woman is hidden, protected; you can enter but not see her display; and, if this isn't enough, she both creates and bleeds away the human race. Why does this scare you so? Scare you to the point you have to take the sexless child as the safer option, then beat the woman out of her before she appears and, if that doesn't work, dispose of her before the musk of woman emerges?

"Moreover, do not simply wait for us to specify the orders we would have you execute: a gesture, a glance, often simply one of our internal feelings will announce our desire, and you will be as harshly punished for not having divined it as you would be were you, after having been notified, to ignore that desire or flout it. It is up to you... [t]o interpret our movements, our glances, our gestures, to interpret our expressions, and above all not to be mistaken as to our desires." – Duc.

The grandeur abusers have of themselves never ceased to amaze me. Again, nothing new, same rules to the game, generation after generation. But is it not interesting that extremely quickly a child can anticipate the requirements of the abuser? Whether he or she always complies or not is another matter, but they are always correctly anticipated. Remind me again why de Sade and his modern counterparts claim this as their power. Reading the abuser can make the difference between life and death and certainly control the level of physical and mental pain. The rules are so simple and learned so quickly, in ongoing abuse of a sexual nature they want to avoid detection, thus leave very little evidence, marks and so forth. The blows will always come to the back of the head, where the hair covers the purple bruises, but what a useful tool to know their fear of evidence. Thus, they have two options: they can, as de Sade did, either kill you or ensure you are relatively uninjured. Blood is evidence, and so that knowledge a great comfort. Of course, as a child you don't know the meaning of paedophilia or their fear of women, so assume the worst is to come after puberty, that fear eating away at the mind and soul, so much so you vow to remove your life before adulthood.

Following Duc's speech, de Sade betrays his assumed air of power with excuses for what he is about to write. During this de Sade often directly addresses his reader, alludes to them, but more interestingly and perhaps subconsciously he discloses his own multiplicity.

"Many of the extravagances you are about to see illustrated will doubtless displease you, yes, I am well aware of it, but there are among you them a few which will warm you to the point of costing you some fuck, and that, reader, is all we ask of you; if we have not said everything, analysed everything, tax us not with partiality for you cannot expect us to have guessed what suits you best." – de Sade.

There was no storm last summer.

Stormless hunger

Our eyes met, and that meeting induced all: the tender longing, understanding, the synchronicity of body and mind, primal lust. An invisible bubble circled us, excluding all else. Our breathing drew faster with the rhythm of each other. We merged a contrary mixture of warm soft caresses and hot raw hunger, those initial sweet kisses giving way to the urgent starvation we needed satisfying. Tongues gracefully dancing together, exploring the recesses of pleasure, then, as the stirring within beat too much, suddenly hard and pushing deeply into each other, bodies melting into one. My fingers stroking your soft dark curls would long to scrunch your hair tightly within them, forcing your head to mine. My hands caressing your cheek reach to your wrists, bending my palms within your delicate dip, desperate for you. Our softly writhing hips would increase to a powerful thrusting grind. We wanted it all, the honeyed caresses, the frenzied desperate bites. Exploring every cell slowly, all we could see and deep inside the darkness we couldn't. I could spend hours teasing your every curve, wondering at the textures deep within, until the urgency bucked the pit of my stomach and I'd have to take you hard and fast, commanding the muscle lining you inside and out to rise and swell under my touch. Wanting everything at once, the taste, touch of you, your beautiful full ripe breasts, your curvaceous stomach, your sensual throat, your writhing hips, your full teasing thighs, your pert arse, I wanted it all, took it all. My arms would flail limply, desperate to be pinned. My breasts pout for your attention. My hips and arse lapping up your soft caresses, teased until I needed hard, firm, fast, raw. I ached for you to explore slowly, to make me moan and beg and then take me with such thrusts, feel my reactions swell and clasp so hard to nearly break your bones, and you nearly did mine, scream my brains out. I heard your soft whispers of commentary and fantasy, your sensual moans and your beautiful primal screams. Always I wanted to make you scream louder, harder, your stomach to thrash in two emitting a primal, uncontrollable howl and wanted you to hear my loudest ripping screams, to give you my deepest, uniquely sexiest, longest orgasm, to share that with you and surpass any with Cline. Cline the instinctual lover is nothing compared with my hunger for you.

Day Eleven

There was a story in the local papers last week of a primary school head who was caught by CCTV using the services of a prostitute. Part of the reason the head and de Sade are in print is that they make people feel terribly comfortable and smug. You'd never have a four-month orgy in a gothic Bastille. No, you can't afford to. You wouldn't use the services of a prostitute. No, buying drinks in a nightclub is cheaper. De Sade didn't leave the womb a frightening powerful figure of torture. You are guilty of the very same thing as de Sade. He forgets what it is like to be a child, thus how he can arouse himself on the mutilation and pain of children, and you forget de Sade was a child, an infant even, a neonate. How anyone can forget the most profound formative years is beyond me. With de Sade and the head, we share nine months in the womb, the first breath, learning, growing years. We also share the grotesque sexual flashes we quickly bury and pretend we never had, don't deny it.

But you are different: you don't do what de Sade does; you don't do what the head does; you are better, yes? When I was about nineteen I went to the shop, young woman, nothing spectacular, ordinary event, two minutes to the local Co-op to – I don't even remember – maybe fetch bread. It was on a high street, in a dusty town, just a mundane working-class shop. Sitting on the concrete beneath the neon sign was a beautiful, black-haired, olive-skinned young woman busking, a raven on her shoulder. I kid you not – reality is often more surreal than fantasy. Five minutes later we were in my tatty poor girl's flat, the sun streaking our naked lovemaking forms. Am I any different from de Sade or the head? Or maybe you are different from me, too. All I know is I still smile when I remember that summer afternoon filled with innocent pleasures with the exotic busker, her parents' circus acrobats.

Innocent beginnings

We made love, sweetly, tenderly, intensely, passionately, probably not differently from any young lovers deeply connected and chemically in tune. We shared the fantasies we wanted to do in the future and some just fantasy for fantasy's sake. They were the sensual fantasies that thousands of lovers all over the world, unbeknown to us, were probably sharing for the first time at that very moment, mirrors, watching each other, blindfolding, food, sweet, tender, beautiful innocent fantasies. We started looking at leather together in shops on websites. I'd smile so much inside at your excitement as you described exactly what you wanted to find.

"Babe?"

"Yes, Hon."

"You busy?"

"Just typing stuff for work but I can stop for ten."

"I've been looking on Yahoo! for leather. I want a pair of black leather shorts that zip all the way round. What do you think?"

"Mmm, sounds good!"

"Check this site, hon."

"You found shorts, babe?"

"No, not yet, but the second page has a fab leather top."

We're trawling sites looking at leather tops, high necks, corseted waists, studded leather, leather and chains, pages of leather, dresses, trousers, catsuits, bras, thongs, gloves, collars, harnesses. Just leather, we just like leather.

Day Twelve

The Bastille has statutes compiled by the four "heroes". These include what time everyone is to rise, what they are to wear, when to eat, when to wash, when the orgies begin and end. The females apart from the narrators are all to kneel when in the presence of a "hero". What is it about kneeling that makes it an immediately subservient act? I recall the knee rests in church pews as a child but never felt the desire to kneel upon them. It could be all the usual things: it makes the kneeling person smaller and totally innocuous; more than that it makes them directly level to the groin they are submitting to, thus the "dominants" are thrusting out their genitals with a huge "take that" to the world, metaphorically saying that is all you are worth. Is it coincidental, I wonder, that the genitals are also the location of human excretion? De Sade's love of bodily waste is apparent from Day One. Personally, I'm tickle-stomached and prefer the body contained, finding any expulsions repulsive enough to trigger expelling within myself. I saw a documentary on de Sade two months ago, which claimed de Sade was deeply into submission. I expect some would read from his love of taking bodily fluids that that is the case. I don't know whether de Sade was into submission or not – I know nothing of his sex life – but the taking of bodily fluids is an act of dominance. The closest thing I can compare it to is orgasm. As a woman I control my orgasm: whether to give it, how intense, how long it will last; my mind controls that, not my body, and certainly not a lover's body. If I decide to give my orgasm, that is what I'm doing: I'm giving it, in a way submitting to the other person by giving them a precious offering.

Wasted

I'd read about water sports and scat in Pat Califia's Saphistory *when I was about eighteen, written it off as a stomach-churning chapter of no interest to a healthy full-bloodied woman, lent Pat to my friend Ian, the doctor's son, and never saw it again. By the time I met you I'd all but forgotten water sports and scat as something that didn't concern me anyway. Discussions of fantasy increased in tempo. You talked of exes who liked to watch you defecate, and others you'd urinated with. With distance between us I kept bravado, but a small part of me nagged fear, apprehension and inadequacy. Nagged an awe of your experience and that in the long run I couldn't and wouldn't satisfy your needs.*

When apart, as well as the world, the universe, we'd talk of masturbation, which – seeing that I'd do it when horny, tired, stressed or just to ensure all was working – I'd recite to you only if particularly interesting. You'd "save it" and have a huge orgasmic binge. It was during such discussion when you told me about masturbating on a full bladder and passing water on the point of orgasm.

"It's the most amazing sensation – try it."

Duly, I did as I was told, but, alas, my body is too well trained in appropriate control and etiquette, thus, would not comply, giving but a mere trickle and shrivelling in disgust at being expected to pleasure anywhere near the enamel tunnel to the sewers.

Day Thirteen

The four wives shall have no prerogatives of any kind over the other women; on the contrary, they shall at all times be treated with a maximum of rigor and inhumanity, and they shall be frequently employed upon the vilest and most painful enterprises, such as for example the cleaning of the private and common privies established in the chapel. These privies shall be emptied only once every week, but always by them, and they shall be severely punished if they resist the work or accomplish it poorly.

The wives are treated with the utmost hatred, as they are the epitome of womankind. The crones and narrators are detached from gender somewhat; the children are not quite women. The wives, however, are not only young women: they are the buggered daughters of the "heroes" and the battered and used "wives". They are collectively owned, no detachment, no mistake, these are women, thus, they are to be claimed, dominated and used as such.

During my time "spying" in the dungeon, fascinated by this novel phenomenon I'd not before come across, I concluded two observations. The first was that in many cases both the dominants and submissives, along with other visitors to the room – the scope for human confabulation noted, of course – had experienced some kind of abuse throughout their lives. I could understand why this might be the case for the dominants but not yet the reason why this would be the case for the submissives. The second thing I concluded was the whole thing was a useless pretentious exercise carried out by people who wanted to feel they were somehow different. I observed their behaviour and the behaviour in any relationship and saw no difference apart from the formality of calling the dominant ma'am or sir. All relationships have power dynamics. Equality is driven by power dynamics: one partner guards "her" kitchen, and the other pins down her lover in the bedroom. All these people did was put a spotlight on those aspects. When I raised this I was metaphorically lynched and given the sadomasochistic evidence. Domination and submission are different from sadomasochism. Although sometimes the two co-exist, they also both exist separately. When does a relationship stop being "vanilla", as vanilla as a relationship can be with all its power dynamics, and move along the continuum to sadomasochism, biting, scratching, hair scrunching, ice, candle wax, blindfolding, tying, slapping? Most intimate relationships incorporate all of those at some point during healthy varied lovemaking. Maybe the distinction is if all is carried out using something other than flesh and items of clothing such as silk scarves: other household items such as the decorative candles, ice in pretty shapes out of the freezer sitting next to the Sunday roast. Does liking the smell and texture of leather move it along the continuum to sadomasochism? So silk scarves are vanilla, soft bondage rope is sadomasochism, palms spanking buttocks is vanilla, leather softly trailed over the body is sadomasochism, pinning your lover roughly against a passing tree is vanilla, sweetly calling her Mistress is domination and submission. The differences are so clear – can't think why I didn't see them before.

Bound by love

You know everything about me: my favourite colour, favourite foods, my deepest fears, my phobia of dentists and smear tests. I know how you sleep badly at the moment, your love of lattes, Chardonnay and bacon butties and smear tests. We trawl the net for a speculum. Once you have something in your head you won't rest until you have it. That's something about you that's always made me smile; inside I'd be screaming, "Slow down, I want to know you, know your body with my body, slowly." Yet I can't help but smile and oblige your whims.

"They have them here, babe: www.fetteredpleasures.co.uk, and loads of gothic things."

"Hon, look at the leg spreaders."

"What are they? Hold on: I'm looking at the eighteenth-century cuffs."

"They have them on the eighteenth-century page – scroll down."

"Aha! I see them."

"What do you think?"

"Yeah, kinda sexy. I like this gothic eighteenth-century stuff."

"I want some leg spreaders, and some cuffs."

"And the leather shorts and a speculum."

"Shush! Hey, look at the thick steel cuffs, sixty pounds, they're fab. I want those."

"And you shall have them eventually, no rush. I want a collar, too, not for any reason, not into that D/S crap or owt, just want a collar, think it'll look good."

"Yeah, I want a collar, too."

Day Fourteen

The children in *One Hundred and Twenty Days of Sodom* must have felt as if their lives were suddenly being pulled out of their bodies from their innermost flesh. What is trust? I never trusted anyone until I met Colette. All were potential de Sades, with the potential to do all his atrocities and more. My body would close itself tightly in fearful anticipation. I was immune to pain – not immune, but so *in* pain that any addition would pass unfelt. My very first lover was the beautiful, middle-class blonde at school that all the boys wanted. We'd been friends for about a year, intimate in that innocent schoolgirl way of holding hands, linking arms. It was surreal how it happened. I dreamed we made love and swiftly tried to block it. Though afraid, I often dream things before they occur. But she was my friend, my best friend, she understood me completely. I stayed over at her house, a huge old vicarage. Apart from her younger siblings and grandparents, we were alone. We messed around in the garage, put paint on the walls and she set fire to it, just the usual teenage angst. It was a warm night and well lit, maybe by the moon, or maybe just by the traffic on the crossroads. We wandered among the trees in the garden, holding hands and swaying and whispering the private things only best friends say and know, walked past the swimming pool, and just danced by the summer house. There was no music, but we could hear the rhythm and we danced to it in each other's arms. As the night drew close we ventured inside, watched her red portable TV, cuddled together in her double bed. Our cheeks brushing closely, softly, passionately with no ounce of clumsiness, we began to kiss, then make love.

She didn't speak to me the next day or the day after that or the day after that. My friends were her friends, were our friends. I saw none, and, most of all, my best friend, whom I loved more than any, was no longer there, just me sitting eating lunch on the doctor's wall alone, me sitting on the steps to the science block. I felt air scuffle past me, the school ruffians, the smokers. They asked me what was wrong, seemed genuinely concerned. I'd not spoken to anyone for two weeks, maybe three. "You can trust us," they said gently, so I did.

The following day all my friends were in isolation. My best friend denied all knowledge. I answered the teacher's interrogation truthfully: I'd done nothing wrong, nothing to be ashamed of. I was ordered to see a doctor, and the school psychologist. My mum was called in and informed of my "sexuality", and I was unofficially suspended for a month. My best friend carried on as usual; she was innocent for not telling the truth. The final two years of my school life continued in more or less total silence, with no students talking to me and few of the teachers. I never trusted any since until Colette.

Trust

We were closer than any humans could be. I was working on an ICT project at work, with the plan of paying off as much of my debts as I could, then returning to university to continue research and you were heading for Oxford. I was so excited, we had no limits, we were going to storm the world. Daily I asked you if you'd heard from Oxford yet, my fingers practically permanently crossed. Then I got your email:

Hey sweet – great news. I'm been nominated for a scholarship for Oxford!!!!!! i just have to fill in a couple of forms, send them off and then wait to see if my nomination has been approved. I'm trying not to get too excited 'cos I got to this same stage last year and then failed at the approval part but since they have changed the rules this year there

should be no problems this time – I hope!!!! so keep your fingers crossed
for me hon… and I'll speak to ya soon… take care my love, hope work
goes well today. C.x.x.x.x.x.x.

>From: "Gale Halshaw"
>To: Colette@hotsmail.com
>Subject: Re: female insecurities
>Date: Wed, 09 May 2001 14:53:11 -0000
>
>Listen hon if I have neglected you then I am sorry. Work is
>horrendous to say the least. I am just glad I did come up and relax
>with you otherwise I would have been ill (mentally and physically
>lol!). Do you think for one minute that just because I do not ring
>you, I stop thinking about you?
>As for your hotpant cladded arse (I am taking the fifth amendment
>US citizen or not on that) you know exactly what I think. Suffice to
>say the thought of those two ripe peaches is enough to distract any
>dyke.
>As for the world revolving around you… hon I wish it did… life
>would be so much more beautiful and the thought of waking up to
>seeing your cheeks rise in the west rather than the sun is much
>prefered (god I'm such a dirty bastard even if sincere). I wonder
>why you doubt my affection for you when it is so blatant and when
>you also know I would say if I had a problem with you. I will be
>on-line tonight for most of the evening so I hope to see you then.
>Lots of love Colette… and I miss you too!"

I read your news about Oxford grinning ecstatically, and scrolled
down. You had signed off "C x.x.x.x", but the words underneath your
message were foreign to me. This wasn't a reply to a mail I had sent you.
I knew Gale Halshaw. She was some friend of yours from Manchester. I
never really took much notice, assumed you were casual friends. You
rarely said much good about her, unless one counts contrived and bald.

I sat at my computer and burst into tears. Every night you phoned me, told me how you'd never before felt the depth for anyone you had for me, that there was only me, held me in your arms pledging soft whispers of committed love excluding all others, and now I sit here and read something that can have only been written by a lover:

Hey you – I know your doubting me right now but id like you to see the original message I sent to gale – gale and I are only friends and we haven't talked much since her visit up here… she has had a lot of stuff going on for her with work, g/fs etc… and i was worried about her cos she usually confides in me… and yes I have missed her..just like I miss talking to Helen or Jo if we haven't talked for a while… it genuinely is only a friendship thing sweet – I'm not treating you like a fool and gale's reply to my email was one of humour and affection at my paranoia in thinking I had upset her… nothing more… its just my insecure nature that if i don't speak to a mate regularly then i must have done something to offend them..gale was only reassuring me that that wasn't the case. Anyway the email goes like this –

"Hey pal… listen, correct me if I'm wrong, but you seem a little distant lately. well since the visit anyways… have i upset you or something?? id like to think that if i have our friendship is important enough for you to tell me… it just seems weird that we rarely talk on MSN, phone etc… is there something I've done that I'm oblivious too or is this just another example of me thinking the world revolves around myself and my cute hotpants clad arse ??. lol"

You obviously have gales response to this email… so make of it what you will. I've told you the truth love. I would never play you as I consider what we have to be too special… but you will believe what you will..i only hope you decide that I'm telling the truth, cos i am – anyway .I'll talk later bye C.x.x.x.x"

I wanted to believe you. I wanted to believe you so badly; after all, all we shared, all we said, our complete acceptance and closeness, could it all be false?

Day Fifteen

How must it have felt, for all the bewildered confused, captured children and of course for de Sade himself? Yes, for de Sade, too, sitting alone, isolated from the world, bar the odd servant and visitor. Not just isolated, but isolated with those constant pounding thoughts of pain and destruction. Was he a psychopath or a projecting depressive? Humour me, imagine it: you spend every breath, every day for months, years, thinking of nothing but the most cruel tortures you can inflict, the most cruel routes to death you can drive (in this space garrotting is for amateurs). Now imagine you are eleven years old. Adults appear to have a great deal of difficulty with this. You've been there, you are that eleven-year-old child that grew up, that child is there within you. S/he didn't just disappear, get thrown out with the toys and old annuals. You are that eleven-year-old child safe in the confines of your room, the covers snug around your toes, your toys peeping down from the shelves, and suddenly you are taken from your life, by strange men that smell of adult and earth. The journey is long; you have no idea where you are going; you try to talk and you get struck; you cry and you're struck harder. You arrive at your destination, unaware of your surroundings and fate, surrounded by men and women who poke and prod and beat you and, worst of all, you don't know what is going to happen, whether you are going to live or die. Now back to de Sade. Imagine being locked up with nothing but thoughts of the worst possible abominations known – and, if you're not thinking at the level of slicing of millimetre layers of flesh over a period of a year until the person either bleeds to death or dies from continual infection, you're not touching the level of de Sade. Back to the eleven-year-old.

Concentrate, again, to imagine his/her pain and confusion. It has to be at a minimum on the level of the stench of sex hitting your senses while the ugliest old man sucks the fluid from your nose before expelling himself on your virgin flesh.

Now switch between de Sade and the child fifty times, until you lose total sanity. Or, alternatively, read on.

I never experienced the confusion of de Sade or the children in the orgy. My earliest memory is sitting on my mother's knee and moving to take the hand full on my lip, as she was about to get struck. My split lip and I were put to bed. I chewed my lips ever since until I don't know when I stopped. Maybe I was seventeen, maybe twenty-three. The fear of the unknown was never an issue, as it was a permanent fixture. I didn't stop to think whether I would live or die. I constantly thought I'd die; therefore, if I lived, it was a bonus or a nightmare. I learned very early that one of the easiest ways to forget everything and sleep was to tell myself I'd never wake up. It still works now, better than progressive relaxation therapy for inducing a good night's sleep. Consistency was a luxury I never had the opportunity to experience, unlike smoked salmon and caviar. Some days a smile could receive a smile in return; other days it could receive a crack across the back of the head; some days the answer to, "Do you agree with me?" was yes, other days no, other days no win. In the case of inconsistency there are no rules, and every rule is subject to a moment's change. Do you get the picture? You don't know if you are going to live or die; you don't know whether the answer is yes or no; there are no rules, but if you don't anticipate them you risk your life. You don't own your body: it's there for adults to touch several times a day and expel over while you vomit in the corner. There is no safe place, no snug covers warming toes; there are no captors to fear, just to pray for; there was no other knowledge. This didn't begin at eleven, but since you existed.

Cycles of confusion

I couldn't concentrate on work: the email from Gale bothered me. I flicked over to the suburbs to see if you were about there. You were in the "lesbian love nest", under your own name but with a small c as usual, with Gale, in under her nom de plume, "PUTTYCAT". I found it crude: an educated woman with a nom de plume complete in uppercase. I'm sitting at my computer, confused, looking at the name list. You don't talk – well, type – in chatrooms: there is no point my going in. After five minutes I find myself in the room as "sally". No one is going to notice a sally; "sally" is no one. I sit and watch, waiting to be reassured, because being here will confirm what I know, confirm that you love me, that you don't play games and quieten that horrible voice of experience.

There are about seven other chatters in the room. Some know we met, became a couple offline. I sit and watch, watch the two of you exchange words of crudity, the things you are fantasising you are doing to each other with no holds barred, displayed for all to see. I always find online communication rather psychotic: people type nonsense such as "circling your nipples with my tongue". No, you're not! You're sitting alone in a chair. Gale wasn't an online stranger: she was your real-life friend; you stayed at her house, she at yours; friends, you said. Tears shook through my body as I switched off the horrid plastic machine, bypassing shutdown.

Day Sixteen

When they realised their fate, the children couldn't cry: they'd be killed or at the least severely beaten for crying. De Sade could cry, realising his thoughts, de Sade could cry. When I was a child my father would play this game where his middle finger would force my chin level with his staring into my eyes, until I cried, then hit me for crying. But I never cried; my mum did, but not I. I'd stare him out until my eyes stung so much they burned and he'd wander away, bewildered at my resilience. It was a tricky game averting the eyes, though submissive could also be seen as insolent. Crying, although submissive, would be rewarded with a beating, thus, staying in the staring position where put was the safest option. I had a problem with eye contact for years after, though having my school friend push me off a counter because I apparently had "evil eyes" and having various lovers catch my eye and call me the "Antichrist" or say I possessed the eyes of a killer, I must say didn't speed my recovery.

I imagine that de Sade's "heroes" and their modern contemporaries punish crying because each tear is the manifesto of their behavioural politics and only parties sure that their aims will bring the greatest benefit to the majority can bear to read their own manifesto. It was also years before I could cry. Once I'd found the strength to open the floodgates I didn't suppress that beautiful and much-needed expression any longer. When the gases of pain are stored inside for years, the fear of the explosion when finally opening the lid is greater than the fear of the experience. Years and years of storage and I didn't know it, didn't know myself, what dark demons lingered in the depths, just robotically took each event and filed it away. I could have been darker than de Sade, darker than any extremity he could imagine, darker than my deepest fears. I didn't know – I was just the filing clerk of my soul. As with the characters in de Sade's macabre tale, it is only the adults who can afford tears.

Tears

I rise from my bed unrested. I try to phone you. No answer. Throughout the day I try. No answer. I fire up the computer and log on to await your return. There in the suburbs "PUTTYCAT" taunts my confusion. Tears soak my face from nowhere. I enter the chatroom, ask "PUTTYCAT" if she has heard from you and say I witnessed the sexual exchange between the two of you and I'm obviously very confused and upset about it. "PUTTYCAT" promptly admonishes me for possessiveness and assumptions, arguing that you are your own woman and do what you please with whom you please and I shouldn't assume commitment. I feebly try to defend myself: I have never demanded, would never demand, anything of you. The exclusivity, commitment, love were all things expressed by you. By now the tears are bouncing off the keyboard and I can barely see to type. I asked you so many times if, due to the distance and knowing each other only three months, you wanted to keep things casual, and so many times you replied your feelings were more deep, serious, exclusive; and now "PUTTYCAT" was telling me you saw us as casual all along. Why had you told others this? Why not me?

Eventually you entered the room. I tried to open a private room with you. You blocked me. I was even more confused and hurt. You were my lover, I needed to talk to you, sort this out, find out what was going on, listen to what you had to say. You wouldn't talk to me anywhere but the main room, so I was put through the humiliation of asking why you wouldn't talk about it properly as well as asking why you'd had your sexual exchange.

Meanwhile, as my body shook with tears, the vultures in the room, seeing a weakling, attacked me. You would neither talk to me properly on the telephone or on MSN, nor reassure my fears. "PUTTYCAT" mocked my naïveté and you joined in. The tears continued to soak grooves down my neck, salt stinging into my skin. I understood nothing, couldn't fathom what was going on. My mind, previously in confusion, accelerated to complete turmoil. I was lost in a strange and horrible game, yet again with no rules, not knowing how I arrived here or why. All I had done was fall in love for the first time in my life.

I don't remember if it was the following day or that night when you ended our affair, citing my behaviour. It was your email, your sexual exchange, your refusal to talk, your public mocking, your total indifference to my broken state, yet you cited my behaviour. I believed you, I trusted you, you must be right.

You said so, "PUTTYCAT" said so and several strangers from Outer Mongolia and the US and Scotland said so. Reader, forgive me, I had no insight.

Day Seventeen

The Bishop is de Sade's child self. The wanton, demanding self. The brother of Duc, the Bishop is moody and temperamental, prone to neurosis and cold-blooded murder. The bishop is thin and cunning, possibly urchin-like. He executes what Duc cannot. Why the child? The Bishop is completely concerned with the satisfaction of his needs, like an infant with no regard for anything other than milk and warmth. The children in de Sade's novel are weak and accepting. People accolade the acceptance and sweetness of the child. Yet it is the child who throws the tantrum, stamps the foot, spits out the food, complains and always fights for his/her needs and rights one way or another.

Bishop is an ugly, dark, mutated child, a child created from a lack of imagination and underdevelopment of all but hedonistic sexual pleasure, a child who has not successfully passed through the phallic stage, but rather is stuck within it, preoccupied with naught but the fascination of his own genitals.

My reachable inner child is actually a teenager, the complete opposite of Bishop with no sexual drives. She's a bratty little number, happy when shopping, dancing, listening to music and generally having fun, but prone to foot stamping if the credit card runs out or the shop doesn't have the chosen colour. She whines if ill, pouts to get her own way and grins when satisfied, and never takes any feat seriously, yet sneaks herself into all the wrong places. I'm sure you all recognise your child self. Immune to adult emotions, she will run wild through the sea and sulkily express any apparent injustice or displeasure.

The adults have left the building

I don't remember what happened next, whether I ever went to bed over the next two weeks or simply went from the computer to the shower to work and back again. I had shut down, shut down to stop the tears flowing. We were everything and more, and now, without ever falling out, without so much as a tiff, without falling out of love, of passion, we weren't anything, with the flick of a switch. My head pounded, full of broken cogs, full of guilt for I didn't know what, but I must have done something, something very bad for you to remove your loving arms, your soft warm curves, your complete understanding and love of me and project me into the cold. The fault must be mine, thus I drowned in my tears until I was no more, watching my actions being performed, vaguely aware I had to take control, get back, or I'd lose my job, my home everything. At the helm the bratty child scampered around for chocolate, went to work, playing at being the professional.

My younger self was angry and scared and rather unconcerned for you and all but a return to stability and a steady supply of chocolate, clothes and fun. Angry with you and angry with myself for trusting you, falling for you and then taking the blame, angry that I'd failed to protect. Whether rightly or wrongly she saw you as a charlatan, a liar, a fraud, a game player, with little integrity or responsibility, and as someone who had played, hurt deeply, then to rub salt in the wound had humiliated me while I sat breaking down and she had no qualms telling you so. You had no choice but to listen. She had no wish to telephone you or waste breath talking to you. Instead she entered thesuburbs.com with profiles such as "No liars today please" and "Integrity is for life not just for fools" – the usual teenage impertinence.

Something attracted me to the banners on the site, you were playing me, and somehow I instinctively clicked the banner for alt.com. There was no reason: alt.com, was a BDSM dating site; no reason why you would be here. But our mental frequency took me there nonetheless. I spent hours, stayed up all night, and the next, the next, browsing the thousands of women advertising, looking for you. I had to sign up to search the whole database, felt contaminated signing up to nothing but sexual exchange, like the women who offer sex in the back of Loot, or some pornographic magazine. Days I searched and found nothing, but, among the offers of domination, submission, water sports, rope play, group sex, transvestite maids, I knew you were there somewhere.

Day Eighteen

I know not if art imitates life or life imitates art, or I'm simply falling into insanity without Colette. Imagine the setting: it's 2 a.m. in a tidy city flat, a small delicate man is tied with black bonds to a wooden chair facing an external window, his legs cuffed together with black leather cuffs, blindfolded with black satin, immobile other than quiet, necessary breaths. He listens, listens to words I write, words I speak, until I steal his soul and make him too part of the words.

The hermaphrodite is such in its completeness, for it is not recognising the masculine and feminine self. Hermaphrodites are not both sexes, but neither, thus, it is presence, it is totality, shadow, anima, animus, persona, all that constitutes, yet also a transcendence of the physical.

The route to self-acceptance includes every opposite and contradiction, and for a woman her masculine self, the animus, for a man his feminine self, the anima. De Sade's anima is represented by Durcet, "his entire body, and principally his hips and buttocks, absolutely like a woman's". Durcet is impotent, and any orgasms he *does* have he cannot cope with, leading him to crime. More than anything Durcet loves to be taken, sodomised. He is weak, sexually inept, sweet, soft-skinned and high-voiced; he is a vessel and de Sade's version of women. Jung proposed that the anima and animus existed in order to understand the opposite sex. Durcet is de Sade's understanding and perception of woman.

If we all have an anima and animus, my animus is rather unconventional compared with the stereotypical male. He is a romantic dreamer and poet, with little interest in sex or arousal. He has a fine appreciation for art and refinement. His floppy fringe falls over his intense yet gentle eyes. He adores manners and style and is feverishly protective of women. Chivalrous to the point of self-sacrifice, yet without an ounce of fight. His gentle easy temperament shields him from the realities of life. His demeanour is sunny and presence fair-weathered, brief and somewhat infrequent.

The lady can do no wrong

I accepted your love as true, you wouldn't say such for a mere infatuation, wouldn't betray your previous but still deep love for such. I trusted and believed you, had faith in you. You were the woman I'd met, held and laughed with, not this cold dark stranger. Maybe you were ill, scared, misunderstood, whatever, it wasn't you, not your fault.

We'd hardly spoken since your online playing with Gale, but I wanted you to know that whatever, however far apart, whether we'd ever see each other again or not, that my love would always remain. I sent you flowers, chocolates, picked carefully to ensure your favourites, and Chardonnay, for no reason but to let you know I love you and was thinking about you no matter what had passed. This angered you. You ate the chocolates, smelled the flowers, drank the wine and called me disturbing. I hung my head in shame, feeling contaminated and confused, but knowing not why, knowing not what I had done that was so abhorrent – only you knew that.

Day Nineteen

Sixteen children locked in a deadly Bastille and no one cares. Perhaps the most confusing of all, no one considers dependent lives their responsibility. No one will interfere. People condemn de Sade and the paedophile rings taking children off the streets to abuse and kill. People point fingers and raise their noses in superiority. People assume themselves to be better than de Sade, Robert Black, Fred West, Roy Whiting, and the man next door who has fathered two of his daughter's children. All together now, you are better, you have morals and social mores, you know right from wrong. That's good to know, because the sixteen children in the Bastille are relying on you to save them. Duc, the Bishop, Curval and Durcet do not confuse them. The "heroes" are demons, their worst nightmare, they expect nothing less of them. The person who assumes the air of superiority, who boasts morals – it is not expected that you collude with the abuser by pleading ignorance. You live next door, you hear the screams, see the men. You teach the child, you vaccinate, fill his/her teeth, you pass the child back to the torturers. More than a hundred thousand children go missing in the UK every year – that's not the odd one you accidentally missed. "I didn't know" is not a defence. What did you do, soundproof your house, walk around blind, deaf and intellectually challenged? All of you? Forgive me: you are *innocent*? You did *nothing*? You are *not* innocent, because that's precisely what you did: nothing. The children in de Sade's Bastille, in some Thai backstreet, in the mansions and terraces of Britain, the parks, the brothels of Europe were waiting for you. Just before the phallus and the hand squeezed the last breath of life from them, they were looking towards the door expecting you, just one of you, just once, to open it.

Not as they seem

For the two weeks that we split, if I go online "Dyana" follows, "Dyana", "Victoria", "Xena", all the same person. "Dyana" never shows until the slightest playful tiff we'd had or times like this. "Dyana" always knows when I'm low, knows our situation. On top of everything else I'm somewhat unnerved by this. After you have privately ranted, "Dyana" shows; if chatters get abusive "Dyana" shows. Always "Dyana" flirts, no matter how much I'm uninterested in all but you; "Dyana" offers comfort then flirts. You denied knowing "Dyana", let alone disclosing any of our private exchanges to her.

"Dyana" emails me. I recognise the address straightaway: it's the address a guy who called himself "Sir C" had been looking for the sender of, due to his having received a flux of abusive mails. "Dyana" has signed her mail to me, but I can see his problem: in the section where the name of the sender usually appears, Dyana's mails just say "me".

Politely, I reply to her mail, attempting to uncover the enigma. We share a strange exchange discussing the philosophical dark recesses of the mind. Her next mail arrives rather quickly and turns the situation even more surreal. "It started as a bet," the words reveal, "to see how long I could last undetected as a woman and a domme." I reel back in my chair. Have I entered insanity itself? Maybe none of this is real and I never switched the computer on that fateful night; I never met you; you don't even exist and this just isn't happening. Maybe I have a chronic case of psychosis, so extreme that I imagine I'm still living in my house; my neighbours still say hi; I'm still going to work, and no one has noticed. Maybe I'm really in a padded cell on the local acute psychiatric ward. Surely it has to be me; the world itself can't be psychotic, can it?

I know there is more to "Dyana", whoever he is, because a switch in gender still doesn't explain how he knows all about us. I reply sweetly but with an edge, saying I'm sure that's not all the mystery of Dyana, along with the usual dark observations of chatroom antic to bait him. He accepts my hand and duly replies, signing off, "one more surprise John xxx". Even though this was my number-one suspect I'm still frozen in shock. John is Joan, and now John is Joan is Dyana is Victoria is Xena, and not forgetting Wendy and Nan. You were friends with John, spoke to him on the telephone, had him on your MSN. While we were still flirting online before we met, John did his best to cause animosity between us. When I went to chat in another room because you were having cybersex with some American woman, John came in as Wendy and tried to engage me in crude sexual exchanges. I ignored him. Dyana then came into the room. I'd known Dyana online before you and we'd always flirted. This occasion was no different, especially as you were cybersexing the American. Wendy joined in the flirtations, which I backed away from as they fell into lewd sexual typescripts. After I joined you in the room you were in, John came in and revealed himself as being Wendy and the two of you laughed at my humiliation. At the time I didn't realise Dyana was also John. I never understood why you considered him as a friend when you also said he'd caused trouble between you and a woman you flew over to America for a month to be with.

I was now in a complete panic about this strange game and I was scared, worried about you; this guy obviously had an obsession with you and if he was on your MSN he could easily get your address, because you had your full and real name on it. I called you, told you with garbled fear all that had happened and you confirmed you had told John the things "Dyana" knew about us. You said, "So it wasn't you making the phone calls?"

"What phone calls?"

Now I was hurt, confused, panicked and angry. How dare this man enter our realities. Online games were bad enough, but to intrude your reality, phone you silently, then comfort you when you assumed the calls were from me and pretend to be someone different altogether and comfort me while I was bewildered about how s/he knew my private reality. I was fuming, wanted to protect you, yet you seemed remarkably calm and unconcerned.

Day Twenty

The third day the "heroes" drew up a programme for the seventeen orgies planned for the end of each week. The programme includes several "marriages". Not the conventional marriage, but couplings between men and woman and men and men. The sodomisers are called husbands and the sodomised wives. The girls are to remain virgins until December (the novel begins on 1 November) and the boys until January. The taking of each child's virginity is dated and the perpetrator stated clinically as though recording a plan of medical procedures. De Sade mocks the marriage institution and monogamy. His mockery isn't an endorsement of free choice, but rather an oppression of it, bigotry as bad as the bigotry sometimes perceived to be from institutions.

Marriage is sexist, financial, religious, all those things, yet on another level it is also a choice between two people. Two people, who may not be choosing marriage for sexism, finance, politics, religion, two people who are individuals, not part of an institution, not a group who may or may not be bigots. De Sade was too weak-livered to assert his own wishes, thus he prefers to see marriage as a forced situation with no other options. De Sade's wife was moneyed, he had options. Polygamy is quickly becoming the norm. I think that, like fashion, sexual behaviours return in cycles. From the Victorian era, we have had the pretence of majority monogamy, serial monogamy and back to the polygamy of the 1700s. I neither disagree nor agree with any. I think all should be tailored to suit individual rather than societal needs. I don't intentionally choose any myself, but find if in love or mentally connected to another I don't have any interest or arousal in others. Her body and hers only becomes sacred to me and more attractive the longer I know her. I find de Sade's mockery of such offensive. I don't mock or judge polygamy.

Connections

We made up almost as quickly as we split up. You asked me to come to you and within a day I was on the train. Unlike the first time you met me at the station, you didn't have your wry smile, but instead paced a tight circle in front of the coffee kiosk. I was wary, very wary, and you were subdued and apologetic. I rested my drained form in your bath, while you sat leaning against the opposite wall, your head down, looking for the entire world like a naughty child. I so wanted to raise my wet body and hold you, whisper how I forgave you, but I didn't. You needed to apologise and I needed to feel my fear and hear it.

We spent the evening relaxing in our closeness, just relieved to be together again, occasionally whispering how much we'd missed each other, then sitting, our hands or thighs touching in gentle silence and understanding. You'd reach up and stroke my hair and neck and I'd caress your forearm or skin that was resting on my thigh, sometimes falling into the arms you'd wrap around me. My head nestled onto your soft breast while we watched a film. My eyes would drift into heaviness as your gentle breathing lulled me as only you can. We talked, asked each other if either had slept with anyone else in the two weeks apart, to which we both replied no, but we didn't talk long, didn't need to discuss: just being together, close again, we knew.

The weather was muggy, and now I couldn't see the city and beyond from your flat as I had before – not that it mattered, since we spent little time outside our tender sweet whispers, embraces and passionate lovemaking. One day you left to visit your ex, Helen, for a few hours. I took a lazy soak in the bath, wandered the city alone, familiarising myself with the shops, scents, people, sights and textures. I brought groceries, Fenwick's chocolate cake, smoked salmon, fruit, bacon, and stopped for a snack of I can't remember what in Fenwick's café, sitting happily watching the buzz of life around. I tidied up, collecting our dirty clothes from the bedroom, and your laundry basket, sorting them into darks and lights, before tidying myself for your return and snuggling down with the day's papers. Your gentle movements alerted my ears to your return, and, much as I'd enjoyed my space to wander, tidy and just be, I couldn't suppress the soft smile that graced my face at your soft "Hey, you."

I muttered about having just put a wash in the machine, moved to the laundry basket, pulling out the beautiful navy flannelette sheets. "I couldn't fit these in." Horror flickered across your face, only for a second, but I registered it, being sensitive to the slightest change in gesture and expression. "No rush – they're just old anyway." The sheets certainly weren't old: they felt brand new and expensively luxurious. But my confusion lasted barely a moment. Whatever it was, it couldn't be important. We were entwined in love, mentally, emotionally and physically, nothing else mattered.

I returned home and once more we were apart, but only in body – our connection will never leave mentally. Every spare second, we spoke, messaged and emailed. One of my emails was from alt.com. It was you. You had been there all along, lurking, hiding under a pseudonym. You *were annoyed, asked why I was registered there. I said I'd been looking for you. You denied playing me, said you'd put the advert there before we met. I believed you, loved you and I had no reason not to. Still, it confused me. I couldn't understand why, if you weren't into BDSM, and you hadn't been interested in casual sex since your youth, you would put a sex advert on a BDSM site. It mattered not: we were together again, deeply in love; all else I'd learn in time. You hadn't been playing games, just a misunderstanding; it mattered not.*

Day Twenty-One

Reading de Sade is like sexual tennis. I have to remain totally self-analytical and read it fragmentally. There is nothing erotic about the situations de Sade describes. Thus, the mind and body start cold, intellectual, but profanities flood every page – profanities, such heavily sex-soaked profanities. My schemas don't possess separate files for profanities huskily voiced during orgasmic euphoria with Colette, and academic, derogatory, other-context profanities. My mind and body simply hear a profanity and raise hormone levels and rush the blood, filling nerve endings in anticipation. De Sade must play havoc with the endocrine system. The words "fuck", "ass", "cunt" flutter across the page and, before they are registered, the breasts, ovaries and vulva are on red alert, just as quickly shrivelling when context catches up – another profanity, bang, reaction, context, bang counter-reaction. And so it goes, this conundrum of abhorrence, inciting the contradictory, arousal, horror, guilt, confusion, loathing and fear. Fear that anything so abusive could induce arousal, however momentary. This is why such a level of self-awareness so one doesn't go insane is needed. Not insanity from de Sade's horrors, but from a fear that somewhere locked in the darkness of the mind there dwells a pleasure from his horrors. Fear that the profanities – beautiful profanities, profanities said in love, profanities of passionate, tender, sensual acts – would merge with his revulsions and pain, resulting in arousal from such. Like when infants get a sudden initial sexual rush coinciding with a smack, heels, a wayside carcass. It is the profanities alone causing the reaction; my body rises then jolts cold, shuddering at the context. It's OK to feel arousal at any usual source, even if that source is within the most detested frame. It's OK to feel revulsion, even if that revulsion is also laced with sources of pleasure. De Sade is the verbalisation of my worst nightmare, watching short sharp flashes of the most loving passionate intimacy within a movie of death, blood, guts, nausea, abuse, paedophilia, pain, brutality, rape. It is rather like those subliminal messages advertisers use in films that the viewer never actually sees. I have to see them, be aware of them. Life takes so much that, if you can hold onto anything, make it your sanity.

De Sade mirrors human hang-ups. Bit by bit, Colette and I peeled them aware, replacing them with honesty. Nude bodies, sexual acts are arousing. Whether you want those bodies or to do those acts matters not – they are arousing. Men, women, two men, two women, men and women, images of coupling arouse because they remind us of our own. Phalluses of all kinds, textures, shapes, are arousing: the muscles clench and contract into oblivion, simple as that. Instead of honesty, there exist invisible, unwritten barriers: "heterosexual women don't find women attractive"; "heterosexual men don't find men attractive"; "viewing random acts of sex is not arousing to women"; "friendly flirting is not arousing"; "lesbians don't do raw primal penetrative sex"; "there is a difference between kinky and vanilla". So it goes. Instead of voicing the natural and true reactions, we recycle the "rules" of fake communities. Community? The place that provides support nurturing, practical help, sharing, advice, keeps its members healthy, warm, dry, fed, housed? Where exactly is this community, other than the guardian angels, who are random members of the human race, fitting into no pigeonhole and related by nothing? Books and magazines speak of the mythical "gay community".

What gay community? There is no housing, education, advice sharing. Oh, do you mean the drug-filled, alcohol-filled, violence-filled, hedonistic, selfish, lonely, random-sex-hungry nightclubs? That's a business, not a community, and there is nothing else – just people not lying in a drunken heap every night, getting on with their lives. I defy mythical communities that cause more pain than good to lay down invisible rules. Bodies, sex, textures, shapes, acts, poignant images, it's all OK.

Dusty

We talk love, passion, sex; we talk fucking, grinding, tribalism, and headily mixing at all. Nothing can compare to our skin on skin, our bodies entering each other, the world's most skilful, gentle, slow, fast, hard, thrusting hands, but we want more, always more. We want all that, nothing to change, and yet to be physically closer than separate bodies, to look into each other's eyes constantly, see the throes of our love, to cover every inch of flesh with each other, to completely enfold. We want to grind, legs wrapped in legs, thighs against thighs, hips dancing to a shared rhythm, sex merging with sex, stomachs moulding into each other, breast against breast, hands holding hands above our kissing heads.

I'm not sure about having latex in between us: I want nothing to come in between us, nothing to touch your skin but me, to touch my skin but you. I want to know you slowly; I can recite every curve of your flesh, yet still I want to know it more. I want to soak in our tenderness. I want to wallow in what we have; I don't want it to change yet. The passion we share is explosive; I want to stay in the explosion. Our fantasies will still be there as the explosion grows bigger, blowing up the universe. Let it do that first – our fantasies will still be there. We talk of silk, leather, lace, latex, silicone, rubber, truncheons, fruit, vegetables; of dildos, big, small, narrow, wide, harnessed, unharnessed, double-ended, doubly penetrative. We look everywhere at everything, excited in fantasy. We land on a site with the softest leather harnesses and dildos in all shapes, all colours, the finest. We wander for hours in awe, both exhilarated. When we want to incorporate this fantasy into our explosive passions, we will return here. You want it now, want Paris, the slenderest, softest leather harness now, want Marlene the medium dildo in marble purple, now, want Dusty in marble blue, now. You want them sent to you, want to see them as soon as possible, before we meet again, want to try them on. What you want you get. I love you infinitely, refuse you nothing, want you to have all that makes you happy, all that makes you smile:

hey sweet heart – just wanted to tell ya that our final package came today and the dildos are fab… very sexy and soft!!! but you were right to get dusty hon..marlene looks scarily large but I'm sure I can work up to it np The colours look great too. I'm dead pleased with your choice hon and that we used babes cos the leather is like silk..so soft and the quality is good too. u take care of yourself and enjoy the sunshine today and eat loads of icecream..I'll cya later hon cos I'm chainsmoking before I have a morning session at the gym C xxxx.

Day Twenty-Two

The storm never erupted but finally it has cleared, replaced by a dry instead of sticky head, and I can once again breathe. The days I've read so far of de Sade all repeat the same passion for buttocks and distaste for cunts, thus the title is rather apt. De Sade pays great homage to the bottom, almost worshipping it. All kinds of bottoms, narrow, big, young, old, peachy and pile-ridden. The bottom and all its attributes are sacred and, as with all things he holds in adoration, it must be defiled, torn, destroyed and in all possible ways dominated. Indeed, one of the eight "fuckers" is actually called "bum cleaver". The images de Sade supplies around the bottom are sufficiently horrifying to cause permanent constipation because the body is trying desperately to hide itself at the mere thought of such violation. Constance, Durcet's daughter and Duc's wife, "the day after Duc had deflowered her of her maidenhead, sodomistically speaking... had fallen dangerously ill. They believed her rectum had been irreparably damaged". I hate to point out to de Sade with all his sexual prowess and experience that the anus does not have a maidenhead and, had it, the colon would explode shortly after birth, rendering the human race extinct before it began.

The buttocks are all things; they are asexual. Round, pert, small, flabby, toned, matters not, all can be found on males and females. De Sade was not homosexual, heterosexual or bisexual: he fragmented the individual so much, sexuality wasn't a consideration in de Sade's perception of sex. The great thinkers, Freud included, believed humans are all inherently bisexual, mentally if not pragmatically. Bodies are arousing, actions are arousing, situations are arousing, shapes are arousing, textures are arousing, labels are relevant to physical acts only. Labels have no place mentally; they describe an act, not a complete person or a community. Labels describe a singular act in a moment only. We cannot see tomorrow, cannot predict tomorrow. Can we really predict the sex, gender, body type, personality type of our lovers until death? Some people like labels as if they were wearing an identity tag, as though insecure in their actions; thus they have to label them. One of the very first things Colette said was that she'd never sleep with a bisexual woman, even though she herself had experienced sexual intimacy with both men and women. Is human behaviour really extreme enough to be put neatly into pigeonholes? I see sexuality as somewhat of a continuum with none fitting into either extreme. Cline was a strong muscly woman, so strong she could lift me on one arm and her two children on the other. Cline made love like a champion male jock, only expertly. I'd lie under Cline, tasting her sporty salt that fell from her hard flesh, tracing the deltoids, scratching grooves into her back, and taking it. I'd reside in the kitchen; apply lipstick before Cline came in from work, like any respectable fifties housewife. Does that make me heterosexual? I have difficulty understanding distinctions. Where exactly does homosexuality end and heterosexuality begin? To sleep only with women, yet fantasise about, well, everything, really – does that make a person bisexual? To find neither sex's naked form repulsive, to flirt with all – does this define bisexuality? I find male homophobia tedious, as, let's be honest, an arse is an arse is an arse, and not only do men adore anal sex with women, but their G-spot is the prostate gland, located several inches up the rectum.

Distracting bums

I wanted all of you at once, to feel every section of your flesh against every section of mine, leaving no space uncovered. Making love with you drove me insane. I had to be looking into your eyes, kissing you, tasting and moulding your full, demanding, perfect breasts, teasing and biting your hips, running my finger along the fold of your groin, deep inside you, hands caressing your bum, thumb inside your anus, fingers skilfully building your clitoris, taking you everywhere, all at once. I wanted to taste you, bite you, stroke, rub, frig, take, fuck you all at once, everywhere. It can't be impossible, but I hadn't mastered that total completeness. Tasting you while fucking you everywhere, I'd still want to be caressing your breasts, pulling your hair, kissing your mouth. I was never repressed in my greed – you wanted everything, everywhere all at once too. I was constantly pulled in different directions by your sensuality, and our emotions. The love would shout "hold tightly", the tenderness, "kiss softly". Your hair would scream for attention; your neck, "kiss me, taste me, bite me"; our minds, "talk"; your back, "mould me firmly beneath your palms"; the arch of your throat, "run your finger down me, kiss, bite". Our eyes would burn passion, our mouths, "kiss hard, get lost within us"; your breasts, "manipulate us, flick the tip of your tongue over us, wallow deep within us, but don't ever divert from us"; your stomach, "lick me, bite me softly, taste me, run your thumbs and fingertips down my sensual curves". Then the belt of deep, passionate, primal, intrigue, hips, sex, bum and thighs. This is where I melt and you writhe, your power, demanding anything of me. Of course, I'm obeying you, as I follow your pouting sex, writhing hips and pert toned bum. I want you lying sensually on your back, like a seductive Raphaelite, and lazing teasingly on your stomach, your round cheeks gently grinding into my lust. I want your full womanly rise, the vision, the smell, and such euphoric responsive touch. I want your firm pert bum, the vision, the smell and such contracting drawing my touch into you.

Our passion would distract us as much as our love, whole raw aches in our bodies, and sometimes intense burning concentrated in every sensual location at a time, demanding attention, that could never be satisfied immediately. Love and lust distracted me at work, distracted us at fun, while relaxing around the house and while you tried to concentrate on your dissertation:

Hey lover – was checking out the dildos in babes again and none of the butt plugs are suitable for harness use :(:(So....I was thinking of getting one of the smaller and thinner dildos from the babes range – specifically the Naomi (I like primary purple) and wondered if you'd have a look and tell me what you think. its 20 quid so quite reasonable and ill be happy to stick it on my credit card. Speak to you tonight sweet..and I hope you have a good and sticky day. C.x.x.x.x.

Day Twenty-Three

Again the day has dawned; it dawns so early in July, taunting me with my living status. I consider de Sade, the nightmare of the children in the one-hundred-and-twenty-day orgy of violence, and possibly the nightmare of the reader. You close de Sade and the nightmare ends. In the story I'm recounting to you, the nightmare never ends: I'll live it every moment for the rest of my life, like a record stuck in the groove; death is my only escape. Whichever way I turn, whatever I do, it's always in the front of my head, whether dancing in some club, surrounded by beautiful women and men, turning heads, or hiding myself in my small house ignoring the phone, door, computer. You can run from de Sade, close it, shelve it, throw it, burn it, but I can never run from the course of events you will soon discover, nor from myself.

Do you ever feel like a cog in a clock? Totally lost in the momentum, unable to prevent the pendulum from swinging. I've no idea how to stop it. I have periods in my life when I consider running away, just taking some clothes, jumping on a train, any train, the first in the station, wherever it goes, then, when it arrives, jumping on the next train, location is irrelevant. Location is far more irrelevant to change, however. I can run, I can run from streets, houses, the telephone, people, but never can I run from myself. I caused this, Colette and I. We have run from each other, but we can not escape ourselves. If I move location, the cog will still spin, the momentum is flowing, its rhythm too powerful to stop. Events are never a means to an end but a means in themselves. I can intellectualise, look logically, objectively, see reason and the rational, in the same way I do with de Sade, but de Sade is fiction, so removed from reality, so easy to detach from. The intellectual, the logical, the rational – Colette and I were two young attractive women who fell in love, such a beautiful, simple, constantly occurring event. She wasn't de Sade, I wasn't de Sade, there was no grand plan, no gothic mansion, no demands, just respect for our exclusivity. How the momentum swings, gets twisted out of control! And I don't know how or why, cannot predict or prevent it

Steel and fantasy

As we grew together, limits completely ceased. No emotional limits, no material limits, no intellectual limits, no life limits, no sexual limits, we became hedonists drunk on life and our shared energy, intoxicated by acceptance and empathy. I thought it, you said, you thought it, I said, until there was no longer a need for thought or speech. We were adventurers in life's candy shop, and all the colours, flavours; tastes were free, there for the taking. Everything excited us like children seeing the twisted sugar shapes for the first time. We'd laugh, grin, jump, throw arms through the air, never repelled or shocked. With each other we could be that hidden instinctual self. There was no judge, no jury; there were no social mores, no black and white, no right and wrong. Everything was acceptable, everything was right, everything was good and what other people thought mattered not, because there was no deeper love, no one person more important than you and I and we wanted it all. Too soon, but we wanted it all, at once, all together. It was as though someone had opened the door to utopia, it was so overwhelming; we just opened our mouths, eyes, ears, hands and grasped, until we had all we could carry, then returned for more. We were young, and our interaction had caused a catalyst within ourselves to free us, free us of everything, once this reaction had taken place. As with molecules, the structure changed forever, we could never return, never go back, to who we once had been, never lock the open door, never give back the freedom, stop grasping the everything.

Leather turned into blindfolds, and collars. Leather progressed to iron. Iron developed into steel. We looked at steel cuffs, steel restraints, steel batons, steel pokers, steel phalluses. Talked in depth about the attributes, its hard coldness. About the pragmatics, the pain of the grind, how it would have to be stillness against other stimulation. We wanted steel and you wanted it now. Steel is clinical, clinical turned our attention to the thousand-pound red leather gynaecologist chairs, which distracted us to the A-frame, the leather horse, the iron cage, the rack, the Gothic mansion to put them all in, the black, purple and reds we'd decorate it with, the heavy smell of the oil lamps lighting the stone walls. We weren't fetishistic, kinky, dominant, submissive, sadomasochistic, we weren't anything. We didn't want to be anything but ourselves. We wanted loving, tenderness, flowers and chocolates, soft slow lovemaking, hard passionate lovemaking, fucking, role play, *food, pornography, sensuality, textures, vocals, every sense stimulated, leather, chains, clothes, naked flesh, romance, spontaneity, urgency, indoors, outdoors, water, beaches. We wanted to incorporate everything within our love. Not one thing, not a fetish, a paraphilia. We wanted every slight thought we'd ever had, every glimpse, every corner of our minds and beyond, to wrap it all in our love. We labelled nothing, identified with nothing, never being one thing more than another thing. We wanted it all. Slowly, day by day, very slowly, we were going deeper, deeper in love, deeper into the candy store, deeper into complete acceptance not just of each other, but of ourselves and any slight flash of experience, frame of a movie we'd ever seen, deeper into freedom, into wanting it all.*

Day Twenty-Four

Did de Sade write his novel to be erotica, or did he attempt to think of the most horrific acts and deaths and merge them with sex to make it all the more horrific? Was he merely trying to shock, to get the biggest reaction possible, make humanity recognise the reality of selfish hedonism? De Sade could well be appalled that any would see his work as erotic. I'm trying both to be objective and to stay sane, the two not being particularly compatible. I'm thinking who and how anyone could find de Sade, other than the profanities, arousing. Bear with me, because I'm standing on the very edge of sanity to do this and there is a danger of falling off. First, anything can arouse a person given the right conditions, the more common phenomena being shoes and lingerie. Alone those two things are inanimate objects, given a connection with a person or a situation, and they can lead to arousal, or even paraphilia. A logical solution: if all things can be arousing to some, it stands to reason that people will find at least one element of de Sade arousing. I struggle with anything but the profanities. The incest and children paedophiles will find arousing. Many will find the buggery arousing; necrophiliacs will find the corpse arousing;

sadomasochists will find the torture arousing. I really struggle with the vomit, the serpent buggering the man, the women ripped apart by the phalluses of horses and other huge mammals, the miscarriages, the slitting of goats' throats. So I objectively took apart each thing and hopefully returned still mentally whole. The vomit is the surge of fluid, stronger, and faster, than any fantastical ejaculation. It comes from the mouth, itself a sexual organ, and probably symbolises the expulsion every man wants. The serpent, once I'd analysed it, was quite obvious: it is the disembodied penis, the nonhuman, cold, guilt-free fucking penis that resides in the head and belongs to nobody, literally. The horse, bulls and other large mammals are reverse anthropomorphism. Instead of seeing the animals as humans and giving them human qualities, the humans are identifying with the raw prowess of animal mating, rather like watching lions mate on a documentary and mounting your "lioness" with the same vigour. I wondered why they were killing the women and why the women weren't also mammals, but this is a gender difference: the men want to see themselves as fine strong rampant mammals, yet still see their mates as delicate maidens. I can offer no hypothesis for the miscarriages, the slitting of goats' and other animals' throats while the animals are fucking women or men or being buggered. I don't know the experience of a man's orgasm, but for a woman it is the most powerful bodily experience, not missing a single nerve, contracting through the mind and entire body, leaving the body spasming for a long time afterwards. Slitting a throat is another powerful act: it will result in immediate death – indeed orgasms are called *"petites morts"*. Female orgasms don't have an immediate death; male orgasms ejaculate from hard to limp in less than sixty seconds – the throat slitting symbolises the immediacy. The goat or ram symbolises the phallus, the death of the goat, the "death" of the phallus. It's the subconscious wish that the phallus should have such power and stamina and ejaculate with the pressure similar to the burst of blood from the jugular. Action movies have burst dams, machine guns and explosions in them; de Sade brings the subconscious wish for that greatest spurt closer to humanity and the living. Understanding this is a horrible thing to do. I have to read each act as it is, in the literal cold blood, dissect it all to understand the minds that might find eroticism in the acts, then put it all back together and say, Am I still sane? do I find any of this erotic? see the literal again? feel the nausea rising and know I'm still as I was? Sane is the wrong word: it has no meaning other than in legal terminology, ironically.

De Sade will induce a huge dissonance within you, the acts are horrific, you will not want to feel arousal, but if there is honesty between your body and mind you will, even if it's just a reaction to the word "fuck" running all the way through. The story I'm telling is very scary and serious. I don't want to incite any arousal whatsoever, but you have to understand that the whole sequence of events, some of which may be arousing, is my cost for your understanding.

Pornography

We often talked of pornography and I think reading or watching it together would have been different. We'd look at medieval and Victorian drawings and books. You wanted tacky 1970s videos such as Deepthroat and we'd look for them together, and the sleazy 1990s Ben Dover films. You had on your Amazon wish list, sitting under Disney films and criminology texts, The Oyster, The Pearl and De Sade. Oh my naïveté! I assumed de Sade was 1700s erotica, not different from The Oyster, other than in period and location. I wanted to write erotica for you, provide the passionate fantasies we loved with no distractions from another writer's perception. Write erotica for you to read, while I knelt under your naked form, you sitting on a chair, me sitting at you feet. Neither of us moving, complete stillness, just you reading, and me listening, without reaction, as our breathing would naturally uncontrollably deepen, our

breasts rise, hips begin to writhe, sex swell and moisten. Neither of us
would move. You would keep reading and I listening, until the end.

Day Twenty-Five

On the fourth day the "heroes" distinguish whose property each
child is by different-coloured ribbons. A ribbon worn over the face
to represent who owns the cunt and a ribbon worn over the nape,
representing who owns the arse. Sexual pleasure comes from the
pleasure and response of the partner – the greater the response the
more intense the pleasure. I've lain in bed next to a lover before,
stirred by her naked form, turned to trail my fingers down her
spine, the back of her thighs, breathe softly against the nape of her
neck; and, on the occasions that the only response has been the
depth of her sleep, my ardour has quickly deadened against the
stillness. I see rape, necrophilia, sex with sleeping bodies and the
ownership in de Sade's novel as the same thing. They all possess a
commonality. Each sees an object, not a person, a mind, an
individual, not even a whole body, just a cunt or an arse, a hole. A
dehumanised, detached, dead, still, unresponsive hole. An
inanimate object, not different from the house, car, tools,
television, consumer durables of capitalist hedonism, the owned,
inanimate objects, claimed, coveted, fought over, labelled as
belonging to. An alpha wolf owns space, owns the carcass, owns
the trinkets of nature he drops to the pack in gratitude for loyalty;
he doesn't own the alpha female. She responds willingly or turns
her teeth to rip out his throat in preference for a better wolf or
simply because she has no desire at the time. The real confusion
with rape, necrophilia, sex with sleeping partners and de Sade is
how a person reaches a point where s/he sees others on a par with
dead meaningless objects, yet does not see him/herself as an
object? In the case of autism, the emotions exist; the individual
with autism simply cannot read expression, gesture and emotion
of others. Could it be that de Sade, and the others mentioned who

see humans as objects for their entertainment, can feel their own meaning and experience, yet cannot see the life in others, are totally void of empathy? Close to the definition of a psychopath, but psychopaths show charm, no matter how superficial. For the charm to exist there must be an understanding, empathy, however slight, of others and an awareness of response. I struggle to understand the ownership of anything living, plants, animals. Bodies can be forced, but minds and will surely cannot. Humans are not unlike animals at the base reduction; creating physical associations can induce behaviour. Thus taken to its extreme, advertisers could claim ownership. They mass-control the minds of millions, but does that make the mind no different from a dead fragmented object? I imagine Pavlov's dog: a bell rings, s/he gets food, not any different from the association millions of schoolchildren make every day – at the lunch bell, hunger follows. It's a natural bodily response, but that doesn't mean to say that dog and those children are pliable objects like clay. Take the food away and of course the dog will drool, but who's to say s/he isn't feeling, "Where is my food, you bastard?" Ring the lunch bell and provide no food for the children and observe the reaction, conditionable yes, inanimate objects no.

Fetish shops and floggers
We are watching television in your flat, one of those late-night magazine shows. There is a commentary of a group of young people investigating the sex area of I can't remember where – I think New York. They go into a sex shop, comment on the outfits and sex toys, nothing different. They continue on to a sex venue, a huge building with several floors all having different themes, some nurses, some prisons, police, and a dungeon. In the dungeon they watch a flogging and one young man of the group is persuaded to try. The dominatrix uses the two-flogger method, through the distant screen of the television; it looks not dissimilar to a massage, except for the leather shards of the two cat-o'-nines and the masseurs.

You turn to me: "We could try that, that wouldn't hurt: it's just like a gentle massage."

I nod and continue watching, considering how thin straps of leather splaying onto bare flesh can ever not hurt, but you know better than I, don't you? I trust you, trust your judgement.

Another time we're wandering around the fetish shops in my city, criticising the dire quality of the leather and lack of quality clothing. We look at the leg spreaders, the blindfolds, the cuffs.

"Hon, look at this." You're looking at a small version of a suede cat-o'-nine-tails in purple.

"It's so soft babe – feel it."

I feel the flowing tresses, smell the aromatic new hide. "Yeah, it is really soft."

"Something like this wouldn't hurt."

I nod. "No, it wouldn't."

I never stop to think why we are looking at it. We have moved, shifted gear, we are no longer the innocents we were when we first met, and I don't even realise. I don't realise you've changed, we've changed, don't realise I'm not the person I was and, because I don't realise, I don't try to return.

Day Twenty-Six

The Bastille is highly clinical and routined. Not only does each child have a set date for the taking of virginity by a specific "hero", but they are also taught how to "frig", masturbate a phallus, by the narrators, using a dummy. The narrators provide their experience from a life of "training" starting in prepubescent childhood. "Training" gives validity to the paedophilia. The paedophile has changed his/her mindset to eliminate responsibility, instead of seeing his/her actions as abuse without consent; s/he sees the actions almost as a public service, an education of the young, rather than a corruption. The children and "wives" are punished if the "heroes" don't orgasm. The children and "wives" are perceived to be responsible for the arousal of the "heroes", and any decrease of such is blamed on the child's "wife's" lack of skill, thus rendering any punishment just. This distorted view can only come from a serious deficit in development. The perpetrators have no sense of self, no sense of free will, no sense of personal control over their actions. They possess an ID, without an ego and superego. They are for ever trapped in pre-seven-years-of-age egocentricity. Like the infants the psychoanalyst Melanie Klein describes as splitting, a child or wife is completely good when the perpetrators receive their pleasure and completely bad when they don't. Like pre-toilet-trained infants, they don't have a sense of control over their bodies and, worse still, their minds. The fact that the perpetrators are younger and less aware than the children they abuse in no way excuses them. They are adults, they are skilful in adult manipulation and deception, they have developed. They choose to use only the ego, view from the egocentric, split, not take responsibility for their bodies and minds. They choose to abuse others and choose to pass on that responsibility to the abused. They are developed enough to dole out punishment, to desire adult sexual pleasure and know it in all its extremities. They are developed enough to control the schedules and lives of others. In essence they have passed through development, then, in a personal postmodern pick-and-mix have chosen the elements that suit, validate and excuse their behaviour in a very aware and calculated manner. Passing responsibility for one's behaviour to others is not a simple ploy to think, carry out and maintain.

Rushing the innocence
It had been a long yet busy six weeks without each other. You'd had your scholarship for Oxford confirmed:

*Hey you..i know your not a morning person but I just had to try to get you out of bed as I've got my scholarship for Oxford!!!!!!!!!! *yippee**

I just got word in the post earlier and wanted you to be the first to know lol but now your like the last cos I've phoned my family, mates etc and tried to get you out of bed several times but to no avail (but I have to admit to feeling very guilty about ringing you cos I know you need your sleep too....oh, dilemmas, dilemmas lol) Anyway, must dash...have got to email loads of people, especially those snobby buggers down in Oxford itself and tell them that they have the dubious pleasure of my company come October. lol.

love ya loads

C.x.x.x.x. (the very very walking on air excited C today lol).

I met you on the commuting train between the two cities, electricity passing between us as we sat, thighs close together, our breathing quickening. We wanted each other there and then with the rhythm of the train, could have easily stayed there making love, oblivious of the passing stops, but our love was too special, too private. We departed holding hands in a taxi during the short distance of my house. Our hunger continued upstairs without our stopping to drink or eat; you were my food, my liquid. Under black linen trousers, perfectly moulded to your form, you wore the most sensual, the softest of shorts, clinging to the folds of your thighs, your hips. I nestled my head into your body, your breasts so full, so perfect, rising to the sunlight, your thigh warming my cheek. I wanted to stay here for ever, feeling your heat, smelling you, our closeness, not to remove your shorts, just lie with you, cascaded in our love, the emotion and anticipation greater than any act. We made love slowly yet urgently, tenderly yet passionately. I wanted you all at once, to lie in your arms, to hold you, gently caress your face, your hair, your skin once again, smell you, feel your warmth, relax with you. I wanted to kiss you softly full of love, and kiss you hard full of lust. I wanted to watch you, take in your curves. I wanted to taste you, feeling your flavour as part of me once again. I wanted to hold you, and shiver with the intensity of our love. I wanted to grind against you, our bodies so close and intimate once more. I wanted to fuck you hard, take you and never leave you. We did all those things then lay in each other's arms tightly, flesh pressing against trembling flesh, mind pressing against floating mind, intoxicated in love.

After a while you rose and took out the harness and Dusty. You put the harness on; I trailed every finger between the leather and your skin, watched transfixed as the leather binds made your permanently pouting rise swell and redden even more. I bit into your thighs, tasting you and new leather simultaneously. I teased and teased, never wanting to stop, running my fingers down the smooth, black, shiny straps, then your lily-white groin, pushing against your closed, hidebound sex. You wanted me to try it on. I did to please you, and wanted to, but not then. I was menstruating and enjoying you too much. You locked Dusty into the shards of leather. I didn't want this. We agreed to explore the harness and Dusty separately. I still wanted to know your body more with my own flesh, then slowly introduce Dusty, after months, after much more lovemaking, just teasing with it at first, incorporating it now and again, not to replace us. I thrust mechanically, blankly, bored, ignoring the period pains and the discomfort of thrusting away aimlessly in an attempt to please you. For the first time, I was unaroused with you; you were like all the others, unconnected. I couldn't feel your flesh against mine, couldn't feel any intimacy, any intensity, any depth, any love, any us. You turned on your back, on your knees, the edge of the bed, every position imaginable, not talking softly and sensually, as we usually did, not in tune with me. I thrust like a chore, a robot, neither enjoying it nor confident. I didn't know every cell of your body, I didn't know the dildo, I didn't know the harness, I didn't even feel like fucking. None of this was part of us. It was unfamiliar, hadn't been initiated into our intimacy. Nonetheless, I wanted to please you, didn't want to lose you. You pulled away, hurt from a missed thrust. I felt guilty at hurting you, so guilty, yet with hindsight I couldn't feel your body, your responses; there was no communication physically, verbally or mentally, just cold thrusting. I felt dirty, used like a sex object, disregarded, but could say nothing. I'd hurt you and that was more important, though it was an obvious consequence. There was no build-up, no teasing; you weren't turned on; I wasn't turned on. Our connection was missing and so was the necessary physical responses that make lovemaking pleasurable. It wasn't merely my clumsiness: I couldn't feel where I was thrusting. Anyway, you were miles away, I was miles away; it was your urgency to coldly fuck, rather than our usual intense lustful urgency. Neither of us was turned on, there was no passion, electricity, chemical reaction, just an urgency to fuck without arousal or reason and an urgency to please without arousal or reason.

Day Twenty-Seven

De Sade is taking me through a labyrinth of vomit-inducing behaviours. Sentence after sentence thrusts the senses with the sucking of month-long-unwashed feet, the inhaling of wind and every other possible permutation of filth. A friend informs me that the drinking of vomit so often described in de Sade is called a Roman shower. I assumed it to be some fantasy he invented to shock, not something people practised and found arousal from. I'm going deeper underground, hearing, seeing the things de Sade writes.

A couple of weeks ago, I was in a shop that sells leather. I'm talking with the two men; they are recounting tales of people nearly bleeding to death in a private dungeon party. This is real life, not one of de Sade's fantasies. Did I open the novel and step into the middle of it, or did I become embroiled in Colette's dangerous games while de Sade is but a figment of my imagination? I'm trapped in a parallel world. I wonder where the world has gone, the way it was before, before Colette. I feel as though I am going crazy, yet I know, since meeting Colette, the craziness I have encountered far surpasses my fears. How many corpses? How many? How many deaths from infection, vampire paddles, buggery, razors, beatings? How many are hidden away? How many parents scream for their missing children? Children for missing parents? Thirty people dying in de Sade's novel chilled me. Now I wonder how much of what he was writing was fiction and how much worse the reality is. I wonder how many people are getting tugged towards the centre of the earth, how many slip and decide they enjoy living on the soil, sinking into the grave.

The cause of pain is not quite clear, but functionally it is a message from the brain to alert the individual to an injury. Clear unmarked flesh is healthy. Bruises, weals, cuts, scratches, tears, swellings are damage. Urine might be sterile, but vomit, faeces and sputum are infectious, carrying toxins, not the hot sexy hormones that seep through clean flesh. I accept and I try, but I don't understand; moreover, I want to slash the tentacles trying to pull me under.

Summer love

The Dusty experience created a sexual barrier we had never before experienced. Although you did taste me into orgasm, I discouraged you reluctantly. I was menstruating, but you insisted. It felt strange, so conscious yet so intimate, so afraid, yet so bonding. You were the only person who has and ever will do that. Our love was as strong, if not stronger. We laughed in the cinema, shared waffles and knowing looks in Fatty Arbuckle's. Holding hands walking through the streets. You talked of Oxford and how, once you were settled, you'd show me all of its wonders. We talked love and future in the best Chinese restaurant and laughed with chopsticks. I massaged your feet, your back, kneading out your tension while you watched Stuart Little. You were carrying something, something you wouldn't tell me about. I could feel it in your skin, see it in your eyes, read it in your mind. You hugged me in the street, slept on my shoulder, reassured me you loved me deeper than ever, that you were happier than ever, happy with us, just apprehensive about Oxford. I knew it was more than that, something else, but not us.

Six nights you stayed. We held each other close, whispered that we could never go so long again without seeing each other, whispered soft talk of love well into the night, and again as our entwined bodies dawned. We graced Debenham's, Marks and Spencer's and Boots, buying sweet luxuries to share, browsing in the intimacy of a couple who've been together years.

Our sexual barrier broke the day before you left. You'd being studying and I reading. We were tired. We drifted into sleep side by side. Slowly our bodies merged in frequency, like waves dancing, perfectly choreographed. Our breathing quickened together; hips began a slow satin writhe in harmony. Our bodies took over, automatic control; suddenly we were kissing softly, making tender love into sleep, awakening again one with each other, sharing scent, skin. You caught the train about 1 p.m., packed some crisps, Pepsi and chocolate we'd bought the day before. All morning you didn't speak. You had a sadness. I felt your pain, wanted to hold you close, tell you everything would be all right. You wouldn't say what was wrong. I think you were scared of crying if you spoke. I felt so guilty that we hadn't more time to talk, that you hadn't the time to cry. I wanted to kiss away all your fears and pain, but the clock sped you away and your eyes remained straight ahead and choked as your train pulled away, and I just wanted to jump on and reach you.

Day Twenty-Eight

Does a journey begin when you book the train, or when you board? Most boarders of de Sade are merely trainspotters, but my journey began before I knew the train I was on, destination unknown. I ask why, always I ask why. Why are we here? Why is life? Why is de Sade? Why the children? Why pain? Why oppression? Why abuse? Why me? The blonde girl at school when I asked her why, why she lied, why she made love, then cut dead, she said, "There isn't a reason for everything; you have to accept there isn't a reason for everything." Maybe I should stop assuming people are reasonable beings in control of their actions.

All the storytellers in *One Hundred and Twenty Days of Sodom* were introduced to sex and vice from childhood. I want to scream, "No!" Imagine going through the most intense fear and pain, thinking that every day is your last, not that you *might* die but you *will*, and it will be a grotesque, horrific death. Imagine that you want to run away, be put in prison, murdered, fall to your death, anything other than the life you have. Imagine monsters ten times your size that smell strange and bitter, that make you look at the most disturbing images, violate your personal body space, make you touch slimy, greasy, horrible saggy flesh, covering you with their poison until you freeze and vomit with repulsion and fear. That is what sexual abuse is like at four years of age, and the full horror cannot be verbalised intensely enough. There is no way anyone would repeat such pain on another: quite the opposite, the escapee will warn and protect others from the adult ogres behind Taboo Mountain. De Sade writes the narrators as abuse victims to validate paedophilia; they recount it as something they enjoyed, because that takes the guilt away from de Sade, the "heroes" and every other paedophile. It's a strategic game of manipulating perception, facts, expression and gesture, the paedophiles perceive gesture as it suits them. The child has to perceive the slightest gesture accurately as a matter of life or death.

I live with the burden of reading the slightest expressional change, any flicker of body language daily. I know the second eye flash of insincerity, when a person listens, when s/he doesn't, but pretends to be listening, the slightest sexual interest, hidden contempt, insecurity, fear, defence, attack, I see it all. The lie behind the smile, the plea behind the scowl, the deception behind the grin, the mouth is but a mask and I hate seeing behind that mask. I hate looking into people, seeing the reality. I want to live as others live, fall into the same ignorant bliss, see the fabrication; instead I see, therefore react to, truth. I had a counsellor once and

I could catch the flickers of horror cross her face, the oh-so-slight shudders pass through her body, and I felt bad to have disturbed her so. I want to be as far removed from de Sade as possible, but, unfortunately, the cycle is like politics, fascism and communism eventually meet.

Birthday blues

You returned home without calling the next day as you'd arranged, or the next. You mailed to say you'd bumped into friends, and stayed the night with them, drunk. I had a sense, a sense of something wrong. You mailed the next day to say we were over. I felt confused, astounded – we were new, still so madly in love. We had a long conversation, you still persuading me to visit you, I saying I couldn't do that and not touch you, and I doubted you could either. Later that day, or it may have been the next, you mailed saying you did still want us, you were just terrified about Oxford, thus lost and confused. Panic had set in, you were still trying to complete a dissertation for another master's, but the panic blocked your flow, you wrote a word in two weeks.

Your fear wasn't about the deadline, but about yourself. Oxford challenged all your certainties in yourself. You challenged, questioned your ability, your background, but I never did. Oxford was all you ever wanted, and I knew you would succeed, not because you wanted it so badly, but because you are more than capable, and beyond. Nonetheless, nerves ate away at you, not only over your academic ability, but your social status and skills. You are brilliant, witty, your eyes dance and involve those around you when you talk. You propel your passion for all things for life. To me it was obvious everyone would love you. I felt so useless, so helpless, hated to see you in pain, your pain hurt me more than my own. Nothing I could do would change your emotional turmoil; nothing I could say would change the thoughts residing inside you.

September was your birthday. When we met in August, you were full of excitement and anticipation about our sharing it together. During your brief closure into yourself, when I'd said I couldn't see you as anything other than the love of my life, you'd made alternative arrangements to spend it with your ex, Helen. I was two hundred and fifty miles away; Helen was less than half a mile away. You saw Helen daily. I was hurt that you couldn't restore the original plan, not particularly because it was your birthday, but because it was only two weeks before you were about to go away to Oxford. And, with trying to complete your outstanding dissertation, settle in and keep up with the MPhil work, I knew it would be weeks before we'd see each other. You wouldn't even let me call to wish you happy birthday because Helen was there. I was confused, hurt and annoyed. What was the issue? She was an ex, a friend; I was your partner. Oxford and the dissertation were pressuring you; work and money issues were pressuring me; and all in all they were pressuring us, the world was closing in.

Day Twenty-Nine

I'm beginning to think the world is turning into de Sade's vision. A vision of a world driven by nothing but hedonistic pleasures of the senses, themselves oppressive, for one person's sensual pleasure can abuse another. The *Sunday Times* wrote a report about the "debauched" French, being far more "depraved" than the British, as the British held only secret suburban key parties, whereas the French have swingers' clubs in every city. I wonder if a country can sue a paper for misrepresentation of the facts. Previously I assumed there to be an element of investigation in journalism, not quite matching science, but nonetheless at least some attempt at investigation. I'm being unfair: the report did contain investigation in Paris. Any in the comparative United Kingdom? Obviously not, or else they would have found at least one swingers' club in every city and a lot more "debauchery" than France.

De Sade himself has been held responsible for fetishes, particularly those concerning the giving and receiving of pain. Philosophy, psychology, validated doctrines, not just the lay person, all name the giving of pain after de Sade. Even when discussing the combined giving and receiving of pain, de Sade's name tops the bill, no pun intended. Sadism, sadomasochism, sadist, every dictionary, diagnostic manual of psychological disorders and fetish economy immortalises de Sade. I wonder if, as with the *Sunday Times*, this universal immortalisation was based on any investigation, scientific or otherwise. In the same vein as de Sade's being a *comte*, not a *marquis*, buggery, paedophilia, vomit, faeces, urine, prostitution, particularly of children, feature far more – and with increased salience in description – than flagellation. Pain is a constant. The buggery does involve ripped anuses, however. The desire could be for rough sex, as the focus is on the act, not the pain. There was a lot of pain and extreme torture and fatalities in de Sade's work, there is no denying, but sufficient to herald him as the founder of pain rather than paedophilia, buggery, scat and similar? De Sade wasn't the founder of anything. He wrote novels, nothing new. But through words he reached a mass audience and had a sharp, powerful group of letters forming his name. Sade, sadism sound far more like cunt than masochism, though still nowhere near as profound; buggery already had a name; and, as for scat, his name is too stylish for that. Besides, flogging bare behinds was a far more gripping area of study. Pain has been part of human interaction since the pagans and before – throughout evolution. People would beat themselves into a frenzy while giving thanks to their gods. In certain tribes pain is seen as "normal" rather than belonging to the realms of mental illness. In every culture certain pain is seen as "normal". I could never really understand why holes through the ears were seen as different from masochism – if it hurts it hurts. Likewise, how is the tattooist, the dentist, the Saturday-night aggressor distinct from the pain giver, fashionably called the "sadist"? Sadomasochism is different from any coupling animal, including humans. Why? Are the usual bites, scratches, bruises during sex the same as dental pain, which of course for reasons my logic has yet to compute is different from sadomasochistic pain? The truth of de Sade remains far more diverse and extreme than any legend, although he was not the founder of pain.

The admission

I find myself on the Hotmail page that says, "To reset your password, please answer your secret question." I'm staring at the page. You've been distant, or maybe I've been distant, or maybe we both have. It could be the sum of the pressure, or the silly tiffs we had over our not meeting up before you were due to go to Oxford, or your being away every weekend – but I have a feeling and have to follow it.

"What is my vibrator called?"

I'm still staring at the screen. Of course I know the answer: you told me while we relaxed in your lounge. I simply don't want to do it, don't want to reset your password, don't want to enter your account, but, I have to reassure myself, it's nothing more than the mutual pressure. Later that night, you attempted to access your mail and realised your password had been reset. Somehow we got into a "yeah, well" disagreement – the kind that start, "Yeah, well, what was I supposed to think?" and move on to, "Yeah, well, I cybered Carat." I shrank back in my chair. It was a stupid thing to say, not only because it was before we met, but, because I don't cyber. It was a stupid bet with Osiris. I never dreamed for a minute that events would make me wish the playful bet had never occurred. You replied, "Yeah, well, I slept with a guy, or didn't I?"

"What?"

"I slept with a guy"

"Who? When?"

"Bernard, in May, when we split."

"You're joking, aren't you?"

"Am I or aren't I?"

Your MSN went off, I tried to call, you didn't answer. I reset the

password on your email again, reading nothing, just deleting every
message I'd ever sent you from as far back as February. I sat back
stunned, my whole body numb, my face blank as those in grief or those
without awareness.

Day Thirty

It's an odd summer without you and with de Sade – a cold
summer. I expect he'd prefer it cold, somewhat reduce the risk of
pungency in his present state. However, that is my projection, for
de Sade is the grand master of pungency. In a strange way de Sade
is a better man than many, for he takes all that is human and
embraces it. Lay aside the violence and nonconsensual acts for a
moment, though not for long, for we must never forget true
humanness and responsibility. In our society, we view people as
objects, status symbols, and we are all guilty. We make assessments
of height, weight, face structure, body shape, carriage, style,
behaviour and level of education at a very minimum; we all make
those assessments. Think not? I too try to convince myself not,
but reading de Sade brings home to me that a greasy, wart-ridden
women would definitely not be regarded at all as a lover, yet if she
had good communication skills and interesting dialogue she
might be regarded as a friend.

The early "days" of *One Hundred and Twenty Days of Sodom* is
about raw bodies, internal bodies, complete body workings, saliva,
vomit, gases, grime, faeces. It makes me question if I ever love
humanity; the individual or just the external outer layer. I love
Colette, but could I ever stomach her vomit? It's a question I can
never answer honestly because it would never come to pass, but I
like the human containment and have no desire to empty its
contents. Am I loving, then, just the container? Possibly, but less
so than de Sade. De Sade writes hundreds of bodies, hundreds of
acts, many unnamed; he describes a girl breaking wind into a
man's mouth, then, barely a sentence away, another man drinking

champagne in which he has just washed a month's worth of dirt from a woman. Perhaps this is the reason de Sade needs to literally get inside a human body. All he sees is the body, hundreds of bodies, tall bodies, short bodies, thin bodies, big bodies, clean bodies, dirty bodies, clear bodies, ulcerated bodies, young bodies, old bodies, not a human in sight, just lots of bodies, objects. I don't love a container, a vessel: I love that container because of her expression, because of the way her mind weaves, because of her wit, her purity, her wickedness, her shyness, her confidence. I don't need to exchange vomit to know I love her in entirety. I look inside her soul and mind, not the biological tissue, which I love regardless, hence have no need to reduce her to that. If that means the greasy, warted women will be in no area past friendship, so be it. I can't deny my genetic programming, because de Sade's denial of the complete person led him to accept every possible physicality.

Total shock

I didn't sleep again for a long time, weeks, months. I had no stability, would fluctuate from staring blankly into space to pacing with a nauseous rush building. I didn't eat. I went whole days without drinking or even moving. Life demanded of me, swished around me, and my body would move, but I wasn't there. I don't know where I went, still don't. I had no place to go, I was but a protector of myself, an emotionless mechanism, a nothing that had somehow fallen in love. There was no other part of me to hold it all together in times of crisis. I did that and now I was lost. Nothing was holding me together, still isn't. I was the one who worked, organised, paid the bills, kept order. My body was in fear, my adult parts had left the building, abandoned a sinking ship. My life was in the hands of my teenage parts of my psyche, my work, my house all left for someone else to sort while I stared blankly. Any bits of me left with awareness were petrified. Where was the logical adult? Had they died for ever? After days of living off chocolate and television viewing with no limits, the initial teenage bravado turned into fear. Dead adults and scared teenagers aren't the healthiest state.

Day Thirty-One

I'll fetch Monsieur her son along before he's fully done, and I'll toss him off like a sardine.

– Curval, discussing aborting Constance's pregnancy.

He continues, "Why yes, 'tis perfectly true I am not fond of progeny, and that when the beast is laden it quickens a furious loathing in me, but to imagine I killed my wife on that account is to be gravely mistaken. Bitch that you are, get it into your head that I have no need of reasons in order to kill a woman, above all a bitch that, were she mine, I'd very surely keep from whelping."

This clearly illustrates de Sade's hatred of women. A defamation that cuts to the womb of every woman and turns a natural female capability into an animalistic shame, thus undermining female power and insulting her strength. He describes women as disposable and uses language associated with animals. Perhaps more interesting is the repetition of abusive language across generations. De Sade wrote *One Hundred and Twenty Days of Sodom* in 1785, yet dialogue such as "gravely mistaken", "Bitch that you are", "get it into your head" can be clearly identified with present abusers, as I'm sure many battered wives will recognise.

The favourite narrator recounts the mysterious disappearance of her sister, who left the brothel to work for a man who had seen her regularly for six months. Duclos went to the address her sister gave, yet never found her sister again.

" 'I was never able to discover what had become of her.'

" 'I dare say not,' Desgranges observed, 'for, twenty-four hours after having left you, she was no longer alive.'

" 'And spare us any emotional demonstrations, Duclos,' the

Duc said dryly, upon noticing that it was all she could do to keep back a few involuntary tears, 'we don't care for regrets and grievings, you know; as a matter of fact, all the works of Nature could be blown to hell and we'd not emit so much as a sigh. Leave tears to idiots and children, and may they never soil the cheeks of a clearheaded, clear-thinking woman, the sort we esteem.' With these words, our heroine took herself in hand and resumed her narrative at once."

Abortion and killings. Disposable – women and their produce are disposable, irrelevant to the scheme of de Sade's perception. Does this merely disclose de Sade's mental state or was de Sade simply brave or indifferent enough to write those thoughts? How many paedophiles, snuff lovers, wife beaters and the others who don't act, but still think, how many make up the male population, and do they share de Sade's thoughts? De Sade is incredibly brave: few share thoughts, lest they be seen as thinking dysfunctionally, hence nobody really knows if they are thinking within the realms of "healthy". People hold their thought processes so close because they are so afraid. I thought I knew fear until I read de Sade. With such a constant of violent, abusive thoughts, I fail to understand how he didn't lose mental coherence. Thinking is a powerful tool in regulating action. Decisions are so much easier when discussed in one's head. Yes it's perfectly sane to have a narrator sitting in your head, and even to discuss two opposing opinions. The taboo of how people think should be opened. Psychology does so much, yet also so little of what it could do. When people know of my psychology degree, they ask, "Can you tell what I'm thinking?" Of course, what they mean is, "Am I thinking functionally?" Yes, you are, and I don't need to tell what you are thinking because *you* can. What about violent thoughts like de Sade's? I find the level quantity and constancy of de Sade's abusive thoughts very difficult to process and cannot see how such cognitions can be positive. However, a few days ago, I was walking into the city centre and considering Paul Briton's theory of violent material, films or books, and their having no effect on the majority, but being a catalyst for those who – due to abuse or other circumstance – relate to the violence and proceed to carry it out. It was during the debate surrounding the film *Natural Born Killers* that Briton suggested his theory.

Whether films or cathartic thoughts of hunting down, torturing and killing paedophiles, those occasional fixes actually calm and sedate, releasing tension. The more violence is actually acted, the less the thoughts, the more the thoughts the less any action – and I favour thoughts and films to bruises.

The worst attack

I called you, called you and said I was completely broken, but calm and ready to listen. Which bit didn't you hear? When didn't you hear it – when I left the message, when I emphasised it, when you finally called back after four days? "I'm calm, I'm not angry, I love you the same, I want to know everything and I'll just listen and say nothing." That is what I said, consistently what I said. I wasn't angry. You had no reason to defend, let alone attack. I wasn't asking or expecting you to.

"I took my top off as soon as he came in through the door. I fucked him all over the flat. We fucked four times, masturbated each other four times, he went down on me twice and I gave him oral sex twice. He came all over my hair. We fucked all night, in every single room."

You didn't coldly tell me the facts: you revelled in every word, your voice full of excitement and arousal as though you were reliving every minute of it and had loved every minute of it, loved it far more than any passion we had ever shared. You never spoke of our lovemaking in such detail, with such passion, even though you had always emphasised how mind-blowing it was. From the tone in your voice it couldn't compare to this. I listened and listened, for hours, maybe two, maybe four, my body paralysed, my stomach griped with nausea. The night-long fucking

*binge I wasn't angry about: we were split, it wasn't an issue. But this –
what need was there for this? To overtly describe, relive, become aroused
while you were reliving it to me. I wanted cold facts of all that occurred,
not a running commentary of your passionate memories, not a vicious
attack, not how brilliant it was. I was rationally listening, calmly
hearing what you had to say, and what you were saying was your fuck
was so wonderful you couldn't recount it coldly, it surpassed us,
surpassed respecting us. It was so wild you couldn't just tell me the facts
without your arousal interrupting. I asked you why.*

"*I was horny, I wanted him.*"

Day Thirty-Two
An old witch of about seventy came to our house; I was curious
what brought her to us, she seemed to have an expectant air, and,
yes, I was told she was awaiting a customer.

Duclos recounts the grimiest acts with toothless old women
and filthy men. Men inserting unwashed penises into gums. Men
gagging human beings, choking them, dispelling their acrid fluid.
De Sade describes only acts, yet I can see the damp worn walls, feel
the cold unfamiliar linen and smell – how much I can smell that
bitter venom! Lies can mock the ears, mock the eyes, but never the
olfactory senses. Since being exposed to this nausea-inducing
stench from three on my mother's hands, clinging to her like a
rabid virus, incensing great wrath deep within me – and a year
later contaminated with it over my own prepubescent flesh – I
have never understood women's tolerance or mastery of
withholding vomit as it hits the nasal cavity. I can understand
male tolerance of it, since they have to acclimatize to the
pungency from around twelve years of age.

I remember my change from no scents – other than those
clinging from others – to acquiring adult hormones and aroma. I
detested it. I wasn't used to having a scent. I was no longer familiar

within my own body. I would wash several times a day, and even with the soap and water on my skin I could smell this on me. I was conscious that the whole world could smell me. Luckily, it was only the heady musk of female hormones that after several years I finally became accustomed to. I started feeling familiar with the scent and gradually accepting it with Cline, though I probably never truly accepted any scent separate from my own until Colette. I still sometimes find myself walking along the street and being hit by the reek of human as people pass, and my lip curls involuntarily.

Loss of trust

Your words replayed in my head. Not once, but constantly. Not words, but the whole: smells, tastes, touches, actions, expressions. Everything from the reddening of your skin from kneeling on your hands and knees to the greasy coating of perspiration you shared. I smelled all of it and the nausea reeled up from my stomach not once, but constantly. Every time I thought of us, of you now, I saw, smelled, felt your stinging words as though I had been forced to observe. The sickness never left me; for months the animation of your words resided in my forehead from the minute I woke and in all my dreams. Still when I talk to you, spasms of building bile grip me. What you say since, what anyone says since, whatever hits my senses, all I can keep reliving are those words you spat and the arousal with which you spat them, drawing me into that night with him. Drawing me into a place I don't want to be and holding me hostage there for ever.

We decided to try to rebuild what we had not so long ago shared. Decided we had something too close, special, intense, deep, loving to throw away. We had split when you fucked Bernard; apart from the emotional attack, neither of us had done anything wrong. Yet I couldn't trust or believe you. I wanted to, I wanted to so badly. That's why I wanted to listen calmly in the first place, so you could feel safe in our closeness with the truth. You told me it had happened only that once, only with him, and that you'd never slept with anyone while we were together. I wanted to believe you; I tried to, much to the annoyance of myself for acting like a fool. If you were telling the truth, why did you attack so while I calmly listened? If it was a one-off, why did you have about six condoms? Why, when you were obviously so aroused while recounting it, would it just be a one-off? If it occurred six months ago, how could you remember each slight detail so clearly? You said months before in my arms that casual fucks never go back to your place, so it couldn't have been a one-off. If you wanted sex, why not chose a young attractive, fit man or woman? There must have been another reason for choosing a fifty-year-old ugly guy. And so it continued. Why? Why? Why? I needed answers. I will always love you, but no longer trusted you.

Day Thirty-Three

I wonder whether de Sade could have ever stopped writing his novel, stopped writing it as he did, or whether he lost himself becoming part of the momentum, like the narrators and "heroes" in *One Hundred and Twenty Days of Sodom*.

For the first eighty-three days of the story I'm telling, I couldn't have predicted, let alone have stopped the events. Now I'm stuck in a horrible quagmire created by those events and I know not where the force is pulling me. Not becoming like a narrator in de Sade's novel was a more difficult feat than this, so why am I so weak now? Since Colette left I feel nothing, I care for nothing, I want nothing, I can do anything because nothing matters and not wanting something is no longer a deciding factor because I want none of it. Why don't I curl up and die, become all silent, act depressed? Why do I take it all, wanting none? I've also stopped trying to figure out why and instead shrug, saying, "Why not?"

A search for truth

I wanted to move on, my love, for you never waver, but I wanted to regain the intimacy, the truth, and if you wouldn't tell me I'd find out. I asked you for Bernard's number so I could confirm what you had said; you refused. I took your refusal as something you were trying to hide, couldn't see any other explanation. I so much wanted us to be us again, but the sound of your voice, the sight of your name, the constant thoughts of you brought only your act with him and what other hidden possibilities to mind. All I needed was confirmation of your truth, just to ask Bernard what happened and then settle back into us. I wanted to sleep again, to eat again, to rid my body of its continuous nausea. I tried to erase it from my mind, but constantly it would be there, that little voice saying you were taking me for a fool and would persistently deny it without the evidence.

I put out the feelers for his number, made a couple of false starts by relying on the electoral register, but within a day and only two phone calls I had his number through his job. I had it now, but I didn't know what to do; you had no idea I had it, pleaded with me not to contact him, promised you were telling the truth, yet each day I rise in agony of not knowing. The pain was clenching like fists beating inside my head. I held off and held off until the pain became too much.

It was early evening when I called him. I explained who I was and what I was calling about. He was polite, a nice guy. He had no knowledge of me, which I found strange. He did confirm it was just one night, but he said mid- to late summer, whereas, you had said May, which is surely the beginning of summer. He confirmed your lie about the condoms, as I thought they were yours, not his. At the time I was hurting, confused, but with hindsight I salute my astuteness for recognising that a fifty-year-old guy out shopping, not expecting to have sex, might feasibly carry one condom, but not six.

You were fuming when I told you I'd called him and politely asked him to confirm your story.

Day Thirty-Four

In Day Nine de Sade concerns the reader with every possible permutation of scat. Rows of prostitutes defecating in a man's trousers, pots of faeces, any possibility imaginable, de Sade has written it. A Freudian analysis of scat would reduce it to an expulsive fixation in the anal stage of development and I don't disagree, particularly considering the level of maturity of the "heroes". While shit is seen to be an insult, it's also a highly personal result of the churning of the inner body in sorting the nutritious from the waste, and that waste, although unneeded, is very much a part of the person, created by the person as the precious energy. I don't credit de Sade or his "heroes" with any consideration of this, but it is analogous to the products of the mind. Hence the term "don't talk shit", and, of course, for all but scat lovers, this is taken as an insult for whatever resides within us, created by us, is part of us and thus is not to be demeaned. Is any production of the human body or mind less meaningful than others, and if so how do we tell the shit from the gems?

Colette saw style, fashion, and not only of the clothing kind but mental fashion, social fashion, intellectual fashion. I don't see fashion: I look through people like a X-ray, revert them all to cave persons and then make my analysis. I don't see categories: rich, poor, trendy, passé, old, young, animal, human. I see patterns, behaviour, hierarchy. I walk through my Bastille, listening to stories of people on the street – eople who say they've smuggled diamonds, others who say they were held hostage in deepest Africa. I meet hundreds of fascinating people but none stimulate me like Colette. I can talk to none as we talked. I wonder whether de Sade would have been such a libertine had he never had what we shared, then lost, if he'd never met the love of his life or had married her instead of the wife his father chose. I barely notice the passing sixty-five billion people, feeling like a lone member of *Homo sapiens* on a dead planet.

Eating my soul

I try. I hide all my pain. I act as though everything were fine. You can feel my barriers, though. I'm not relaxed with you any more, our naturalness doesn't flow. Our phone calls are now brief. When I hear your voice I hear those words, hear that desire for him, the contempt for us, and you hear the tension that is created in my voice no matter how I try to hide it with the words. My pain doesn't challenge the words. I do love you, I do support you, I do accept you, it does increase by the second, I do miss not being by your side, I always will.

You talk of all the places you are going to show me when you get to Oxford, how we are going to go for a punt ride, explore the grounds, the buildings. You show me websites of where you'll be staying. You are excited; I'm excited, happy for you, happy with you and so, so proud. I tell the world, well everyone I come into contact with, that you are going to Oxford and I'm so proud of you. You go shopping for the things you need and the things you don't, reporting enthusiastically like a child about your steel pan set. I fail to see their use, as you don't cook, but join your enthusiasm, knowing you like them because they're pretty. You buy clothes, bed linen. You have clothes, bed linen already, new. You buy everything, half of Fenwick's. I'm happy that you are, but confused. Where is the poor working-class girl? Why does she need several sets of everything in two locations? How is income support so lucrative? Why does the woman who tells me daily she loves me not recognise my intelligence?

Day Thirty-Five

It's precisely a year since I last saw Colette. I still recall vividly the train pulling out as she looked straight ahead and I walked home alone, feeling scared and oddly out of sorts.

I lie on the grass, trying to feel the sun, trying to feel, but since Colette left I've felt nothing, no pleasure from chocolate, no sensations of hot and cold, no physical pain. I need to nearly die to feel alive again, to want to live again. I need to feel fear to know

I still want to be. Unlike de Sade and his "heroes", I sleep with my door unlocked, even open, since Colette left. I who gently chided her about walking through the city streets alone at night, even though her city has fewer than half the violent attacks and sexual assaults that mine does. Now I have no care to fear the world is my Bastille, and I walk among de Sade's, unprotected and unconcerned. Don't be alarmed: most de Sade's are within the home, anyway. Even with a open door, without a father, a lover, I'm safer than average. Approximately one in two of my lovers has been abusive in some way, physically or mentally. Abuse is supposedly cyclic, but an alternative theory could be that all have a 50 per cent chance of being abused or not and, as with the turn of a coin, some get more heads than tails. It's easy for a theory to say abuse is cyclic. It puts the responsibility back onto the victim, instead of finding a reason and prevention for the perpetrators. It's far more efficient to write off childhood abuse victims as damaged goods for ever destined to a beaten wasted life. It makes de Sade all the more consumable for all those charming intellectuals who preach abuse as a working-class phenomenon, read de Sade purely for research and behind closed doors. It also makes de Sade evade censorship: imagine a working-class wife batterer and abuser of his children recording his activities for the world to read. I can see your upper lip curl in disgust. No need, it will never happen, but what is the difference between that and De Sade's work. There is a difference: the wife batterer's and child abuser's work would never be as extreme and in most cases the victims will have at least some opportunity of getting out alive. De Sade can be published because he's eighteenth-century French aristocracy, but why would anyone want to read him? We all have an element of de Sade in us. We all would like to do as we feel with no restraints. We all do things just because we can. We all oppress others and deny personal responsibility, we drink tea, coffee, eat chocolate, oblivious of the workers who are dying daily at our hands. But we're different from de Sade; we're not violent or depraved. We don't dream of orgies, dream of killing, walk past someone in the street who has bumped us and feel like hitting them, find guns or knives slightly erotic, because none can see that. It's OK, it's just you and a work of fiction. Your dreams, fantasies, private thoughts, anger can't really be seen. The problem with violent partners and abusive parents is they won't admit they are like de Sade or others and come out with, "What a madman", while blaming their lover for hitting him/her, instead of recognising a part of themselves that needs nurture and control.

Oxford fears

It was the first week of October when you travelled down to Oxford. You said you'd call when you got there. You didn't. It was about two weeks before you called and your emails were infrequent. You still had a dissertation to finish for your previous master's by November and you were petrified – petrified of not completing the outstanding dissertation, of being in Oxford, of not being good enough, of failing. You skipped lectures, stayed in your room to complete this dissertation you had neither the inspiration nor the energy for. You were quiet, distant, depressed, out of your natural environment. Sometimes you'd write in awe about the world-renowned researchers lecturing you and the status of your peers. Other times you'd feel out of place among the "toffs". I was worried, wanted you to make friends, to enjoy your time there, tried to support you and talk you out of returning home without pressuring you. I'd dream your tears, your loneliness, the dark depression that veiled you so. You'd come off Prozac suddenly the day you started Oxford and although I've never agreed with Prozac I was well aware of the dangers of suddenly withdrawing from it without a doctor's advice.

Day Thirty-Six

There is a storm finally; perhaps it will clear the air, which hasn't been clear since last summer, though unusually I could breathe through the mugginess, perhaps because I didn't notice my breathing. I sometimes think of cutting de Sade open as he did with many of his characters, to see if he's as rotten inside. I have a naïve belief that violent people smell and eat as they act. There is a correlation between food and behaviour, certain vitamin deficiencies affecting regulation in the parts of the brain related with aggression and lots of fish creating gentle intellects. Excuse me, the kippers on the stove are burning. Colette lived on Marks and Spencer's. Marks and Spencer's pasta bake, Marks and Spencer's shepherd's pie and so on – either Marks and Spencer's or takeouts. She never tasted of Marks and Spencer's burned plastic, full of salt, so I can only assume the local Starbucks slipped vitamin pills into her latte takeout. I live on Sainsbury's, Aldi and the local halal meat shops. Fresh fish, rye bread, hummus, free-trade chocolate from Sainsbury's, smoked salmon from Aldi and fresh sweet potato, pulses, fruit, lamb and bunches of coriander from the halal meat shops. I smell gluten- and dairy-free and look like protein on bones with added fruit.

I've hardly mentioned de Sade, as Days Nine to Sixteen are about little but scat, smearing faeces, eating faeces, inserting faeces into a woman. The only notable event is Duclos telling the story of killing her Madam at the brothel, taking over, and selling the Madam's grandchild after being trusted to distribute the Madam's wealth. All these actions excite Duclos, the "heroes" and no doubt de Sade. I feel a little inadequate when it comes to sex, I find these acts of little interest psychologically, let alone arousing. I find making love arousing, the anticipation of making love, pornography, the writhing of a lover's body, the scent of her, textures, sensual touching, suggestive flirting, and I can honestly say even by this stage of this story, all of which I have not yet written, I have not yet in my experience found anything else arousing. I was in a major city club two weeks ago, two dance floors, café, a huge bustling popular place, not a hidden-away backstreet place. How I came to be there will be apparent later in the story, but, nonetheless, this wasn't a swingers' club, yet there were people having sex in every square of the dance floors and stages, women and women, men and men, men and women. I might add I wasn't expecting such. Imagine being in a huge, flashing, trendy, booming nightclub, dancing away, and two guys are lying on the stage giving each other fellatio. You go downstairs to the high-energy dance floor and two women are naked bent over the balcony overlooking the dance floor, while two men thrust into them, fluffing themselves, showing their penises to all every now and then, the screams drowning out the music. This is not eighteenth-century France, a private orgy, or a hidden-away Bastille. This is here, this is now. There was no one having sex in the toilets or any dark corners by the way.

Dissertation and snappiness

You were panicked; told me you were working around the clock, four days at a time without sleep, just continuous pummelling on your outstanding dissertation. You were angry, tired, frustrated, hurting. I listened, held out my soul and let you release your pain onto me. I trod around you like a fragile feather among high winds. I tried to predict every edge of your voice and calm you before you snapped, yet never responded when you did; and my own worries I locked away, shielded them from you. My new job, my fears, my pressures never came to your notice. I had a week off work, a backlog of paperwork left to me from my predecessor in utter disarray, which would take a year to sort, but I didn't have a year: it needed doing before the week was up. I wanted to do anything to relieve the pressure from you, thus my week's holiday was spent typing your bibliography and organising the paperwork. I had no time to breathe. You snapped about your tiredness, your lack of sleep, while I typed through the night on your work, on mine, taking the odd break to deal with bailiffs during the day unperturbed by all. Just wanting you to be all right, the people I worked with to be all right and the roof over my head to remain. All that mattered to me was that your dissertation was done and you could finally settle into Oxford properly, so we spent a week without sleep and while you recovered I returned to the grindstone, working until the early hours still trying to clear the mess left for me. I worried as you told me about your blurred vision and dizzy spells, and laughed it off when people asked if my tired stumbling body was drunk.

Day Thirty-Seven

I consider the castle used by the "heroes" and mull through the world, seeing the very same hedonism. Was de Sade, like Orwell, a prophet, or has the universe always had such desire for instant gratification? Balance has deserted, there is no yang. All that remains is gaining the maximum amount of pleasure. It seems to have been forgotten that, for pure pleasure, others are receiving pure pain. The lucky few have turned into Ducs, living his principle of feeling only the pleasure and none of the pain their pleasure inflicts on others; if they don't feel it, it's not their responsibility.

It makes me ashamed to see people squirm and manipulate any excuse rather than accept personal responsibility. Child labour, slavery, Third World dependency on the UK, due to phenomenal interest rates – it's their fault, the arms they buy, not ours. It has nothing to do with the coffee, chocolate we consume, the clothes on our backs. Nothing to do with the way we ease our conscience once a year by responding to media images of starvation with food, instead of irrigation systems, thus maintaining the famine and false charity the following year. Likewise, the voices of decadence chant, "There is no need for anyone to starve in this country, people are homeless by their own choice, it is their own fault." It has nothing to do with lack of money, teenagers running from fates like de Sade, then getting caught in the no-address, no-job cycle. Nothing at all, while the middle classes inhale a week's rent in one hit of cocaine, after paying a week's shopping money for entrance into a club, drinking a gas bill and fucking twenty times more than those poor who are killed by AIDS.

Us again

Your dissertation was finally handed in. You could now settle and enjoy Oxford, and we could be us again. I was so relieved, but also so very tired. I'd done nothing but cope through your first few weeks at Oxford, cope and take your frustration. Now all was safe, the panic, fear, worry, exhaustion hit me, I could express now all was safe. I told you all about work, how I'd missed you, how your snappiness had hurt me, how I'd missed our closeness, but you didn't want to know. You had no time to talk, no time to get back to normal, no time to be close again. To be strictly true, you had plenty of time, plenty of time to catch up with Helen, plenty of time to talk for hours with online strangers. But for us, who had gone straight from the Bernard affair to dissertation stress, for us, who needed time, you had none. Us that you said you wanted to work out since the Bernard affair, us that you wanted to spend time getting back to how we were. Yet you insisted that neither your feelings for me nor anything between us had changed. Were you having a different relationship? It had all changed: we used to be closer than two separate individuals can possibly get, not be able to bear spending little intervals every day without talking. We were relaxed about everything, talked easily about everything without thought or prompts. I thought of how we were and every time I thought of giving up, thought you no longer wanted us. You'd somehow plead with me not to give up on you, so I wouldn't, ever, still won't. Then you'd proceed to pick fights by saying how you wanted a threesome with a guy. Your words, your behaviour were becoming more and more erratic and inconsistent and, if ever I questioned this, I was at fault for not being supportive. I remained calm and put it down to your fears of being at Oxford. I tried, I really tried.

Day Thirty-Eight

Damn this dyscalculia. Days slip away as if they'd never existed at all. Did a forgotten moment, day, week, year ever exist at all? I wrote the days, one hundred and twenty-one in all, and later found this dyscalculia had stolen two away. I had to decide to leave the natural state of things or go back for those lost days. On balance, I decided to return one day to her rightful place and leave the other lost for ever, symbolic of both equilibrium and yet dissociation. I've reached the end and slipped back, like a glitch in the matrix, or a premonition of the future. I can't betray the plot. I can't say how deep the rabbit hole goes. I can't tell you how dark the mirth becomes. You know at least I am not dead, unless I was resurrected to come back and correct the tale. I'll give you something of the future. This novel is de Sade, Colette, Cline, Ilona. Now, I am emptiness, with the days complete and this binding of ink ripped from my shoulders; I am alone. Not even alone with me, myself or I, just alone, a nothing. I am somewhere in the midst of these many words. Perhaps still on a station in my mind waiting for Colette, or naked in the summer rain with Cline, or standing still on Canal Street with Ilona, worst of all, maybe still locked in that room, in that house with that de Sade. You have to go on reading, because I had to go on writing and I have to go on living. You too must continue, but, heed my words of warning, beware, tread with care. I did not write this plot to sharpen a knife, plunge it into you and twist your soul into rhythms of agony. Really I did not. Quite the opposite. And, as you read and your heart beats faster, your body freezes, your breathing slows and that tear becomes stuck in the corner of your eye. One day, maybe when you reach the one hundred and twenty-first day, maybe sometime later, I hope you will understand.

Perhaps my subconscious left chapters, like an open door, for my return. There is a pit in my psyche. A dark, frightening, horrible pit. There I kneel in all my innocence trapped in that eternal abyss. There is my core, my essence, the beautiful woman and all her pain. I am the treason of my soul, laughing, living, dipping into the pure and impure diversities of life, while she lies dying. I had to return to de Sade, Colette, Cline, not for any of them, not for the events, but for the key to the pit, the key and the strength. Sometimes the only route to strength is through exhaustion and letting go. Am I exhausted enough? Have I let go?

Now

I have a strange restlessness. I think of you daily, but I don't know if I want you. I don't know if I want myself, if I want anything, what I want. We shared a parallel world in a parallel dimension, and I don't know how many people are parallel people in a parallel time in a parallel universe. I know not whether you and I felt unreal at the time or just with hindsight. A cliché, but it felt too good to be real, then too bad to be real, thus rendering the whole experience surreal, or maybe that is just my memory of us, my memory in general. Walking through life in a dreamlike existence, watching and narrating in my own private movie theatre. Extremes of perfection and pain don't happen in real life, it's not in the script. Real life is – well, I don't know what it is. I can only look at the lives of others and wonder, in a way one might look at the stars and wonder. I wouldn't change anything, you, or me, the intensity, the depth. Nonetheless, am I an actor playing a part, a viewer watching a film? Am I ever living a life? In the scheme of things, it's insignificant: neither you nor I will be but a half-life remaining in the sods of the earth and the momentum will continue regardless.

Day Thirty-Nine

It has been a cold summer, nothing like the heat of last year, which Colette and I shared. De Sade is becoming terribly repetitive and so very arrogant. The female form is repulsive and a crime to be punished for. The only bearable bit is the arse; breasts and cunts are formidable; he could have written the plot in one sentence, so why waste several thousand? Pregnant Constance is made to eat faeces as her punishment instead of being beaten. No, the "heroes" are not being kind: they wish to rip the foetus out of her rather than risk letting a miscarriage spoil their fun. Day Seventeen degenerates into everyone's consuming faeces. I assume this to be one de Sade's favourite pastimes, as he gives such attention to scat, particularly eating shit. I thank myself I've never had a lover into such; I think the very proposition would be sufficient to cause severe constipation. Duclos's narration moves from purely scat to a mixture of flagellation and scat. The whipping is not usual, but consists of variations where the whips are drenched in faeces and urine. Do not try this at home, unless you have an extreme desire for a fatal blood infection.

Now, I've previously mentioned childhood abuse as being a factor in BDSM. Add to that a rhythm, hypnosis, like the chants of a shaman. The whips, floggers, cat-o'-nines, paddles all lash their own distinctive melody and beat. The air becomes a mixed aroma of leather and sweat. The illusion of power is greater with an implement wielded. What about pain? The pain starts at nil, like a weightlifter building up: the first weights feel light, no effort, no pain, and the final weight feels like a rush, an accomplishment. Pain sluts report the same burst of endorphins as athletes. What I haven't fully understood is the relation of pain to sex and arousal, although, as I have said previously, there is much pain inflicted in sex through nails, bites, scratches, but such damage does not register as pain at the time.

Arguments and lies

I was exhausted, had enough, enough of carrying your stress, of being your emotional punchbag, of being blamed for your inconsistencies. Still I loved you but the tension was clawing at me. You called one night.

"Have you been following me?"

"What are you talking about?"

"Slim says you followed me and caught me with a guy."

"Well, if I had, you'd know about it. What are you talking about? I don't even know a Slim."

"Well, he says Carat told him."

"Well, there you go: you never trusted Carat."

"Yes but Silver told her."

"I don't know a Silver, and, Colette, this is crazy. These are online strangers, I'm your lover, we speak several hours a day, you know me inside out and even if you thought I could do something like that you know my every move, for God's sake, and it's five hours from here to you. This is completely absurd."

"So there's no truth in it?"

"I can't believe you're asking me that. I can't believe you're dealing in lies about the woman you love from online strangers."

"Slim's a friend. He's just looking out for me."

"Colette, he's a stranger. You've never even met him, and he's never seen me online, so how could you believe lies from someone who's never spoken to me in any context?"

"He says you've told the room we've cybered too."

"I've said nothing of the sort. I wouldn't. The only person I've asked if you've cybered is you, but that's between you and me."

"And that you mentioned his name in a main room."

"What? The only person I've ever talked to Slim about was Carat and that was only because she asked. All I said was his name is Christian, and he's an actor. I just can't believe you love me yet are dealing in lies about me."

"I'm only asking if it's true."

"You shouldn't have to ask. These people are complete strangers and you know me. I am so mad that complete strangers I don't know other than through you are spreading lies about me and you are listening to them. Why on earth would this guy Slim do that?"

"He's only looking out for me, he's a friend."

I snapped, I was tired, worn down, I'd had the brunt of your pressure for weeks and now you preferred to spend time dealing in lies with strangers instead of our talking as we once did, only talking to me for this. This was the longest conversation we'd had for about four weeks. We'd always talked about real life, real things before, not online psychosis. I didn't even know the people dealing in the lies and the insults about me you passed on, as I had stayed out of chatrooms at your request.

"Look, I've had enough, with Bernard, your snapping, your inconsistency and now you deal with liars. Just fuck off."

Day Forty

Days Eighteen and Nineteen continue the sadomasochism theme with Duclos telling tales from the brothel of men wanting nothing but slaps to the face, men tied to ladders, beaten hard before being released, men bloodied with needles, beaten with nettles. Duclos recounts how another man used her brothel for a year and liked to be humiliated and punished like a schoolchild.

Tying up focuses the attention totally on the body: the tied individual cannot move, writhe; s/he has to accept and cope with every sensation felt by the body, no matter how intense. The restrained individual gives up all control and responsibility; for that period of restraint, s/he does not have to think of anything, for s/he cannot act, so thinking is futile. Total vulnerability has to be accepted. The case of the school role is similar in nature: the chastised individual returns to a time without responsibility, without worry, without thinking for her/himself. Sex is literally about letting go, individuals desiring restraint, school role, cannot let go, they cannot shut off responsibility and anxiety for the duration of sex, thus they pretend such switching into their sexual selves is forced.

Such desire for expressing vulnerability is not confined to the sexual context. In a safe environment, adults will whine, stamp feet, regress to baby talk and in very private realms lose verbal speech altogether. Colette and I would murmur as we fell asleep side by side, saying nothing, wanting nothing, just communicating affection and contentment with a series of sounds, understood by us. Certain sounds are universal, not human, not infant, having no need of thought, heard throughout the network of life and, like screams, understood throughout.

A day at a time

I wrote you mail to apologise, explaining that the last few weeks had stressed me and I'd been hasty; that I still loved you, didn't want to lose you. You refused to carry on as normal; after all, I'd promised never to reject you. I'd promised to just say I felt angry and not reject you, agreed that rejecting each other, then coming back after a couple of hours' cooling off, was damaging. I just couldn't cope, snapped was all, and you wouldn't understand, couldn't see how you were hurting me. You never said sorry, never saw things from my view. My view was some desolate industrial estate that no one was interested in, somewhere unimportant.

We decided to take things a day a time. Meanwhile, Sorcha, who had targeted you in the chatroom before we fell out and I'd spoken to once before, tailed me like a limpet. I thought nothing of it at the time, saw no reason to be suspicious, just assumed she was a friendly person, so chatted with her in private at her request about psychology. I'd just logged on one day when you were talking to her. Seeing that you were busy, I said I'd see you tomorrow.

"No, wait, she's going now, she's just said bye."

So I waited. After an hour I realised long goodbyes like that happened only between us, so I left you a message saying I knew we were taking it a day at a time, but I also knew when I was beat, turned the computer off and sat and cried. You called saying how Sorcha was no threat to us, that you wanted me, no one else, and I believed you; you said daily for nine months you loved me and I trusted you.

Book 2

Day Forty-One

Summer is fading. The leaves fall from the trees and our love acquiesces to the same finality of the seasons. A love so intimate we were inside each other, suddenly falling to the group to be swept away as debris, but leaves layer the womb of earth in preparation for new life. Nothing so unique can ever be debris.

De Sade is a growing journey, to understand him, I have to step inside his life, and that is what I am doing, stepping inside his life, to understand him, Colette, us, our sudden demise, events. When the research goes so deep that I step inside someone's life, I invariably live that life, while still distinguishing my own. I sink into it, breathe and taste it, infiltrating the visage and skull of de Sade. The music while I work now plays sadomasochistic chanting. I didn't even know such music existed four months ago. I wonder how many of de Sade's biographers are brave enough to really step inside his life, and not the odd controlled observation, or candid interview, but to actually immerse themselves fully, surround themselves, until they lose their own scent, stinking of de Sade. I sink into de Sade, to understand, really understand, and I term this "method psychology". Different from method acting, where the actors are sucking in the characters to give realism, to breathe life into them. I've no wish to breathe life into de Sade, merely to understand; not to understand or analyse de Sade, for de Sade is dead, we are now.

A labyrinth of abuse

We both agreed we were getting back on track. All was fine until one day I felt ill. I was quiet, not as entertaining as usual. I awoke the next day in agony, my neck, mouth and throat swollen. I couldn't swallow and could hardly talk. I was scared and in pain. The pain was so bad I was crying when I called you. You slammed the phone down and I wandered off to rest, hurt and confused. Later that day I logged on. I went to message you, ask you what was wrong. You'd blocked me. Confused, I went into the suburbs to ask you what was going on. As soon as I entered the chatroom the browser crashed. I tried again and a webpage came up saying I was banned. Burning a temperature, hurt and confused, I went into a lower room, hoping you'd see me so I could ask what was wrong and explain that I couldn't get in, but I was only ever in for minutes before I was kicked out. Eventually, Sass, an online friend of the website owner, came into the lower room: "You're banned because of Colette and Sorcha so stay away from here."

"What are you talking about?"

"You know what I'm talking about."

But I didn't. I knew all I've recounted and that I was burning a temperature. Beyond that I knew nothing. I entered the nest to try to ask you what was going on. My entry heralded a torrent of verbal abuse from total strangers, other than you: Sorcha, Puttycat, the site owner and Sass. I didn't know these people.

"Get lost, psycho."

"You're not wanted here, nutter."

"Stalker."

Tears flooded my keyboard.

"I don't know any of you, why are you being like this?"

"Just stay away and leave Colette alone," said the site owner.

"But why should I? I've done nothing. Colette, tell them."

"Leave me out of it."

"But they say it's because of you."

"It's not just me that's complained."

"But no one has any reason to complain and why have you?"

"Leave me alone."

"What are you talking about? We were talking on the phone until earlier when I felt ill, we were taking things a day at a time and I've only come in now because I'm confused to ask what's wrong."

"Go on, you've had your say, leave now," the site owner continued.

"But, but I've never fell out with anyone."

Bang – and I was evicted. The abuse was more and more extreme *than the short bit I've recounted. I called Colette; she didn't answer, so I left a message on the answerphone.*

Then I sat and cried. Cried about the abuse, but mainly about the betrayal of someone who until now had told me daily she loved me.

Day Forty-Two

Being immersed in de Sade makes concentration extremely difficult. Ordinary things lose something: food, work, reading the paper, discussing the weather. Opiate and barbiturate users describe the feeling as everything being attenuated. Well, multiply that by ten. Abuse attenuates meaning. It produces a switch. Night after night the body is being damaged. It is never that the horror lessens, merely that if I, anyone, thought about it, insanity would be due to follow. The only way to survive is not to think about it, to turn it off; the flipside is that other switches become created for release. All the while this is subconscious, so there is no control and it continues to function long after the threat has stopped. A functional tool? Not when you consider that anything of less intensity than the abuse has no meaning, thoughts, impact whatsoever, because of that "off" switch. When life or death is uncertain daily throughout childhood, death ceases to be a fear. It has to, or else the fear would consume and ultimately kill. The heart can take only so much fear in a fourteen-year span. Once the capacity has been reached, life instinct kicks in and instead of the heart giving way, the fear does. When death is feared, nothing becomes a fear. When nothing is feared, there is nothing to care about, no need to care. No worries of where the next meal is coming from, because there is no fear of not eating. No fear of humiliation: because people are no longer feared, they can do no more damage. Add this to sinking into de Sade. De Sade is but an add-on. The lewd language means nothing, anyway, but, surrounded with it daily, language itself means nothing; it becomes so difficult to turn the de Sade research off and think, talk in ordinary terms. Consequently, "fuck" slips out in the most inappropriate places. De Sade is full of death, pain extremity, so full of it, it has to become meaningless; I have to become more desensitised than I was to begin with. People spend their lives looking for the occasional extremes, the kicks, the thrills, the anxieties. When everything is extreme, nothing is, and I begin to feel as though I'm walking through innocents, as though every new person I meet is nubile, shy, and every experience numb. I can no longer grasp for extremes. Nothing will be, yet, being human, I will continue to do so, and where will the journey end when I realise there are none left?

Weaving the noose

I discovered the depth of your games. Bit by bit it seeped out that Slim, Carat, Sorcha and you had complained. Slim I didn't know, Carat I had been a friend with for over a year until the lies, Sorcha I'd spoken with twice, politely, both times at her request, and you, well, you know the story so far. It all came out: how much I'd hurt you (what had I done exactly?), how you had to get a restraining order (we've never disagreed face to face). I'm a pacifist, rarely raise my voice, and you are nearly twice my size and strength. Perhaps the restraining order was when I wrinkled my nose at buying Marks and Spencer's ready-cooked rice and you glared at me until I shook and put it in the basket anyway. Of course, there never was any restraining order. You need a reason for a restraining order, but try telling that to God knows how many of the population you'd told that I was apparently disturbed. Every time people told me new information or gave me new abuse, I'd call you to ask why, give you a chance to explain, but always your answerphone was on. You were too cowardly to face your actions, yet at the same time knew I was too poor to take any legal action. You were safe; as long as you didn't approach me and physically assault me you could do anything. Anything at all.

Day Forty-Three

Time rolls away, bills get slung in the bin because they are meaningless disturbances in my search, work gets rushed, food is swallowed, not chewed, energy is endless for this focus, only this, and, if I collapse at the end, so be it, for now it is bountiful. You may question why I am so immersed. You may think me obsessed, crazy even. If being passionate is crazy, then I am. I get a passion, a drive, from a simple query. You can look at anything for a short while and understand it, and your definition will be functional enough, substantive even, but is a definition ever really understanding? I have to remove everything cell by cell, jump in every cell, feel what each is like, drown myself within them, pick apart every molecule, then rebuild to see the whole picture, for as long as it takes until my understanding is fully sated.

Children are always far more interesting thinkers than adults. Adults lose something when they stop asking why, and maybe that is what my search is for, another adult who asks why. None in de Sade question. The children are fearful robots that merely obey. They are such so he can write their pain and deaths. If he wrote their thoughts of why, he would have had to step inside their lives. He would have had to understand. Would he then still have been able to write their pain and deaths? The fuckers and storytellers don't ask why. If they did, de Sade would have been looking into a mirror, and understanding oneself is the most frightening of all.

De Sade didn't question himself and we cannot question him from outside, as we contaminate the understanding. Questioning de Sade can come only from introspecting the method, and that is the most dangerous psychology of all, an extreme form of Gestalt, where instead of talking to the "empty chair" we *become* the "empty chair" and return to ourselves to understand both. You understand the path I am taking. You know what I am asking, what I am doing. I already understand the children in de Sade's novel. I know their whys. I don't know de Sade's why. Biographers say it takes a strong head to read de Sade, so, if you get the gist now, you either imagine I have enormous confidence in myself or am completely mentally suicidal. It's neither, just a lust for understanding, and the only route is empathy. The word "empathy" is often thrown around with ease, and it can for some people be easy to have empathy with the victim, but I already understand the victim. The dilemma is that the answer to their whys lies in the mind of de Sade and his comrades.

A quandary of confusion

Still I love you. I sat daily, crying and staring into midair, you loved me too – you told me so endlessly and deeply and I believed you, so why would you do this? It couldn't be your fault: you were the woman who loved me; I trusted you, knew you'd never hurt me; you promised to always keep me safe while cradling me in your arms.

"We'll always keep each other safe," you said as you stroked my cheek. No, it couldn't be your fault: there would be some explanation, some weird online stranger who had entertained himself by dropping the threads, until we blamed each other, or the pressure of Oxford, or both. There was no way you could suddenly change from the kind, warm, fun-loving person I knew to this. Humans just don't behave like that, without warning signs.

I still sent off your Christmas presents and card, knowing it wasn't your fault, that you wouldn't do this and we'd find out one day what had happened and you'd apologise for doubting me and not defending me while strangers abused me. We'd come through worse, Oxford was big, and this was trivia, silly.

Day Forty-Four

... [A]nd heading at once for the grave our informant had indicated, above which the earth had only recently been broken, we would both fall to work, dig down to the cadaver, and when once we'd uncovered it, I'd frig him over it while he spent his time handling it.

– Duclos.

This is de Sade's first mention of necrophilia in *One Hundred and Twenty Days of Sodom*. It's on the twenty-sixth day, still in Book One. Already we have witnessed incest, paedophilia, beating, whipping flogging, scat, water sports, buggery, rape, scalding, roman showers, every other body fluid, burning, branding, bondage, cutting, wanking over coffins and now necrophilia. When I've discussed the motives for necrophilia, a friend mentioned a possibility I'd not considered that the dead cannot judge the quality of the performance. There are arguments for its being the ultimate submission, but, for submission, power is being given from the submissive to the dominant. The dead cannot give anything. There is no control of the dead: control comes only where something exists to control in the first place. The only person the necrophiliac controls and dominates is him/herself. A projection of him/herself, s/he sees as soulless, an empty vessel, rotting flesh without a mind, without a life. We choose mates who we feel deserve us, are worthy of us, so is the psyche of the necrophiliac feeling unworthy and undeserving of the living? The power boost for the necrophiliac comes from the illusion of total ownership, total possession. I say illusion, because can something that does not exist ever be owned, ever be possessed? The ownership of a strong formidable person may well be considered powerful, but a corpse has no mind to care, nothing to own.

Latency

You went back home for Christmas and for some reason weren't online. I had peace. I missed you, missed us, but I had peace. I had no abuse from anyone, no lies, no games. I could finally grieve our relationship in peace, but it did mean one thing. You were away and I was receiving no hassle. I shut it out, I didn't want to hold you responsible, didn't want to believe our whole nine months together could have been a lie, that nine months of my life weren't real, were false. It's like a warped twilight zone where life isn't real and I couldn't handle that. Already I was questioning my sanity, my instincts, my intuition.

You'd told everyone I was mad, so I must be, mustn't I, because you were always right? Even I had validated your being always right for nine months. Well, you were wrong, I'm not crazy, I'm not the one who took nine months of reality and turned it into a fabrication. I didn't try to play with reality, to go back in time and challenge it. I didn't take a course of events on an unexpected swerve that belongs to the realms of strangers, not lovers. You were wrong, and I was wrong thinking you were right and maybe that was what went wrong. I should have listened to my intuition. And that vulnerable girl I first met off the train – I doubt she wanted to be right even though she convinced so well.

Day Forty-Five

If you were suffering from an orgasmic disorder and murder would cure it, would you kill? Are several minutes of one of life's many pleasures worth a life? The reason I ask is the story Duclos tells on the twenty-seventh day. A judge hires her while watching the executions, the executions he has sentenced. Watching such being the only way he can gain an erection. Duclos questions the ethics of sentencing people to death for his own pleasure; his answer is de Sade's favourite philosophy, that if it gives him pleasure it isn't wrong. Only the person sentenced would find it wrong or harmful and that is not the responsibility of the person causing the pain: his only responsibility is to his own pleasure. This is the egocentricity reflected throughout de Sade's characters, thus the core of de Sade himself. The other recurring theme is the striving to reach orgasm, as though it were some difficult feat. I gather from this that de Sade himself was impotent. What I find difficult to understand about any erectile or orgasmic disorder is that, if orgasm or erection cannot be reached, surely there is no arousal, thus no drive or urge to orgasm anyway. Coincidentally, I stumbled upon some purely accidental insight. A woman I met around eight weeks ago – I'll describe the meeting later – although I fell for her, she never released her orgasm. She was forty-two years of age, had never orgasmed with another person, and had orgasmed with herself only from forty. She experienced arousal, but would stop lovemaking before the throes of orgasm could begin. For four weeks she was the sweetest soul, after which she became cruel and hateful. I'm not suggesting there is a relationship between cruelty and erectile/orgasm disorder; however, in some people whatever causes the cruelty may also cause the orgasm disorder. The fascination is: what is our friend the confounding variable? I'm going to gamble on a little association called "bad", and, a weak ego, an overcritical superego and an out-of-control id overcompensating for the overcritical superego by doing a little trick that I believe Melanie Klein called splitting. Bad is the confounding variable.

In a certain group of people, cruelty has been associated with "bad", as it is in most of us. Nothing unusual so far. Sex has also been associated with "bad" and, because bad is associated with cruelty, sex is also associated with cruelty, as both are bad. Too simple? I did specify only in a certain group of people. It works exactly the same applied to the racism example: crime is "bad"; people who commit crime are arrested; a higher representation of black people are arrested. Now, one would think, why are more black people arrested, and look back to the suss laws. However, a racist would just make the connection, arrest bad, more black individuals arrested, black people bad. Where do the overcritical superego and out-of-control id come in? The superego is generally the internalised voice of the individual's primary carer(s) as a child. If the carer was firm but fair, the adult superego will be firm but fair. If the carer was cruel, critical and negative, the adult superego will be cruel, critical and negative. Add that to the association of sex with bad and you have the erectile/orgasm-dysfunction reason for a certain type of person. Now for the cruelty aspect of the self-cure. The id is badly undernurtured, feeling trapped and hurt by the superego. There is no ego to mediate. Or it is not strong enough to mediate, so, when the id boils up to gain its needs, it is angry, and aggressive and loving all things the superego holds in contempt and such things become associated.

So what has Melanie Klein got to do with all this? Her theory of splitting is that adults with a weak ego continue to use an infantile perception of events around them. Infants see their mother as good when she produces the milk they want. The infant loves her, sees her breast as good, as a source of nourishment and comfort. When the infant cannot get any milk from the mother's breast, s/he sees her and the breast as bad and hates her, until the next time the milk flows, when s/he will love again. This simplicity is expected in infants. As adults we condemn behaviour or situations we might not like, but do not love the person any less, apart from the people who have never grown out of the "splitting" pattern. Such people do not love and disagree: they love absolutely, then hate absolutely. They see good absolutely and bad absolutely, like the girl with the curl right in the middle of her forehead. When she was good she was very, very good, and when she was bad she was horrid.

De Sade saw the world in simple childlike ways such as splitting. Not unlike the modern fascist, he saw people as absolutely strong or absolutely weak. The labels were always attached to the people – he could never see circumstance. On his deathbed de Sade gave his confession. He also removed the names of the people who imprisoned him from a list that would lead to their death. When he was good, he was very, very good, but he saw sex as bad, so to gain any sexual release he had to be horrid.

Defying the feelings

My friend with the IT knowledge introduced me to a cute blonde female friend of his. I dated her, I slept with her, I smothered myself in her scent, anything to get you out of my head. Still, while I slept next to her, your eyes would be pleading with me to stop, but you could plead all you liked: as long as I was with someone else I was recovered, I was over you, over us. And, even though I wasn't over us, even though I breathe you every second, I had to get away from the madness and into the world, the mundane, boring, shallow, empty world that existed before we met. I tried to deny you, slept with the blonde, even spoke with her and pretended to be remotely interested to myself as much as her.

Day Forty-Six

I'm still trying to get inside de Sade. To understand what he must have felt like writing the things he wrote and doing some of them. I'm trying to go about it by stepping inside a serial killer's head first, because that somehow seems easier than stepping into de Sade's life directly. Method psychology. You're honoured to see the process. Just don't try this at home. Before anyone raises the question "How can one who doesn't kill ever step into such a mindset?" we are all capable of everything – we simply don't all do it. That's why de Sade invokes such reaction. The reaction is not to him. De Sade is dead, not even a corpse, decomposed, gone. The reaction is to the shadow in every individual. It is oneself people recoil from, not a dead ex-prisoner. What de Sade wrote would have no impact if his words were not recognised when read. Before I read de Sade I thought it would be a mundane, outdated horror story, thought I could write something far more extreme and stirring of every known human emotion, but all I can do is hold a mirror to his words. De Sade is read, the reader feels repelled, labels de Sade, not his behaviour, as evil, pushes the words as far away from him/herself as s/he can and feels good about him/herself because s/he feels so far removed from the focus of evil.

Who is feeling the evil? Not de Sade – de Sade is dead. I spend several hours trying to step into a killer; the destruction is a mere extension of the instinctual urge for the destruction of all things, Thanatos. As with a hunger or any state of arousal, food is required, the throat needs to be filled. What if hunger, thirst and lust are not recognised, if there is just a need, an instinct, an urge, a desperation that needs to be met? It may be something so simple as a protein craving, but the message from the brain hitting the stomach, the throat, the parasympathetic nervous system is not working correctly. You are running around knowing something is needed but with no idea what. The kill doesn't fill you, doesn't fill that space. On the contrary, it is a huge anticlimax. The biggest anticlimax you can feel. There in your hands is something hot, alive, energy-filled, powerful and as the final breath exhales it demises in front of your very eyes, in your hands. That toy, you loved and then smashed on the floor until it broke and became nothing, not a toy any more, not anything, the anticlimax. The cup you released from your hand as a toddler to watch what would happen – the fascination and pleasure lasted only seconds while gravity pulled it to the floor and you watched the surfaces meet and the china splay, and, once it lay in tiny white splinters, the anticlimax, because it was nothing, no longer a cup, and you could not regain the fascination and pleasure with that particular smashed china again. We want to observe all the curiosities we will definitely experience. The only guarantee is death. We will definitely die, but will we feel the experience or will it be like birth and we don't feel the fascination, miss the experience? We can't consciously experience our own birth, so there is a fascination with the birth of others – and not just in humans: pack animals watch the labour and delivery of the pregnant pack member. We don't know if we can consciously experience death, but unlike birth, where the energy and fascination remain, death is an anticlimax.

Jacqueline Phillips

The extent of the lies

People crawled out of the cyberworld woodwork eager to rub your lies into my wounds. They exposed the number of people you had told we were nothing, while, at the same time, you were holding me, phoning me with your declaration of the deepest love. Although we'd never so much as argued, I was a violent, crazed stalker according to the people who'd come into contact with you. While loving and gentle to my face, you had mocked me behind my back, laughing with online people and friends like PUTTYCAT alike, calling me a bunny boiler. All the time you were jealous over my slightest differences in routine, and emphasised our exclusivity, to others you said you were single. It was the greatest humiliation of all. You challenged my sense of sanity. I continually asked myself if you were right and I was insane. Your denial made our love a farce, so maybe I had imagined it all, imagined meeting you, our time together, the almost daily eight-hour phone calls, your emails, messages, during my lunch hours at work. You introduced me to none and refused to meet my friends. If you'd planned such a game you couldn't have prepared for any eventuality better.

My Christmas holidays consisted of trying to find out what and why. I was working on paperwork one day, the suburbs was down and replaced temporarily by onlyfruit.com I had the room minimised, taking breaks every now and then while I worked. Sorcha entered. It was the first time I'd seen her since her fraudulent complaint. She disappeared as soon as she arrived, reappearing minutes later. I politely asked her to talk in private. She agreed, at which I asked her how I had offended her in two conversations to put in a complaint about me. She denied any complaint, could not explain why she hadn't spoken up when I stated to the webmistress that I'd spoken to her only twice, politely, both times at her request, and denied any knowledge of the whole thing. You were an Oxford student with the gift of the gab and flirtation to seduce all behind a screen; you were there constantly, an intelligent among sheep; you were validated. Few had the independence of thought to question you.

Day Forty-Seven

Colette signed in on MSN last night for the first time since July. Three months without word, three months of equilibrium and again my emotions are on a rack, stretched beyond reasonable capacity. My heart always softens, whenever I see her, hear her, read her. I cannot but soften. This is the nature of love. It is only afterwards when it hits me, the lies – meaningless behind her words, all her words – then the anger. Words of how she misses me. At the time words of how there was no deeper love, how she had never been so relaxed, so close, wanting to be with someone, missing someone so much. It makes a fool of me, a fool for believing, trusting empty words, when the actions with others and myself were totally inconsistent with the words. So why did I believe the words? Anger is never towards a love. I could never be angry with her, merely angry because of her. Angry at myself, generalised angry, and this explains another reason for murder, but, unlike de Sade, not a sexual murder. Nor a domestic murder. A deep build of pain, humiliation and ever-multiplying wrath gripping every skin cell of the soul like the sweat of a virus.

The aggression isn't caused by the anger, but, rather, the object experiencing the aggression becomes the focus of the anger and the beating and destruction of the object, the beating and destruction of the anger. When anger grips you to the point of wanting to squeeze the life out of somebody, anybody, a nobody, not a lover, a friend, anyone you know, the person's life becomes the epicentre of the anger and with the demise of his/her heartbeat comes the demise of the anger. With each understanding I get closer to stepping into de Sade's life, though de Sade was more extreme, far more extreme, more than your most entertaining nightmare.

New Year return

It was the second week of January. I was on the telephone to a friend, chatting, laughing, totally oblivious. I replaced the receiver and returned to my research. There on the screen was an MSN message. I looked at the name: it was you. I sat shaking, confused, I was a nutter, stalker, demon from Hades, you'd blocked and deleted me and warned the world and her daughter.

"Hey. Sorry to disturb you."

You had typed. Eventually I braved a reply: "Sorry, I was on the telephone."

I was confused, what did you want? What could you want?

"How are you?"

"How do you think I am after your games? I've had a peaceful few weeks, no hassle while you've been gone."

"I'm sorry."

"Why did you do it?"

"I don't know."

"You did it, you must know, only you do know."

"I was on self-destruct, I was hurting everyone close to me."

The conversation was stilted, you were trying to act as though nothing had happened, but I didn't – I couldn't – trust you. I wanted to, but a louder voice said you would do the same again, worse if I allowed you to, that this was a sequel to your game. Still you were adamant you meant all the things you said while we were together; that you loved me deeply.

It was into the early hours before the conversation ended. When we were a couple I'd always waited for you to shut your computer down before going; tonight you typed, "You shut down, I've rejected you enough."

I was confused, bewildered, hurt, and still I loved you. What sanity was this? I was the violent nutter you feared so much, whom total strangers abused, yet now you were sorry and guilty for rejecting me?

Day Forty-Eight

I read some of de Sade out to the man ironing in my kitchen, his ears almost visibly close in front of me. We discuss the prose, the simplistic sentence after simplistic sentence of nothing but lewdness. Both agreed that anyone could sit in a room and think of the most atrocious experiences, mutilations that could be inflicted on adult, child and animal. You could do it. You could think of the worst situations that could happen to yourself. You don't have to live, to enjoy the sensations of expression, the weather, texture, foods. Instead, you could imagine the systematic removal of each paperlike layer of your skin, each hair pulled from its roots one by one, followed by boiling water poured over the now bald, skinned frame of yourself. You could, or you could live. Choices, choices, and not a drop of free will. Where is the line between de Sade and inflicting pain, and living negatively drawn? If you make a shop assistant feel inferior are you any better than de Sade? If you tell your lover she is the bane of your life in temper, are you better than de Sade?

The little man in my kitchen disagrees with my continuum, saying we don't always have a choice when behaving negatively. No choice? Not in control of our behaviour? Then who or what *does* control it? The same man only days ago recounted how he sometimes felt like kicking people who were bent in front of him, but always refrained. How many people do you pass in the street and feel like hitting? But you don't, and as quickly as it came the feeling passes; yet at home after a hard day you've taken your lover flowers, she picks a fight and you end up calling her a selfish bitch – the most precious part of your life, the woman you love, but you waste the life being negative, having chosen not to hit the stranger who means nothing. The damage would have been less had you hit the stranger, than a few cruel words to the woman who trusts and loves you. De Sade reflects the hypocrisy in us all. He reaches inside and pulls out the shadow, and when we vomit at his words we do so only because we can picture the acts, we are choosing to picture them, they are not so far removed that we cannot imagine.

Missing us

Out of the blue you asked about the fling I had over Christmas. When I asked how you knew, you said Sorcha told you. I was livid, confused, in a quagmire of emotion. How on earth would Sorcha know my business? Other than the one conversation I'd had with her, I hadn't seen her. You cross-examined me about my fling for days. Was she prettier than you were? Did I like her more? Was she sexier? Why did I do it?

"Did you sleep with her in our bed?"

"Yes, I did. I wasn't going to, but after all the hurt it was metaphorically putting two fingers up at you."

"It's OK: I was going to get in with you, but I don't want to sleep in her come stains."

"There are no come stains!"

"Snuggles under the duvet beside you."

"Turns my back."

"Pulls you towards me."

"Snuggles into your neck, shaking, hiding my face from you."

"Turns your face towards me kissing your tears away."

I answered all your questions openly, no matter how many times they were repeated. I felt guilty even though we were split; even after all we'd done, guilty at the time, guilty afterwards.

Day Forty-Nine

There is a certain finality about October, as though the year should end here and not in December. Today I walked into the cold air from an hour in a superstore and the sky was covered in a blackness. Blackness from the storms, the gunpowder, the smoke. Daylight was dulled, attenuated from a coating, a cultural statement of ending. October is a very Gothic month. The "new black" is black. Grand buildings host ghostly displays commentated by eerie whispers. Hot chestnuts burn through blue hands, before the streets empty to the darkness.

Duclos recounts tales of men ejaculating into the faces of beaten children. The end of October symbolises the enemy of the child. Nights draw, leaving shorter days. Shorter days mean more time indoors. Behind those doors, those doors where the people living in the light never see or hear what happens, behind closed doors. Doors where "de Sade" hits them into corners of the room, and they go to school unable to breathe, but still the people can't see beyond those doors – the child is diagnosed with asthma, bronchitis. It's broken ribs, not rocket science, you fools! These are the "de Sades", the people smiling insincerely, pretending to be kind, playing the "good cop", like the storytellers in de Sade's novel, then handing the children to their deaths, their tormentors. Doors where "de Sade" enters their bedrooms, their "safety", forcing his penis against thighs not the size of your arm, trying to enter vaginas that are not yet anything but a continuation of child. The doctor says their pain on urinating is thrush, cystitis. Children don't get thrush or cystitis. It isn't nuclear physics, fools! Fools or Sadists?

October ends, but the pain doesn't, the children grow. They hate the de Sade. They hate you next door: you heard their screams and turned up the TV. They hate you, the teacher: you saw their pain and pushed them further away. They hate you, the social worker: where were you until it was all over? They hate you, the psychologist: you are no use now, you should have prevented it. They hate you, the doctor: for colluding. They hate you, the passer-by: you saw the pain in their eyes, the tiny arm trying to pull away from the adult hand; you heard the "if you don't stop crying now, I'll fucking batter you, you little bastard", and you turned away. They hate you and you and you, every single one of you. You are all de Sade in that grown-up child's eyes.

Seducing the scared
Daily you were blowing hot and cold, and daily I'd begged you: no more

games, no more inconsistency, no more repetition of November. No matter what you did, what lies you told, I wouldn't react. I'd sit and cry, curl up in a ball on the floor wanting to die, unsure of how I got to bed the next morning, but I'd not react to you, just keep pleading with you to stop, stop the games. I said I'd talk to you, but nothing else, wanted the games to stop; and when you were blowing hot you'd assure me I'd trust you again and you'd be there no matter how long it took. Days would go by when you'd correct me for calling you honey, saying it was inappropriate now we weren't a couple, and other times you'd talk of our future together or attempt to seduce.

"What ya doin'?"

"Writing my novel."

"Sneaks up behind you and distracts you."

"Ignores you and continues to write."

"Goes upstairs and gets into bed."

"Ignores you, continuing to write."

"Calls Lightning upstairs and cuddles her."

"Concentrates on my novel."

"Writhes and rubs hips."

"Hears you writhing about tries to ignore you."

"Turns on my front, writhing and stroking my thighs and hips."

"Decides the dogs need a walk, looks at your writhing naked body and turns away."

"When did you come upstairs?"

"To get Lightning, puts Lightning's lead on and heads for the door."

The tears stung into my cheeks. I put on my coat, really heading for the door. I had to get away from you, even though you were two hundred miles away. Without turning off my computer, I couldn't escape you and even then I couldn't escape the pain.

Day Fifty

Sooner or later the victims become de Sade. There doesn't go a day when you don't want to make your territory, your surrounding, your space safe. Not a day when you don't want to take a gun to every paedophile, abuser, violent psychopath, rapist. Even knowing you'd probably halve the population of Earth doesn't bother you. But it's not about revenge. It's about safety and needing to get rid of these "de Sades" crawling under your flesh, tormenting your every waking breath. If you could just, could just only, get rid of them, that's all, that's all you want, peace, simple peace, something you've always wanted yet never known, simple peace.

The "heroes" have a new rule, that, whenever they shit, they shit only in the mouths of their wives. I wonder if battered wives would prefer such. Interesting choice, isn't it, broken arm or shit today? Battered wives, you've never met one, it doesn't happen that often, we don't get them in this street, in this village, in this group. They don't hit the face or the hands; she has high-neck clothes to cover her neck. She doesn't have arthritis – she's twenty-three, not seventy-three. Her trousers cover her legs. She can work with broken ribs, fingers, toes, a perforated eardrum, cigarette burns rubbing against the cotton on her back. She didn't do her broken arm falling from a horse; she wasn't in hospital having gallstones removed. He isn't the nice charming man you talk dotcom shares and have a sherry with over Christmas. You weren't born yesterday.

De Sade and his contemporaries, who hate their wives yet see them as property to do as they please with, show a strange contradiction. If you hate something, truly you don't want the object of detestation near you, but want to own something. You are consuming it, making it belong to you, become a part of you. In their wives they put all the parts of themselves they hate, and then destroy those parts and their wives in the process.

Alpha again
You had claimed me again, demanding knowledge on whom I spoke to

*and why, and my attention now. We no longer spoke on the telephone,
but you still treated me like your property, calling me rude and sulking
if I spoke to others when you were online, or even if I was working but
you assumed I was speaking to others. You became a walking
contradiction, telling me you were happy separated and your life was
none of my business any more, yet getting upset with needless jealousy.
You'd taunt me, saying people didn't like my abruptness, yet if I was my
usual friendly self you'd accuse me of flirting and I'd spend hours
reassuring you I wasn't, never biting, never reacting. The games were
bizarre, your biggest being having cybersex with Slim, the man who had
ultimately split us up, by telling lies about me, having never spoken to
me in any context. I was astounded, thought I knew you, began to
wonder who the woman I'd spent nine months with was. Since your
taunts about Slim, I wandered around in a permanent daze, totally
confused as to your behaviour, even though we had split. How could you
be so intimate with the complete stranger who broke up your
relationship? Did our reality, our flesh, our words, our love count for
nothing? I knew nothing, understood nothing but the fear of being blind
in the fog of an emotional matrix. Maybe it is me: it may be perfectly
rational behaviour to identify total strangers you've never met, who have
intruded and violated your real life as "close friends" whom you
"implicitly trust". I have no answers. I can see only from inside.*

*You said you had stopped having cybersex with Slim since we'd been
talking again, yet within ten days, "Have you cybered Slim again?"*

"Yes."

"You said you weren't going to."

"It's none of your concern, we're not a couple."

"So it's OK if I cyber and sleep with people."

*"Cyber who you want as long as it's no one I want, then I'd be pissed
off."*

*A woman you'd flirted with for a year and obviously liked you was
talking to us both afterwards. You were livid. I didn't take you seriously
when you cross-examined me about the woman you had always flirted*

with – I assumed you were being sarcastic.

"Do you like Claire?" I was confused it was an odd thing for you to say.

"Not like that, C, no, I love you."

You kept on, "She thinks you're sweet."

"No she doesn't, C, it's you she likes, don't take the piss."

"I'm not taking the piss – she keeps flirting with you."

"Colette, it's you she's flirting with. quit playing games."

"I'm not playing games: she's flirting with you and it's pissing me off."

"Why, do you fancy her? Well I'm not interested and it's you she likes, so you've no need to be jealous of me."

"I'm not jealous of you. I'm jealous of her."

"You said you didn't care what I did and you'd only be jealous if it was someone you liked, so quit taking the piss."

"What I say and what I mean are two different things."

Day Fifty-One

Power corrupts. Corruption is a weakness. Real strength doesn't need to corrupt, control, oppress, feel superior. Real strength is happy to be equal, to just be.

I'm in the shower while I'm thinking about this, in the shower while I consider, power, strength, Foucault, de Sade, Colette and myself. I let go a lot since Colette. For years I've been letting go. Power, power, power, the cogs of my brain dance a harmony with the hot jets of water, and the thoughts flash by more quickly than my conscious can catch them. The only reason power corrupts is that the corrupters are weak. To oppress another in order to gain power, they do not possess true strength, being so afraid of another having equal strength. Power is an illusion, the status that goes with power the very epitome of weakness. The "powerful" need the control over other countries, businesses, people, the big house, the sports car, the wide-screen TV. They are slaves to objects, slaves to fear, afraid of letting go, feeling nothing without objects, and, if all had the same objects, the weak would need more to feel better, to gain esteem, thus status is relative. De Sade saw a distinction between libertine and victim, strong and weak; he thought the weak received all they deserved and that, if a person could be killed, s/he didn't deserve to live. De Sade is weak. He feels strong only by perceiving others as being less than he is, by controlling them, dismissing them as inferior. He is unable to let go, to accept, to see others as equal yet still see himself as worthy, strong. His power is meaningless, gained only from downing others.

If I lose control, say the wrong thing, lose my temper, I feel bad, inferior, wrong, for not choosing the right choice, having a moment where I am not responsible, yet if I let go, if I just let go, stopped trying to control, stopped trying to choose, stopped trying to be responsible, I'd have more choices. I struggle with the falling-down house, because I'm afraid, afraid to let go and have no house. A house does not define me. I work because I'm afraid, afraid of not eating. I don't let go and just walk, walk the world, because I'm afraid, afraid of being attacked, falling ill. All our lives, we are told you should, you must, you ought, should use manners, should be responsible, ought to achieve the wide-screen TV, the sports car. Follow the social mores, those socially constructed ones. Behave morally. What are morals? Whose morals? What is right and wrong? Who decides? Still, none realise. They follow these "rules" because they are "right" and the opposite is "wrong", yet they do not know why, or what is "right" and "wrong", just like the times table they learn by rote. The fear of behaving out of character, as though character were a square rigid box.

I struggle with Colette, Cline, colleagues, passers-by, because they don't just accept, because they aren't free, they don't let go, don't enjoy the moment, accept themselves. The thighs are too big, or the desire too wrong, the top not new enough, the hair not good enough, the body a shame, the mind never quite perfect, that thought a little weird. The irony is that, all the while I became frustrated at their lack of freedom, I was not being, not just letting go. If I had instead of trying to make them let go, trying to control, they might just have seen the point and stopped reaching for and abusing that illusionary "power" they never had.

The dildo is on the linen basket, Dusty. When Colette returned it, I didn't look at it for months after she left – I couldn't bear to. No one else has ever seen or touched it, and the leather straps still smell of Colette, whitened by her sex. I've taken the straps out of the box only once. I can't bear to clean them, look at them, remember. I wash Dusty in the shower, rubbing soap up and down its marble-blue shaft. Thinking too many pushes, a need in my cunt, a need to let go. It's not a desire, a sexual lust, and simply a deep need for release. No teasing, just release as the shaft races along my clitoris, until my cunt quickly reaches the point of begging. The blue flat base sits against the cold white tiles, my body riding against it, my cheek pushing against the hard tiles. Colette and Cline never enter my thoughts, just quick urgent flashes, flashes of genitals, none I know, none I've seen, anonymous cunts, cocks, anonymous, wet, my moans escaping, my head hitting the windowsill, free.

Passing the lies
While you'd been gone I'd chatted to a young Australian living in London. It was innocent, close but innocent. You brought her up. I asked how you knew whom I spoke to.

"Slim told me," you replied.

"That is impossible. I've never seen Slim. I don't know Slim. I've never seen the illusive Slim in any room and I'm very private. None know who I talk to but I, so how would Slim know?"

"His subs told him."

"Colette, I've never met his subs either, and no one knows my

business, and why on earth is he sending people to spy on me and report back to you?"

"He's not spying on you."

It certainly felt like that: I had no privacy, no sanctuary; Colette knew everything and supposedly others were telling her. Why would they? Why would strangers waste time watching me instead of chatting about the weather? How could strangers hear and know about my private conversations that Atlanta and other friends knew nothing of? I was hurting, wanting out of this situation, out of this life and scared.

Day Fifty-Two

I spent a long time getting uptight about how uptight people were. Hiding their bodies, concentrating on orgasms, it all annoyed me and I felt so much was missing from their lives. Of course, feeling such, and being annoyed and uptight about the situation, was being just as uptight myself. I was an inverted hang-up. De Sade is hung up, uptight, oh, certainly: the "heroes" eat shit, cause pain, kill, which many argue is sexual freedom. I consider it precisely the opposite. As a child, when first abused, you don't know what an orgasm is: all you know at, say, four years is that strange feeling stops it continuing for that moment. The problem is that the feeling is pleasurable, it is comforting; however, it's not, thus, under situations of intense fear, confusion and abuse.

The very thing causing pain causes comfort alone, which then causes confusion because of its association with pain, which causes guilt and more pain and so the cycle continues. Until eventually the painful, abusive orgasm used as an end to the fear at that moment becomes split from the self-comforting one. The former is concentrated on and over with as quickly as possible. It's a simple uncomplicated tool of escape from pain. The latter developed as I did, becoming self-indulgence, self-nurturing, always enjoyed for the sensation, appreciation of the self, never concentrated on and – by, I don't remember the age, maybe fourteen – only ever multiple. It's free, totally free, I could type now, and orgasm. It's not difficult, it's not a chore, it's a pleasure, like eating chocolate, and, when I consensually give my orgasm to others, I'm proud, I think it's totally mind-blowing and beautiful. My body, this body, this beautiful innocent body that was abused – hang-ups I've none – I don't think of as any more beautiful than another, other than for the fact that it is mine. Therefore, of course, more beautiful to me. It is my own flesh, my own skin, I know so well; it enables me to see the things I see, do the things I do, taste the things I taste. I would never show it off in a superior way, but I'm proud, protective, comfortable in nudity or clothed. I hate the abuser that hurt my flesh, but not my body that experience the pain, not my brave beautiful body. I see all bodies as beautiful, which is why I find people's hang-ups and hatred of their own forms difficult to understand. De Sade's "heroes" cannot just feel pleasure, they have no freedom. They cannot feel pleasure sitting reading, alone, with a love, in comfort with new sheets, in the summer rain, on the M6, by a tree, in the kitchen, softly, tenderly, roughly, urgently. They can't. They are controlled, uptight, bound, locked in tension, which is released only by extremes, by the pain of others, the humiliation, torment, deaths of others. They are as sexually repressed and tense as the woman who concentrates, afraid of giving herself, afraid that my pleasure lost in her body is some chore or obligation, afraid her beauty and expression are somehow repulsive, bad, wrong.

Quit the games
Daily I begged you to stop the games; daily I wouldn't react to whatever you threw. Instead, I didn't sleep, didn't eat, didn't live. I lay and cried waiting for death, no longer able to cope with or understand the confusion or contradictions. Unable to understand how our strong deep love had accelerated into this, whatever this was. I tried to be everything you wanted me to be, spiralled further into debt buying food from Marks

and Spencer's, clothes from Next. Nothing concerned me, as I was going to die anyway. I couldn't live, not like this any longer. I worried about your behaviour, about you, why you were so unstable. I'd have nightmares of waking up and finding you'd quit university, which you still sometimes talked of, or had been found dead somewhere. You associated with people you previously would never have tolerated, people you'd always dismissed as game players, behaviours you had previously detested. I was scared for you, scared for me.

Day Fifty-Three

I neglect everything to research de Sade, for this. It isn't de Sade: de Sade is dead, not even a corpse, but mere decomposed chemicals. De Sade could be anyone. It isn't for Colette: Colette could be anyone. It isn't for me. It is to tell this particular story and make this particular journey. When the journey is complete, I can return and collect the things that belong, that were neglected and abandoned, while sorting through the new. Sometimes we fear being ourselves for fear of losing ourselves, thus resign to being, doing nothing. So what if I get lost somewhere in the dendrites of my neural pathways? Do I need a map in my own home? De Sade never pushed life. He wrote sentence after sentence of fucking, beating, disembowelling, never once describing it step by step. He wrote the outside, the surface; he listed, and catalogued. He never took apart any act. Never makes the reader feel the pain. So she poured scalding water over him, so what? Where are the blood blisters, the skin-ripping agony, the torment, the need to rip away his flesh to rid the deep searing burning soaking into his muscles, gripping his mind into a focus of nothing else?

Days later the flesh doesn't peel away from the bone, green doesn't replace red in infection, his mind doesn't move into delirium, the fear doesn't taunt his heartbeat as he hangs onto dear life, alone in the bed he will die in. I find his lack of depth disappointing: if he was determined in destroying lives, taking them apart cell by cell, he could at least attach some meaning to it, take some meaning from it, some passion, an urgent nagging hunger, anything, just not nothing. I suppose this is my failing: I want it all, I want anything, I want everything; I just don't want nothing, cannot tolerate nothing. The sweet double negative that is meant to be, "I didn't do nothing" – well, thank God for that: you did something, then! Not that the something has to be work, or anything apparently "productive". "Something" is always relative. Some might say I'm wasting time, neglecting a life, on this journey, this story. Well, let it waste, then, let go.

Playing the stranger

You would rave about Slim; rave about the man you didn't know who had phoned you with lies that had split us. Your game consisted of teasing me, telling me how much you still loved me, then later that day or the next revelling about how wonderful and sexual Slim was.

"He's teaching me French."

I couldn't understand how you could trust someone who had gone out of his way to trespass and damage our personal life; your personal life, reality, but you just kept saying you trusted him implicitly. I was real, your ex-lover, the lover you'd been totally open with, the lover you'd been so close to.

I felt inadequate. You had always said we shared the most passionate, mind-blowing lovemaking you had ever experienced, yet now, Slim, a total stranger you'd had no physical contact with, was sexier. You'd taunt me with how you wanted to do threesomes, be tied up by Slim, so many things, things I'd never considered, things I'd not do. I felt inexperienced, inadequate, nothing, felt you'd left me because I was the world's worst lover. My previous sexual confidence, awareness of my own passion had all but disappeared. I became nonsexual. How could I think of sex when I was so appalled that my lover rated a stranger higher?

You'd frequently pass on insults Slim had said about me; you'd type away two hundred miles away and I'd sit tears drenching my clothes, my workspace. I was nothing, worthless, worse than the lowest life form. I had to be, even complete strangers who'd had no contact with me in any form hated me, insulted me. They could be hundreds of miles away, thousands of miles away, they didn't even need typescript, didn't need a simple "Hello", didn't need any observation of me, all it needed was to know I existed to hate me. Allow me to introduce myself, I am the universe's lowest; feel free to abuse and insult me; I deserve nothing more. I was but an innocent, a young tiny woman, trying to keep her head above water who'd fallen in love, is all.

Day Fifty-Four

I like walking in the rain, my feet wet where the water leaks through my boots, my socks, onto my skin, and those drips sneaking onto the nape of my neck. Occasionally I think everything is a social construction. I certainly think comfort is while I'm walking over these cold, dark, wet fields. Soggy, cold skin is a different sensation from dry, warm skin – not a worse or better one, merely a different one. I've slept under damp for years. I've stayed a night in a launderette; I can't say it was uncomfortable, the two twenty-pence pieces I had for the dryers were an interesting alternative to the cold and the door locked out any draft. I slept on the settees of men I'd just met. The fear of what might become of me simply made an interesting interlude. I can't say I was ever uncomfortable – some even gave up their bed, some sent me away filled with bacon and cheese the following day. Afterwards the crowds would mutter their disapproval against the "rough", "cruel", "hard" men. "Kill you as soon as look at you, he would." Their beer would splutter onto my face, but I'd have to hold my head and as much drink as they could, because soon these drunks would seek out food. It was a service: they needed to dispel verbal diarrhoea and I needed to eat. A fair exchange of services I thought – my ears for a meal.

It was only ever uncomfortable on the few times I was hungry. I think the YMCA hostel before had been more uncomfortable. The banging threats on the door, the blood-splattered walls chilled my psyche. The sheer insecurity of it all. The manager, Mavis, was an alcoholic, a fairly unreasonable one. Masses of miners were kicked out because a couple had dated her daughter. I fought for the rights of others, simple things such as asking her to provide a washing line in the more than ample grounds. The others made me a representative and Mavis eyed me suspiciously as I quietly observed the two four-litre bottles of wine diminish in her presence night after night. She had a lucky break. I was sixteen, seeing a really rough woman, a woman more alcoholic than Mavis; she'd beat me black and blue and tease around the edge of the female crime-gang world. I learned many things alongside Chaucer, that most of the brothels were owned by lesbian women, the unofficial blues clubs in basements of huge rundown houses.

Mavis's lucky break came in the form of one of her social workers. It was much later when I knew the whole story. The social worker had asked two men living in the hostel and two of the female gang members to steal and burn her car for the insurance one drunken night. They arrived at the agreed time; the car wasn't there, so they broke into her house. Mavis immediately pointed the finger at me, clean, legal, recordless me. I was confused, knew nothing. Because it was known that I was an academic with distaste for crime, I was never told anything the gang did. Nonetheless, Mavis gave me a week to leave, unless, we agreed, I could prove my total innocence. I went to the police station; it was on the day of the poll tax protests. I was asked through a door, which I obediently entered assuming the interview rooms were through there. The door immediately locked behind me and I was read my rights and fingerprinted while I stood trembling.

The cell was empty bar a thin plastic mattress, but they gave me hot, sweet, milky tea, although I don't drink tea, or sugar, or milk. They gave me burger, cold chips and peas, some of which I ate, although burgers make me sick. The only uncomfortable bit was that I was menstruating and hadn't realised I would be there so long, so I had to press a button and swallow my pride to ask for a sanitary towel. I told them all I knew, which was nothing. When the interview was over, one of the policemen got a coin, and said, "Heads or tails? If you get it right you can go." I was so scared, so naïve, so confused. I didn't realise being innocent meant I could go, anyway. With hindsight I would have possibly just walked away and refused to humour him with his coin game, but I didn't have hindsight. I returned to the hostel, with a day to spare, gave Mavis the evidence of my innocence, but she hadn't kept her bargain. With nowhere to go, I had to walk into the cold the next morning. I had to postpone my education. I couldn't study from the streets. I had to get a job. I didn't have an address. Have you any idea how difficult it is to gain work without an address?

Jealousy and defiance

I asked you to stop, yet daily you persisted in switching between taunts of how you were going to fuck others and jealousy. I tried to ignore you, would turn off my MSN while researching, but you'd find an excuse to mail. I was under total control, prohibited from living my life, rewarded by declarations of love, affection, future meetings, then dispelled with coldness, abruptness, abused by taunts. You'd try to lull me into talking sexually and when I wouldn't comply you'd go, saying you just felt horny.

You put down my city, my clothes, my music, my body, my life, my profession, my degree. All you had done, all you wore, all you listened to, ate, lived was superior.

Day Fifty-Five

Last night I went to the cinema, the big Warner Brothers one with the stadium seating. The show was *Red Dragon*, to complete the trilogy. I'd read the books, seen the respective prequels and vaguely remember seeing the original *Manhunter* as I child, although my memory could be mistaken. Lector fascinates me. He fascinates me more than de Sade, and only in Harris's first two books, where he is the perfect example of the psychopath, fitting every item of the psychologist Hervey Cleckley's checklist of psychopaths. De Sade on the contrary has too much hate, and hate is an emotion, neither does de Sade come across as particularly charming, his behaviour seems too aggressive. Recently, psychopathy and anti-social personality disorder became synonymous terms, but, I think they are definitely distinct phenomena, Lector being the heart rate never "rise past seventy psychopath" and de Sade being the antisocial personality. Psychopaths are frequently misunderstood, they are not all cruel or killers. The psychopath doesn't feel the same pleasure, emotion, interest, and exhilaration as the majority of individuals. Their heart rate doesn't rise in situations that might ordinarily elicit fear or excitement; thus, the psychopath has to find extremes, something more to hold a focus, to entertain. Some take up dangerous sports, some become great scientists, politicians. They make up 1% of the population; that's around four people in an average street of a hundred houses with four persons living in each house. I try to avoid Cleckley's checklist, and, when I can't, I hope to say "no", that one doesn't fit Colette. Glibness and superficial charm, compulsive lying, lack of remorse, lack of deep emotion, impulsive behaviour, sexual impulsiveness, lack of attachment. No, no, no, no, no, no. "Yes" makes our nine months a farce, unreal, it makes everything I believe to be true unreal, it makes nine months of my life unreal. Eighteen years, twenty years, were unreal enough. A life based on lies, deceit, covertness. Will it ever be real? Is anything ever real?

Hot or cold?

Some days we were so close we could talk again about our love, our future, our hopes, our dreams. You'd say that deep down, in the flesh, you wanted none but me, that you missed our lovemaking, could still smell me, taste me, still thought about our intimacy, longed for it. I tried not to be lulled by you, knowing that in an hour, a day, you'd damn me for speaking to you or disclose your want for threesomes, group sex, casual encounters of the third kind now you were single. You'd contradict yourself, saying you couldn't go without sex for a week, then reassuring that you'd always been faithful during our relationship. I didn't believe you any more, didn't believe anything. You had challenged my reality. I didn't believe in existence itself. I didn't disbelieve either. I simply didn't believe or disbelieve, I didn't know. Some days you were demure, warm, like the woman I met; other days you acted as if you had a string of lovers or soon would have. I no longer went from smiling to crying: instead I remained in a permanent tearful state of confusion, tearful with worry for you as much as anything else.

Day Fifty-Seven

MI5 are advertising for jobs for the first time. I was tempted, very tempted, but, no doubt, sooner or later, they would read this journal, or delve a few inches into my skin, and the skills on my application form would be illegible with the spillage of red. What was coincidental was that at the same time Colette had visited the MI5 website and also considered applying, her reason for not doing so being salary, not a primary colour. MI5 is like de Sade, a fascination, a dance with the very opposed, and there is a fine line between fighting against and joining. The boy said I'd end up becoming a double agent, exposing Psyops. Psyops is the systematic brainwashing programme begun by MI5 in the Thatcher years. It involves various propaganda exercises against anything socialist, the former USSR and the unions, and promoting anything capitalist. An extremely clever and successful tool. Probably the only tool enabling the election of a "right" Labour government. It is difficult to realise how much brainwashing we have been subjected to, unless you look back twenty years and imagine being told that a "right" Labour would emerge. The very thought would have been farcical, and I doubt that during the 1997 election many made the subliminal connection between "New Labour" and "New Right".

We have a macro-living de Sade. A society of hedonists and no apologies. De Sade lives in the cutthroat world of the city. De Sade lives in every momentary coupling, where each party's concern is his/her own pleasure. De Sade lives in the fast food, fast roads to the quick thrills. Society is balanced on a hidden motion of immediate gratification. Until Colette opened my eyes, I never knew it existed. The clubs of sex, serving until the early hours in every city, swing, leather, pain, orgies. No city is without such, and clearly visible once the blinkers have been removed is the very tip of the iceberg. Maybe I would have become a double agent, maybe I have.

Internet gossip

As soon as I logged on you were there, furious, saying somebody had told you someone had been asking about me because they wanted a real relationship with me. I laughed, it was so absurd, I was a tearful suicidal mess. I never cyber, let alone did I consider being with anyone at that time. I was at the end of my tether, fed up with games, fed up with lies, fed up with your dealing in lies. You snapped at me, "This is making me upset and insecure and you won't listen, you just blame me for lies."

I couldn't cope; you who wanted strangers, you who wanted threesomes, single adventure, you who said your business was none of my concern, you were upset and insecure about some crazy lie? You were lying still to me, lying about me.

Day Fifty-Eight

Which is worse, physical or emotional pain? The contention of many women is not with the wielder of pain, but with the mother. The mother who didn't stop the father, or the teacher, or the bullies. The mother whose approval is sought and whose criticism aches more than any number of broken bones. The mother whose dismissal of the pain is the worst rejection of self. With de Sade, a rapist, an aggressor, a tormentor, an abuser, you know what will happen: the pain is expected, it is clear to see. There is no confusion. De Sade doesn't pretend to be a counsellor, friend, mentor, lover; he makes no bones about being and wanting to be your worst nightmare. The only question is whether you will live or die; other than that, every bit of your life will be complete and utter torture. There is no pretence. You know the danger, the pain you will feel.

You never feel trust. There is no doubt that you can ever reason with de Sade. He is big, you are small. He is right, you are wrong. He is God, you are nothing. No mistaking de Sade's motives. He will never demand affection, never encourage with a compliment, never listen to your opinion – you don't have one. The only aim with de Sade is to escape him. You can hate, be angry, want to kill him, or even lock him in a box as the "demon monster", but, once free, never will that pain be as bad as confusion. De Sade will never reject you, you want to escape, rejection is felt only when you want to stay. The pain is raw, but it is understood. Monster hurt me; the only confusion there is why and the why soon becomes why not when it becomes clear: de Sade hurts, all he does is hurt.

The only damage he causes is pain; he doesn't damage the deep emotional artery with love. He never pretends to be protector and saviour, lulling, then watching with disdain while you burn in the fires of hell, the flames of the tormentor licking at flesh, flames fuelled by the "protector".

The block

I needed a break, at least for a few days, so I blocked you from my MSN. I began to balance again after a couple of days, go without shaking, crying. I worried about you, but it was only for a few days' reprieve. I logged on one day, and my MSN, which opened automatically concurrently with the Internet, gave the message, "You cannot sign in because you are signed in elsewhere."

I knew immediately it was you checking my account, checking my mail, checking my MSN list, checking whether you were blocked or not. In temper at being blocked, you blocked and deleted me on your MSN. I sent you mail, telling you to stay out of my account just because I take a few days' space from you.

Day Fifty-Nine

Sundays are like waiting time, sleep, the *Sunday Times* and preparation for work. Waiting, waiting for the week to begin or end again; like a full circle, it begins, it ends, it always ends, there is no such thing as a full circle, the only guarantee is finality, that finality may be replaced, transform, but its particular form ends. What stays is the transformation, the compost heap of your life, the remains that feed the next circle. I become so many circles, the child circle, the teenage circle, the boring adult circle, the wild circle. Each damaged circle became reinvented with a new circle. The wounded, broken, neglected teenager became a carefree, playful, bratty girl who could have not all she desired, but the same as the average clothes-hungry teen. There were so many reinventions, too many circles. Some days I know not where one circle ends and another begins. I ceased knowing which circle I am long ago, or whether I'm a circle at all, or maybe an oval. A shy, coy, submissive, feminine, vulnerable circle met Cline. Cline damaged the circle so much, chipped away at every edge with every type of abuse. By the time I met Colette, I'd being along a year and metamorphosed into a strong, protective, androgynous circle, but it was only one circle some of the time, not the only one, not all the time, not the main one, not the oval. When Colette left, a new circle was invented, a circle she invented, a circle I don't know or recognise, a circle of circles, a circle of fragments.

I wonder how many people are fragmented selves of their former self. Do they ever find themselves before death strikes or is reality lost for ever in the pools of the tormentor's pleasures? Schizophrenia springs to mind when considering the fragmented person, and in some ways, schizophrenia is akin to a fragmented self, the psychosis and the "crazy talk", but, when a schizophrenic is in reality, s/he is in that reality, and in fantasy, s/he is in that fantasy. Fragmented selves are the drunks who were the businessmen the economy relied on, now with no recognition of their former selves, the graduate from the underclass who no longer "fits" anywhere. Fragmented selves are not a reality or a fantasy, everything is real, it's all too real.

Pleading

I wouldn't defend myself, I wouldn't attack you. Instead, I begged you to stop. Stop the games, stop the lies, stop playing Slim against me, Sorcha against me. Strangers against me. Stop the hot; stop the cold, the whole damn inconsistency. Stop claiming me, demanding of me, then rejecting me as a worthless splinter in your finger. I'd do anything for you, I still will, always. I became your puppet, your puppet to toy with. You'd give me words of love and warmth, of the future, then laugh, dismiss me as weak, a wimp, a doormat, not ruthless enough for you. You'd praise our lovemaking as the best ever, say how you could be so sexually open only with me, then tell me how it had never been enough. How it was inadequate, compared with your cyber fantasies with Slim, the stranger, compared with your orgiastic plans, your water-sport lusts. I was lost beyond my league, trusted you, believed you when you had persistently said you loved, accepted and wanted me, me for me, nothing more, that nothing could match your love or attraction for me. I was a fool, a simple, naïve, innocent fool, stupid and rotten to the core and begging you, begging you so much to stop, to stop hurting me.

Day Sixty

Life has become a bag of pick-and-mix. One day is now a thousand. I wake late, taste my lover in the shower, walk dogs, stop at an organic restaurant for lunch, tour around sex shops, then department stores, before returning to view a play with my mum. This is normality. Everything is normality. I remember the homework at primary school, where we had to write about our weekend, it would go something like, "I went to Tesco with my mum. Outside we saw a big fluffy dog." I'd be struggling to fill the page, thus complete trivialities like the cans of beans that were brought, waiting for a bus, carrying the shopping would have been included. What did they want me to put? "I woke up wanting to die, my mum was badly bruised from a beating the night before. We sneaked out of the house before my father woke, brought the essentials, adding everything up as we went along. I was cold waiting for the bus and my arms ached, fingers cut from the carrier bags. Later that night while watching *Nicholas Nickleby*, I fixed my eyes on the television, while my father touched my nonsexual, child vagina and masturbated himself."

These teachers ask too much. Make it interesting? Seven years old, and I looked at them with contempt, they knew nothing. They thought interesting was a theme park, a bottle of wine, a cricket match, a foreign holiday, but reality, depth, they had none, and even then I knew. I vowed I'd never be like that – a stupid vow, really, as I never could be like that: I had no choice in the matter. For years I thought I'd been through hell and come back, but the truth is, I hadn't been there, I'd started there, I knew nothing else, I had none else to come back to, I had no metaphorical place to come back to, to call home. Question on everybody's lips is how did a young, attractive, professional woman such as I function through the heat of hell?

What I'm about to tell you is the most important thing in this story, but do not try it at home. I created a parallel universe, subconsciously, and literally. I didn't sit there at four contemplating my fate and decided that reality stank so I would reinvent it. You have to understand the process. Every child has a vast suspension of disbelief. I cannot say how it started, only how phenomenal and long-lasting my parallel universe was, as I developed, so did it. I was living in hell, but I was not living in hell. I had all the suckers fooled and was very pleased with myself. They were abusing me, but they were not, because nothing could touch me. I had a world, a whole world; I could and did draw maps of it. It contained houses, schools, an army, a police force, shops, everything a society could need and want. I had sisters, brothers, a moat around my castle, where my mum lived, and the laughing man was locked away, but I rarely stayed, choosing to live with my "sisters" instead. I would wake up in my world, go to school, and during assembly slip into my world. Often, I would be chastised for not concentrating, for daydreaming, but I wasn't daydreaming: I was living, I was in school, my school, and my high scores on the end-of-year tests proved as much. Teachers could slap, hit, shout, but they can never deny black-and-white test results. Ask me what the lesson was about immediately after and I couldn't tell you, but, within my own world, all the information was absorbed. Now it concerns only others and not myself that I cannot recall immediately after an event. I know I retain every important fact; not knowing where I learned what fact is irrelevant.

Absurdities and lies

"Sorcha says you're having a relationship with the webmistress."

"Don't be so ridiculous, Colette, if she's going to lie, she should at least

say something believable and for you to even give that the time of day."

"So it is true?"

"Of course it's not true, it's completely absurd, and I'm getting fed up with you dealing with lies. Do what you want but don't pass them on to me."

"I don't see how it's absurd. Anyway, she didn't lie when I challenged her about it, she said she just thought it looked like that."

"And Sorcha would know how? I've never even seen her in the room."

I was getting more and more scared and paranoid, and this time I wasn't going to wait until Colette put her Internet plan into action. I reported all the lies, so they couldn't be used against me later. Colette was furious: "So every time I tell you something you go running to the webmistress?"

"No, but this involves her too and I had enough games before Christmas. I'm covering my back, C."

I couldn't believe your hypocrisy. You'd involved the webmistress and a whole bunch of strangers in our relationship for no reason whatsoever, yet I try to protect myself from a repeat of those games and you insult me.

Day Sixty-One

Necrophilia is a theme running through *One Hundred and Twenty Days of Sodom*. On the twenty-ninth day Duclos describes a girl in a meeting with a libertine, whereby to receive her money she has to act completely dead. After telling the story, the Duc becomes so aroused he fucks his daughter, while pretending she too is dead. His language, like all the language running through the novel, pure sleaze. Not language on the level of tacky pornography, but really slimy, contrived sleaze, sleaze on the level of Ben Dover or a man with few social skills, comical in performance and verbosity. The language of the "heroes" in some way explains the passion for necrophilia. The women are not people, not individuals, not human: they are merely empty vessels, objects, sex toys, solely for the entertainment of men. They are not created to move, feel, talk, think, just to provide a tunnel collecting the sperm of men. To de Sade and his libertines, women are a flesh tube, more sensual than glass, plastic, leather, and the sensuality is their use, purpose and reason for living.

If de Sade were alive today, I doubt he'd be writing books, though he might turn his hand to filmmaking: *I Fuck Dead People*. Necrophilia isn't amusing and snuff even less so, but it is also no good hiding *One Hundred and Twenty Days of Sodom* behind one's hand when reading. This journey isn't about understanding de Sade. De Sade is tree food. The only thing that exists is the present moment, but de Sade provides the catalyst to understand. Not understand society, behaviour, the individual, just understand. Necrophilia could be an attraction because the libertine may hate the woman, yet love the female form and the physical sensations, and, from de Sade's repetition of misogyny, hatred of females is certainly a possibility. However, actions say more about the actor than the object of direction.

By nature necrophilia cuts off all feelings and emotion, focusing purely on the second pinnacle of pleasure, almost as though that pleasure were not to be enjoyed, so the act is as distanced and cold as possible, due to perhaps an association of sex with guilt? The closest thing to such distance during physical pleasure is the orgasm created not out of desire or any sexual need but as an immediate cure for insomnia, or the cold distance when sometimes exploring the mechanics of the body, such as timing the speed to orgasm or timing the duration.

Questions and lies
Constantly you question my movements, and where I am, what I'm doing, am I with anyone, why am I in a chatroom? I'm there to find Slim and find out how he knows my business and why he is so interested anyway. Eventually, you reveal he didn't tell you any of my business:

you'd seen me talk to the Australian woman before Christmas, while you were slinging abuse, and assumed we were intimate. You had lied that Slim had said any such thing about his subs seeing me and reporting back, and that Sorcha had told you about my fling over Christmas. I had to face the worst possible scenario: you were the only connection to all abuse, all lies, you, the woman who loved me, held me, promised never to hurt me, to keep me safe. Still I didn't want to accept it, didn't want to accept that you would behave like this, and I couldn't figure out a reason.

Day Sixty-Two

The dark nights drain my energy, or maybe de Sade drains my energy. Long journeys are exciting, stimulating, usually, always profound, and the effects rarely show on the body or mind until the destination has been reached. All the while I take this journey, the novel, myself alone in my study with my thoughts, the people, the places, the learning, the experiences, I am alive, stimulated, energised, but, outside the journey, into the realms of the ordinary, the days are long and tiring, my patience resentful, impatient to return to the beaten trail. I begin to forget where the journey ends and life, myself, begins. I need to retain a magnitude of strength to remain an explorer of the journey and not merge into the surroundings and become a part of it.

We merge so much throughout our lives; it is difficult to retain the reality and the self. Merge into parents, lovers, children, work, friends, propaganda, advertising, the system. People begin to define themselves by the places they live or holiday. A personality becomes the label it wears: "I am a Gap girl". Food invents whole personae. Politics become the sinews of minds. A child changes a woman from an individual into a "mother". People become their colour, sexuality, class. They answer those little "Who am I?" questions with labels that belong to suitcases or bear left at stations for fear their owners might lose them. "Who am I?" "I am a submissive male." "I am a mother of two." "I am a gay woman." "I am an entrepreneur." "I am a left-winger." "I am a Gap-wearing, Punto-driving, Hackney-living label of my former self."

Damn, where have all the individuals gone? I am no paediatrician, but I do hold the assumption that infants and sponges are rather different in their characteristics. I could hold a label prohibition, a revolution scouring the earth, cutting all labels from everything, "What's in this can?" It's food, just eat it, just be, understand the statement behind the label, understand it's about you, not inanimate objects.

Cybersex

The extent of your hidden sides slowly trickled out since we split. I thought you were in a room, under another name, spying on me one day. You replied that you never changed your nick other than when you were having cybersex with men in the lower rooms. You explained how you would seduce them in a main room, then suggest a few of you go into an empty room together so you could type dirty with several at once. You revealed how you had continued having cybersex with the American woman while we were a couple.

I felt tarnished, uncertain; all that I knew about you, about us, was being challenged; yet still you expected me to believe you'd slept with none other than me during our relationship. I didn't believe it, I didn't believe anything. Your truths were too unstable, too changeable. You were a chameleon, a broken kaleidoscope, disjointed and neglected by some child because you could no longer reveal the whole array of pictures. Many times the DSM entered my head, most of the classifications I know by heart, and Cleckley's checklist.

Day Sixty-Three

Myra Hindley has died. The papers are filled with hate, showering ink into "Rot in Hell"; "The Witch is dead". Internet boards are full of hatred and abuse. Ironic, considering that the writing of de Sade awoke the sadist in Brady, yet de Sade is revered as a revolutionary. Myra Hindley is the flesh of us all. She is the innocent baby we all were. The mother she never was, that we could be. The friend we would trust with adolescent secrets. Myra is so close to home, she almost coexists within us.

Those who hate and judge, run away from their own shadows, hate their own lack of control, fear themselves, refuse to accept their wholeness. They perpetuate the pain in society by seeing de Sade and Myra as so far removed from themselves, so alien to humanity, that they fail to understand humanity. The heart of understanding begins with the self. De Sade, his "heroes" and Myra Hindley are no different from the rest of society. Their behaviour was different at times, but were their thoughts really so different? The affirmative assumes we think before we act.

I consider the shadow within me, the shadow that raises my voice, the shadow that ignores the plea, the shadow within us all, Thanatos, instinct. I push the stranger against the cold tiled wall of a club, because I want to. I have no thoughts before, I don't consider whether I should or not, I just do, because at that moment it is myself, my raw animal without thought. It is easy to say I wouldn't do it if the woman pinned didn't want to be. I can make all the excuses in the world, differentiate myself from de Sade and his contemporaries, I can do that, because she responded with passion, but had she responded with horror, the action had already been done. We are base animals with the schemas of intellect. Walking oxymorons of reason, passion, emotion and instinct. The reason built upon and secondary to the animal.

Sometimes I try to catch my thoughts, not just thoughts but the urges, the lightning visual flashes, often more colour than sense. How can de Sade, his "heroes", any of us understand the urges, feelings, instincts, flashes that are not coded by language or cinematic Technicolor?

Lucy

You told me you'd slept with a girl called Lucy. I asked you about her. You said she was just a fuck, that you regretted that you didn't have the feelings for her that you had for me, it was not like us. A mistake you called fucking her. Were you and I a mistake? I couldn't believe some trendy intellectual Oxford babe could be a mistake and you didn't consider us to be so. I hurt, ached so much, tears spilled onto the keyboard, the chair, the floor, stinging so much they should have eroded deep ugly scars down my cheeks, along my neck. All you said, all I thought I meant to you, all the heat you still turned up, the confusion, the love you still spoke, yet you could bear to touch another, fuck another, claim her as yours. You bewitched everyone in your path, men, women, young, old, with your charm, your energy, your mystery, the depth you never allowed yourself.

I sat day after day in darkness. My life crumbling, my work, my flesh, my mind. If all you said was untrue, if our love was untrue, if the nine months we shared was untrue, what was real? My life was thrown into the pit of question. If your feelings weren't real, were mine? If everything we experienced didn't exist, then how did anything else in my life? How did anything in life, how did I? I could no longer trust my own senses, emotions, judgement, reality.

Day Sixty-Four

Colette is barely a myth now. It seems as though we were never lovers at all. I see our time together through a painful, black-and-white, hazed photograph. I look at those photographs, the history of our ancestors, the suffragettes, the pioneers, the inventors, the poor, the repressed Victorians, the hidden, the invisible, the brave, the indulged. Look and see they no longer exist, and one day I too may not even be a black-and-white photograph someone will look upon and realise life is so very fragile. Since losing Colette, I care about little. Not caring is very liberating. I do. I am. I be. I am beginning to let go, not of Colette, of everything. I am still a long way from letting go. I hold on much too hard. It takes time, but gradually I am watching it all slip away, allowing myself to slip away, seeking release. I am asked of my plans. I have no plans. I want to do everything. I don't want to choose. I don't want restriction. I don't want limit. I don't want labels. I want to be. I want to run away from all the masks of social mores, cleanse every layer of paint that hides life, rip up each social construction, tear the designers off the bodies revealing the truth. I live a contradiction, trying to do everything at once, yet let go. I don't know when I sleep or if I do. By trying so hard to let go, I'm actually doing the very opposite.

I am so exhausted, life has become so much work, research and fight, I can almost see the attraction of de Sade and Hindley. How must they have felt to revert to the animal all humans are? I eat the Green & Black's chocolate, nurturing the inner child ethically. I pull the scowl, nurturing the teenager. I contribute to the reasoned debate, nurturing the adult. I flirt with the underworlds, nurturing the shadow and the base underclass flesh I was born as. I fight the world oppression, nurturing the pain in my soul. I have too many I's. When do I nurture the animal I am?

Cold and inconsistent

You would flirt, then taunt. I would ignore you, continue with my work, and the familiar beep of MSN would herald your calling. After demanding my attention you'd coldly tell me I wasn't ambitious enough for a place in your life. I didn't desire Prada, instead I valued talent. I had no passion for money, instead I wanted to end oppression. I had no drive, I expect walking the world with me is out of the question. My degree was worthlessly from a new university. My accent too working-class Midlands, rather than trendy North or pretentious South.

Where was the woman I met, the you who hated snobbery, who held me close, who rated love, emotion, intelligence, passion for life over the brainwashing of labels; the woman I laughed with, kissed softly, whispered love to, heard it from? Where had you gone? Had that poor girl from a northeast village been swallowed up by her insecurities and Oxford plasticity? You didn't even talk about your MPhil, never sounded excited about it, or life in Oxford. You talked empty stranger sex, about how many people in what combination you could fuck, pornography and all that glittered, the designer clothes, expensive accessories. My head was splitting in all directions trying to see through the fog, but your words were so changeable, so sporadic and contradictory. You loved me, you hated me. You wanted your MPhil, you wanted to leave and head back north. You wanted threesomes with strangers; you wanted warmth and love. You demanded attention, then complained you needed to be left alone. You were the woman I met, the studious, the passionate, the insecure, the pretentious, the deep, the shallow, the impulsive, the confusing and I was confused.

Day Sixty-Five

I'm listening to Alanis Morisette. She recommends walking round naked in your living room. I still remember Colette walking around in her tight shorts and a tighter vest. It felt the most natural thing in the world to laze half dressed or nude, to gently lean against each other, softly smile, in a nest of love. Now I rarely claim my space naked. My self, my body, undermined by her words and condemnation. What I once thought of as mine, as beautiful, is tarnished as inferior. My form hasn't changed – only my perception and her derogatory judgement, the first negative commentary that has ever been my experience. I still stand at five foot four. My eyes are still dark brown with flecks of red and a blue circle round. My body is still petite, with a button nose and small full lips. My breasts still thirty-four B to C, depending on my menstrual cycle. My waist still measures twenty-three inches, twenty-four or twenty five after I've eaten. My hips still measure thirty-four inches. My hair is flecked with grey, but no wrinkles grace my body yet. It's all fact now, not beautiful, familiar, positive, just horrid, horrid facts. Life, horrid, horrid facts. Food a means to an end. Activity, the exploration of more horrid, horrid facts. My new lover, a person within a life of horrid, horrid facts. I am nothing but a statistic in her eighty or so lovers, the random figure she cannot remember. I am a random figure. I have an unknown number tattooed upon my soul. I have a quality control of her orgasms stamped on my heart.

I can only wonder where identity begins. My earliest memory is age three or four. I don't remember that period as though it was I, but rather like an observer. I am the eyes behind the camera in my head. Four years old, you have to understand have to get the picture, look around the house, please. See the slugs on the toilet cistern in winter, how dark each tiny room is, the plaster falling from the ceiling and the curtains in that front room, green-patterned curtains. I was staring at those green-patterned curtains while he undid his trousers and lifted me. I was a tiny four-year-old, I am a tiny adult, lifted me so his penis was in between my naked thighs. He moved me to and fro, rubbing against and burning my undeveloped infant vagina, telling me it was a game of see saw. I didn't reply, didn't see any "game", just concentrated on the green-patterned curtains. Patterns that fall together, moving and creating more patterns, memorising the eyes to follow timeless patterns, patterns of shutdown.

No deeper love

You were still cybering Slim. I asked you if you cared for him loved him, if he turned you on more than I. I asked everything.

"Does slim turn you on, then?"

"No, hon, it's my fantasies that turn me on. He was just there"

"Just hurts, hon, you used to love me."

"I still do."

"Really?"

"Deeply."

Deeply, she loves me deeply, so why? Why? Why the constant pain? Why the inability to sleep? Why does my body pace unable to rest, to settle? Why does my soul scream out confusion? Why do the tears never stop falling? Why do I want so desperately to die? Why does she keep hurting me so?

Day Sixty-Six

The patterns in the curtains evolved into the flames of the fire. He would sit in the pitch black apart from the flames dancing around the black fire food. Darkness has very strange effects, I assume it was the darkness. Everything would be silent and dark, eyes straight ahead. This was for safety, any noise, movement and I could be hit at the back of the head, sent across the room. Four-years-olds very quickly learn to avoid experiences that are unpleasant. Staring stilly into the darkness caused things to have a hazy edge and eventually disappear totally; as an adult, I fear this. It is a little similar to losing consciousness, fainting, falling, but I didn't fear it as a four-year-old: I went with it, didn't try to fight. The other odd effect of the darkness, is in itself. It is terrifying, yet somehow it calms the fear that you might be about to die, calms the pain of the events.

Fire is more comforting than curtains. Fire dances, fire turns into faces, fire communicates and I'd hear its soft whispers of comfort, see its protection, obey its command to keep staring and concentrate. I wasn't psychotic, I was four. Later, in my bedroom, I'd see the imaginary white horses appear at the end of my bed to take me to the "real" world and out of the nightmare that was life. The "real" world had many more characters than the nightmare and rules were far more fluid. It started off as a land with my castle, the queen, who resembled my mum, the laughing man, who was locked in a tiny room, my "sister" Jill and "sister" Chris, who were both eighteen, yet they weren't twins, an example of the fluidity of rules. There was a female police force and army, a school (the head was Santa), a sweetshop and rows of terraces with a few entertaining characters in. Rules of logic are very different at four: I could take my old scruffy teddy bears with me and they could be a character, genders could change with a character change, that simple.

I owned the whole land, but most often lived in a terrace with Jill. More often than not I was myself, and Chris and Jill were the sisters who would look after me, feed me, talk to me, tell me what to do and generally nurture me; other times I would step into Chris or Jill. I'm trying to remember the rules of a four-year-old I can remember only by observation rather than remember being. In its simplest form, I was primarily a four-year-old, but, would "step into" Jill when Jill was talking to me as that four-year-old, as time went by, particularly as I got older; or perhaps I merely remember older better. I would sometimes refuse the inner world as "myself", seeing it from Chris or Jill. The world has modernised significantly; it has undergone many gradual changes, so gradual I don't notice them, or indeed for a long time never linked the present with the past. There is no school, police or army any more and it's called a visualisation now, not a "reality". It's healthy to visualise nightly and daily. I was four years old, five years old, six years old, seven years old, eight years old, nine years old, ten years old, eleven years old, twelve years old, thirteen years old, fourteen years old... twenty nine years old. I knew nothing else. It is the way to wake, to sleep. You go to bed, you turn the light off, you do this every night for years, you will never stop doing it. It is ingrained in your soul; it's no conscious process, just completely automatic. Try learning how not to ride a bike, how not to walk.

To fuck or not to fuck

You would act jealous, try to seduce me, stake your claim on me, and always I wanted to believe you, I love you. After you'd set the scene, when I'd later say, "Hey, sweetheart", you would correct and chastise me. "I'm not your sweetheart." I'd limp away inside myself, confused and alone, like a pup that's learned the trick and follows the rules, yet suddenly no rules work. You talked incessantly about Slim. I didn't want to hear, but you would tell me anyway. You'd go on and on about how you trusted him implicitly, how he was such a good friend, so clever, witty, cultured, good-looking; you'd never met him. You told me how he was an actor; he had a girlfriend, but came online to see whom he could meet up with for a casual fuck. You seemed to think this was wonderful; I merely wondered where you had gone. Slim might as well have been the world's greatest lover, you thought he was sexy, adventurous, and you'd not even met him.

You couldn't decide whether to go to London to meet him to fuck or not. You were only in Oxford – it wasn't a distance. Sometimes you would say he was just a friend you found sexy, others how you desperately wanted to fuck him. We'd been split up two months. I loved you more than the oxygen I breathed, you mocked that, mocked everything we shared by wanting some total stranger, some fantasy in your head and holding higher than the reality we shared.

Day Sixty-Seven

I have a head cold. It saps my energy. I drink a horrible mixture of garlic, chilli and ginger, adding some cinnamon to make it bearable. I can't afford to be out of action, such is life. My whole life, I can never recall resting. When you're born out of the underclass, you work, work to eat, work to study, work for warmth, work for the falling-down roof, work for the debts of the food, study, warmth, the work just didn't cover. I am grateful each job is always better than the last. If I stopped working I'd reach what I want to be. I'd be the eternal black-market underclass workhorse, dead or sectioned by thirty.

There are always behaviours learned from each class, ingrained in infancy. The working class learn the "American Dream". They aim for the wide-screen TV and the Axminster carpet. The underclass run and hide and evade the invisible enemy of the invisible people. All through university I thought they would catch me as an impostor and turf me out. The working-class "heroes" who slip out of the system making illegitimate thousands treat us with caution in our professional suits. They return to suburbia, we to our comfortable ghettos, the police rarely pass through. The underclass say nothing, we fight quietly.

My fight is getting up every time you hit me down. My fight was getting a job without an address, then getting an address without money. Ignoring the disbelievers and doing it anyway. from hostel to streets, to job, to bedsit, to breakdown, to job, to night class to university. We are the scum of the country according to Charles Murray. We are the cause of all social evils. We are the drain on your system. I worked from fifteen; I cleaned toilets, waited, scrubbed floors, bathed adults, quite literally handled shit. I did anything, but claim from your system. I claimed for eight months during my breakdown, shoot me for being ill. The Victorians would have treated us to a lifetime of asylum. Eugenics, I believe you call it. Still we run from sectioning. Possibly paranoid, but, then, how many middle-, working-class do you find in the acute psychiatric ward for depression, anxiety, borderline dissociation? The underclass suffer from chronically painful necks from always looking over their shoulder. I look for ever. "my father's" final words to me sixteen years ago were, "Wherever you go, I will find you and kill you, you won't know when to expect it." Safety comes before life, no electoral registration, immediately you are breaking the law, no vote, no credit rating, no voice.

Water sports and orgies

I'd wake, work, return and sit in my inner darkness and confusion. I didn't know if you were going crazy, if I was or we both were. I'd sit back despondent, exhausted, confused, while you fired words of cold, clinical, hedonistic sex. You wanted threesomes, you wanted orgies, you wanted water sports, you wanted bondage, you wanted domination and submission, you wanted men, you wanted women, you wanted all of it, from anyone, at once. You'd put adverts on websites asking for couples, singles, groups, listing your likes: water sports, chains, asphyxiation, power play, whips, leather, domination, submission, pain, anal, voyeurism, and more.

I'd stare at the screen in shock, not shocked by any of your desires, but, because you had emphasised over and over how close we were and how you felt more relaxed and open sexually with me than anyone, yet I knew none of this. My mind reeled. Is that why you didn't want us? Had you become bored sexually? All the times you said it was mind-blowing, was that all a pretence? Was I not adventurous enough? Was I sexually repressed? Boring? Did I come across as too prudish for you to share these fantasies with? All the time I thought I was a good lover, that lovemaking was better in the context of two people in love, but I was wrong, I'd failed.

Day Sixty-Eight

Life is like a series of doors. As a child I'd awake in a hallway with several doors. I'd go downstairs and see my mother, who I thought was a princess with her long, almost black, glossy straight hair. A certain door would open as I watched her mixing firelighters with newspaper in the hearth. She would give me breakfast and walk me to school. It was always in assembly that the other door opened. I don't know how I know this, but I do. It's always the same with doors. I'd be sitting cross-legged on the cold wooden floor and maybe I'd shut my eyes, maybe it just went hazy, but, that's all I can remember, watching my mum make the fire, walking to school, assembly, the door closes, the next memory is walking home. If the "father" was home or out of bed another door would open, a dark door, a cold door, a door that never cried, a door that would stare him out when he'd hold my chin, staring, waiting for me to cry, to hit me as he did my mum. This door would stare defiantly back, this door wouldn't cry, this door wouldn't get hit, at least not for crying.

I know not if you understand, but this is life. This is how I can be suicidal, desperate and in debt, functional at work, flexible in yoga, the life of the party, doors, all doors. When one opens the others are forgotten, until it opens again hours, days, weeks, months later and I wonder why the bills are piling up referencing letters I never received, why I'm still alive, the answers to the questions the new people ask me.

Everything functions; like the orchestration of a navy submarine, everything functions. Doors for emotional expression, doors for intellectual stimulation, doors for practical necessity, doors for social interaction. Dysfunctional? Sounds too functional to be true, like a magic pill that allows efficient happy work, a party mood to order the release of tears at the right time, never interfering with other parts of life. Each item on the plate of life is devoured and processed separately, but pray tell, do the potatoes know the lamb is also being eaten?

Day Sixty-Nine

The journey with de Sade takes me way beyond his words on pages in a book. It takes me to Manchester, Birmingham, all the way into another life. With everything in life, reading is only part of the understanding, experience provides the insight. I'm not spending one hundred and twenty-one days living as de Sade, in his footsteps. I can't afford to live as de Sade. I don't have the luxury of that decadence, perhaps a little smoked salmon and ten minutes watching a portable TV. I am spending one hundred and twenty-one days delving into aspects of de Sade. This is the benefit of being educated, underclass, abused, poor, rough, cultured, professional. I don't fit anywhere, therefore I can infiltrate most places. I am the invisible face in the crowd, the hidden wolf among the herd.

Since a child, I have always stumbled upon things without looking and, days after beginning my journey with de Sade, I had a phone call. It was a male-to-female transsexual friend. She excitedly told me about the domination and submission club she had been to for the first time, and she was intending to go to a similar club in my city that weekend. Would I like to go? Would I? Would I? I looked at de Sade's novel and the journey we had begun, that easy, the exploration was practically thrown at me. From the comfort of my living room, without effort, I suddenly had access. Access to a journey, access to fascination, access to insight. A privilege I was going to respect. If I search for de Sade, I will miss the wonders. I didn't set out searching for de Sade or searching at all. I explored with an open mind, like a sponge, absorbed my new surroundings. Seeing the sights, smelling the smells, hearing the cracks, tasting the heat, touching the flesh. Welcome to fetishland, please hang your clothes in the cloakroom, the forecast is hot, and the itinerary busy.

Domination, submission? Before meeting Colette, I'd never heard of such things, and then I thought they were Internet fantasies for bored people. I had no idea it was a huge community, that every major city in the UK has at least one domination and submission nightclub that I'd innocently walked past several times none the wiser, until now. I'm using domination and submission rather broadly. It isn't domination and submission: it is domination, submission, sadism, masochism, leather, polygamy, water sports, voyeurism, transvestism, shoes, boots, role play, exhibitionism, discipline, orgies, bondage, spanking, rubber, suspension, asphyxiation, feminisation, electrocution, vampirism, humiliation.

Pleading no more

I was losing the ability to cope. Days of your teasing me began to tear at my soul and sanity. I was falling apart. Tears filled my surroundings, leaving pools of pain and confusion. I stood staring for hours, knowing not what I was doing. I would go to bed at 3 a.m. or sometimes, 4 a.m., 5 a.m., 6 a.m., and be up again at 7 a.m., feeling through the day in a fog. Skin began to peel away from me, every cell of my body trying to commit mutiny from a sinking ship. I would fall into a corner crying and shaking, not knowing how I got to bed. My door was permanently unlocked, for I didn't care, didn't care if I lived or died, just wanted freedom from this pain.

I begged you, pleaded with you to stop, to stop hurting me or stop talking to me altogether. Your games continued, your hot and cold continued, and I merely sat empty, a void, an empty vessel, a body without a soul, my eyes already dead. All that was still working was my lungs, heart and organs. My mind had eloped into pain when it needed, more than anything, safety. I told you I couldn't cope, that I was breaking down, that I wouldn't retaliate but you had to stop. Did you listen? Did you care? I can't play the game. I don't know the rules. I see love as a warm feeling inside, not as a power struggle, a strategic plot of winners and losers. I lust flesh, not points, want affection, not war, warmth, not cold.

Day Seventy

The first book of *One Hundred and Twenty Days of Sodom* has ended. The second consists of what de Sade calls, "150 complex passions" and is narrated by Madame Champville: "1. Won't depucelate any save those aged between three and seven, but only cuntishly. 'Tis he who deflowers Champville at the age of five." And so we begin. All of Champville's narrations are short and snappy; all refer to the libertine as "he". Champville does not provide the colour of Duclos. Her words are cold and detached, removing herself from the situation. It doesn't belong to her, she didn't witness these events, she isn't saying these words.

On the evening of the 4th of December, at the orgies, the Duc depucelates Fanny, who is held by the four governesses and ministered by Duclos. He fucks her twice in a row, she faints, the second time he fucks her while she is unconscious.

I'm still so far from understanding de Sade, his contemporaries, their desires, their actions. I can feel the pain of the victim, feel it physically, my body shakes and clenches, feel it mentally, but I cannot feel empathy with the libertines. I'm trying to understand by thinking of situations of lesser force. I have no desire to force someone to sit, lift his or her arm. Perhaps wanting to guide people in reaching their potential could be interpreted as force and a desire for obedience. If I want someone to think freely, to hold an opinion, to express, on some level I'm wanting an obedience to that; by wanting them to think independently, I'm trying to force independent thought. It doesn't give me any sense of power, merely an arrogant pleasure that someone is enlightened by his/her own independent thought. A belief, whether misguided or not, that, by knowledge and being able to think, the informed choices individuals can gain from such will make their life safer and more secure. Nonetheless, I am in a sense forcing my values and preconceptions onto others, as no doubt de Sade's "heroes" thought they were.

Completely erratic

Everything about you was erratic: you hated me you loved me, you were skint, you were loaded, you were studious, you never attended lectures. I hurt and worried, you were not the woman I knew, you were inconsistency personified. I could see your faces in my head, many of your faces in my head. Angry faces, sorrowful faces, wicked faces, blank faces, anxious faces, lonely faces, too many faces. I knew not who you were or who I was. You would treat me like a stranger you didn't know , then discuss the things we would do the next time we met. Still we were taking things a day at a time, but I didn't know what you were taking a day at a time. Some days it was strangers, other times friendship, and, if I acted like a single woman, it was the love we once shared.

Day Seventy-One

My new lover suggested de Sade was mentally ill. The problem I have with mental illness is I don't believe it exists. I think all behaviours are a valid reaction to an event or an expression of something. It came to me. I was trying to sleep when it came to me. In such a flash it came to me. I visualised the iceberg. The mind is like an iceberg, consciousness is the visible tip, but the larger matter is buried in the sea of unconsciousness. The difference between the labels "sane" and "mentally ill" is this iceberg. The "mentally ill" have no ice in the water; very little is subconscious. De Sade could write what he did, feel little restraint because his shadow, id, every abhorrent thought that passes, that we push down into the water was accessible to him. The ego is undeveloped because the id was always conscious. All things that are usually unconscious are far bigger and stronger than the conscious.

Think of that iceberg. Schizophrenics are repeating every unconscious thought and contradiction, there is no conscious filter, everything is now and it's information overload. The irony is that those labelled "mentally ill" are actually too aware. We spend years trying to unlock the unconscious, treat anxiety by attempting to unlock the unconscious, and there it is already unlocked. Cognitive therapy works on raising the sea around that iceberg, by burying half the thoughts and keeping those that would have originally been conscious. The unawares are "well" and "functional", "mental illness" is an expression of everything. Everything in confusion because it is all present at once. Fear, killing, pain, confusion, want are all things we experience thoughts of then quickly push away. Away where? Where do you think that thought goes when you walk past someone in the street and feel like hitting him/her? Do you think it just disappears into thin air, because you have promptly forgotten about it? That is your iceberg. That is your wellness. Normality thrives on forgetting and lack of awareness. Would you rather be unaware than like de Sade? You are like de Sade, you are no different from de Sade, your iceberg is simply hidden, it is still there, within you, hidden by fear.

A year to the day

It was February the thirteenth, two thousand and two, a year to the day we first spoke online, or thereabouts. You had been flirting with me via email, via MSN and in the chatroom amid the inconsistencies over the last six weeks. I suggested we meet in the dungeon for old time's sake, where we had met a year before. You refused, said you were busy. Still I waited, crying, confused, alone, I waited, I trusted. Busy you were not. You were in the lesbian room above, said you were meeting someone. I didn't know if you were or if it was another one of your games. I was finally losing control. I had taken six weeks of your hot and cold games, six weeks of total confusion, six weeks of mockery and pain. I went into the room you were in, you mocked me. I felt so helpless, so weak, so churned by weeks of sleep deprivation, hunger, the banging in my head that wouldn't go away, the utter isolation and deep, deep pain. I was a wimp, unattractive, undesirable, powerless, stupid, foolish. All I had when I met you was gone, gone, gone. Like a madwoman I clicked random names in the room list, asking if they were meeting you, because I didn't know. I knew nothing. You told me so much, but you told me nothing. You played games of telling me you were going to fuck random strangers, then you weren't, you were meeting online people, then you hated the Internet, you were going to fuck Slim, then you weren't, and you absolutely weren't bisexual. I didn't know any truth, didn't know who I was, what we were, what you wanted didn't know what was true, if anything.

Day Seventy-Two

Life is strangely calm now. Horribly calm. It consists of work and sleep. At least with madness there is reason to live. I always wondered why impulsive behaviour is listed as a symptom of many mental illnesses. What is so dysfunctional with impulse? I'm not talking murder or abuse, just not thinking, not deciding, not planning, just doing. We are born to do, to act. Is it really so dysfunctional if you go out in Birmingham and wake up in Manchester, if you kiss without any reason at all, if you make love without any reason, then ask her name? Why can't streets be used to dance and sing in? What is wrong with wading in fountains, walking through parks at midnight? What is wrong with doing all this completely sober?

De Sade, abusers, paedophiles, wife batterers are not impulsive. They carry out their actions with almost military precision. They are cold, calculating, not acting out of instinct or wrath. De Sade's "heroes" have a whole list of "rules", dates by which certain things will happen to each child. The one hundred and twenty days are planned out precisely: who will lose their virginity vaginally and anally, who will lose their limbs, who will die how and when.

The man they call my father would stare into our eyes, to make us cry, so he could hit us for crying. My mum weakened more than I, but, nonetheless, the point is he had no reason or rage, he set up the situation. One year, just a few days before Christmas, he called me upstairs. I went and on the bed was a keyboard. "This is the Christmas present your mum has bought you," he said. My whole insides crumpled on the day, I had to feign surprise. I've always hated Christmas, usually spend the day cleaning or writing. No psychopaths are impulsive.

Harassed by the root

February the fourteenth, two thousand and two. We were both in the lesbian chatroom. You taunted and taunted me that you were going to meet Janine the American and cyber her. You had already told me that all the time we were a couple you had continued to cyber Janine. When she came into the room, I asked her about cybering you when we were

Jacqueline Phillips

still a couple. She called me a nutter. Before I could defend myself, Slim came into the room; this was the first time I had met the person who had split us up.

"Why did you lie about me?" I asked.

The reply I received was a torrent of abuse, along the lines of fucking nutter psycho bitch. I folded in half, sobbing confused. I'd never met this man. Why would he talk to me like this, abuse me thus? He clicked me into a private chat. In private chat, he spoke rationally, giving excuses for his lies, while continuing to abuse me in the main room.

Slim set about taunting me in private. He mocked the relationship we had, said I'd never meant anything to you and beat upon my wounds how he was going to meet and fuck you. I sat shaking uncontrollably as this person assassinated my character as the psychotic scum of the earth. You just sat there, allowing this attack on the woman you had loved deeply, held closely. I couldn't understand, needed to know what was going on, begged you to talk to me, to explain, you didn't, until Slim asked you to, then you denied all responsibility.

"What other people do is nothing to do with me."

"But, I don't know this guy from Adam. Why would he attack someone he doesn't know and knows nothing about? What have you said to him?"

"I haven't said anything."

"He says you're going to meet and fuck."

"We might."

"You said you weren't, that it was just a fantasy. I can't cope with this any more, Colette, I've taken your games for six weeks and before that. I've never retaliated, but I can't cope any more. I have to stop you, because if I don't you won't stop, you will just keep playing hot and cold inconsistent games, it will hurt me far more than you to hurt you, but you are killing me, I have to stop you."

Day Seventy-Three

'Tis the evening of the 4th of December, at the orgies, the Duc depucelates Fanny, who is held by the four governesses and ministered by Duclos. He fucks her twice in a row, she faints, the second time he fucks her while she is unconscious.

Fanny is one of the oldest of the little girls. She is fourteen. I thought of her age and almost felt relieved, then total horror at my own relief. I am becoming too sucked into de Sade. It's almost as though certain acts aren't as bad as others, when actually they are all equally as bad. Here is a fourteen-year-old girl being held hostage and raped and I'm thinking, Well, she's fourteen, it's not as bad as the twelve-year-olds, and she hasn't been beaten, had her limbs removed or killed yet.

Well it *is* as bad, it *is* as bad, it's worse because she knew she would get raped on this day, she knows she will lose her limbs, she knows she will lose her life, and the others know their fate. The difference with stranger shorter-term abuse and familiar abuse is evidence. The familiar abusers want long-term access to their prey; they don't want evidence or too much damage to jeopardise their permanent toys. Stranger abusers, like de Sade's "heroes", have little concern for evidence or damage: if their victims live they might tell, and if they die they can easily get more.

Imagine being a six-year-old child, an adult looming over you, everything about him looks huge, emphasised against your size, his teeth more yellow, his breath heavy with stale alcohol, his male hormones strong against your non-scent. Imagine he is pushing against the skin of your vagina that won't go anywhere. It hurts, really hurts. He tells you you are too small, but maybe next year you will be big enough for him to put his penis bigger than his arm inside you. Imagine it, next year you are not big enough, or the next, so the threat remains. Imagine it. You don't want to? Neither do I.

Killing me softly with your words
I tried to understand, I didn't want to react, but I needed this to end. I

was completely losing myself to your power. I trusted you, loved you, had always believed whatever you told me, trusted your judgement more than mine and I still did now, when you were telling me how worthless I was. I just kept repeating, "This has gone too far, Colette, you have to stop this game, I have to stop it, I cannot cope any more, you are killing me." You were killing me, my lungs moved up and down, my heart pumped, but within me all substance had died. My eyes were as still and blank as any corpse, gone was the shining twinkle. I couldn't say when food or liquid passed my lips.

Day Seventy-Four

Yesterday my brother told me that the step-aunts I never saw were abused by my maternal grandfather. All sense of known reality had dropped beneath zero. Take a return trip back to the beginning of de Sade's novel, the "heroes" were the husbands of the others' daughters, all of whom were fucked in every way by their fathers and husbands, some of their husbands being their uncles. I have found de Sade. De Sade is my family. De Sade is all reality. De Sade is the lies never to be told. De Sade is the secrets tearing souls. De Sade is the flash in someone's eye that invokes fear. He is the faraway screams in the night that are unknown but to the person woken by them. De Sade is the pain in the head long after the fist is removed. De Sade is the teacher's handprint embedded in flesh. De Sade is the reason for crouching in the corner. The always expectant horrific death. De Sade is the exhaustion that never recovers. De Sade is the thrusting vein in the temple. The clenched fist, the murderous thought before restraint. De Sade is the fire and brimstone of the universal soul that emblazons itself on all.

The fields are hard with frost, the air bites, like a giant mouth taking chunks out of cheeks, ears and the nose. The trees so real and free, nude, from aesthetics. Sometimes I walk, yet I don't feel the ground. Colours swirl around me I don't see. My hand explores the other, yet feels nothing, so explores more in an attempt to induce a response, a recognition. My head gains snippets of awareness before a quagmire of fragments and sometimes loss. This has no clinical term. There is depersonalisation. There is dissociation. There is no term for the occasional states of collision. How ironic when dissociation is the healthy state and collision is the breakdown or momentary crisis of pain. It occurs when there is a glitch in the system, no immediate threat, no immediate need for function, yet increased pain. It could be drawn as a formula, a little diagnostic tool. NIT + NIF + IP = C. The outcome of de Sade reduced to a formula. The children in the castle reduced to a formula. Life reduced to a formula.

Trying to escape

I left you that night begging and pleading with you, warning you I could take no more abuse. The next day I woke up, I knew there was only one way out, to get rid of you for ever, to retaliate, until you finally left me alone. I went in every chatroom you were likely to use. Put in the handles, railasietteloC, reyalpevisubaasimilS, not to mention, reknawasimilS, you get the picture. I left the handles sitting absently in the chatrooms while I went away to cry. I wanted you to leave me alone. I had to do whatever it took to rid myself of this pain. I became cruel. I dug inside your soul and took out your insecurities, or at least some, and every torturous word I said gripped my soul, vicing my head, cramping my stomach, giving the mother of all pains. Hurting you hurt me more than the accumulation of all your games, lies and insults. I was turning a key, a key that worked in only one direction. I knew I would stop you hurting me and I knew there was no going back.

Day Seventy-Five

I am experiencing an emotional glitch. I don't have any white-hot wrath, or immediate pain. It is that fuzzy feeling right in the centre of my forehead and the thoughts that are not slow enough or stable enough to catch. There is a pain in my body but it's not definite, not an ache, not a pounding, not a burning. It is the sensation of being in a daydream, but not in the daydream, but not outside the daydream either. A place where nothing is real, it isn't false, it simply may as well not exist, I simply may as well not exist. Nothing feels, looks, smells familiar. My hair, my hands, my body, it moves, but I cannot get any hold on it. The skin I feel, I see, I know it is mine because I'm sitting inside my head and logically it cannot belong to another. The mindspace I dwell in must be mine, but I simply cannot get a hold of me. It's not that I feel out of sorts, I feel as though I do not exist, there is an incompleteness with momentary recognition that is too fleeting to grasp. I cannot do or respond to anything, or wait for it to pass, for I am not whole enough to control it. Glass eyes and corpses don't have feelings, but that is as close as description comes. I can feel the emptiness in my eyes and I can't connect them to another frequency, odd how you can feel how eyes are looking.

Death threats

Slim continued to click in and out of rooms, abusing me. He would come in wherever I was, private-chat me, insult me and disappear into cyberspace. I needed to understand he was a total stranger. Why did he hate me so much, need to taunt me so much? I couldn't ask him, as he disappeared before I could say anything. In my confused logic, I went into a room under "Slim" to try to bring him back so I could discuss why he was behaving the way he was towards me. I didn't expect the complication that occurred.

All of a sudden I was in a private chat with a woman, a friend of his. I'd forgotten I was under his handle, until she asked me something unfamiliar. I was mad, all you had put me through, for weeks and before that for months, all Slim had put me through, a complete stranger without reason. While the complete stranger was telling "Slim" her problems in one room, I was repeating them in another. Slim didn't act like a reasonable person: he had phoned you with atrocious lies when we were still a couple, had lied about and then abused a total stranger. Perhaps he would understand his own behaviour.

It was an hour before Slim came into the lesbian room.

Slim: hi all again

Slim: Woman, listen up. this is the last thing I am ever gonna say to you OK?

Me: What??? how about sorry and what are you doing here yet again?

Slim: if you ever talk to Beth again pretending to be me... and if you carry on trying to hurt Colette... I am going to fucking kill you. OK..you understand? So fuck off and die somewhere... and leave Colette alone...

Me: I think your the one hurting and playing games you lying two crossing wanker

Slim: – or honestly, you are gonna find yourself in real trouble

Me: she lets you talk to the woman she loves like this

Voice: go on you've got the right one LMAO colette is shit in bed

Slim: and as for Colette, if I see her upset by you one more time you cunt, I will fuck you up and make your life hell... trust me

Me: You better quit you've lied abused me...

Slim: Watch out..sleep well

Day Seventy-Six

Sometimes I sit, and the empty feeling isn't quite the empty feel, but rather the feeling of fullness, that all in my head is trapped and squashed up against an imaginary wall, I can feel it, yet not release it. The walls appear to close in and even outside the sky will close in, as there is no escape. De Sade is within my flesh every day, he is now more than half my genetics, he is all my genes. I am no longer merely half rotten to the core: I am *wholly* rotten to the core. This is the effect of incest or familiar abuse, there is no escape from your own DNA, the flesh that was made by de Sade. How can

I slice it open from the inside and crawl out? You look at me in my blatant naked honesty, de Sade's hide under superficial charm, but you see the darkness running through my veins, you see the poison pumping around my organs. There's a label on my head, runs through the family via sperm and egg, "genetically fucked". If I were livestock my parents would never have been mated, they'd long since have been dog food, not the steak in the exclusive restaurant.

As a child, I parted company with the genetics I so hated. I was not part of them, not from them. I was a changeling, Neptune's child, a completely different person in a completely different reality whose parents died at my birth. In every sense I was an orphan, and they were weird, weird strangers I had to share a house with. I'd walk two metres away from them, raise my brow behind them if they spoke to anybody, all the things a child can do to say, "Don't associate me with these people." To me, they were definitely not of sound mind and rather stupid with delusions of their own intelligence and power. It was only as I grew older and had still not escaped that I grew to fear them. I tried to escape, but not hard enough; had I not been afraid for my mum's life, I would have simply run off, taken a train to another city until the police picked me up and put me into care. At ten, I tried shoplifting to get put into care. I didn't want any of the stuff, threw it into the bin, as I exited the shops. The shops were too stupid to catch me, though. I made it easy, asked for a carrier bag from the till as I walked in and simply filled it. How difficult is that? Who asks for an empty carrier bag as they enter the shop?

All the while I kept waiting for someone to rescue me, take me to safety. The neighbours who heard the crying and screams. The teachers who constantly told me off for daydreaming. The relatives who thought I was a strange child. The shopkeepers I talked to, pleading with my eyes. One of them must telephone the police one day. I waited. My fourth year, I waited. My fifth year, I waited. My sixth year, I waited. My seventh year, I waited. My eightieth year, I waited. My ninth year, I waited. My tenth year, I waited. My eleventh, year I waited. My twelfth year, I lost hope. Duc told the children in the castle, that there was no point in screaming or trying to escape: nobody would come to rescue them. De Sade is everyone who does nothing.

Charlotte's defence

You refused to give Slim's name and address, so I could report his threats to the police. I can't pretend I wasn't perturbed. I had completely lost it and broken down. You were acting very inconsistently and Slim, whom you trusted implicitly, had wreaked complete havoc, via telephone and Internet, yet knowing neither of us. You knew everything there was to know, my address, my job, my routine and I no longer trusted or knew you. I no longer felt safe from people like Slim.

You took over the site, you, your friends, Slim. I had no logic left, nothing left but tears and fear. Somewhere I figured, if he wanted me he wouldn't want to kill me, so into the nest "Charlotte" trooped. He fell hook, line and sinker for the false name and the laughter after his lame comments, the fake interest. Soon enough he private-chatted for cybersex. Even in my biased state I couldn't believe how clumsy and unsensual he was. I had to take control, regardless of the person or medium; I could never interact in something so utterly unsexy. His ardour increased: he talked of meeting "me" in London for sex. I typed back affirmations while I considered a tube in the opposite direction would be the closest he would get to my body.

He chattered non-stop and all the while I just kept directing him back to sex and looking at the clock, adding up the hours I was wasting with him. My aim was quite simply to make him orgasm then go, he was holding off, trying to convince me that he never masturbated during cybersex, that he wanted to wait until we met. Surprising how a little encouragement weakens the resolve: as soon as "Charlotte" convinced Slim she really wanted him to come, he was halfway there. I expected him to disappear as soon as his orgasm was reached. He didn't. As I was making my excuses to leave he asked for my email address. I thought about it, then typed, certain he would realise once he saw the address on the screen; he didn't. No doubt you told him, when "Charlotte" PC'd you afterwards.

Day Seventy-Seven

Life is a predetermined waiting room. Freewill is the illusion for those who forget thought precedes behaviour. State of mind is not a choice. Hold on while this great brute of an adult is ripping out my soul. If I change my mental frequency to happy all will be fine and we'll live in a world with rainbows and little bells on the end. Hell, I'd rather be insane than psychotic. Humans really are the Shire horses wearing the little leather blinkers. Suffering where? I can't see it. Adjust your blinkers out of your egocentric vision, you fools. If predetermination of thought isn't enough, then there are the steel doors so many seem to be blind to. Homeless, under eighteen, no, we can't help you, go away. Steel door closes, and the little whispers of, "It's their own fault, you know, they have a choice." Of course it is, of course they do, they were stabbed by a parent, they were raped, they were abused, they were beaten, they were starved, they were thrown out for being gay, having a black/white boyfriend/girlfriend. Education, underclass, yes, you can have it; money to live on, no, definitely not. Steel door closes. They have a choice, we live in a free society, they don't want to better themselves. Food, basic need, forgetting. Dialect? Work here? No, go away, we can't employ that kind of talk here. Steel door closes. It's their own fault, they should learn to talk properly, have no aspirations of working on a production line.

There is a correct way to talk, isn't there? It must be correct, because the people in power say so, and they are right, everyone else is wrong. Language is for talking correctly. What did you think it was for? Communication? Mental illness, job, education, health, yes, just don't tell anyone, bluff it off as elite eccentricity, get caught and all the steel doors close, literally, right behind you. Don't forget, it's your own fault, you have a choice, you can pull your socks up, don't ask me how that's going to help when it's your emotions that are hurt, but several million people pulling socks up every two minutes will certainly make mental illness more visible.

Still playing

After finally retaliating against you, I mainly hung in the dungeon trying to avoid everything and heal my pain. You came by one day, clicked on my name, called me pathetic and said you were now with Sorcha. Only last week you were going to meet Slim to fuck him, and only two weeks previously you had blocked Sorcha from your MSN. I couldn't keep up with you, you were unstable and I wanted no part of it, wanted to be left alone. How could the woman I love and thought I knew be behaving so sporadically? I had retaliated, washed my hands of you. You had Oxford. You had the world at your feet. My heart ached with every twist of your knife, Slim, Sorcha, complete strangers, you didn't know, hadn't met, yet you wanted them all, wanted to bewitch them all, wanted to be loved by them all. You wanted to feel good. You didn't need to: Oxford confirmed your brilliance and you were certainly gorgeous. You broke my heart, my trust, challenged my reality, broke me down for your insecurity.

Day Seventy-Eight

Question is, what do I do now I've found de Sade? Shoot the nation's paedophiles? Then what? Shoot myself, because I'm of the same genetics? Taking life isn't an option or any harm, revenge is only an excuse for abuse, due to a latent desire for it. The reason de Sade is so difficult to deal with is that he is everywhere. The press has just reported that Pete Townsend has been allegedly subscribing to a site that has downloads of child pornography.

Pete Townsend was apparently carrying out research for a book. The question remains: why aren't the police closing down and prosecuting child pornography sites? Operation Ore, as the police investigation that uncovered seven thousand two hundred subscribers to various child pornography sites was called, was the largest investigation into child abuse yet. Why? Occasional individuals are prosecuted for having pornography on their hard drive, computers are seized, such computers will reveal details about the sites, so why isn't there a prosecution of the site and other users of them? Why don't credit card companies report such sites to the police? Why don't the press and the public pick up on this discrepancy? We have a principle of innocent until proven guilty, so until prosecuted I don't see it appropriate to make conclusions about Pete Townsend.

Libby Purves makes an interesting point in *The Times* today. She comments that we are all aware what child abuse, including child pornography is; we do not have to abuse a child, including looking at the pornography, to know it exists or to research it. Yet de Sade is still on the shelves. De Sade is the forerunner of Internet child pornography. We could delude ourselves that no children were actually harmed for the construction of de Sade's work. All literature has its reference in reality. When anyone subscribes to child pornography, he or she is indirectly responsible for the abuse of those children by providing a market. When anyone buys a copy of *One Hundred and Twenty Days of Sodom*, he or she is validating abuse of children and women, and snuff.

I would question the motives of any who do buy de Sade and validate potential facilitative material that may encourage abusers to act. Unlikely? Ian Brady was highly influenced by the works of de Sade. The reading didn't force him to commit any action, but de Sade is really only of interest to abusive members of society, he does not stand as an example of intricate plot or beautiful prose.

De Sade is running the country. De Sade is running the world.

Forget patriarchy. We are in a state of Sadiarchy. Oh, I be one of those extreme feminists. Abuse of males is terribly underreported due to the stigma. What now? What label will you give me now? Whatever it be, remember, I am spawn from you. I am one of your many daughters. I am a child of your culture. I am a product of your system. Frightening, isn't it? There is nowhere to run. We are your doctors. We are your teachers. We are your cooks. We are your nurses. We are your drivers. We are your lawyers. We are your accountants. We are your computer programmers. We are your system.

Sorching the soul

I was minding my own business in the dungeon when you came in precisely ten days after Slim's death threat. Hand in hand with Sorcha, throwing abuse. First the games you played between us all, then the death threats of Slim, now this. I didn't understand. I didn't understand you any more. I didn't understand the situation.

Me: so why you brought you new lover here to rub my face in yet again

Colette: not at all

Me: Your last question Sorcha, no I didn't hound you, I hadn't seen you for weeks

Sorcha: what?! whats kind of an answer is that

Colette: cos I wanted to know why you were lying ..I'm tired of being the accused

Colette: you denied hounding sorcha when I asked

Me: yes I didn't hound her I asked politely to pc and she agreed

Sorcha: what?!

Colette: well that's a different story to the one I heard woman

Me: she said she wanted to know why I was lying which I am not as you well know colette I might have said cruel things to you and you me but you ask me something I tell you

Colette: so sorcha is lying?

Me: yes Colette we already established Slim and Sorcha have lied for 3 months

Colette: so all of this is sorcha lying to get me away from you?

Me: I don't know why she is lying colette

Sorcha: er excuse me... what am i sposed to be lying about???!!

Me: I don' know why she pced me twice in the dungeon I don't know any of this craziness

Sorcha: what???!!!

Sorcha: are you talkin about me?

Me: I don't know why a silver I didn't know lied why Slim insulted me and lied for 3 months without knowing me

Sorcha: I find it hard following deluded rubbish Woman...sorry but thats just me

Day Seventy-Nine

In de Sade's world, everything is enclosed in the "safety" of the castle. The only defence is to keep everything open on leaving the castle. Pull down the steel fences. Smash the locks. Leave nothing covered. Truth is the defence. Direct, open, cards face up on the table. Leave your door open. Tell everyone your facts. Regret nothing, don't do what you will regret. Deal not in secrets or lies, these are the tools of de Sade, once away from de Sade we no longer have to see them again. At the same time the castle traps us for ever. Locked in its slimy walls, our hands infected from trying to crawl out and in there, we'll die. The castle infects. Out of a running shower my body feels contaminated. In work my mind feels prostituted. I smell humans all around stimulating nausea in the pit of my psyche. I still feel the alien sweat on my hair, my skin. I breathe the heavy male hormones of de Sade in my lungs.

Posting truths

When you continued your games after my retaliation, adding Slim and

Sorcha to the pyre, I decided to end them once and for all. I tried to remember every conversation we had in the last six weeks and post it on the suburbs message board. You had not only broken my heart, you had lied to me, to others, about me, about others and only your reputation was left in tact.

Day Eighty

My shower is producing only cold water, so, I'm in the bath. A bath that hasn't been used for over twenty years. I had to clear it of rubbish first, and scrub at the marks, which are probably damaged enamel. There's still a full bookcase, wallpaper, tools, boots and a host of other junk sharing this six-by-four room with me. The taps are neither silver nor gold, nor green, and they chug when turned on. I can lie in only a quarter of water, after which the hot tap throws out brown liquid. I have to get in immediately, as the temperature isn't exceptionally hot. Meanwhile, the tank, filling up, sounds like an industrial plant about to blast under pressure.

Houses mirror their owners. This place is a living, breathing, damaged and neglected place that was loved once. I love it now, but I'm not happy with its structure or the damage, and I don't have the funds to put the house into therapy. Houses are places people enter, therefore the house ultimately becomes that person, whether through neglect or abuse; house damage is caused by the inhabitant, or the previous inhabitants. The inhabitants who damage a house have been damaged in exactly the same way, by someone entering them. We inhale de Sade, and by doing so keep de Sade alive by becoming him. In the trade it's called "internalisation". The world is full of de Sades and what are we who are non-de-Sades? Victims? Do we walk around with shorn heads and a tattoo to mark us out? In a sense we are de Sade absorbers. We have allowed that which we detest to enter and control. What logic. Yet, he is there residing within our heads.

De Sade is the abusive teacher: "You stupid ignorant child."

De Sade is the abusive lover: "You fucking bitch, if you contradict me one more time, I'm going to break every bone in your fucking body."

De Sade is the abusive parent: "You say no to me? You say fucking no to me? You want to end up like the rest of the morons watching shit, eating shit? Next time I tell you to take your clothes off you do it. Understand? You say no to me again, you fucking little cunt, and I'll make you an orphan. That what you want? That what you want? Your mother six foot under? Get out of my fucking sight. Now."

Question is, if we are not going to be the victims, how do we ever get those children out of de Sade's castle? How do we expel de Sade from within ourselves and replace the original undamaged self? How can we do that for the "victims" who were damaged at four, three, before their earliest memory? Do they have an undamaged self to reinstate?

Wanting to die

I left you, I left wherever you would be. I had made a huge mistake. I believed our love, our closeness, our tender words, our nine months together were a reality that from your behaviour they obviously weren't. The thoughts wouldn't stop hitting my psyche. How could I reconcile with the confusion of those words, the loving we shared and how you behaved in the last three months? All a lie. I should've known, really. How could I expect to be loved by any? How could I be so stupid to believe love off any? People had said those words, but nobody in my life ever had, nobody in my life ever would. I was unwanted before I was born and unloved afterwards, unless I was a useful shoulder to cry on, a distraction, a safety net, a source of entertainment, a sex toy, but just I without a means of exchange am nothing.

People claim my body, until they fear I might have self-worth, then they will still want my body at their command, once it's been ripped to shreds by their tongue and the only sensation is numbness. I as a person, without any offering, the core of me, stripped of flesh, stripped of intellect, my fundamental soul, is worthless, unloved. I started the beat, beat, beating of my head against stone, rocking back, hitting forth, muttering the mantra, "I want to die, I want to die" at fourteen years of age and now I'm left with nothing but my confusion and bewilderment at what I did to the world, for all to hate me so, my hypnotic mantra beats once more. Imagining not waking up in the morning is the best, if not the only, cure I have found for insomnia yet.

Book 3

Day Eighty-One

I thought I nearly lost de Sade, and the panic was phenomenal. Luckily, he was just under a pile of papers in this neglected old house. Fear not, I didn't panic because I am considering pledging alliance to his cause and taking an apprenticeship in "how to fill four months with as much human suffering as possible". I simply haven't completed my journey yet. This old corpse and I are stuck with each other a little while longer.

Although I've now found de Sade, I still am not able to find any empathy for him. I'm trying to gain limited empathy, not so I can excuse or condone any behaviour, but to gain insight. The children are still in the castle, a huge proportion of different generations are walking around with internalised de Sades within them. We might never rescue those children from that castle, but what about the next generation and the next? I've always tried to keep an open mind; until evidence suggests differently assume the same number of male and female abusers. Operation Ore are arresting 99.9 per cent males, and seven thousand two hundred is not a small sample. All that figure suggests is that females do not look at child pornography, not that there is not an equal number of female child sexual abusers, and it doesn't imply there are fewer females involved in physical and mental abuses of both children and adults. It's not simply the case that keeping males away from children will prevent abuse, thus why insight is needed if the next generation are going to be prevented from entering that castle, because once they're in there it might be too late to rescue them.

Separation is not a possible prevention, because unfortunately infants and children need adult carers. Kelly, Regan and Burton found that 21% of females and 7% of males have experienced child sexual abuse. Prior, Glazer and Lynch (1997) found that 27% of females and 16% of males have experienced sexual abuse as children. Finkelhor et al. (1990) found 90–95% of all sexual abuse cases go unreported to the police.

Females cannot place all the responsibility of abuse onto males. If between two and three out of ten of our girls are getting sexually abused, mostly in the home, and one to two out of ten of our boys are getting abused, that extent of abuse cannot just go unnoticed by the female members of our society. Even if the majority of child sex abusers did happen to be male, 50% of our society is female and to my knowledge they are not all blind. The majority of abuse is ongoing within the child's own home. In comparison, stranger abuse is rare, and if the reverse were the case would be more easily preventable. De Sade is not just the person directly abusing the child, or the person directly abusing their partner. De Sade is also every person in their daily lives who knows about it, and if they "don't know" it's because they don't want to – well, not wanting to is an evasion of responsibility and makes him/her no less de Sade.

The suicidal era

Nine months you lied to me. Nine months of a reality I couldn't trust. The confusion is dense, a fog in my head, everything else is attenuated. The sounds dull muffles, sensations semiconscious, a distinct inability to feel, touch, I bite myself to feel and still can't, vision is blurred with that familiar haze of grey dots. I can't stand this pain, this confusion, these questions racing through my head; I can't make sense of. I have to get out of it, away from it, escape it. My head beat, beat, beats bounding bruises by the wall, any wall, every wall, and the mantra, the familiar hypnotic mantra, "I want to die, I want to die, I want to die". If I wish something enough it will happen. There's pills, or high buildings, easiest foolproof ways. I'm scared of heights, but it's the only way; if the pills don't work, I'll be in agony and I'd have to let the dogs out; if I took pills at home, somebody could see them running wild and find me and everything would be worse and so humiliating. The corner is best, just fall into the corner crying and stay there, never to get up again. I do this every night. Sometimes I cry onto clothes I'm ironing and fall, sometimes

I pace around afraid before eventually hitting the wall and crumbling to the floor. Every night I do this. I'm going to stay here in the corner, my corner, crying, and die, only every morning I awake in bed, so I try the next night and the next. If I keep doing it and keep staying there without food and water, just beating my mantra, I will leave this pain for ever. If only I would stop waking up in bed, if only I would stop waking up at all, if only.

Day Eighty-Two

This is roughly where we began. I hadn't heard from Colette for weeks. Within the space of a year, I'd been ecstatically happy, in love, sensual, hurt, confused, suicidal. The weeks passed, I busied myself completing a novel, and I longed for understanding, answers. For some reason I focused on Colette's intrigue in de Sade and on writing her a novel. I suppose this could be considered the beginning of the story and the previous two books merely the background. Days after the novel arrived, I received the telephone call from my transsexual friend asking if I wanted to attend a fetish club with her. From that day on my journey spilt me into ordinary working professional, a reader of de Sade and an infiltrate of a very thriving diverse underworld. I last heard from Colette about two months ago when she appeared on MSN to ask about my new lover and other things she had read from my email account. Let the journey begin!

Followed to Gaydar

I ran and ran from you. I spent every dream trying to push you out of my mind space. I turned the computer off, other than for work. The nights were long. I wanted to die. I didn't want to face people, didn't want to go out, but felt so afraid. I'd stare at my work for hours, unable to make sense of the jumbled words, exhausted through an inability to concentrate and too guilty if I didn't try. I began to take my ten-minute breaks at Gaydar, wanting human company, but not feeling strong enough for physical human company. After about two weeks, I saw a profile, "Lustful lesbian lawyer". It could only be you. Why, why, why? I came here for sanctuary, out of a necessity to have communication at a time I was too suicidal to go out and interact. I couldn't escape from you, wherever I went you were there. The cycle continued on Gaydar, flirt, cold, argue, put down. Sorcha the total stranger was already better than me. You hadn't met her yet, nonetheless, you were totally in love, had never loved like this before, and I'd heard it before, the words you'd said to me and no doubt Helen. I was rendered worthless, lower than a complete stranger. I was unlovable, unwanted, useless, discarded, and hated by complete strangers.

I found more and more about you, the lies, the sites you were registered on, the various email addresses you'd had for months. Every now and then I'd go to the suburbs trying to get to the bottom of everything to get told I was dangerous, mad, crazy, violent, that you'd taken an injunction out. You denied saying all these things, said they were all mad:

I have never said I was getting a restraining order ffs lol. I haven't talked to Prophet about you at all, whatever he's saying, take with a pinch of salt, you know who i trust online and proph ain't one of them.

No, you trusted Slim implicitly – Slim, who told lies that ultimately split us, Slim who made threats to kill.

Day Eighty-Three

Still wroth with the lovely Constance, Curval maintains that there is no reason under the sun why one cannot successfully bear a child even though one has a broken limb, and therefore they fracture that unlucky creature's arm the same evening. Durcet slices off one of Marie's nipples after she has been well warmed by the lash and made copiously to shit.

Damn, think we need to get into that castle pretty quickly. Why would anyone want to take a perfectly healthy body and damage it, not kill it for the intrigue, but actually damage it? Is it the same principle as vandalism? Why do people vandalise? To destroy something beautiful, to destroy something they think they will never attain? Depression affects more women than men, and it is internal anger, a huge self-destruction. Is the act of injuring the body of another the reverse of that, a hatred of the self that is taken out on others? Only Duc is the strong, "perfect" male and we've already ascertained that Duc is de Sade's "ideal", how he would like to be, how he would like to see himself; therefore it is probably safe to assume that de Sade had a very low self-image, whether consciously or not.

The old "crones" have to be damaged because they are the complete and utter shadow of de Sade's internalisation, they are his worst reflection, the mirrors that have to be smashed. The women are beautiful, they are superior, but, de Sade cackles, they won't be for long. They think they are so pretty, so perfect, so clever and de Sade is about to change all that. Look how powerful he is, how quickly he can render everyone to become less than he is. His arm might be ugly, it might be gammy, but look, as he laughs at Constance, it works. De Sade is now superior. Any healthy arm will always look better than a purple, black, red, yellow, hanging, fractured limb.

The children, they were loved by someone, they are worthy, wanted children, people would stop these children in the street and comment on their cuteness. How dare they? De Sade wasn't loved, de Sade wasn't wanted. Why not? Was he such a horrible child, an ugly child, unworthy of life? Well, he's showing them, because it is the "perfect" children's bodies that are damaged, not his. He will make them look how he sees himself, worse, yes; he will make them look worse. They will feel his pain, they will feel deformed, they will experience what he is going through, all of it.

Duc will avenge de Sade's image. It's such a lack of power that causes the abuse.

Cocaine and insanity

You finally admitted you'd been taking cocaine at Oxford. My stomach dropped a level. Had you merely pushed down your demons all along, instead of confronting them? You had everything, Oxford, the world, looks, brains, charm. It explained your forgetfulness, how sometimes I couldn't make sense of the conversation, the extremes you swung to and from about everything. You were afraid, you were invincible, you were alone, interesting wonderful people surrounded you. You were short of money, you were buying platinum rings and talking of a Prada outfit for the ball. Why were you risking everything? Where had you gone? What had happened to the sensual woman with the coy smile I met on the station? Had you been kidnapped, another taken your place? I didn't know if it was my insanity, yours, the cocaine or all three. It was like being on a motorway with no rules, cars driving on the left and right, from side to side, if in doubt freeze and wait for the two possibilities: survival until organisation or death.

Day Eighty-Four

I'm eating rusks in hot soya milk. Baby food? Well, technically, yes, but this is life. Life is yin, yang, life is balance, nurturing the inner child. Some people seem to have a complete inability to identify with children, to understand a child's perspective. When we grow, we add an age, we don't lose one. The child we were doesn't suddenly vanish into thin air; like Russian dolls, we go into the adult as the child. Those years of experience and perception are not lost, they don't cease to have happened because a new year has occurred. Being a director at thirty doesn't change drooling on Mum's shoulder at four. Being a doctor at forty will never change the snowman built at six, or the fact that that particular snowman was real. That snowman will always be "real".

To believe the snowman was real is enough to make him real and different beliefs at forty don't change the beliefs at six or invalidate them. You can't go back and rewrite all the scripts. You can only ever rewrite the scripts in the moment.

In childhood, everything is fluid; the only limitations are the limitations of the mind and a child's mind possesses few. Very quickly as a child you realise you can change everything with belief. Sex can change, bodies, people, size, age, skin colour, environment, everything can change form. Things are labelled thus only because adults tell you they are; well, adults are wrong, every child knows that. Adults may well be adults but they aren't the brightest candles in the pack; if they were they would know what you know, and they don't. There is a very elaborate practising going on with the child. First is the knowledge that nothing is fixed; this knowledge is practised on small things at first. An adult tells you a colour is blue, so you see the colour blue, then change it to red, yellow, sky-blue pink if you so wish. A child can do this, because a child knows what all these colours look like, therefore knows what to change the perception or belief to.

The second knowledge gained is that adults don't have this skill. Not only do they not possess this skill, but they have a very strange belief that, if they do not have the skill, the skill does not exist, thus the child practises hiding their magical awareness. Not only are phenomena not fluid, but some things can be invented or shifted. If a child doesn't like fish, but is forced to eat it, as long as a child knows what chocolate tastes like, the fish is edible, because knowing the perception is enough to experience the perception. De Sade is pretty mean, not an individual or group the child likes. Child kills de Sade. No matter what de Sade does, it can't hurt child because de Sade is really dead. A new carer is created, who is protective, entertaining, funny, nurturing. This "carer" allows you to eat ten bars of chocolate at once if you really want to, and you can make as much noise as you like, and loads of mess. In fact the only restrictions are restrictions to your safety. A perfect de Sade/parent substitute. The really brilliant thing is that de Sade never becomes internalised, because the child only listens to her carer, who tells the child not to listen to, obey or behave like de Sade. It's almost perfect, the child doesn't need rescuing from the castle, because the child didn't like anything about the castle, therefore changed it all. People affected by de Sade later than the fluid childhood don't have that "get out of jail card", but for now this particular adult and the child within her can rip that victim sticker right away.

It's a matter of yin and yang, a matter of balance, of trusting the only person to trust and letting go.

Erotica and trust

We were separated yet jealous. Hateful yet attracted. Angry yet loving. I'd ask you about your behaviour and sometimes you would apologise and say you just didn't know why; other times we would escalate into petty – petty being both of us asking why the other was on Gaydar. "I'm here for the erotica," you said. "The erotica is in the lifestyle section under 'sex stories' lol most are crap but some are good, I like the one called 'it'll be lonely this Xmas' the best."

I could write better stories than that. I hadn't read them yet, but I could. Erotica wasn't my forte, but it wasn't rocket science, either. I have a very competitive edge when it comes to writing and suddenly you had exposed it. I wrote a story, then another, then another. When you read them, you'd ask for more and, when a story not written by me was printed, I'd write more. I'd write them while taking a break from paperwork or de Sade. I write to entertain you, you ask for the stories, but, in truth, anything you ask for I would do.

Day Eighty-Five

Generally de Sades have terrible insecurities and low self-images. This is why de Sade's "heroes" are currently pulling teeth out of the children, cutting off fingers, toes, nipples and ears and breaking limbs in One Hundred and Twenty Days of Sodom. All de Sades do this physical, sexual, verbal or multiple. They demise every cell of the body until nothing is sacred. Children don't have insecurities, hence they are physically and mentally perfect, everybody is beautiful, it is only when that perfection is vandalised that people feel unattractive. De Sade maintains the cycle of ugliness. It doesn't exist: it's a sadistic construct, which, yes, is the same as a social construct in its structure.

I should have really low self-image. I should hate the whole of my body, detest it in fact. I simply don't. What went wrong? So many de Sades and so little physical insecurity. I'm not big on my face, there's nothing specifically I would change about it, it just feels weird, it doesn't match my self-perception. I don't think I have a wonderful body or anything. I simply feel fine with it and I personally like it, I really don't care what others think, whether it is attractive or not is irrelevant. I like it and I prefer it to anyone else's, not because I find it more attractive – I don't – but because it's mine to fold into, with my scent. Why?

"Bad thing, he hurt it because it's bad, dirty."

"It's not bad, it's just a little baby, it's been hurt, needs love."

Would I really hold a conversation like this with myself? More than likely, and the more he hurt it, the more it had to be protected and the worse he was. Everything would be softly nurtured and washed clean with the soap. It was analysed, however childishly, and thrown out, not internalised, but let go. In-tray, deal with, out-tray. Some residue is natural, so what if other adults don't sleep with their hand over their pubic mound?

Surpassing all

You talked more and more of Sorcha, a stranger you hadn't yet met. I felt my emotion being ripped into tiny shreds, my perception of truth, reality smashed with your words. I was the woman you loved more deeply than your ten-year relationship with Helen. We were closer than two souls in one body. I felt your skin on mine, your warmth against me. Our scent known only to each other, recognised as home immediately, I could smell you even when you were three hundred miles away.

A lie, all a lie, now I had been so loved, so special, we had been so close that a complete and utter stranger could surpass me. You had never met this woman. What did that make me? What mockery of us? How little your thoughts of me. How empty your daily words for nine months. I never trust "I love you", but now I can't trust "I've never felt so passionate, intense, I didn't think I could feel so deeply about any, until I met you". I didn't trust it for a week, I didn't trust it for a month, but by six months I began to. Now all I can trust is that all words are lies, there is no meaning, the depth I feel is not the depth others say but do not mean.

A total stranger surpassed your feelings for me, feelings that had grown, developed, shared the rough and smooth with. Your words stung like ribbons of wire upon my face. Your words threw my body hard against a wall. Turned every part of my body into lines, spots, warts, every hair on my head grey, dry, greasy, every aspect of my persona boring, plain, unremarkable. I was nothing, so important even strangers were more attractive, more passionate, more alluring. I lost the you I met and I lost myself that met you. You had taken me, swallowed me within you and spat out my shadow, destined to live for ever in darkness without my fire.

Day Eighty-Six

I get angry. I mean really angry. Not annoyed, not irritated, merely homicidal. This life, these figures, the myths, the system perpetuating abuse and violence. If one in four to one in three females experience sexual abuse as a child, based on those figures, logically there are around one in five abusers of children. Statistics saying that the average paedophile/abuser abuses seventy children are a myth to play down the number of abusers. Considering that the majority of abuse takes place in the child's own home, is ongoing over a number of years and there is an average of 1.8 children in every family, it is unlikely that the abuser is abusing more than four children on average. If the "de Sades" who physically and emotionally abuse children and adults are added to this figure, there could exist around one in four abusers of children or adults in society. Subtract those who are too young or too old to abuse, and the figure begins to hit one-third of the population. On a normal distribution curve one-third would not lie in the poles of "abnormal". The reason it is practically impossible to break into de Sade's castle and rescue the children and wives from their fate, to stop the continual production line of victims, is because abuse in its various facets is almost "normal".

Child abuse was not recognised until 1908, although incest between father and daughter was made illegal in 1898. Before 1908, children could be sold, battered, raped, starved, killed; exactly what de Sade described could and did happen, and it wasn't illegal. Children did not matter. Adults using them as entertainment and commodities was probably the norm. There are still adults who could be reading this who were in no way protected from abuse by the law. There are still adults alive who may have been born towards the end of that period when the usage and abusage of children was legitimate, and some of them will have spawn and reared a generation to believe exactly what their own experience was. We think we are so advanced with our virtual superhighways, the men on the moon that may or may not have happened, the age of digital and silicon. We are at the end of a barbaric age. I remember VCRs as being strange and new, the microwave, the CD, the touch-tone telephone, square light switches, and I'm not old. Rape within marriage wasn't made illegal until 1997. The working class did not get the vote until 1918. Homosexuality was not decriminalised until 1967; it was not removed as a "mental illness" until 1973. We still executed people fifty years ago. We are not an enlightened, healthy, non-oppressive society. The only way we can have any ammunition against de Sade is by lifting the carpets, taboos, stigmas, embarrassments, confronting the truth and accepting that abuse of various kinds is a huge part of our society. Creating a myth that only a minority of deviant individuals from certain sections in society abuse does not help prevent it. Quite the opposite: it maintains the cycle. We are so concerned with fears of accusing innocent people that we do not listen to, believe or protect our many thousands being beaten, raped, molested, buggered, not once, not occasionally, but every day. Every day, breathing the perpetrators' sex, choking on their own vomit, tasting their own blood. Well, rally for the "innocents" – it would be interesting to define which of us oppressive hedonists can be defined as innocent. Would you take a thousand pounds less a year to erase LEDC debt? Would you take put-downs such as stupid, clumsy, idiot, crazy, ugly, victim, promiscuous, fat, skinny, in all their variations and covert forms out of your vocabulary? Would you stand up and get involved with the child who is being abused, the woman/man who is being battered, protect that person, report the perpetrator and finally say that, whether it is the norm or not, de Sade is no longer acceptable?

A new Domme on the block

Have you ever wondered what it is like in another person's life, but you can never actually experience it? An alternate reality without chemicals? Ever wanted to dive into the book you read? A snapshot in a film? I'm stepping towards the door of the Sphere club, it opens, I step inside and I leave myself outside, one body gets out of the taxi, another steps into the club. Everything looks familiar, yet it is nothing I've never seen before. I feel strangely comfortable in a completely different, yet not alien, environment. I'm tall, I'm stronger, I'm breathing the heat, the leather, the steel, upstairs, downstairs. I listen to the cracks of whips and floggers, watching idly.

Dawn introduces me to two transvestite friends, Sally and Shona, and a man who speaks most eloquently, Charles. I handshake and open my vessels, my pupils, my scanner, my pores, my ears, my lungs, so much to take in. A woman walks past in a leather corset exposing her ample full breasts, my head turns to stare. I somehow suggest she enter the grope box and in a flash arms surround the holes like Medusa's hair in what looks like a magician's box.

Back upstairs, I'm still scanning, looking, researching, thinking, processing, and getting heavily intoxicated by the heat mingled with that sweet musky smell of leather. I find myself in a conversation with a slim man, Neo, and an equally slim petite women, Ell. Neo is drawing from his cigarette and running his hands through his hair. "I'm a switch, well mainly sub, but I do switch."

Ell has responded with similar sentiments and they are looking at me.

"Dom."

What? And why? Sometimes words just escape from the mouth and somewhere, sometimes, in the back of my head, I'm sitting in total disbelief saying "Whoahhh!"

Neo asks if the Ell and I will have a "little play" with him. Ell agrees, and I say I'll join them when I return from the ladies'. The cubicles are very white. What the hell is a "little play"? I don't suppose you ever find yourself agreeing to an experience you have no idea of or arguing in your mind that whatever it is is OK, because we can just watch.

Neo is bent over a black box with wooden bars across the top, Ell doing something with a flogger, "something" being the operative word. But why should that annoy me and incite me into picking up two floggers. All of a sudden weals are forming on Neo's flesh, his back, his buttocks, wherever. The floggers twirling in synchrony above him, beating their own rhythm, starting firmly, getting harder and harder, until the blows become thrashes. I'm thrashing away you, away Slim, away my childhood, away the pain, I'm destroying it, destroying it all.

I'm not de Sade, I'm not you. I will never be de Sade or you, I am the personification of my experience, I am all your games and abuse stamped into me. I am the scar that won't heal. I am the steam that never condenses. I am white-hot rage. I am the result you created. I am protection. I am vengeance. I see nothing now, no room, no people, no Neo, the floggers move by themselves, all is black but the face in the fire.

"Amber."

"Amber, Ma'am"

I hear, I think, the second time, maybe it was the third. I throw the floggers down and stand back by the bar. Ell approaches Neo, talks to him, then walks away.

A man with a ponytail approaches me. "That was the best flogging technique I've seen in years."

"Thanks."

What the fuck? What have I done? Tell him you saw it on the television.

Neo joins me at the bar. "That was great, thanks. If you ever want to play again here is my number."

I slip the piece of paper into my back pocket.

Tell him. Shush. I'm telling him.

"That was the first time I've flogged someone."

"I don't believe you."

"It's true, it's her first time," *Dawn confirms looking at me kind of strangely.*

Dawn and I come out of the night air into my house and, bang, I'm different from the person who unlocked the door.

"Damn, fuck, shit, Dawn, what have I done?"

Dawn laughed, "I didn't expect you to start flogging."

"Neither did I. I mean, how could I? I'm as bad as an abuser. How could I hurt another human being."

"It's consensual, it's not the same as abuse, it's what they want."

"It is the same, it is violence, it is worse, to them it's sexual, it's not sexual to me, yet they don't know that. Would they consent if they knew *it wasn't sexual?*

"Probably."

"Besides consent has nothing to do with this. The bottom line is I'm hurting another person."

"Look, it's OK, you haven't done anything wrong, but if it makes you feel so bad don't do it again."

"It makes me feel bad that I did it in the first place."

Could I ever reconcile with myself? Was I any different from de Sade at all?

Day Eighty-Seven

Every day I am bound by the system. I am a prisoner, my life is not my own. When I sleep, rise, eat, move, relax, all decided, all commanded. I am a slave for a small shelter and sustainable food. I won't be a slave all week. I fight it, return to my natural pattern and in doing so continue the cycles that damage only myself. I am not a machine, not a clone, not an object. I am not tame or domesticated. I am a wandering mind. I need now. Now I want to eat, now I want to research, now I want to walk. Instead I am forced into a little timetable, the institution of society. I don't even want to be a part of society. In fact I want to blow it to a thousand pieces. Society is one big lie. Society is why the children and wives are trapped in de Sade's castle and can never escape. How can I rescue them without my own life and a note to say why? Society is ruled by and supports de Sade. Most children are abused in their own homes. The abusers with an ongoing victim are rarely stupid enough to leave physical evidence. The abusers cannot be prosecuted without physical evidence or corroboration. Stranger abuse, a one-off incident, can often be corroborated, therefore prosecuted. Abuse every day of a child's life, for ten years, fifteen years, is unlikely to be corroborated unless s/he had siblings who were also abused. Society punishes one-off incidents, and dismisses living in hell and fear every day of your life, giving out the message: If it's your own child carry on. Did I say I feel like suicide today? It isn't because of de Sade that the children cannot be rescued from the castle: it's the society surrounding the castle stopping anyone entering, watching, listening, while the children are slowly murdered, every single one as bad as de Sade.

Every year another damaged generation is spawned, and the previous one shakes its collective head at the "state of society". What do you expect? Your law does not protect children. Your law causes drug dependence, mental illness, violence, suicide, physical illness, ghettos, prostitution. Your society is a lie. You propagate myths, thinking we are too damaged to challenge them. For children to be protected would mean accepting that there are a huge number of paedophiles, abusers in every stratum: nobility, doctors, lawyers, teachers, politicians, judges, police. Confronting that would kill the status quo, which is more important than children. The damaged children serve their purpose as bribes and scapegoats in the next generation. "Look what will happen if you don't work and stay with societies 'norms'," instead of "This has happened because of the abuse of the previous generation." The few abusers who are reported and prosecuted – which is doubtful given John Denham's words at the 2002 UN Convention on the Rights of the Child: "Parenting can be difficult, but we must avoid bringing the police and criminal law into family life" – have such small sentences. Sentencing provides no protection for the children or adults who prosecute their abusers. Abuse isn't reported because survivors are in fear for their lives. Where is the protection that enables individuals who have experienced abuse to prosecute and vote, and remain safe? Is there any good reason for the electoral register to be public? Why aren't children and adults who were abused as children provided with protection from the abuser?

Society doesn't want to prevent domestic violence. Men carry out most domestic violence. It is not healthy for men to live alone, hence why society encourages living together and discourages living alone through excessive costs and "rewards" such as family tax credit for those who do live together. The largest population of single householders is women. Women are the lowest earners. If domestic violence were taken seriously there would be more women leaving relationships, which isn't healthy for men. It's like the old chlamydia syndrome: it's ignored because, other than their carrying it, chlamydia has few negative effects to men, and it is women who get all the negative effects. We live in a wonderful society as long as you are neither a child nor female.

Lashing nights

Lash was the place to be. Somehow since that night at the fetish club I had arranged to go to Lash with Neo, Sally and Shona. I had to go: it was the place to be, a huge chunk of the journey. That's how I found myself in the back of a Land Rover with two transvestites and a male submissive I hardly knew on my way to Manchester. Greeting us at the door was a goddess who looked as if she had walked directly off the set of The Night Porter. *A huge changing room and shop to the left, the bar to the right, upstairs the dance floor and along the corridor the dungeon, if you can clamour through the throng of sexy Amazonian women, that is. Forget Vivienne Westwood, Prada: if you want to see something really cutting-edge, go to Lash. Candy pinstripe rubber suits, pirates who look as though they had just stepped off a seventeenth-century ship.*

The dungeon, wow! Wow, I stand and stare at the giant spider's web made out of rope, complete with human hostage, the rope spun around her body like a spider's cocoon, at the women dressed as Gestapo, at the mass of people and more queuing for equipment that won't be unused all night. The horse, the rack, the box, the A-frame, the stocks, not accommodating one person, but binding three or four to the various corners. Crowds watch the dungeon, crowds wait, submissive males in maid outfits looking for masters and mistresses they can serve with drinks, some already standing to attention with trays. Look behind, just look behind, now on the ceiling, brain click, this is a lecture theatre, well, accurately speaking, right at this moment it isn't a lecture theatre. I didn't want to leave. I wanted to stay at Lash and dance, talk to all the friendly people, feast my senses on all the outfits and look up at all the six-foot women who wore dresses that stopped at the smalls of their backs.

Welcome to another world, familiarise yourself with the music, the colours, black, red purple, stay and learn the lingo, why not be measured for a candy-stripe suit of rubber or get suspended eight foot above the ground on a rope web? Huge cognitive-dissonance problem: de Sade and Lash are totally different. Lash is a big, fun, fantastical, giggly, party. De Sade is dark and dangerous. I suppose I just have to stick with the journey.

Day Eighty-Eight

De Sade has introduced me to a huge new world. An alternate society. This world of Mistresses and Masters, submissives, slaves, pain sluts, stone butches, gimps, is made up of social workers, lawyers, lecturers, teachers, consultants, civil servants, graduates. I could open the trapdoor and shout, "All your missing professionals, the redundant, the sick, the retired, they're all down here." I suspect there are levels to the reality, levels I haven't seen yet. The first, most visible, level is jovial and supportive. Whether seduced by domination and pain or not and there are many within this reality who are not, who are just along for the ride, the community is addictive. Everyone communicates with everyone. Secrets are few. If anyone has a problem, whether it be practical or personal, people offer skills.

How this reality can be so big yet so invisible I cannot fathom. Less than a year ago I knew nothing of its existence and before meeting Colette I knew nothing of domination and submission. "Domination and submission" seems the wrong description of it.

There are power dynamics – domination and submission – in every relationship, real domination and submission; this community is nothing like that. Those who "submit" know how they want to submit and the dominants oblige; what exactly the submissives who ask for what they want and get it are submitting to, I'm not quite sure. With interactions that aren't specifically D/S, the dominant partner in a given situation makes the decisions. Most of the submissives are males. For many, sex is secondary, if a part of their lives at all. Sexuality distinctions become blurred, because sex is not a core element: men will flog men, women flog women, submissives flog submissives, dominants flog dominants. The identified sexuality is irrelevant.

There is a core of lesbian women who don't merge with the others, and in some ways are closer to de Sade. I admit to researching them very little. The few things I did learn about that core group included slavery, age play where they would pretend to be six years old during sex, daddy fantasies, the butches' use of male pronouns. Not only did I not want to get involved as a very monogamous lesbian woman, but I admit I was scared. Reading the abuse to the children in de Sade's novel isn't the easiest thing to do: at times it does evoke the demon of reliving the childhood I never had. People talking about age play in real life doesn't summon just my demons: it summons my anger, an inner rage that these people are mocking the pain and reality children have and are presently experiencing. Being subjected to sex by an adult as a four-, five-, six-, seven-, eight-, nine-, ten-year-old is not a fantasy: it's a life sentence. It's waiting time.

Floggers and straps

My journey continued to Manchester, where I met Dawn for a "munch". A "munch", is as the word describes, a lunchtime meeting of people who identify as being D/S. Dawn met me off the train and took me to a nearby pub. Narrow stairs led down to a basement room, which was jam-packed with people. The aroma of Canadian steak and leather crawled into my nostrils. There were stalls selling clothes, floggers, straps, paddles, handcuffs, collars, bullwhips, all handmade. I wandered around the packed small room, people introducing themselves and asking where I was from. At one of the stalls I picked up the various floggers and felt their textures, some rough, some very soft suede and leather, with honey wooden handles; long floggers, short cute floggers. I looked on the table, an array of implements, picking up cuffs and collars, running my fingers around the edges. There were black leather straps that looked like half-belts; I flicked one across the palm of my hand.

"They have titanium in." A man's voice drew my attention.

"Titanium?"

"Yes, in between the leather is a layer of titanium. And in these," he continued, picking up a fish-shaped, slim, leather paddle and handing it to me. I was impressed, titanium, and only £6, and the cutest, softest flogger was just £15. A woman came and paid for a cat-o'-nine-tails while I stood feeling the sensual softness of the flogger, smelling the new leather, and the smoothness of the strap and paddle, bending them this way and that, fascinated by the titanium. Suddenly I'd handed over cash and made a purchase.

Dawn walked me back to the station. The realisation hit: I had brought a flogger, no matter how cute, and a strap and paddle. Why? I didn't need tools to research. I never took the flogger, strap and paddle out with me, and it didn't hurt to have a souvenir after months of travelling with de Sade.

Day Eighty-Nine

Colette MSN'd yesterday. She apologised. We have different demons that affect us in similar ways. Colette's de Sade was an abusive lover when she was still not out of teens, not a child, but not a woman. The mind has an immune system that operates not dissimilarly to the physical immunity. Every time it's under stress, the body's immune system hunts for a threat. If a threat can't be found, but the stress continues, the immune system eventually becomes confused and attacks its own cells, causing anything from asthma, allergies, psoriasis, arthritis to heart disease and cancer. This is why so many abused children grow up to develop chronic illness. Their stress hormones, cortisol and adrenalin tick over at the same level as if there *were* a stress, so, when there *is* a stress, they go through the roof and the immune system is prematurely exhausted.

The psyche has its own immune protection, which works while the threat is present, but, if that threat is ongoing and severe, the immune system goes into overdrive, causing the protection to attack anything, so, instead of protecting it becomes destructive. The psyche has several levels of protection: a total shutdown, dissociation, confronting the experience through speed-thought flashbacks, anxiety, social shutdown and emotional shutdown. In its striving to protect the self from further harm, the doors close to others, yet at the same time the psyche needs others, so a conflict ensues. Intimacy grows so far, until the protection seeks and destroys like a natural killer cell. In protecting, the system is self-destroying, reducing life to solitude and pain.

There is a cycle with abuse, no matter how much the survivor attempts to avoid the pain of his/her childhood, of the last abusive relationship. No matter how different each new partner chosen is, abuse continues. Colette was the first person to completely break my every defence and confirmed their necessity and reinstated them, through her own internalised de Sade, not intention.

Meeting Chuck
Suddenly everyone was D/S, everyone was polygamous and I was a lone monogamous woman who thought relationships were for sharing time, supporting, coming home and discussing the day over food. Take Chuck. Chuck was a bright, artistic, intelligent woman on Gaydar. She was also

polygamous, D/S. Was there no getting away from the journey, no time out? I went to Birmingham one day to meet her for coffee, and, oh, God, hasn't Birmingham changed? It never had the cosmopolitan smartness of Manchester, but now, where the Bullring was is just a huge iron carcass. We went to a café bar, though it had the hard wooden chairs and traditional round tables, not the sinking leather sofas and soft décor I associate with coffee bars.

In the flesh Chuck was attractive, petite, quirky and girlie, her smile hiding a tension I couldn't quite pinpoint, her eyes an unnecessary insecurity. I couldn't help but notice how small her hands were. Hands are important. It isn't like saying cute face, good hips, oh, but such small hands! After all, hands say so much. Anyway, Chuck was animated and the conversation was good. Intermittently, I would build stacks out of sugar cubes or my eyes would wander out of the window, because I didn't like the environment. These are little cues that say, OK, I'm bored in here now, I want to go somewhere else. You always knew even subtler cues.

Day Ninety

Zelmire's ass is made the evening's treat, but before being served up, she is subjected to a trial, and is advised that she will be killed that night; she believes what she is told but, instead of depatching her, Messieurs are content each to give her a hundred lashes after having generously embuggered her, and Curval takes her to bed with him. She is further embuggered all night.

Imagine it. No, really imagine it. Step inside the experience, lock yourself up for a hundred and twenty days with twenty people older than you, bigger than you. Listen to nothing but abuse of yourself and your sexuality. Experience nothing but abuse of your body and threats of worse, followed by threats of inevitable death, a slow painful death, lasting days and weeks, not hours. Imagine your fingers being cut without anaesthetic, your legs being broken, your flesh slashed and scalded. You just cannot, you cannot come anywhere near to imagining that experience. Neither can de Sade, neither can all the de Sades in society who are excited by his words, carry out his actions on a daily basis, sometimes to the death. What pleasure is there in causing torture until every cell of the body is feeling nothing but intense pain, evoking such fear that the heart beats so hard it bruises itself beating against the breast bone trying to force itself out of the condemned body? How can I possibly step inside this mindset? It's not a hate, it's not a rage, wrath is quick, immediate, uncontrollable, irrational. This is calculating, this is excitement. Even if my superego and ego left my psyche, my id would have no desire to torture, or threaten – blow up the odd empty building maybe, punch the odd person, possibly pull a trigger, certainly a few destructive things that are immediately gratifying. Even then, my id would have to perceive being wronged to deflect from chocolate and sensual pleasure and react. I can categorically say I would never torture.

Fantasise about torture? Yes, of course I do. I fantasise about cleaning the world of paedophiles, other abusive people, systematically, taking them hostage and doing far worse than de Sade could ever write, but that's for another novel. In what situation would I imagine torturing an innocent, however? Every now and again the brain thinks a them-and-us mindset. Torture fantasies about abusers, I humour as harmless catharsis, like watching a violent film. Taking a twentysomething, attractive, innocent man tying him to a chair while he is seduced by an unknown woman, then chopping through his penis with a cleaver at the point of his orgasm, before leaving him to die, does disturb me. I am not part of this fantasy: as with a violent film, I watch it roll past, while trying to bury it down feeling guilt with every frame that passes. The key to understanding de Sade is honesty. Do not be mistaken: the fantasies about torturing abusers of any kind are purely anger and vengeance. They are cathartic. Torturing the young innocent man isn't cathartic, it isn't about "taking one of theirs" and damaging him, as they have ours. That's a lie of the conscious to provide a rationale and hide the truth and resolve cognitive dissonance. One cannot desire anything associated, however loosely, with one's pain and the object of one's rage and hate, thus any desire must be destroyed.

De Sade and his modern contemporaries associate something they desire with hate. The desire will be different, depending on the abuse, it is not necessarily sexual. In the case of the children, de Sade's "heroes", as much as they have no feelings, no morals, no empathy, actually hate the parts of themselves that desire children and women, and by destroying the child they are destroying that part of themselves that they hate. Unfortunately, their defence mechanisms are too solid, their motive too subconscious, their awareness too lacking for this realisation.

Breaking Charles

I'm back in the Sphere, trying to find a link, trying to understand de Sade, to understand power. Charles visits several clubs a week. In each one he stays bound and flogged all night. The dominants get tired and still Charles wants more beating. Charles has several degrees, master's, doctorate. He is incredibly articulate and confident, tells the dominants exactly what he wants. Why does he need to do this? It's like a compulsion, an obsession. I get it into my head that I want to break Charles. I don't know why. I want to understand him. I want him to say stop to someone for once. I want him to react, wake up, be the enigmatic lecturer he was. More frighteningly, I want to be invincible. I start the rhythm softly and build the beat to the background music, the lashes raining harder and harder, covering flesh, but no redness appears, no weals, his breathing doesn't quicken, no movement from the stillness of his form, nothing but the conversation about interesting places and people. My whole body is working, my shoulders circling as fast and hard as they can, crafting the floggers, the thrash breaking the low hum of people as the impact hits. I'm beating down leather for my life. Thirty minutes pass, an hour passes, five hundred lashes, maybe a thousand. I have to get a reaction. I continue in hypnosis to the music. He hasn't flinched, his flesh gives no marks, his posture as calm and fresh as he entered the club. I'm tiring, I feel as though I'd walked thirty miles, danced for five hours, my blows are weakening. I try to visualise all I detest. What am I doing? I'm intentionally trying to provoke my own anger to gain a reaction, to beat harder. My body is exhausted, I let the floggers fall from my hands and walk to the bar in submission.

"Thought you were trying to kill him," a voice muttered.

I am eternal shame. Charles is bouncing towards the bar, chatting to people, full of energy. I am total disappointment. The music and the people haze away. I am a living cell of guilt. Why would I try to hurt someone until he breaks, just because he likes being hurt anyway? I am complete disgust. I am dark base. I am vile behaviour.

Day Ninety-One

De Sade is creeping about between the layers of my flesh. For months I've lived and breathed him; daily he drowns me more. I don't want to be on this journey any more. I have to flounder through the desert because there is no way out but to travel it. I want to reach my destination, to shower every strand of de Sade away from me. I want to feel my own skin again, to return to myself, leave de Sade behind in the sodden earth, never to step over him again. The end beckons me; I can already feel myself racing ahead, walking away and back towards myself again. I'll not only leave de Sade, but, also the undercurrents in every city, all the people along the way, who helped my understanding of de Sade. I'll keep a flogger as a souvenir, throw it in the bottom of a wardrobe. De Sade has infiltrated my brain; my only thoughts are understanding every angle, every colour of his spectrum.

The castle frustrates me. I am helpless, useless, I have done nothing, a pain, an experience wasted, a life not worth living. I've fought obstacles, many obstacles, huge brick walls, the odd mountain, but this, this is fighting power itself. De Sade and I head to head. I stand no chance. I'm not fighting the abusers of the children with an army. I'm fighting a system. De Sade makes up the system. De Sade is in power. De Sade looks after his own. De Sade brainwashes the people. De Sade has tools and the system uses these tools.

The tool of taboo: abuse is something not to be discussed; if society does not discuss abuse, de Sade can continue in safety. The tool of stereotype: the typical abuser is poorly educated and underclass; abuse is not a social problem, it's an antisocial problem, not a concern of mainstream society. The tool of stigma: if people experiencing abuse do not come forward, then it doesn't exist. The tool of spite: children lie; everybody knows children lie; they are not to be believed. The tool of psychology: memories are subjective, not accurate, and are heavily influenced by imagination. Is everybody in the population psychotic, then? The tool of sexual myth: men are sexual beings and cannot help it if their sexual needs are not gratified elsewhere. The tool of stress: he was under great stress; this excuses him from killing his wife, raping his daughter, shaking his six-week-old baby to death, any other torture he so please to release his stress; if any try to defend themselves and that results in his death, they will be sentenced to fifteen years. The tool of blame: children are not innocent, they are sexual creatures who seduce and taunt; women are not innocent, they nag, or wear revealing clothes. The tool of double standards: she deserved it, she was a prostitute, she was drunk, she led him on, she dared walk alone.

This is their system, these are their tools, they are in charge, and they are our teachers, doctors, lawmakers, and criminal justice system. There are as many of us as there are them; where is our system? We who have experienced de Sade allow him to run the country, we sit back and let it happen, we allow the next generation and the next to experience the pain we feel every second, a pain we wouldn't wish on any.

Pride and tears

It was the beginning of June. I'd pace, wondering, waiting. Eventually you mailed. You had passed. I was so happy, so proud. I cried onto the keyboard, I shut down the mail and walked and cried, cried and smiled. I knew you'd do it, was worried that your own fears and insecurities would make you quit, not try at all. Sometimes it's better to not take part than try to fail. You thought everyone at Oxford was better than you, brighter than you, I just thought they were richer. I read your mail and cried, for months I'd been afraid of your returning to Newcastle, not completing your dissertation, taking too many drugs. You had to fight your insecurities to achieve your dream and if that meant being afraid, being up and down, snappish, hot and cold, it was all worth it. You could do anything. You could take on the world – in a sense you already had. I was so, so proud, you the woman I love had come from poverty and alone had achieved the world with nothing but your brain. There was a spanner thrown into Burt and Eysenck's theory and you the woman I love had thrown it. We were the opposition of every working-class apathy who said, "I can't" and you were the sexy Antichrist. For nine months I listened to your dreams, your fears, and afterwards I'd taken your pain, absorbed it, felt it as though it were mine. I'd heard your thoughts, seen your confusion, listened to the confident woman and the vulnerable child in your voice. I knew going to Oxford wasn't just a three-hundred-mile journey, that the lectures weren't just listening to words, the students weren't just peers, your work wasn't just words on a page. I felt the passion in your research, the power in your words, I could hear your voice so intense so animated; whenever I read your deconstructions, you wrote your soul.

Day Ninety-Two

I am in a place I cannot even begin to explain. I'll call it unadopted space. This is what happens when no part of the personality structure wants to own the mindspace. It's a glitch in the matrix. The ultimate fragmentation. A lost time. I go upstairs, I stand, simply stand, not even wondering what I came up for, just stand trying to get a grip, to recognise the room, that I walked the stairs. Things fall onto the floor around me, the fingers of the clock turn, yet I don't notice, just glimmers, glimmers of fear wondering where the seconds went, the day it is, the task I should be doing. I look for a lighter, the lighter is there, where? Maybe I look for ten minutes, maybe an hour, it's still there, yet when I take my eyes away its location is a mystery again. I switch the kettle on, once, twice, three times, who knows, I don't, only to fill a cup already full, though no doubt cold. There is a glimmer, a mindset, a set of views and then gone again, like strobe lights, quick flashes of control that disappear in horror as soon as the subject is illuminated. It's hardly surprising no responsibility wants ownership of this mind. This damaged, sick, festering mind, this mind spoiled before it developed, this mind of a victim, this feeble mind, this mind taking a journey with de Sade, this mind of impulse, the actions, the thoughts, the images, the blood, the deaths, the women, the childish subversions, worth nothing but rot. Beautiful things are owned, intelligent things, logical things, wonderful things, responsibility is taken for potential perfection, not potential destruction. There is no memory here, not an error with the long-term store or the short-term store, both simply cease to exist, a memory is a split-second flash that disappears the moment it is recognised. There is a vague feeling that something is wrong, but that feeling is like dandelion clock in the wind, too fragile to grasp, too floaty to transfer to logical thought, a little feeling somewhere far away, with no idea what the problem is.

It's terrifying, or would be if terrifying if it could be expressed or held close, like standing alone on a tiny rock with nothing else in existence, only standing alone on that rock, the self exists, I would feel the rock under my feet, I would feel my feet, I would feel the flow and pattern of my biology, know the thoughts in my mind. It's like standing alone on a rock with nothing else in existence and not even being there, losing all lucidity, not existing inside, not existing outside, not existing at all, being a filler, not the substance, knowing nothing, feeling nothing, a forever neonate without a history, a vision, a memory store. I becomes nothing, there *is* no I in this space, there is no them, no we, no us, no ownership. This is waiting time, no will, no purpose, nothing but a vacuum. Always it passes, the waiting time passes and the benefits outweigh the costs. Those who have never been labelled as not always lucid pass on such opportunities for fear of being in this place. Fear of being lucid, but not remembering, fear of not being in control every second, fear of letting go.

There is always control, merely varying definitions. De Sade had control, his own version, every cell of a person has control, the other cells merely don't think so when the definition doesn't fit with their own. Only this place has no control, but it doesn't need to control, there is nothing to control. De Sade didn't let go: everything was calculated according to rule and order. Letting go isn't about acting selfishly, causing damage: it's a trust in an alternative mindset a transference. De Sade wrote lists, numbers after numbers of ultimate tortures, each torture corresponding to a pain within himself. What he forgot to do was write a transferring list. He feared death and wrote death; instead of transferring the bad to the good, he transferred the pain to others, so he became death to others, for if he was death he no longer had reason to fear, in principle. In practice de Sade became the pain, the concepts he feared so and in doing so lost all substance of himself. He didn't remove the women and children: he removed himself, dehumanised himself. De Sade was so afraid of letting go, he held on, held on to everything and became his own nightmares.

The irony of worthlessness

You talked Sorcha. I asked if she still surpassed what you felt for me. "She's different," you said. "It's tender, fluffy, she's shy and wary, inexperienced, so it's not as heavy." I felt the rise of tears well from my whole form. I was shy, coy, wary and scared. You wanted it all and all at once. I tried to slow you. I told you so much, I loved our openness, sharing every possible fantasy, but we were new. I wanted to just be with you, caress you, lie naked, explore your every soft niche and curve with my every sense. My whispers fell deaf against the wind of your determined experience. Some fantasies were that, to be more would soil them, as arousing as they are in the safe confines of the mind, release them and they become dangerous and grotesque. I was scared, I didn't want to bare all in front of strangers, didn't want to be touched by any but you, touch any but you, didn't want others touching you, didn't want our love out of our private space.

You were repeating all the things you'd said about us. If the tears hadn't spilled in contrast to your cold words I would have laughed. Every time we made love was so tender, loving, close and passionate, but for three times. The only time you properly made love to me. It was after your liaison, we'd just made up, had made love so tenderly for days. You wanted me kneeling across your settee. I was hurt that you didn't want me intimately the first time, but silenced by your experience. You never took me properly again, used the excuse that you thought you couldn't satisfy me. You could so easily had you made love to me, instead of the cold clinical act that left me confused and hollow. Our lovemaking had always been loving no matter how passionate, but not this time. I could feel any part of you next to me, there was no caresses, no kisses, you must have been standing several feet away, reaching out as one would with de Sade's repulsive crones and a gun to the head. I feel pleasure from my lover's pleasure. I just wanted it over and you didn't protest.

I'd been in that position so many times before with Cline and others without the love we shared, with no love declared by them daily as it was by you, yet I could feel every part of their warmth, thighs pressed into mine, back curving over me, my whole body caressed and kissed, but not from you. The second cold time was that week, you began to make love to me and your eyes were so, so cold, just for a flash second, but long enough to put such fear in me. Fear that didn't know if you were going to love me or take a knife to me, fear that seriously considered running, packing my things and running.

The third time our lovemaking was cold; you had pushed and pushed for a strap-on and, although I wanted us to explore one at some point, we were still so new, I just wanted you, but your experience shadowed me and I agreed, not thinking we would use it for months. We met after two months apart. It had been so long I just wanted to take you in my arms and feel your embrace around me. We kissed passionately, hungrily, lovingly. You unpacked the dildo. I wanted to see it too, although I had no interest in anything but you. You unpacked the leather straps. It was beautiful, thin soft shards of intoxicating black leather. I wanted to make love, close to you, first teasing you through the leather, taking so much time, making up for lost time, tracing my lips and body across all of you, taking in the scent and taste of you. That never happened, you wanted the dildo. I wanted you, not some latex, nothing between us. I hated every second, but clumsily hurt you, through my innocence, so held my peace, assuming you knew all I was feeling with you knowing and loving me so well anyway.

Without you I'm left in this horrible quagmire, de Sade and I, the world our Bastille, desperately trying to be who I thought you wanted me to be and lost in this misty bog we created desperately trying to scramble out, but without the strength. Without the strength to be who I was, who I am again. Irony making as much sense as this obfuscation we stumbled into.

Day Ninety-Three

To gain Nirvana, you have to let go. Have nothing, lose everything. I write a poem, if it doesn't work, I screw up the page, throw it and write anew, I start again. It is not as easy with de Sade:

the experience cannot be rewritten, the script cannot be changed, though the castle can be smashed and torn and destroyed. Without a castle de Sade has no place to turn, no place to torture and kill more children. The script as it was cannot be rewritten, but, as it is, in the present, it can be trashed and built again. We're still hostages of the castle, pained by the torture, pained by the desperation to escape and landing our debts to "society" by doing so. Society is de Sade, it keeps the children locked in those castles, supports the de Sades, punishes the children for trying to escape, hide, get away. We are slaves; we are slaves to our escape. We tried to live in a system that tortured and punished us further. Lived by those laws, norms, values, because we believed, trusted.

De Sade was imprisoned; 95 per cent of abusers are never tried, although de Sade was. His prison was a huge grand castle; with him were his servants, his dogs, his art, his fine clothes and fine food, wine, the odd friend, maybe he played chess, or went hunting; he couldn't work because he was in prison, so he had to stay home, home in his castle with the wine and prostitutes he brought. De Sade rules your country. De Sade rules your world. The abusers are in their castles; their victims are kicked by the system.

The media reported two politicians on the list of Operation Ore, the child Internet pornography exercise, who were investigated by the police. The government has issued a media blackout on the story, and no politicians have as yet been reported to have been sacked or resigned. There has been no mention of the judges uncovered in Operation Ore or the results of any trial, if any trials of the system's hierarchy have taken or will take place. De Sade is running the world. Children are not important, they are worthless, we the victims are worthless. The de Sades are protected by other de Sades in the police, in the criminal justice system, in the Cabinet, on the back benches, in the Lords, they are superior, they are worth more than women and children. We are dispensable, we have no voice, we have no power, just the illusion of equality and a civilised society compared with a hundred years ago. There is the illusion of human rights. De Sade has rights, the heroes have rights. The children are having their fingers removed, chopped with rusty knives, no anaesthetic, and, if they faint while being forced to watch, one of the heroes will rape them while they are unconscious, until they wake bleeding and increasingly infectious, kept alive just enough, until the "heroes" take the pleasure of killing them. This is de Sade writing in the 1730s. This is the runaway taken from the streets of London and Manchester used for snuff movies or Internet pornography in the 2000s. This is the child in the home, not all killed immediately, several will live out their lives in prison, acute psychiatric wards, commit suicide later on. We are shut up, can't talk about the de Sades running this world, can't voice its commonplace, its normality, its virulence in every stratum. Prison and psychiatric wards shut people up very well. Believe the politicians, the judges, the doctors, the councillors, while they abuse a few more children, they are the victims from these ranting "mad" people. Jeffery Dahmer killed his last victim, a schoolboy, after police believed he was "crazy" during a "lovers' tiff". He was ranting. Of course he wasn't an innocent boy who had been lured, then drugged and later murdered.

Falling

I'm dressed in black from head to toe. You don't leave my thoughts for a breath. Will I for ever be in mourning? Thrashing out my wrath on transgenders in a well-populated Hades? I have a rhythm, "Amber" is called, I stop my rhythm to tease with textures rough and smooth on the rounded moons filling my vision. It's becoming frighteningly ordinary. I'm angry with you and myself that I'm here in this space, this life. An old friend disturbs my thoughts to direct my attention to the veil-covered room. She's in the middle of the floor. Lying with her corset under her naked breasts, above her naked waist, her sex being serviced by her husband's tongue. The men lace the pews, surrounding them, fools! Young, attractive, bright, not you, I feel nothing but I can have and I will, because I can have more than you. I casually sit on the edge of the mattress, looking down, watching her face intently, only three breaths away from her flesh, their coupling. She tilts her head in my direction, her mouth curving into a smile at the sight of me, her hand reaching out to mine. I stroke her cropped auburn hair, scrunching it, spanning her small feminine skull within my palm. My mouth takes her finger deep within me, investigating each ridge and crease with every bud and nerve of my tongue. Firmly sucking the shaft, tightly sealed by my full lips, teasing the tip with my fast, flicking, formidable, muscle of breath, nourishment, and expression. The chains of restraint falling fast.

Her husband disappeared, I don't know where. I fell into oblivion and her flesh, fingers sinking deep within her, suspended in space where only her body and mine existed. I saw her eyes roll, her body writhe. I felt her soft fleshy ball of her front wall, the external button of flesh, the two parallel partners of pleasure manipulated together in a beat with my digits. I heard her moans and quick shallow breaths. I received her touch, raising cotton and lowering linen, exposing my arousal against her. I lay in afterwards, holding her naked warmth to my form, lazily pulling her hair through my fingers, her head lolling my shoulder.

When I rose from oblivion, they had gone. The pews surrounding me were empty, but still steaming from human heat. I looked at the emptiness, thinking it could have always been like that; that possibly, maybe, I could walk out as inconspicuously as I'd entered veiled voyeurism; that the sense of time I'd lost had really been only seconds, not hours, and the silence was evidence of our solitude, not their attention; that they hadn't all crept out during our meditative holding.

But they had.

Day Ninety-Four

Do you ever wake up and think not, Where is my life? but, Where is myself? I've done that for months throughout this journey with de Sade. I am the sum of all I'm trying to understand. Flipping from de Sade to the children, desperately trying to smash that castle. I fear lots of things, yet I fear nothing. Once you've felt the flames of hell, nothing else can ever hurt as much. Life is waiting time and, as with all waiting times, sometimes interesting people are met and stimulating events occur, but, mostly, it's sitting in the waiting room watching. I find most things illogical. If you take a risk you might die. The only guarantee is death; whether you take a risk or not, you are going to die. You are not special, no supreme force is going to stop your death. I like death: it breaks the myth of superiority. Look at your designer clothes, your wealth, on your corpse. Power is not gained from people or things. Power is gained only from the one truth, opinions are relative, truth is definite.

De Sade's truth? His behaviour is the truth, the consequences are the truth. In understanding de Sade, sight must never be lost of the outward, observable, action. All else is opinion, relative. "He's mentally ill." Is he? All one in four of them? Does mental illness exist? Regardless of any "mental illness", is he not in control of his actions? "He was abused as a child." Was he? Anyone who was abused knows the pain and would not want to put others through it. If all the abusers were abused as a child, the next generation of abusers should be mostly female. "He's emotionally immature." About a tenth of *One Hundred and Twenty Days of Sodom* is about sex, the rest is about control and power. Many people are immature emotionally; nonetheless the adult sexual hormones that direct arousal are working correctly. Children do not have the hormones, smell or shape of an adult to denote sexual maturity and evoke a sexual response. Sexual abuse is very rarely only sexual; mental and physical abuses are generally concurrent; they are not concurrent in consenting adult sexual relationships as a rule. De Sade's example of physical abuse was towards the extreme end of the spectrum, but his example of mental abuse was probably understated. One thing de Sade does highlight in the castle, which is common with much abuse, is the cold calculation and planning of every event, which doesn't suggest any type of immaturity. Children don't calculate long-term plans: they stamp feet and want now, yesterday; so do many adults in a given context.

Accidental submissive

It started with an innocent phone call. I loved talking to Neo, he is sweet, intelligent, interesting and extremely sincere. He asked if I needed anything doing.

"Well, erm…"

"Any ironing or anything?"

Ironing? Well would you have done different? There is a pile of the stuff in my kitchen, head turn to the kitchen, the mouthpiece. I can't deny it, I enjoy having that time to do paperwork or even just sit and do nothing while my ironing is being taken care of, popping my head round now and again, checking the creases are in the right places, knowing the garment will be ironed again if they aren't. It was after all, getting closer to the research. Neo is probably a rare true example of a submissive.

It might have been during shopping, when Neo told me he'd stopped working for his Mistress, because he had a new closer one, meaning me. Reality, hit that by me again. I was terrified, I wasn't a Mistress. I decided I'd have to talk to him, explain about the research, especially when he dropped "… being in love with a gay Mistress". Oh, hell. Only thing was, he didn't invade my space, he put up with my moods, he is a constant calm, and when shopping and I say I only want a few items, so trolleyless, he is hidden under a basket, balancing Andrex on his head, he looks so funny.

Day Ninety-Five

De Sade is swallowing me. My life has ceased to be. I am but my research, I am the journey. The line between research and reality is dangerously blurring, I frequently have to pencil it in again, pull myself back to the other side. I see the world in de Sades and non-de-Sades, in dominants and submissives, though the dominants and submissives are, up to now, totally different from de Sade. I find the dominants and submissives no different from the usual patriarchy, the male submissives know what they want and the female dominants provide it. The dominants and submissives of the alternative world are totally opposite to dominance and submission in the mainstream world. In the alternative world the male submissives ask and get exactly what they want; they are extremely confident and only ever humiliated and flogged if and because they want to be; any physical damage is superficial, the majority of the tools sensual rather than damaging. In the mainstream world, women submit out of fear – physical fear or fear of losing her mate, fear of an argument. She is not receiving or doing what she wishes, the male dominant is in charge, she pleases him. In the mainstream world any humiliation is unwanted and designed to chip away at her esteem, she will not be asked to kneel and wait while he walks around her in flimsy tantalising clothes, she will be told she is fat, lazy, useless, worthless. In the mainstream world physical damage will injure her, it will be painful, not sensual, her flesh will be deeply bruised, not lightly pinked, fists will pummel against her, she may break a bone or two, her immune system will lower, her life expectancy decrease, she will fear for her life, she doesn't want this. Although de Sade was the purpose of my research on the domination–submission scene, I haven't found de Sade, but what I have found is an exact copy of mainstream society, in its supposed reverse. In submission, males are dominant, in dominance, females are submissive.

I have the jigsaw, I can see the picture, but the details are in those missing pieces. Excuse me, while I examine the plot so far.

The victims don't like the abuser, except battered wives, so theory doesn't follow.

Not instinct, too calculated.

Victim is dehumanised, yet so much attention is given to her/him?

Abuser does not like him/herself?

Abuser dehumanises him/herself? But how?

Projection onto victim?

Looking-glass self?

Eyes? Pain invokes fear in others, or disgust, eyes mirror, reflection, abusers use eye contact?

Eyes can reflect only as much as their colour and muscles will allow. The only frame of reference is the other person: if his or her eyes flash back fear or disgust, we feel hurt and disgusted, maybe angry, not with the other person but with ourselves. Is it possible that the abuser is trying to smash the human mirror, but because, s/he likes, loves, obsesses the person, s/he doesn't want to lose the person?

Submerging

I find myself in a local gay club with a group from the fetish scene. They are dancing to camp 80's melody's upstairs, I'm being beckoned onto the downstairs dance floor by the beautiful girl from Birmingham. I look up to take water and the dancers have cleared a circle around us, they are standing in awe watching our movements. I return upstairs to my fetish friends, the older sexy Helen Mirren lookalike is giving me the eye. Beautiful young woman from Birmingham, or sexy older woman? I need to take a break and use the toilet. I'm standing in the queue, it's been sunny all day, I'm hot, I'm hungry for flesh, I feel the heat of the woman next to me. I flick water at her as I wash my hands. She mutters, "Don't start what you can't finish" as she leaves, but I'm full of – of what? A complete disregard for limits and sanity, possibly. I pull her into the alcove. "I can finish it." I breathe into her neck, pinning her arms above her head against the cold tiles. I kiss her hungrily, lifting her top, tasting her firm, toned stomach, biting into it. It tastes of nature and sun, whetting my appetite further, every time I let her go, I pull her back once again, until eventually I let her go appropriately teased and bewildered. I spend the rest of the night flirting between the group I came with, which includes the "straight" Helen Mirren lookalike, my beautiful Birmingham friend, the woman I pinned, and hugging friends of old in between.

Day Ninety-Six

De Sade is personification of an attempt to control chaos. Life is chaos. Existence is chaos. There is no grand plan. There is no reason or meaning, and, because people cannot accept that things just are, life just is, they continually fight against it, trying to control. There is no scheme of things, no organisation. Organisation is a social construct via which we then try to rationalise spontaneous events as though they were organised all along.

God made the earth in six days. The earth came from the big bang. Wrong, wrong, wrong, on every account wrong. In truth there are no facts. In truth theories are meaningless. In truth events are insignificant. Maybe the human brain is too small, truth sends a mind insane. Who cares where the earth came from? There is no wall put around the universe. If there were there would be something beyond that wall – even nothing is something. We are not special, we are not different, we are not unique. There are no limits. No limits on time, no limits on existence. I once asked my mum who made God. She couldn't answer me, told me to ask my nana, who told me to ask the preacher. When I received no answer, I lost belief in all they told me.

Not only did I lose belief, but I began to think about time. Go back until you cannot go back any more and there are no limits. Time is not linear. There was no beginning, there is no end. The earth didn't begin, it was already part of something, merely changed form, and before that there were other forms, other energies. Energy cannot be destroyed. No great scheme, just chaos in an infinite energy pool. Chaos internally and externally. The body and mind are not stagnant. The only reality is the moment, which has gone before it is recognised. A moment could be cold, hunger, logic, passion, Thanatos, slipping in and out with no control, no organisation. Days are constructed with organisation, but still the moment's flutter like paper in the wind.

Abusers try to control chaos. They have a fear of letting go. A fear of being. Unable to control their own chaos, they try to control others, attempt to possess power. Sex is a tool of control. In chaos, sex is a burst of emotion and chemicals, a total loss of thought, a return to instinct and sensation. Sex is jumping off a cliff without restraint. Sex is abandonment, biting, swallowing, moving, freedom, thrusting, arching, scratching, touching. Sex is the animal within. Sex is the animal that wants to take, wants to give, or both at once. De Sade is afraid of letting go; by fearing the animal, de Sade becomes a monster, always going to further extremes to seek satisfaction, to achieve ecstasy by control, contriving the instinct. Sex will make you dizzy, sex will remove all thought, sex will take your breath, sex will remove any socialised personality, sex will remove control from your muscles, sex will release chemicals sending unique sensations through your body, sex will take you into a semiconscious state and heighten awareness. Deal with it. Sex cannot be thought about or calculated. Orgasms are not quadratic equations. De Sade's characters either have problems with orgasm, or plan the time, place, method. Who thinks about the way food is chewed, swallowed, its passage down to the stomach? Who considers the motor actions of walking? Instinctual behaviours – feel them, don't think them.

Brave new world
Relatively quickly I learned a whole new world. The research was easy,

no bars, no barriers. Every city has a members-only club. Membership is a simple process of writing one's name and address at the door, signing on the cross and entering the dungeon. This world isn't de Sade. It isn't sadomasochism. It isn't domination and submission. This is a world, living, thriving in every city, the suburbs, the country dwellings. This world is not different. This world is an exhibition of the boudoir. Wear leather, wear a dress, wear rubber, wear last century, wear nothing. Males are males are females. Females are females are males. This is a world of every reflection, power dynamics, vampires, blindfolds, food, reversing gender, dressing up, dressing down, smells, textures, pain, abstinence, voyeurism, every consensual sexual plausibility exists here.

Gem was a social worker turned swinger turned sex worker turned dominatrix. Gem quickly became a friend, as Neo did. However, whereas Neo was a submissive for ever, I could witness the passage of Gem first hand. Gem was the swinger in the fetish club on my very first visit, as my head turned to view her full exposed breasts. That night Gem was a swinger who just thought she would come along to the fetish night. I could visibly see her change from a playful viewer who began chatting and flirting to a fully fledged dominatrix, complete with smart shiny-handled floggers and canes.

Most of this world is strictly no sex, but some of the clubs are swingers' clubs on other nights, where sex can go on; other clubs are gay clubs that just turn a blind eye. I would go from the high of observing and talking to people in the Sphere, wander into another room where people would be naked, sweating and rutting like animals, my stomach feeling the clenched fist of revulsion on invading somebody's private mating. There is something distasteful about exhibited sex that is not so when two people naturally make love outside when consumed by passion. I think it comes back to the planning, the whole thing being contrived. If lovemaking is purposely exhibited, the mind is on the exhibition, not on the sensations and passion.

Day Ninety-Seven

One million people marched against war in Iraq. One million. The children are still trapped in de Sade's castle. Here is my impotence. I have more power to stop a world war than to rescue one child, let alone a hundred thousand. There are lives empty lives, torture, deaths. This is a life sentence, not a regime. I don't see a million people marching. I have an impossible mission, a castle in every street, every country, a silence protecting de Sade. I could read de Sade a thousand times and never risk insanity. I've tried every second of my life to find the castle, to rescue the children before we all die, and slowly sanity is chipped away from me.

How long before I agree to enter the castle with guns, making me no better than de Sade? How much abuse in any form before it is too much? How many souls must die worldwide? How about fifty million? Not enough? What is your price? Wear a poppy on Remembrance Day, do you? Does it make you feel good? I'm trying to break into de Sade's castle for millions more dead souls that have ever died in all your wars put together and you wear a fucking poppy. How can I begin to challenge anybody who has had enough and opens fire randomly with a rifle when you wear goddamn poppies? Maybe if I plant a poppy for every child presently being abused, every wife being battered, every slave picking your cocoa, you can wear the real thing, instead of those stupid paper bits. I do apologise if I offend you, I find your priorities offensive.

Let's imagine most of the research is overestimated and at a conservative estimate there is only one victim in ten of de Sade. That's one in ten of every doctor you see, every shop you enter, every teacher you see. One in ten of me, and we are angry – very angry. Be afraid, be very afraid. Create Frankenstein, you might get a monster. You have no idea of the dichotomy of thought caused. Coexisting are a deep empathy for pain, a value of respect and at the other end of the spectrum a lack of attachment in the critical period of development. In other words, although strongly against abuse or harm to others, I'd feel nothing if you all died tomorrow. It shouldn't be the children in the castle against society. It should be society against de Sade, but, it never has been. We are contagious. We will poison your minds by lifting up the carpets, opening the taboos, we will create a "myth" of the commonness of abuse in society. We are offensive to the population. Every day you touch us, you stand on a train and touch us, you walk through a busy mall and touch us, you go to a club and touch us. You can shower every cell of us from your skin, but you will touch us again tomorrow, shame we don't touch you.

Your threats to follow to Lash

You wanted to know everything about the fetish world. I told you. I told you the bruises from the lashes on bare flesh were real. I told you it was the hedonism of mainstream society without any responsibility. Still you romanticised it, said you wanted a Mistress. I knew what you wanted, but it wasn't what you would find in any fetish club. What you wanted possibly didn't exist. You wanted the ultimate fantasy, the fantasy I know so well, ultimate perfection. A woman strong, yet womanly, dark, yet safe, passionate, yet loving, dominant, yet understanding. She will know instinctively your needs. She will encase with her strong arms, but only when her strong arms are wanted. She will have an independence that won't be owned, yet at the same time be trusted. She will pin down, make love hard and rough, but not when soft and tender is wanted. She will decide confidently, yet treat as an equal. She will take responsibility, but not often enough to disempower. She will open herself, yet not be needy. She will listen, but not necessarily agree. She will bite, only where bites are sensual. She will tease, but not when urgency is desired. She is Cline without the abuse. She is you with more passion and less inconsistency.

Having previously read my mails knowing I was planning to go to Lash, you decided all of a sudden you had been to private parties, knew people on the fetish scene and would go to Lash with them. I never completely knew when you were bluffing or telling the truth; either way, the last thing I needed was my world being turned upside down by seeing you again, or disappointment from not seeing you. A part of me felt this was something I had done. I had taken a journey with de Sade that you only talked about. I had uncovered another world that you only talked about. If you invaded that now, you would take it all away. This was my life, my journey since you, something you weren't a part of, something you knew nothing of, a period of me you couldn't invade, a period of me I didn't want you to invade.

Day Ninety-Eight

Occasionally I consider the present and the past. Put them all together, the relationships, and no matter how I try to escape the cycle drummed in through childhood it returns with vengeance. My first lover from sixteen to nineteen was a violent, drug-dealing, prostitute, lesbian gang member. She was a mixture of my father and mother, violent yet needy, aggressive yet womanly, abusive yet manipulative, loud yet secretive. The next serious love I had was never really serious in my mind. We had only just started dating, she stayed for a weekend and I spent the next three years asking when she was intending to go home. She wasn't violent, lied considerably about irrelevant things, was pretty needy, but, apart from that a decent person. Cline was clever, charming, incredibly charming, successful without doing anything, stronger than most men and equally as masculine, yet every inch a woman. Cline had the body of pure perfection, a finely sculptured face, soft curls, long toned arms and legs, full firm breasts, a flat toned stomach, a broad strong back, narrow waist, buttocks so firm and taut. Cline was the most passionate person living, bias aside; lovemaking was every part of life. Go to the shops? Make love. Do the gardening? Make love. Cook a meal? Make love. Cline was aggressive, intimidating, fascinating, volatile, controlling and alcoholic. I was physically and emotionally broken after eighteen months with

Cline, never completely recovering. Leaving Cline was like leaving part of myself. I didn't want the abuse, but I knew I'd never find a lover like Cline, particularly as, after a year when I was healed somewhat, I was going out of my way to find a lover as different from Cline as possible.

Colette was the result. I knew I was lying to myself, burying a part of myself that would just return to that inevitable cycle, just long enough for it to recover. Cline and my first lover, flings in between are just like returning to de Sade. It hurts to know that, no matter what, even I can't escape the castle. It isn't, as some think, an enjoyment of abuse. Abusive relationships kill, every minute is revisiting hell. The only definite I can pinpoint is that childhood experience of relationships is that of power dynamics and extremes, flaws and strength become ingrained, not as part of the abuser but as parts of the self, and these parts of the self are looked for in others, only without the abuse. In the child, the strong self protects from the abuser; as the child grows, the protector becomes an attractive ideal for the young woman, the ideal lover, ideal mate. When she looks for this, but finds abuse rather than strength, the strong self rescues her yet again and so the cycle continues. It isn't abuse she looks for – that is an unfortunate side effect of some strong personalities, it is a compliment to her opposite, the other side of herself, who in return looks for someone soft and gentle to love and protect. Irony is when searching for part of the self plays into the hands of de Sade. How can several different choices of mate be reconciled? Can one person be all things? The biggest insult is that de Sade became his own de Sades. Nearly all the characters in the stories told by the narrators are priests, pointing strongly to some experience de Sade had with abusive priests either as a child or an adult. If the experiences were as a child instead of his defence mechanisms working to fight the abuse, they somehow identified with it. De Sade's own defences may have created the monsters he should have defended himself against, thus perpetuating his own pain onto others. Generation upon generations of pain is reproduced; those who don't create identifications with the abuser, as de Sade possibly did, create protection like the castle trapping the children, Colette's protection, my protection. Cruelty personified is that the whole thing has being created by the abuser; without the abuse the protection would never have been created, so ultimately right up until the last breath the abuser retains the control, a control over a lack of control. De Sade may have been desperately hanging on for some sense of control, over others if he couldn't achieve it within himself.

Musical clubs

It was the night of the Sphere and Toyah Wilcox was playing at the local gay club. Several of the Sphere members were going to watch Toyah and I wanted a night away from research, a night back to myself. Neo reminded me that Zoë the dominatrix I made an unintentional exhibition with would be expecting me at the Sphere. More reason not to go, surely, but, nonetheless, I sensed Neo wanted to go. I entered the Sphere with high spirits and not in the slightest mood of researching anything. After about five minutes I realised I didn't want to be there, I wanted my time back, not de Sade's, so decided to walk back out again and go to the gay club three miles away. Neo followed, as did Gem, and Zoë, her husband Marc and a few others only known by sight. It was a mass exodus. One by one we passed the bouncers in the gay club, their eyes turning at the leather and chains, wolf-whistling as we passed. Half a dozen from the Sphere, including Shona and Sonja, were already in the club on the dance floor, in a prime spot to view Toyah.

Zoë and I swayed to the music and began to kiss, innocently enough. This particular night she was wearing a black basque, stockings and a black tutu, and she looked fantastic. We're dancing close, real close, our bare thighs touching, hands scrunching each other's hair, kisses passionate. My hands explore her back, her hips, her thighs, my fingers rimming around the top of her stockings under their joining straps, exploring that sexy space between her stocking and her, her, her naked cunt, calm my sexual controller, the woman is wearing no underwear. Now the brain ceases to work. I'm alone with Zoë, dancing, only I aware of what is or isn't under her clothes. My hands caressing her bare arse in sexy secret, fingers teasing her inner thighs, the more I'm teasing her the more I'm teasing myself. Until everybody else ceases to exist and beneath that basque, the rhythm we dance is to the thrust of my fingers deep inside her cunt. We come up for air oblivious of the fact that Toyah has been and gone only a few feet away and apparently not greatly amused. I vaguely remember an image of Toyah standing with two gold cups over her breasts, but the truth is I missed Toyah Wilcox because I was fucking a dominatrix three feet away, all as part of research into de Sade.

Day Ninety-Nine

Insanity is a route to reason. Reason is the questions to the answer why. Why is the answer given to the experience. Why is the answer to the pain. Why not? why me? why now? what did I do? why hurt me? are a few of the questions to the answer why. I could fill a book with the questions to the answer why. The infinity of the questions to the answer why is the reason and the insanity. This is consciousness at its best. Insanity is the total of chaos, every thought exposed and flying freely faster than atomic collision. Insanity is thinking out of the box, in every which way direction, seeing the whole, not the part, and seeing it all at once. Insanity is insight, awareness and enlightenment pounding at once, all at heightened alertness. There is no such thing as a cognitive distortion: the individual's thought is influenced by mood, experience, hormones, chemicals, emotions, context. Every thought is valid in the whole picture. Sanity is but a piece of the jigsaw, sanity is now within this specific context, not the whole picture. Sanity is a tiny percentage of conscious awareness. The mind is a whole, a buzzing, booming, disorganised chaos. One situation is not even a trillionth of the internal picture, throw in some emotion, experience, infinite interpretations, several other variables such as esteem, efficacy, and there is a snapshot of a single thought, feeling, action. When consciousness is so pure the whole picture is viewed, felt, sensed, thought, touched at once, focus is locked inside, literally immobilised by the total of the surrounding data. In such an extreme awareness the person would be frozen for ever; in essence, control has to be lost to be gained. The plug has to be pulled on total awareness, without losing its insight.

It is this contradiction that reveals de Sade as being both in control and out of control. He sees a lot of the picture, but it misses important variables, through some heightened exploration of consciousness he has control, of that which is uncontrolled chaos. His fear of the data exposed drives him to fight it and attempt to control chaos. This can't be done internally, for it is inside he fears and runs from; instead he modifies the variables, thus perspective of the data, using it to control others through realisation of his lack of internal control. Instead of recognising not just his own abuse but the variables, the feelings, the pain, the esteem that goes with it, he sees the abuse, but gains control over the variables by changing them to identify with the abuse by perpetuating the cycle onto others. This is reflected in de Sade's love affair with all that he despises. De Sade hates religion, yet it features on every page of his work, is the main character in every story told by the narrators. Whether blasphemous or not, de Sade is associating so closely with religion, he spends all his time with it. By giving religion so much space and time, de Sade gives both publicity and credence to it. Religion wasn't de Sade's hatred, it was his obsession, and like an unrequited lover he hated it with a passion because it hurt and rejected him. In his obsession, de Sade was looking for reason. It takes a strong person to step into reason.

De Sade wasn't strong enough.

Escorting the truth

I wanted answers and you wanted games. How did your emotions change so quickly? Why did you fuck Bernard all night long? Why had you even got condoms? You said you'd last slept with a guy twelve years ago, so why have condoms? It's not a usual household item, sitting next to the salt just in case a stray man calls who needs spontaneously fucking. Maybe it's perfectly normal, it is my perspective in me that is out of synch, the literal virgin in me that can't understand. Nonetheless, why did you have condoms?

"I got them free with my job, I was an escort, OK?"

Of course you are being sarcastic.

"I was in Birmingham, it was brought up in a random conversation about a TV programme et cetera, thought I'd check it out on the Internet, saw some ads and thought I'd give it a go, did, and got some contacts very quickly."

Hold onto your seatbelts while the psyche plunges several thousand feet below sea level. This can't be happening, can't be true. Is it or isn't it? How can I know you so well, yet never have known you at all? Why?

"I only did it a few times and it made me feel so shit; I liked the money but not the emotional effects – I really felt dirty."

You played some games, but the more I asked the more this sounded the truth.

"You didn't have any bad experiences?"

"I did, yes, he just liked it rough is all – got a bit carried away."

I couldn't believe what I'd heard: you, my shy trendy lover, a whore? The only woman I'd ever love a mould of my mother, my violent first lover. Did I believe you or not? You were certainly convincing, too convincing. I spent three days and three nights trawling every Internet site ever known listing escorts, clicked any that remotely fitted your characteristics. Three days and three nights staring at the face of my childhood, swimming back in hell, hating these women and their punters more. It's impossible to judge something you've grown up with, but the images of my mother putting on heavy makeup in bedsits, having photographs taken, waking in London hotels next to her and her punter in the bed, seeing his penis, then closing my eyes again, pretending to be asleep. How that man they call my father sold me to her punter to touch for twenty-five pounds. You'd think it'd be OK being abused every night and all. None of it's OK, I can smell both their stale breath, the fear when her punter stuck his foul tongue in my mouth, in my bedroom, in my window, the neighbour across the way watching, not caring about my pain. It was on the landing he touched me, fuck knows why they chose the landing, the father standing but feet away watching, and I had to lie on the floor like some corpse, while her punter leaned over me, his greasy hair, stale sweat, clammy hands touching my body, my vagina, mine. I live it every day, so it wasn't that your words and searching every warped site for you made me relive it as such: the smells, the pain simply intensify; it never goes away, is just attenuated enough for some semblance of function. It was her husband, her punter, her fault, everything tainted by women. I'm tainted, my mother tainted and now you tainted. I feel the vomit rise, as though my body is trying to reject every one of your toxins, all you that poisoned me, and that nausea has haunted me all my life. I feel the bile in my throat, the putrid sickness in the basin and I see all the poison inside me, the pain written in the colours of my evil inside. I see you all in my vomit, and for ever I will be trying to expel you, the smell, touch, fluid, every contamination you invaded me with. I can't expel my genes. Will I begin to smell like you both did? Will my own toxins for ever remind me, will your toxins become mine, your skin become mine, will I revulse myself as much as you do me?

Day One Hundred

Tiredness stings my eyes and lulls my brain. I cannot give in to lethargy while the children remain in the castle. There is a storm brewing, an internal storm, a fire of wrath inside. There are no limits. We were taught from birth there are no limits. Life is of no concern to me. Whether people live or die is of no concern to me. I have a spreading fire, flames that will either protect or engulf. One way or another, I will enter the castle of de Sade and release the children, if my hands bleed to the bone from deconstructing it brick by brick. I sense it will be another mission, one I may not complete on this journey, one that may take one hundred and twenty-one years, not days. I call to all with any shred of integrity to take your arms. We are going to war. Bombard Parliament with queries about the Operation Ore blackout and why the one in three experiencing abuse is not a priority issue. I fight, yet fail. I am no tall, dark, strong, invincible woman, I am a coward. I didn't stop the abuse. I allowed the child to hang her head and cry. I didn't kill him, didn't even hit him, didn't fight, just managed the odd meek no. I let the blows rain, never raised my voice above a whisper, or pummelled my fists into his huge frame. I haven't built a mansion or a safe place. I've provided a life with more work than play, a rotten falling-down house, insufficient money to subsist, enough debt to imprison for a lifetime. I pretend to be some strong woman, the protector of my soul, and I've yet to do anything to protect. I try, but don't succeed, and half the time I don't know how to get into that castle, provide a life, not a slavery, a home, not a mortgaged squat.

The truth is, I've failed, failed myself, and that child, that long-ago child who waited and waited to be rescued; nobody came and neither did I. I hurt the child more by researching de Sade, the reality; I can almost convince myself I am some strong protector, yet at the same time release my wrath in knowing I've failed. My own castle can't be rescued by leather pseudo-revenge. Rescuing from the castle will never remove the years imprisoned within it, it will never take away that pain, but perhaps part of the rescue is acknowledging that. No matter how urgent the situation, going in and ripping down the walls with my bare hands is worthless if I die of exhaustion at the gates and none are rescued. Taking years to rescue one child at a time is preferable to saving none.

Domme's deception

Love Street club was brilliant, a real tacky, dingy place, nothing like Sphere or Lash, the kind of seedy joint I'd have expected. The paint was peeling, the air musty, the toilets decorated with graffiti and without seats, soap, towels. Not content with the journey in Gem's car, Neo was locked in the box, while Marc leaned over the top at the mercy of the lashes doled out by Zoë and me. A few feet away, a somewhat large woman in high heels was walking over a man lying face down on the floor. This was all right, seedy joints generally are, but it was really all right. About 11 p.m. food was served, and not the odd stale, processed ham bap, but potato wedges and a huge pot of chilli. If I learn nothing else from this journey with de Sade, the one thing I will take away is that flogging makes one extremely hungry. I stood chatting to Gem and Neo, soaking in the atmosphere and letting my food go down. Zoë came over, after already saying she was going to spend some time with Marc.

"Marc's at the bar, come with me for a few minutes," she giggled, taking my hand. I followed her through the dungeon, through some curtains, where I hadn't realised a room existed. This room was dark and smoky with heavy red couches. I could see naked flesh, buttocks thrusting, hear the breathing, smell the sex, this was how I imagined a swingers' club and I didn't like it, the hackles on my back rose. Zoë found an empty couch.

"Kiss me you." She pulled my head towards her. We kissed. I was aware of her stretching her body to lie down, pulling me on top of her, the opening of her hips the way women prepare for sex. My logic wanted to stop, my animal continued kissing her, hands exploring her body in response to her hands on mine. She handed me a dildo.

"Use this."

I didn't want to, I didn't want public sex. part of me felt obliged because I'd started, but, what I'd started was kissing. I pushed the latex inside her, conscious of the people around me and not fixed with passion. Out of nowhere Marc appeared, he began to kiss Zoë, undoing his shirt. No, whatever this was, I didn't want it, I walked away, evil with rage, feeling framed into a situation on the premise of a quick kiss while Marc was at the bar. What was I doing kissing a married woman anyway?

I walked out of the curtains straight to my box, looked at Neo, clicked my fingers.

"Here now," I commanded.

Obediently he hurried across the room placing his flesh on the box. I beat and I beat and I beat, I beat until Neo ceased to exist. In front of me were Zoë's actions, and you, your lies, your dirty income, images of you and punters. I beat your sordid smells from my soul. I thrashed your painful lies from my psyche. I stood on the floor, jumped on the box, wielding down the blows. I stopped smoked a cigarette, I leaned against the iron equipment, rage painting my expression, until the images burned my mind too much, and then I beat some more. Two floggers, one in each hand, swinging with speed and power from my shoulders, flying high and hitting low, alternate, together, figures-of-eight, circles, any way they go. I'm not hitting a person, not desiring to inflict pain, it's not a violence. I'm thrashing Zoë out of my mind, thrashing you out of my mind, thrashing the stench of rutting men out of my mind, thrashing every punter of every woman out of my mind, thrashing every whore out of my mind.

"Red."

And I'm beating harder, faster, but never enough to chase the demons away.

"Red, Mistress."

I'm still standing on the box possessed, muscles throbbing for more. Some guy is standing in front of the box, I stare straight at him, eyes boring red, demonic.

"You want some?"

He nods, head lowering, shifts his body to the box.

"You call me Mistress; your safe words are red, amber and green. Use them. Do you understand?"

Feebly he answers, "Yes, Mistress".

My blows are harder, faster, meaner, just as accurate, but twice as powerful. There is no recognition of a human in front of my blows: this is a stranger. A stranger who just happens to be under the images, the pain I am beating from my soul. I am nowhere. I am not in a club, there are no people around me. I am within the demons in my head, chasing them away with strands of leather, pushing them into hellfire. I am belting away the shame, the dirt, the contamination. I am killing it all. I am fighting it out of my castle with almighty sweeps.

"Mistress."

I am locking you out of my castle for ever. I am barring the gates with anger, after I have thrust my sword into every member of the enemy.

"Mistress?"

"What?" And the blows never stop.

"Mistress, the club is closing," Neo whispers.

The thrashes rain down and down. I throw a flogger behind me, putting all my anger behind one, raising my shoulder back, leaning my whole body, giving each blow an almighty high curve, and again, and again, and again, until I jump off the box,

"You're done."

"Thank you, thank you." He stumbles, but I don't want to hear it, I'm walking away, still wielding floggers into thin air. Still forcing air against the drive of the leather while Gem and Neo are putting on their boots.

"Mistress, are you OK?"

My eyes alone answer, not questioning me. Whether right or wrong, for the first time in nights, I sleep like a baby.

Day One Hundred and One

There is a fearful calm within me. A release, yet an anxiety. I'm at the castle gates, now armed with the knowledge that I can't rescue all the children, at least not at once and not all now. I still have the problem of how to rescue even the one child from de Sade's castle. The real battle between de Sade and me will begin at the end of this journey. I cannot break into the castle and remove the child while I am travelling with the enemy. Maybe I will burn his novel. The people I have met through the research I will never see again. I have sufficient research, I could end the ties now, I keep them open for the remaining twenty days, in case there are more questions to ask.

Neo asked me a while ago, whether I was just going to walk away into the distance as suddenly as I appeared, to be found with a team of fly fishers if I decided in the future to research that. The cold reality is yes, I will and have to walk away. I am an impostor. I am not a dominant so to speak. I have an inner child who needs rescuing. I have to consider her, the damage I did to her over the weeks I wore a flogger over my shoulder in the name of research. I forsook the child, the gentle parts of myself to express myself and affirm my strength, only to realise I wasn't providing that strength. What kind of protection eats into those I am defending? I forsook them to run away from my guilt of loving Colette, the guilt of my pain and stupidity. I sought to regain my strength and looked for it in the wrong places. I ran away instead of facing my responsibility. I didn't only not try to rescue my child, I totally abandoned the castle, danced with de Sade, ignoring the tears carving the child's face at this betrayal. I betrayed them to eradicate my own pain, to beat Colette from my mind, to strike out at love and attempt to validate my lost power and worth. I undermined every principle I hold and every fear of the child and the gentle parts within. I outwardly oppose any aggression, violence, intimidation, even slightly raised voices. I value civility, equality and respect. My actions mocked all I hold in esteem, mocked my doctrine for behaviour, for life, mocked the pain experienced, mocked the abuse of the child. In trying to find reason, trying to understand why, trying to understand de Sade, I have become a hypocrite. I have flirted with the enemy by behaving like the enemy. I have inflicted pain upon another human being. I am my worst nightmare. I wouldn't allow the child near anyone who behaved as I did during my journey with de Sade. In behaving as the enemy does, I have become a clone of the mother who never protected the child. I thought I was infallible, that other emotional parts of myself were screwed up, and made mistakes, not I. It comes as something as a shock, having to accept being human. I always thought I was created for a purpose, that purpose alone, and nothing would influence or distract from that; like a part in a machine, emotions and other variables were nothing to do with me, not part of my job specification. Nothing could hurt me because I was just a worker bee, defending the queen. Life could knock my psyche, but never impact on me, I would always remain a constant, true to my purpose, a tool in the box with one use. To admit my scar takes more strength than defending the world's children.

Denying the admission

Only days after I returned from Chester did you deny your original admission of being an escort. Why would you make up something so potent? Knowing how much bringing the whole sexual exchange to the forc of my mind would destroy me, why on earth would you make something like that up? Your love and rejection flung me back in hell. Wasn't that enough? I spent sleepless days and nights in confusion, I beat total strangers into oblivion trying to gain just a moment of peace in my mind, to no avail, only physical pain to them and emotional damage to me. I acted like an abuser to run away from your words in my head. You say you escort, they are not empty words that stop at you, bang, my mother slept with men throughout my childhood, bang, I smelled their spunk on her hands from my earliest memories when she came in to kiss me goodnight. I would swallow my vomit. It spoiled my sleep, spoiled my mum's kissing me goodnight, took it away from me. They stole my goodnight, any security, any constant, they stole it. It doesn't end there: a word links to an experience over here in the mind and in turn that shares a junction with another, cue, the father selling me at twelve and my fear that it was the beginning of my being sold out like my mother. I live this every day. I know I have never known constant, never known truth, never known openness, never known security, never known protection. I didn't need reminding.

I didn't believe you, either way I didn't believe you. You may have been an escort, I didn't believe you were, I didn't believe you weren't. Lies are what abuse relies on, lies and secrets and all that is hidden. Parent A doesn't know what parent B is doing, or do they? Parent A tells child about parent B, but parent B doesn't know, parent B tells child about parent A, but parent A doesn't know and it's all a great big secret, only child heard parent A discuss with parent B what parent A told child not to discuss, and nobody knows what's going on, but the child sees it all, yet both A and B think the child doesn't know. It is the biggest mindfuck in existence. I cannot cope with inconsistency, lies, deceit, indirectness. It was all I knew for sixteen years. I cannot understand or function with it.

Day One Hundred and Two

I think more and more about my funeral. I want Macy Gray's "The Letter" to play while my body slips gently away into the Atlantic, swallowed up in her vast womb. It's a taboo, death, dying, many things are taboos, when really nothing should be. Society becomes the thought police, telling each other what and more precisely what not to think about. Thoughts do not equate to action. I may think of killing every day for a thousand years, it doesn't mean I ever want to fulfil the action of plunging a knife into someone's flesh. Actions remove thoughts. In the months I've actively researched de Sade, many thoughts have disappeared. Gone are the dreams, gone are the nightmares, and I miss them; in many instances I would choose the thoughts over the actions any day. Is it better to act like de Sade or to think freely? De Sade acted, tried to control his thoughts by shutting them off to control action instead. De Sade was afraid of letting go. Thought-policing is nonsensical: nobody will admit how they think in case others don't think the same, so there are no guidelines on logical thought. Accepting every thought, every feeling has a profound impact. It causes a whole perceptual shift. Right and wrong become replaced with acceptance. Letting go is irresponsible, but what is irresponsible? It's used as a negative, as doing the wrong thing, when it's actually entering reality and admitting having no control of everything. Control is bandied about as a positive and a negative. Some events are wrong to control, some right, it's wrong to control others, but not the self. Is the self not the most important? I'm not suggesting violence: violence is not a natural state, so is it ever really uncontrolled? We live in a myth of control, an assumption of anarchy without a governing body. There are fifty-nine million individuals living in Britain. Do you really think if society naturally lived in a state of anarchy without "control" those fifty-nine million individuals wouldn't be? Pray tell, how do you control fifty-nine million into doing anything they don't want to? If anarchy doesn't exist it is because people do not want to live in it. There are no universal rules. Every pod, every unit has its own values. There is no universal right and wrong, in any level of the hierarchy. Evil is merely a subjective description of the things an individual does not like; good is the description of the things the individual does like. The two dichotomies are an elaboration of infantile splitting. All the understanding in the world doesn't reconcile an abuser finding good in pain.

Tree girl
I saw the girl I'd pinned against the cold tiles of the gay club a few more times. She was a lumberjack and such an unusual specimen of

androgyny, a tiny lithe body, perfectly flat-muscled chest, slim waist that didn't widen into the equally slim hips. It was nothing serious, but still I wanted to know her soft internalism, this untamed, yet gentle creature. Chuck talked to my Tree Girl on Gaydar. Chuck the coincidental submissive. The world had suddenly shrunk and become too small. My eyes were meeting Tree Girl's too closely, her body was too warm next to mine when she told me she had arranged to meet Chuck for the first time the following day. My stomach sank as though a premonition hit. I remember drifting into sleep and her asking me if I would mind her sleeping with Chuck, and replying yes I would, but deep down I knew. They were just meeting for coffee, Tree Girl said she'd call when she got back if it wasn't too late. I was working with de Sade until the early hours, and I knew.

I switched the computer on to work the next day. Chuck breezily said hello over MSN while I opened my mail. Tree Girl's words echoed on the screen: "Just wanted to tell you, I did sleep with Chuck, will call you later." My stomach was punched out of my soul. How could she? How could Chuck? She knew I was seeing Tree Girl. I knew Chuck was polygamous. So what? I wasn't. Chuck couldn't see any wrong in her actions and I couldn't believe the situation. How could de Sade tie in a coincidental woman from Birmingham and my newest lover from my city. It seemed I couldn't escape, couldn't escape the research, couldn't escape de Sade, couldn't escape the hedonistic world I was ever only visiting during research hours. Chuck thought I was crazy, wrong to be upset. Maybe I was but I didn't come from a polygamous perspective, even in non-serious fun.

Charlie mocked my pain, my values, suggested a threesome. I have to run away. I have to get away from de Sade. I have to return to myself. The world is too small. De Sade is too omnipresent. De Sade is swallowing me up in a vast sea of damaged souls. De Sade is undermining my substance. I am not an object. I am not solely a sexual being. I am not the sum of my orgasms. I am not a submissive. I am not a dominant. I am not a giver. I am not a taker. I am not de Sade. I am *a mental, emotional, intellectual, physical being. My needs are not sex, not violence, momentary excitement, immediate gratification. Do not insult me with your sexual separatism from your soul and life. No, I do not want sex for the sake of sex. I am not desperate for an orgasm. I can give myself multiple and still retain my substance. I do not need a fuck to prove my worth and esteem. I respect a woman for her soul, her words, the way she moves, the food we share, the idiosyncrasies of her mind, her favourite music, colours, clothes. I make love to her, not her cunt.*

Day One Hundred and Three

I am in a parallel universe with de Sade, knowing the faster I walk the journey, the quicker it will be over. There may not be any world, any people left when I am finished. It could be crumbling beneath my feet right now, but I care not. Many rely so much on people, even total strangers, people they don't know. They will approach me and a second later I am a long-lost friend. I am not your people. I am not your friend. I am not like you. I do not need you, any of you. I am made to feel eternally guilty for this disposition. I am sorry. I am sorry I do not need contact. I am sorry I do not need to be with people. I see them all day at work, when I walk out of my house. I cannot avoid them. Why would I want to spend my time with them? I am sorry I do not. I do not miss you when you are not there. I do not even think about you, at least not most of you. There are few I attach to and even fewer who touch me.

Parts of me attached to my mother. The umbilical attachment is a complicated one. The mother is needed, yet protected. By proxy of there being only two parents and one being the complete de Sade, it's not compulsory to attach to one, but, when the actions of the child are thought to defend the mother, an attachment occurs. The father told me he would kill the mother if I told anyone. That was the choice: put up with daily abuse or the mother gets it. She would cry on my infant shoulder, tell me her pain, share with me the simple things we weren't allowed to do. For fourteen years we were allies against the enemy, or so I thought. It never occurred to me she might be a double agent. In complete honesty, it did, but I buried the thoughts to bear life. There will always be irony, always be barriers, always be de Sade, one way or another.

Scarlet

Chuck had told me about Scarlet, before we fell out over Tree Girl. I'd already told her about the leather shorts I'd made for myself and agreed to make her a leather skirt with the remaining material. I still made it, even though we hadn't spoken since arguing over Tree Girl.

We knocked at the big steel doors and waited. Scarlet is an education. Inside it is huge, the lobby is the size of a dance floor, of which there were two big ones, a café upstairs, two balconies, a shopping area, and the dank, tiny, stone dungeon. It was past the first dance floor, into the shopping area, where Neo met and introduced me to his transsexual friend Pammy. Pammy was a gorgeous guy/girl, sexy olive skin, dark long curly hair, beautiful high cheekbones and a gentle sincere smile. Pammy showed us the dungeon. The equipment was squashed into dangerous, dark, narrow corridors, where none could stretch an arm, let alone swing a flogger. Pammy showed us each piece of equipment within the corridors. In the alcoves groups were having sex; women were bent over the equipment with guys thrusting behind them. I was confused: this wasn't a swingers' club, this was a gay club holding a fetish night. This didn't happen at Lash. I mentioned this to Pammy after the tour while we rested by the rack.

"It was worse last time. One woman was like a human train: she must have had nine men one after the other, and where you are sitting now a guy tried to fist his girlfriend and when he couldn't he fisted her best friend instead. He was just flinging her body about with his arm."

Neo and I listened with mouths open and brows raised.

"Is this a sex club?"

"No," Pammy continued, "it's not supposed to be, but that's how a lot of the people that come here use it and the management just turn a blind eye."

How disgusting! Dungeon equipment used for sex. We weren't having any of that. Neo lay on the rack and we began our display, even without enough swinging room. The light above was two inches from my head and burning into me and the floggers kept catching on the wooden frame of the rack. Nonetheless, no one else was flogging and a crowd formed, as did a queue. I couldn't flog Neo very hard by now: as soon as someone ceased to be a stranger, my arms lost their power. I couldn't hurt him, he was no longer nothing in front of me. I knew my arms didn't contain their usual power, but that didn't stop the applause from the crowd after our display, or a guy from the queue asking if he could be flogged next.

There were two dance floors in this place. I was in no mood for flogging when there was dancing to be done, but fuckers took the rest of the equipment and there were no other dominants. I had a position to maintain, and maintain it I did. I never showed my boredom or exhaustion at the end of the two hours' flogging. Some guys rejoined the queue again. I flogged until I couldn't flog any more, gently with first-timers, even with the guy who repeated, "Is that as hard as you can do it?" knowing the next day he would be bruised and in pain.

Ready to drop, I left the dungeon and headed upstairs to the dance floor. We'd been there hours before I saw Chuck. I sent Neo to give her the leather shirt and carried on dancing. After a while I decided to talk to her, make up. I don't like bad feeling, but she looked good in a tiny corset, with wide hips, breasts pushed up, pillar-box-red head, and my brain had left my senses, replaced by the swelling in my cunt. She didn't want to make up and it isn't easy to talk to someone with eyes flaming a fire of passion. How I hate this crazy illogical animal. Thank God she didn't want resolve because I don't know that I would have restrained from fucking her.

It was about a quarter to four in the morning when we were moved to the heavier (trance) downstairs dance floor. With fifteen minutes left we continued dancing there. Innocently I looked up and on the balcony above two women were bent over the railings, a man thrusting into one of them, while another was fluffing himself over the railings next to the other. Open-mouthed and speechless, I nudged Neo; we stood and stared aghast. A blonde security woman behind who noticed us looking, laughed. "Oh, they've been at that all night."

I swallowed, ouch. It seemed sex was going on all over this club, on every dance floor, the balconies, women and women, men and men, men and women, everywhere like wildebeests, everywhere other than the privacy of the toilets, which were constantly surprisingly empty.

Scarlet seemed to have more in common with de Sade than anything I had yet witnessed.

Day One Hundred and Four

The winter is mild this year and as damp as autumn. I want it to bite. I want to feel the cold wind chafe my skin. I want to feel alive. We wake up day after day and do we really know we are alive? Life is but an assumption of the individual. If this is death, the events aren't mortal, so is the pain? When do you die: at the moment your heart stops or the moment your soul stops? I felt I lost my soul at four, felt it had died, there was no more me. I was but an empty vessel, carrying blood and plasma and neural networks, but no person, no meaning, no soul, no life. Apparently, we should be grateful for life. The pain, the aches, the hunger, the cold, the fear, the guilt, the shame, the numbness, the stigma, I am so very grateful. It is all the fault of mortality. Without a body I would have no pain, because, although the pain is emotional, the cause was physical. My body was controlled because my mind couldn't be. My mind was violated only through my body. If I had no head, it couldn't be hit. If I had no flesh it couldn't be touched. My carrier, the thing that simply moves around me, was the thing that killed my soul and injured my mind. Something so unimportant caused damage to the most precious things.

There is always a stubborn fight inside, a knowledge that, whatever they did, they could torture my flesh, but they couldn't get me, couldn't control me, couldn't enter my psyche. Every time they hurt me, I would sit in the back of my head, watching, watching and glaring, and scorning. Fools never even knew my scorn.

Some people are photographs, and photogenic they may be, and some are truly alive. I sleep like a foetus, eat what I crave when I crave it, sit, stand, slump in any position my body so wishes. I sway or dance when I want to, where I want to. We are so controlled by culture, walk this way, talk this way, eat this way, sleep this way. No. Walk backwards if you want to, don't walk at all, hop, skip, run, jump, dance. If you don't do what you want, it's your problem, if you do, it's theirs, let them have the problem, they'll work it out. The biggest thing de Sade does is control, control everything.

Lash for lasses

Devil's Abyss was a fantastic venue. The four women who ran Lash had done it again. Outside is old Gothic stone and iron bars; inside is a fake grey stone wall, low lighting, an alter on the dance floor, and stone pillars. Dawn met us inside and we all just stood a while, soaking in the atmosphere, eerie music, low lighting, mass of women. A mass of oestrogen, no contamination, pure oestrogen. My eyes caught a tall woman, dark hair scraped back into a ponytail, a leather trench coat gracing her tall strong frame. She had a certain air of depth, of power. We sat and chatted about something and nothing, the way easy conversation ebbs and flows. We danced around the altar, until her friends were suddenly on and around it. I don't like striking women. I have no wish or desire to, but here were about five gorgeous women screaming out to be touched in some way. I am this totally monogamous woman, stick me in a group wanting sex and I would run away; nonetheless, there is something about the harem fantasy the ego loves. It's not merely attention: it's lots of attention. The tall trench-coated woman would walk past me, teasing my neck with ice, then I'd walk past her and drip wax on her arm, and she'd pass me and lightly strap my shoulder, all the time both slowly moving around the alter in opposite directions. All in all, Dawn and I spent most of the night with these five gorgeous women, never striking hard, never overtly sexual, just softly flirting. The tall dark babe and I kissed gently as she left with her friends, never to be seen again.

The streets were still heaving with people when Gem and I left into the madness of the night. At some point we had decided it would be funny to walk through the streets with Gem on a lead. We walked around aimlessly for fifteen minutes trying to decide whether to eat, dance some more, or both, followed by a lean, young, drunken guy, who kept trying to talk to us. It was on the corner of Canal Street that I turned to say something to this guy, when my eyes locked with the most gorgeous woman. I stood rooted to the spot, just staring at her finely carved cheekbones, strong jaw and shy blue eyes, her hair barely half an inch long, emphasising her perfect features more.

"Have you two been to Lash?" she asked.

I nodded, maybe I said something. Gem was definitely talking. I reached out as though in a dream to touch those sharply defined cheekbones. She stepped back, she stepped forwards, all the while we spoke. I learned that, although she lived in Chester, she was from our home city and visited most weeks. We swapped emails, and this was my first meeting with Ilona.

Day One Hundred and Five

Amelia cut my hair. She's very good. For years, and still now, I cut my own. I suddenly developed an averseness to hairdressers for no particular reason and just began cutting my own, continued doing so through university and beyond. I became good enough that, although the cut wasn't spectacular, it wasn't obviously a home cut. I started going to Amelia now and again, because she has those special scissors that can create the texture I can't. I like how she washes my hair absent-mindedly continuing to talk to colleagues while her fingers automatically massage my scalp and I can drift without having to hold court. Amelia has been cutting hair for five years. I don't talk much to her, just the odd word, for no reason other than that I'm usually relaxing and she is concentrating; but today I ask her if she ever gets frustrated cutting fixed styles and just feels like letting her imagination run wild and creating whatever her artistic flow desires. She informs me of often feeling thus, so I say I will go in the long holidays and she can have free licence over my head. I must remember to call back then and do that. I like the way I hold up my hand and screw my lip in disgust rejecting the hairspray, and she sneaks a little jet just to tease.

I look at my gamine features graced with short fine hair and see the victim reflection. It throws me back, like looking at the reflection of unexpected exhaustion etched onto my face and hair that looks all too faded. Sometimes it looks too round, too young, too undefined, too vulnerable, too different, until I stare into the eyes and recognise myself, those eyes that sometimes fire fear in my reflection. I see a reflection through my eyes. I hate the mirror in front of me at the hairdresser's, don't look in it. I look down at the black smock around me, counting the grey hairs, and listen to the mundane conversations.

People go to hairdressers to discuss holidays; I think having their hair tidied is merely a side effect. Amelia never expects me to indulge in this mundaneness, or maybe it is blatantly obvious I just will not. Neo says it is an abruptness about me, though I prefer the description "directness". It hurts me to think I scare people. I intend no harm, no intimidation, just like to confirm my boundaries. I don't think I talked to the first counsellor I had for around six months. I saw her on and off and never totally trusted her. I withheld things, maybe important things. I was passed on to Claudia just as I was starting my journey with de Sade. I remember that first meeting as if it were yesterday. I went with no intention of allowing a total stranger to know me, judge me, label me, no intention of showing myself, any vulnerability, weakness, trusting. I managed to maintain it for almost an hour. Pretended to ignore the acknowledgement I could read in her eyes, but I couldn't keep it up for an hour, let alone six months. It would have been a lie that would have mocked all. I go through life and occasionally meet someone with a recognition and inside there is a knowledge of some shared path and understanding. I never meant to scare her, never knew I could do such, certainly never wanted to, and the thought pains me.

Denying such is like defecting to de Sade's army. Being labelled, boxed up and sent to some psychiatric unit is such a huge fear, because it's like being imprisoned by de Sade. The freedom, choice, control, life would be taken away. I can bluff through life sufficiently that any such measures are unnecessary, but I don't constantly want to live a pretence to all. I am a hypocrite for doing so at all, since my biggest distaste is deceit. Pretence is that double-edged sword that both causes and protects the pain. In truth, none of my life is pretence: it is more the case that most people know only one face in the reflection, sometimes the face I *don't* recognise.

The party

Ilona and I had swapped emails for several weeks. I explained that night in Manchester as research for de Sade, always having to reinforce my stance as she returned to the striking woman in the collar. By now I wanted to scream to all, she does not exist, she is not real. I am not the participant observer of my research, I am not the sum of a journey through de Sade. There is no striking woman in black with a studded collar, just me with my easy drawstring trousers and flirtatious movement. She doesn't exist, and, if she does, she is no whip-donning dominant, she'd be a strong, gentle soul, detesting of de Sade, rejecting of pain and control, with more integrity than the world and I could ever reach for. Leave her alone, all of you, just leave her alone.

I wanted to see Ilona, her cheekbones, to reveal the contradictions in her words, the intrigue behind her eyes. I was in lust and fascination. Her closed disposition frustrated and captured me. My touch held no restraint as we met. I needed to feel the arch of those cheekbones, needed her heat next to me. After her initial shyness, our mouths entwined with the passion of animals, hungrily tearing at each other from room to room. I don't know how we had ended pushed by each other into the unused spare room, on the unused single bed. Suddenly I was breathless under her silhouette in the moonlight, her back long and straight and powerful. The image of her sitting upright, strong arms removing her thick, black leather belt, holding it with flexed muscles while I lay immobilised by her thigh caught my breath. It was but an image, not an intention, and, as we ran from the room laughing, minds know different and that unspoken knowledge sets a dynamic.

Shona held a party. Well, I say a party, it was a small affair, with Shona, Neo, Gem, Ilona and myself. Shona lives in a small, quaint cottage, all low ceilings and wooden beams. I've never met the male behind the transvestite, but Shona is incredibly reserved, softly spoken and civilised. She is an enigma. We follow up her winding stairs to view her contradictory masterpiece. It is a mixture between Meccano, a dentist's chair and an object of torture. A strange but fixating metal contraption. None will sit in it, other than Shona, to demonstrate. I do, I want to, I'm amused, I want to just sit and not move, until Ilona and Shona joke about strapping me in, then I get out.

Back downstairs, Neo is chained to the ceiling and flogged by Gem and Shona. I meander in and out of the kitchen, nibbling and sipping water, at one point Ilona has followed me, pushing me against the worktop, bending my head down, taking my arse, until disturbed by

Gem. I relax on the sofa, while they chatter and bind Neo, as he mutters theories of oxytocin being the chemical cause of love. Apparently when skin is touched it produces oxytocin, that same chemical produced by the female G-spot on the frontal wall of the vagina, which incidentally is hit during childbirth by the baby's head, producing the biggest blast of oxytocin. Ilona constantly suggesting I flog Neo. She is playing with my mind, I am not the person she thinks I am. How many times must I repeat myself? I relent and feebly strike Neo, because then she will be silent.

Day One Hundred and Six

The day is new. Well, no doubt every day is, yet today seems newer; the more it disappears into night, the newer it seems. An era is ending. The journey is nearly over, and frankly de Sade stinks the more he decomposes. I advise against travelling with a corpse unless you possess a strong constitution. The closer to the journey's end, the closer to the deaths of the children in the castle. Sixteen children, eight boys and eight girls. Most victims of de Sade are never killed, at least not literally. If they were, according to some figures, a third of female children would be dead. Instead, we are the living dead. I don't know if I can ever give that undead life back, or what I can do. I am playing by ear, travelling without a map, walking by instinct. I know I have to find the source to the bloody river of pain. I know I have to piece together the whole. I know I have to reconcile, but not *what* I have to reconcile. There is not one feeling, not one pain, not one need, but hundreds, and some conflict with others. Like everything before, the conflicts will slowly have to be transferred to resolutions, this time without causing more conflicts.

I am something of a fraud. I feign strength, even believe it myself, yet I have fear. I have to reconcile that contradiction of strength and fear. I fear the most urgent need. I fear that which I strive, which is probably what mars my success. I fear admitting my fear, admitting my weakness, yet know my strength lies in doing thus. I fear voicing this fear. I fear the dreams of my fear. I fear, as my voice betrays my persona and shrinks to a shameful whisper, de Sade's castle. Yes, I admit it, damn you, I fear rescuing the children before they die. I fear her. I run from her in dreams, dreams I never admit. I fear the damage. I fear entering the castle, seeing the destruction, fear they may already be dead. Fear looking down and seeing her pain, or worse still her corpse because I'm too late, and reflected in it my own guilt and failure. I fear the pleading in her eyes, or the hatred that I never protected her; or, worse, I fear seeing nothing in her eyes, emptiness. I fear being unable to hold her, comfort, take away her pain, fear no matter how tight I hold her, she won't feel it. I fear that more than giving her back her life and in doing so losing mine, I fear rescuing her, then leaving her, fear she won't cope alone. I am terrified of her weakness, the torturous infection that grows within her, the hollowness of a damaged good. I turn away, go nowhere near the pit of festering contamination. I fear my own weakness. I who am so strong, I leave her in pain alone, completely alone. I left her alone. Does that not make me as bad as de Sade? Am I not a colluder? Like the mother, the neighbours, teachers, society, I buried her alive and left her in her isolated, confused, agonising abyss. My detestation of de Sade is a reflection of my own sham, the research a screen of my own weakness. Today is a new day, and I edge closer to the castle, gain strength by finally confronting my weakness.

Strikes

The Sphere was on. Ilona wanted to go. We were in the kitchen. She wanted to see the moves, the handling of the floggers. She took the belt, copying my moves against the bricks, her eyes betraying a pleasure that scared me to the core. Her muscles pumped in arousal as her mind wandered into images only she knows. She asks what dominants say to submissives. I don't know I just carried out some research, only ever used the safe-word drill.

"Your safe words are green, amber and red, use them."

"I like that."

She repeats them with a menace, pins me against the wall, spreading my legs with her foot, her hands rough against my wrists, teeth sinking into my shoulders, her belt marking flesh on my back. I'm a kaleidoscope of emotions. How do I begin to separate and verbalise? It's another perspective to researching de Sade, a perspective I don't need, I know so well. I know as a consenting adult, Cline had no leather, no straps, but her hands busied my wrists far more, her eyes drove fear, her power hurt my soul far more. Is consent valid without feeling safe? I was pinned and hurt, back in Cline space. I felt afraid, hurt, unsafe, vulnerable, wanted, taken, owned, desired, feminine, angry, violated, wanting to give myself, wanting to stop and take control. I am frozen into submission by my own all-feeling confusion.

The Sphere seemed different, unfamiliar strange, the air hazy, the people belonging to another dimension. I shrank by Ilona's side, confused and hurt when she suggested I flog someone. Had she not been with me in my kitchen but an hour ago. Why would I flog anyone? I wanted a dance floor. I wanted to smile softly, to give a little, teasing with my eyes, then look away coyly. Instead I was here. I felt self-conscious, wanted to swim off into the night, or be carried off. Cline wouldn't have brought me here. I stood back while Shona and Ilona covered Gem in wax and ice. My eyes stung with secret jealously, while I passed candles and ice, occasionally dripping it on Gem myself, just because it seemed expected. I felt lonely. Where was my life, my friends? The club was closing, empty but for Gem and the people behind the bar. I swayed teasingly by the horse. Ilona bent me over, her fingers tightly scrunched through my hair, pushing down my back, parting my thighs, this is not the time, this is private. Is nothing sacred? There is a line between teasing and intimacy and my intimacy is precious and personal.

I stepped into the house from the Sphere. I felt I'd missed the night. Ilona pushed me onto the stairs passionately. I raised myself, and pinned her against the wall, looking at her. She was pretty, not as gorgeous as you, but nonetheless womanly; there was a slender vulnerability about her that was appealing; however, I wasn't bothered. While she behaved on my terms, caused no damage, I'd tolerate her presence, while resenting her silently for not being you. Presently she was revealing herself to be far too much like Cline. She frees herself, tries to gain strength over me, her eyes confused that she can't. She thinks it's a game, thinks I'm playing. Oh, this is no game, little one. Slowly I turn to where she wants me. She strikes my shoulder with her belt.

"Does that hurt?"

"No," I reply truthfully.

She strikes harder.

"How about that?"

I don't think she understands, so I explain it.

"No matter how hard you hit me, you will never hurt me."

She wanders upstairs bewildered. Run, rabbit, run. I have a cigarette, a hot drink, sit a while. I suppose I should apologise, not to her, for her, you understand, for me, for now.

Day One Hundred and Seven

I'm at odds, out of sorts, driving sideways down a one-way street. I feel oppressed, repressed, suppressed, depressed, just pressed. Pressed back down. I want balance and holistic positivity, but, there is a hollowness about leaving behind dominance. I owned every city I navigated my way around. I silently sneaked up and powerfully spat my mark. I finally had validation and status for my power. It goes against all my principles of passivity and equality, but I've spent years, mundane years, taking a back seat in the inner-conflict department of my psyche. Years being appropriate and rational, rarely outwardly expressing other than in times of crisis, until the crises became too frequent, too extreme. I lose myself, my demeanour that was labelled in some sexual context as dominant. Fools. I always look thus, talk thus, have always expected respect from males. The flogging was an entertainment, a sport they asked me to take part in, only the prey were males instead of animals. Suited me: I like animals. I really can't see the harm: they were reddened, a good circulatory massage, never damaged, and I had a channel for my wrath, not to mention a performance of my status and an interesting way of toning. I had my expression in the shadows where my persona resides without revenge, without slaughter, genocide. I met needs and kept principles, harming none, beating plenty. There is no substitution, since losing Colette. I dwell in a limbo, overseeing, organising, resolving, but never actually living. Thinking and doing the best for all parts of my psyche. Balance has always seemed the fairest compromise and I will take my slither now and again. I am not a dominatrix. I have no trade, or desire. I am who I am, who I was naturally created as, I can't apologise for how others respond to the indifference in my eyes, the power in my movements. Is it not a good thing for the security of the soul to maintain the exercises of survival, to service the ammunition, to keep the edges sharp and the alarm system alert? Freedom is not part of my person specification. Maybe I am just being selfish. Since tasting it, my purpose was to assist in the murkier depths of de Sade, to shield, and my mission is complete. I should protect needs, not have them, so why do I feel so? Well, soon it will be goodbye, de Sade, and back to the grindstone, to "deal with the real issues", as Claudia would say. Bless.

Stepping back and forth

Ever since that initial meeting in Manchester, Ilona had continued to step back and forth, in a contradiction of intense and closed, passionate and coy. Ilona was a part-time lover and a half-sentence woman, and I was nothing. When it suited her, which was probably every couple of weeks, I'd see her late in the evening and she'd leave early in the morning. Getting to know her was like trying to climb Snowdon in bad ice: she would only ever start a sentence and asking for the other half was asking too much; she would step away, ending whatever we were. She would step away if I even questioned what we were, or asked where I stood. We weren't going out together, weren't lovers, she wasn't a girlfriend, but she would deny, offended, that we were just sex. Her words were, "Let's just get to know one another", which was fine by me, but we never did get to know one another.

I felt her body heat next to mine before I drifted into sleep. She knew my town, my home, my life, my friends, my territory, she was a part of it. It was open for her to get to know, but I knew nothing but half-sentences. It hurt, the confusion, the emotional blackmail of accepting her way or no way. I felt like the last person on her list, under the friends who would see her awake, have a conversation, under her ex-husband, who saw her more than I did, but not because they shared children (that wasn't the issue), but because he saw her to eat, converse, spend quality time with.

The little time we did share I loved. The woman was a walking, breathing oxymoron, a delicious one at that, simple yet cultured, illusive yet striking, a shallow stream flowing into a deep river. Lovemaking maintained her theme of contradiction. It was just the stepping back and forth, her hands would command every nerve under my skin, within my skin, within my soul, fuck me to explosion. Sometimes on my stomach, her wet writhing into my arse, sometimes lying on her, many ways, many times. My whole body becoming a living work of ecstasy. My mind losing all but sensation, the feeling of passing out, but instead of passing out it passes into another realm. A realm of pure nothing, but everything. A realm where all but pleasure and intensity is lost. I want to take her smell, her kisses, every inch of her flesh and soul, I want to take her touch, her taste, I want to take her breath away. I want to trail my claim over her neck, the little dip just there, mould her firm pert breasts into my mind, trace my touch over the tension in her stomach, *and make her hips mine for eternity. Hips are mortal heaven. I could lie all day with my head resting in that space between the hip and thigh. Lie and sink into universal woman. Close as I can get to her womb, her oestrogen, and there is no atmosphere around me when I lie within her hips. I am swimming in universal woman, held by universal woman. This is the essence of woman. Her coyness was endearing, teasing. The teasing was phenomenal, the air lingering with what I want to taste, licking and gently biting those smooth firm hips, onto her defined petite mound, only to be pulled away. The throat swallows empty, the tongue flicks her anticipation into the oxygen. Eventually I reached everywhere I wanted to be, my appetite satisfied, savouring the sexy clear musk of woman and for the first time the red streams of the ovaries themselves, grinning at her embarrassment as I rose from the shower tiles like Dracula herself. It only served to increase my frustration further, for she never completely gave herself. The first time my confidence in my passion has ever been challenged, but she wouldn't let go. She would stop me, terrified of being unable to breathe, or feeling dizzy, the tension in her stomach. Breathe? Who has ever heard of breathing during such intense pleasure? What need is there of breathing when flying away on another dimension? Is this not why orgasm is called "la petite mort"? It hurt that she was even aware of her breathing instead of lost in the sensations. I reassured her she wouldn't actually pass out, wouldn't stop breathing, wouldn't suddenly die, but she wouldn't let go, just would not be and let go.*

Day One Hundred and Eight

I'm not happy. I feel like a wild beast, bound and restrained, seeking a pack I shouldn't be seeking and, to add insult to injury, having to give up my displays of alpha. I am exiled to the desert alone other than de Sade, back whence I came. The journey will continue, yet I will remain in the hot sandy hell for ever, bound in principles to fight de Sade. Imprisoned with his pungent corpse, imprisoned by this insanity caused by de Sade. Imprisoned by a will to escape, freeing all but myself. I accept my fate, albeit grudgingly and not without rebelling wrath spilling onto the pale grains like tears of blood. Why do you pursue my honesty so? Pursue it, until it chases me, confronts me like a bursting box of denial exploding in my face. Yes, the wrath is my pain, my frustration, my isolation. I said it. How strong do I have to prove myself to be, until I can finally relax into myself? How far will you challenge my strength? Until I finally rescue my pain and carry her bleeding and worn out of the pit, and what if she doesn't want to leave its slimy walls, what then?

There was de Sade the first, de Sade the second, the first "lover", de Sade the third, Ellie, de Sade the fourth, Cline, and then Ilona. Ilona was so obviously a return to Cline, who was tolerated for a long time, before I finally carried away my dying soul. No matter what, I will never deny my love for Colette, she is a lost soul, with her own de Sade, not a mistake, a bad decision. There were no alarm bells, no deliberate harm. Colette is a gentle soul. She would nestle her head into my shoulder, her soft dark curls caressing my neck, while through the night I would hold her. My arms around her warm womanly flesh, her smell imprinted in my mind, not around some inner self, not doing a duty for the vulnerables in de Sade's castle, but around Colette, my lover.

Now, I'm here in exile, never to love again, never to hold again, back to the monster of Frankenstein, back on gate duty. In exile, but not without that feeling now awakened ringing in my soul. Soft eyes with smouldering embers I can never look into, care I can never show, a tenderness within me that will never, can never, be known. The more I beat, the more seedy establishments I entered the more my gentle desire is distanced. I can want, but none will want me and, as de Sade removed the choice, so de Sade can create the distance. Ignore my manner with Colette. You've read the evidence. I'm crazy, cruel, arrogant, dark. Ignore the sunshine of Colette. I live in the shadows, reside in the darkness, wear the flesh of cattle. Ignore my soft looks at Colette, if you catch my eyes, you will catch the menace, the wrath. The evidence is there, it must be the truth, your truth, it must be because it's what I want you to believe. Not what I want, but what has to be, and it would be better to believe the worst. Belief is not truth, but I know my truth and am strong enough to carry it alone. Before Colette, I always liked the loneliness of the desert; I will learn to like it again. Learn not to want, not to want what I can't express. Can't or won't? I see my integrity as a force, therefore can't and won't. Is the right thing ever a choice not to take? Before the internal dialogue sets yet more challenges, I do not wish to discuss the subjectivity of "the right thing". The subject is officially closed.

Rejection

Ilona and I had now been off and on whatever we were for about three months. I still didn't know where we stood and this unsettled me. I was unsettled, she was evasive. It was this tension that preceded my visit to her. She was evasive when it came to the arrangements, thus, when I boarded the train, waiting on cold station changes, I felt hassled rather than excited. At the station I waited, in the cold, I waited, for forty minutes I waited before she turned up. She had things to do, things more important than meeting a lover on a cold autumn day. I stared out of the car window at the meaningless world going past. I was unimportant, nothing, unwanted, and that tear strode down my face like a trespasser, not a sob, or a cry, just a solitary statement. She was hateful to me that, acted as if I didn't exist, and the very fact I did was an invasion. Still, as I curled myself away as small as possible when it came to sleep, her passion awoke next to my heat and I don't know what I felt. I wanted to be wanted, but the taste of rejection was fresh in my senses, thus confusion resumed.

The next day she apologised and we breakfasted at Tesco, wandered around shops. Shops with things, pretty things, as you would call them; she likes pretty things too. That afternoon we relaxed in front of the television, softly talking. Even her ex-husband calling six times didn't make the hairs on my neck stand to attention. It was a stupid argument, really pathetic. Mickey Blue Eyes *was on the television. My wariness returned as I sensed a tension, then she seemed to sleep. When she woke she wanted the volume down. I was falling asleep anyway, so told her to turn it off if she wanted to sleep, since I wasn't bothered either way. She stormed to the set, turned it off and muttered something about wanting to watch it, at which I said to leave it on, then, which resulted in more storming. I turned over, said I'd go home the next day. I couldn't cope with the tension after the previous day. Spoke to a woman who started stroking Lightning and learned more about her in ten minutes than I knew of Ilona in four months.*

Day One Hundred and Nine

I'm here, I'm there, nowhere and everywhere, told to slow, yet not knowing where I am, I rarely put everything together and see the extent of my labour. How do I work full time, research de Sade primarily and secondary, then log my findings and tell the story of Colette and beyond. I try to think of today, partly because as always I forgot all but the part of today I was on. I wake, I dream, am I awake when I dream or dreaming when I'm awake? I prepare for work, and prepare again, not knowing I've already prepared. If I think I've prepared for work, have I and what if I don't think I have at all yet have? I give the work I know at the time I've prepared, then sometimes find the other preparation and back track to that too. My house is a tip. I clean up, at points forget I'm cleaning and the cleaner stays wherever. I take out paperwork, a chequebook, a letter, to deal with, then at a later date panic because it isn't where I put it. I live on cookies when there's no food, only to throw out the past use by things later. Yet, I'm so productive, without realising it. I panic wondering the day, and the date, even the year, luckily I can ask the date without arousing strange looks most days. I am a professional, I can give many facts from the top of my head, some of the time, just don't ask me the season, or what the weather was yesterday. I get on a bus and sit. I panic, why am I on the bus? Am I on the right bus? Where am I going? No, that was last year, what is this year? Where should I be? Should I be here at this time? Am I late? Should I be here at all on this day? Is this work time or holiday time? Am I wearing the right clothes? I switch the light on, I switch it off because I don't realise I've switched it on. Have I eaten? I presume I have when I haven't, presume I haven't when I have. Do I know you, or do you just have a familiar face? Why are you asking me this? What have I done with my life? I've done those things? When? How? Why? My mother, "you know such a body?" No I don't know such a body. Why do you even ask me, because the answer is no, always no. My best friend, "you remember that girl at school?" No I don't, though I'm aware I was at school, then we go through a whole class or two, "well what about such a body?" "No", "You must remember?" "No I don't".

It's a life within a life, without a life, it's two lives, three lives, how much can one person fit into a life, it's no lives. I'm trying to fix together my day like a jigsaw. I woke, I know I woke, because I'm assuming I'm awake. I worked straight through without a break, yet also managed to fit in marking thirty mock exam papers within two hours of the exam. I know I did this because they are marked, but, the pragmatics seem impossible, particularly seeing as I planned a parents evening, went to the shops, did the laundry, fed and walked *Lightning*, arranged a meeting, dealt with mail, researched de Sade, cooked, ate, wrote three thousand words, smoked numerous cigarettes, researched and printed out Iraq's reason for invading Kuwait, read and sent emails, spoke to neighbours, read a newspaper. I can't recall any more pieces in the jigsaw, so I assume that is all I've done. I am a researcher, a worker, a writer, and more. I forget and start doing something else. I had five employers at one point. I am all things, I am no things, I am tired. It's all so easy. I'm composed other than when I'm not. I do things right, thorough, so, while I'm doing A, the people don't know about B, C, D, E, F, G, and neither do I – but *they* don't know about them to know that *I* don't.

Label me as you wish. Just remember I am not de Sade, though many would probably rather know, trust, sane de Sade. It is impossible to be such a small child, with such a large man looming, the fear of death and the contamination, pain, night after night, then carry that outside and function. It had to be cut; once the cutting starts, everything gets cut, because it becomes a developed automatic process from infancy, from a critical period of development, so normal, so natural, so always been. Thinking just happens, it's not thought about, so the dialogue isn't questioned, the blanks are explained as long-term-memory effects of the abuse, the rest absent-mindedness, strangers who wave are just downright weird. Being used to not always remembering what people have said, nodding politely becomes ingrained, natural, something everyone does. What else was I supposed to think? Why would I have thought other people experienced life any differently? I cannot step into their heads. I have not developed into their thoughts.

Everyone reflects how "level" I am; why would I think I was any different? It has always been, nothing acute, nothing different than ever was, nothing sudden, nothing to suspect. I worked round the where am I?, the where should I be?, when did I do that for ever?, why would I think it odd? Like a dog shaking away the rain, I was used to feeling odd, missing the days, the years, sitting watching thoughts, or thinking them here. I had no reason to question, or maybe I just didn't dare, until Cline. Now I have half-days of recognition and half-days of oblivion.

The child will play
I'm not sure what Neo came to my house for that day, probably

something mundane such as shopping. He walked through my door and I directed him back out again, along with Lightning.

"Let's go."

"Where?" he asked.

"Anywhere, wherever we end up."

He headed over to his car.

"Not in the car – cars are boring. We want to be on the ground level where we see the people." I was already at the end of the road; Neo was running behind me to catch up.

"The plan is," I continued, "we go to the station and catch the first train that comes."

"Yes, Mistress."

How cute is that: whatever I say we do, I get called Mistress. It's like being rich with free rein of the hired help for the day, and there are no adults but Mary Poppins types and you can do anything, anything at all.

The first train to come in was going to Manchester. Lightning took the window seat and Neo sat opposite. Stations came and went like frames of a film.

"Ever been to Stockport?" I asked.

"Passed through it."

"We'll stop there see what it's like nowadays and if we don't like it hop to somewhere else."

Stockport was a dusty, littered, dump full of fumes from 1970s double-deckers, nothing like how I remembered it. We bought samosas from a rundown takeaway on the high street, not the homemade quality of the Eastern Grill, but filling nonetheless. I just had to get away, get out of this dead town, run from the dust, run from the neglect, run from the people whose souls had deserted them. Next stop Manchester. The conductor called on the way from Stockport, hence Neo and I had to pay two whole pounds for our mini-adventure. I phoned Dawn on arriving in Manchester, since she lived there, but received no answer.

There is something fundamentally empowering about walking

without intention or plan. I owned the ground beneath my feet, the surrounding air, the huge buildings that folded in, the lights from the closed shops, illuminating my step. We stopped at the takeaway in the village for chicken and salad. Just three doors down is a shop, though many could walk this road daily and never know of its existence. This shop is a basement shop, it is beneath pavement level, beneath the life above. It sells chocolate, aspirin, alcohol and tanning, and it sells Ritter Sport. Ritter Sport is that sought-after chocolate hardly sold in the largest places, let alone a little basement. This is why I love Manchester: it is sensually understated. It was after I'd eaten the chicken and stocked up on chocolate that Dawn came walking down the street. The coincidence! Manchester is a big city, but the world, the world is a tiny place. We chatted a while until Dawn went elsewhere to eat, Neo and I parted company with her and continued walking aimlessly, but not lifelessly. Now it was without this sense of direction that we hit the Arndale centre, one pair of highly original jeans at ten pounds, thank you very much, and then on to the Printworks. The Printworks is outside, inside, or is it inside outside? Perhaps it's just an alternative world beneath the same sky. Anyway, we were sitting outside a café inside with a drink and some kind of dessert. I'm reading the paper nonchalantly letting the world wander past; the lit-up stall fascinates Neo across the way.

"Do you think that's a fish stall?" he asks.

Oh, God, the guy is two score and five and he's never experienced a Donkey Derby.

"We'll go on that when I've finished my drink and the paper."

"But what is it?"

"Shush, we'll go when I've finished."

He continues sitting, staring like a little child, fascinated. By the time I'd finished the paper there were some women already on the seats, giggly and excited, dressed for their night out. We took two spare seats. Neo soon figured out how to play and acted like a little excited boy during the races. Of course the women were cheating, using three balls instead of two, so when I could obtain extra balls I did. After five games and a blow-up cowboy later, we wandered back to the station.

We settled into the seats on the train, Lightning and I stretched out one side, Neo opposite. A guy plonked himself on the adjacent table, his eyes glazed from alcohol, his grin childlike.

"That's a nice dog."

He went to stroke Lightning, who immediately crawled further onto me – dogs really don't like the smell of alcohol.

"I'm Lee." He grinned, holding out his hand to Neo and then to me. He looked around him, took a sip of some lager from a pop bottle.

"I haven't got a ticket."

"Yeah, well, shush, then," I utter. Ticket, ticket, who would buy train tickets since they took the barriers off the stations years ago?

"Have you got a cigarette?"

"No," I reply.

"You've some in your pocket there," he insists, pointing to the pale blue Mayfair packet jutting out of my black leather. I take one out and give it to him; immediately he lights up.

"What are you doing? Go to a smoking carriage – you'll draw the conductor's attention."

"Aw, I'll be OK."

Yeah, sure he'd be OK, and so would we if the conductor came by and assumed we were all together in some ticket-dodging mission. Nonetheless, we learned Lee was going to Macclesfield and had nowhere to live. I ended up giving him another couple of cigarettes. Although he looked about thirty he was immensely childlike. He departed at Macclesfield and waved at us through the window.

"Do you think Lee's the One, Mistress?" Neo has this thing about The Matrix.

The train was two miles from the station; we could see the landmarks of home. At the other end of the carriage was the conductor.

"Agents, Mistress."

"I know. We're nearly there, we can make it, the train will get to the

station first."

Closer, and closer he was creeping and so was the station, and when he was halfway down the carriage we stood up to wait at the door, willing the station, willing the train.

"The bridge, we've over the bridge, we've done it" – and a second later the train stopped.

"Oh, God!" Neo held his chest laughing. "That was so close. I kept thinking he was just behind me and would tap me on the shoulder at any minute."

I just smiled and proceeded the walk home with Neo lagging behind giggling.

Day One Hundred and Ten

I'm cold, the day is damp, my hormones are pondering the fate of my womb lining. The menstrual cycle is taught so clinically: on the fourteenth day ovulation will happen; on the twenty-eighth day bleeding will start. In reality a given body will have a cycle that is anything between fourteen and thirty-plus days, depending on age and individual differences. The hormones don't do this neat clinical-stages thing (guess they can't read). Instead, they spend a week preparing. Preparing for the pregnancy that hasn't happened. Hormones must be psychopaths: they do not learn from experience, rather they consider that after ovulation that egg might be fertilised and they rush around the body shouting, "Fertilised egg coming through!" Immediately they call for fluid, fat, fat on the breasts making them swell painfully, fluid in the womb, blood to the thighs and the ultimate defence of that precious egg. Oestrogen and her comrades begin to tease, "Shall we open the gates of the womb and release the power within or not?" "Wouldn't you like to know? Are those cramps the movement of fluid we're building inside or the pain of the removal van? Is that moisture clear or red?" I can almost imagine the hormones within sticking out their tongues, chanting, "Na, na, na-na, na!" as a week's supply of sanitary towels are wasted, then, realising it is a hoax and forgoing the wings, there appear those devilish red spots.

I return from my second cleansing of the day. It never ceases to astound me that some people don't shower or bath at least once daily. Where is the animal in them? It is just so natural to wake and wash away the contamination of the night, and later cleanse away the contamination of the day, the smoke, the hormones. I'm never clean unless under water. I smell my hormones like aromatic measures of stress. Sweet or sour today, ma'am? Upright, thumb-wielding mammals, rejoice and take pride with your generic peers. You might be male, female, black, white, British, French, cockney, rich, poor, educated, but you are not bird, reptile, fish, insect: ultimately you are mammal. An abused individual doesn't need words. I have only to look into the eyes to recognise a sister or brother who resides in this hell.

I'd crawl after the dog as a toddler, seek her protection. The first dog in my childhood was kicked so many times, she would protect me only from fires or traffic, never the real evil. I suppose her only redeeming feature was that she was two and a half stone compared with the father's fourteen stone, and my mother was seven stone. Size is something that adults cannot relate to when looking at abuse. Adults are giants to children. I was a small child, so small that adults and even older children are still giants to me now. I am digressing. The original dog died when I was ten. Upset? I was inconsolable. Now I was totally alone, until a new dog came along. She was from a rescue centre, she was starved to the bone and had been beaten so much in her puppyhood that she cowered and shook all the way home. That first day, try to stroke her and she cowered; say her name, she cowered. However, that night when the abuse began, she tried to bite him. He locked her in the stairs, so she barked and barked and he had to stop. I was saved, only for one night, as she was sent away the next day, but I was saved. The consolation was that my mum took her to the man she moved in with four years later ,so we were reunited, and, when I left at sixteen, I took her with me as soon as I could. We were inseparable until she died in my arms. I was twenty-three, she was sixteen. Together we'd fought abuse, starvation, cold, homelessness, illness, she protected me through it all and never left my side, until I was in the final year of my degree and the falling-down house with a tiny garden I'd promised her for years. She was one of my guardian angels throughout life. Not all of them are canine, not all are human, but my first unconditional protectors were canine.

Confusion

Ilona has returned. At first we lie in each other's arms, sweeter, yet more intense than before.

"You know that thing Neo said about oxytocin?"

"Aha," I reply. Do I want to hear it? Don't I want to hear it?

"Well, I think I feel it now" – her voice trembles – "in the sense of a chemical reaction. At this moment, I love you." I listen to only the last three words, and I love her too at that moment, not perhaps in the enduring way I love my soulmate, but in the universal way of loving a woman, or possibly in the potential beginnings. I tell her I love her; what would be more honest is that I'm in love with her, which to me means I want her and with more time, more knowing her, if I know what I'm loving then I could love her. I avoided the added oxytocin, pushed it from my mind. I don't want a chemical love.

Things haven't changed. Ilona is a closed book. Christmas is approaching, I offer to stay with her for a few days. She doesn't want me to. I'm an add on, like the side salad on the plate; you just don't mix in the same forkful as the main course, because it will ruin it. Christmas is with her children, her friends, her ex, the father of her children. That suits me. I mean, if I stay for a few days before Christmas, we can take the children out for the day, can't we? No, we can't. We argue. I want to get to know her. I cannot get to know her between 10 p.m. and dawn, every couple of weeks. I know how she sleeps, the profile of her back and her neck. I know the curve of her hips. I don't know what she's like to sit and chat with, watch some inane sitcom with, dance with. We've shopped once for half a day if that, been out for a meal once, and that's the extent of our quality time. She thinks I'm jealous of her ex, because he gets the quality time and I don't, he knows her friends, her life. I'm not jealous, just want to be a part of that main course, treated with respect, as a somebody, a date, a fling, a girlfriend, anything but a nothing. I don't expect to be number one on the list, but number five, or six, or seven, just being on the list at all. I don't ask for more time than we have, just quality time. I'm not asking to know everything about her, just to get to know her. A little bit is too much, I'm demanding, asking for marriage, expecting too much, and I only asked for a date. It was over, she stepped back again, right back, she hated me, didn't want to talk again, and she had nothing to end anyway as we were never actually going out together in her words.

Two days later when it was the works Christmas party, theoretically I'd been single for a year and a half, seeing that the last five on-and-off months with Ilona were nothing. The party was the usual boring shenanigans. You know the routine: sit there while people mumble trivialities, laugh at nothing, consider themselves worldly, then head for some really trashy retro bar that nobody but underage drinkers and certain works parties would ever frequent. Now, one of our party was flirting in the most hostile way. She would do the flirty thing with her eyes, then proceed to whisper that I was really straight. Taking may hand, she dragged me to the ladies'. Now I was angry, confused and hurt. I was hurt by Ilona, confused by Ilona, and angry that this woman in my space wasn't Ilona. I kissed her. I mean, I'm not an aggressive person, I can't hit her, I can't shout, so I kissed her. It was an aggressive, get-out-of-my-space kiss, not a wanton kiss, or a sensual kiss. Then she questioned my sexuality again.

"What was it like to kiss a woman?"

I mean, who was this kid? I mean, women have been my sex mates, my life partners, to the exclusion of all other, since, before I was old enough to even consider sex. There was never any life plan of marrying a guy, or living with a guy, even in its innocence the future tracing of life was to grow up and live with a woman. I think I replied, "Eh?" with the one raised eyebrow, and kissed her again because I was even angrier now.

"You're a psycho," she slurred. She was drunk, but to hell with it. I agreed anyway, it seemed the only source of self-amusement at the time. Cue evil smile.

"Yeah, I am."

I told Ilona the woman and I had kissed. I was the Antichrist! How could I cheat? Cheat? Cheat whom? How could I kiss another woman? How could I be unfaithful? How could I go running to someone else after a little tiff?

"Eh?" Could somebody keep me informed of the rules as they change please?

Day One Hundred and Eleven

Franchon returns to the centre of the stage. After having been beaten with a bull's pizzle, the soles of her feet are burned, each thigh, before and behind, is burned also, her forehead too, and each hand as well, and Messieurs extract all her remaining teeth. The Duc's prick is almost continually wedged into her ass throughout this lengthy operation.

Franchon is one of the old crones, soon to die, as the heroes have decided the storytellers can replace the crones for the short lives the children have left. De Sade, what am I going to do with you? Look at your words, look at them, goddamn you, look. Where is this person, where is Franchon, where is her pain? She happened to be beaten, her flesh torched; did she not scream out, then? Did her face not contort? What fear did she feel? Tell them, de Sade, tell them, tell them the truth. Useless old corpse, I will tell. Franchon is a sixty-nine-year-old woman; you might have a mother like her, or maybe a grandmother. She has experienced much pain in her life, poverty that led her to crime. She is dying from breast cancer and in a great deal of pain from infections throughout her body. She may also have bowel cancer, or Crohn's disease, possibly hiatus hernia, or diverticulitis. Franchon drinks to block out the pain. She has no painkillers, she cannot afford a doctor. Alcohol is her morphine, her morphine for the physical pain and her denial of the mental. How did she end up in this castle? Did she have a choice? Did she think she would live, needed the money for herself, maybe for a family long gone? She's desperate, alone, without love, without a life as such. She looks at these children. Did she know their fate? In their eyes, she sees her pain, wonders if they were loved by someone. Written on their bodies is her guilt. As they get flung and fucked by the "heroes" she sees the triggers of her past. She can't save them, she can't save herself, she can't save anybody. It tears at her soul, glimmers of a wasted life, a life other people know, other people live, a life she merely died. Some people are born living; Franchon was born dying, her soul murdered as her body exited the womb.

We have choices, choices, choices, choices. Franchon had no choices. We all have free will, but some have more free will than others. Franchon had the free will to carry on living or not. Technically, sitting by the scorching flames of hell or suicide is a choice – technically. Do you people understand choice yet? Franchon was once a child, a child seared by de Sade.

Abuse is for life, not just for childhood. The child has no choice other than premature and intentional death. De Sade is deaf, he does not hear no. No, no, *no*, NO, shout louder, waste your oxygen, he will not hear. Look at her, de Sade. Look at Franchon, you wrote her, yet you refuse to look at her. Your words echo a clinical object. She is not a clinical object. Look again. This is

Franchon, everybody. She is a sick, elderly woman being tortured. See her tremble, the beads of sweat falling onto her white knuckles, her knees crumbling beneath her as her screams turn into dying gurgles in her throat. Franchon is your mum, she's your gran, she's your daughter in several decades, she's all the white-haired ladies in the hospital beds you pass. What are you going to do? Are you going to brush the tangles out of her hair, wipe the salty sobs from her cheeks, pull up the pillow to support her neck? Will you sit with her a while and listen to her fears? Will you make her smile, give her that slight chance of recovery? Will you respect her dignity, give her the quality of life she needs? Will you kiss her cheek as you leave, promising to return tomorrow, or will you beat her? Will you burn her? Will you tear out her hair and mock her? Will you cruelly rape and abuse her?

Look at her, de Sade, look at her. This is Franchon. Whatever you do to Franchon, however you treat Franchon, you must and cannot deny her humanity. Franchon is a woman, a living, breathing, feeling woman. Harm her and she hurts. Don't deny her pain; never deny her experience, her suffering. I ask you this, de Sade: throughout our journey, you have consistently denied the life, the feeling, the experience, the substance, the humanness of the children, the wives, the elders, the fuckers; do you also deny yourself? Every time you dehumanise another, you mock life and dehumanise yourself. I wouldn't shoot you, de Sade, if you were a body, not a decomposition. I would merely hold the gun to your temple and make you look; I would drain your ears and make you listen. You would see the pain, the damage, feel the experience, you would hear the screams, you would taste the fear, you would touch life.

New Year's Eve
Christmas had passed like little blanks within the mosaic of the year. I thought Ilona had passed, too, but no: two weeks since last hearing from

her she called to say she was thirty minutes away. It was the day before New Year's Eve, one of those days that don't possess names, face, a substance, thus all but the evening is a blank – and much of the evening. I don't even remember her walking through the door, nothing at all, but a flash of my naked flesh standing against the wall, her teeth biting into my skin, the studs of her belt marking red risen stripes. Maybe she looked good, her arms tense in their powerful stance, maybe the light shone just so, maybe. It hurt, my body wincing at the anticipation of every painful lash. My body should reflect my mind; that is what it exists for, to express my mind. When she reaches between my legs, she should be disappointed, I should be dry, my sex babe shrivelled in fear, but the traitor is wet. I am surprised, I am confused, I am not turned on. I am a child back in the prison of the orgasm paradox. How does that happen? Is it an accident that occurs because it is what the abuser wants and will keep on and on and until one day the bleeding sex relents, or did it happen because the child knew something was on an edge, thus when alone tipped the edge? The child doesn't know what it is. It isn't a source of pleasure, because it's associated with pain and fear. At some point there comes a recognition of this weird sensation as an exit door, a closure. Once the abuser has got what the abuser wants, the abuse will stop, at least at that point. This is the most horrific paradox to recover from. It is the ultimate control and violence to the body. There is no arousal, no enjoyment, just a robotic physical reaction, not of pleasure because the situation is not pleasurable, so the feeling is not pleasurable – in fact it merely initiates tears. Imagine the pleasurable sensations you know. Only the first experiences of them were associated with nausea, fear, death. They are not pleasurable.

I don't remember whether we made love that night or not. The next day I suggested we spend New Year together. I was pretty annoyed when she said no, seeing no reason and all. Ilona was spending it with her children and their father and I was no part of that, subject closed, for she runs off if the subject becomes open.

The club is loud, and dark and bright, the skin on my back burning beneath my clothes. The club is packed, people surrounding my painful flesh, pushing me one way, then another. Gem, Shona, Sally, Mona are on the stage, they wave, but I don't have the energy to wade through the sea of people, it feels too far away, they feel too far away, I feel too far away. It is ten minutes to twelve, at some point I make it to them, with but seconds to go. Across the room I see Tree Girl and Charlie. What? Tree girl and Charlie at the other end of the room. Charlie lives in Birmingham, but she's not there, she's here. Thirty seconds, the balloons will fall in a moment, kids I've worked with, over there and another over there, Claudia over there. The world is too small; it is closing in on me, closing in on me. They are all here, the group I researched, then Tree Girl and Charlie, nothing to do with the research yet they sewed themselves into it nonetheless. The balloons pop, and the arms link, and the tongues invade my mouth. De Sade, can I ever escape you? The world is too small, closing, closing in.

I have to keep a grasp. I can feel I'm not here fully. I need to be here, need to hold on, can't understand why I can't reach, can't just hold on, dance, just keep dancing to the music, no, not hypnotically, aware, pay attention, got to keep hold, grab the stone of now.

I hurt, I hurt so much, I don't want to be here, want to be in a corner and cry, and I feel so weak, so very weak, like I'm about to collapse. I wouldn't hurt like this, shouldn't hurt like this. Ilona wouldn't hurt me if she loved me, she wouldn't, just wouldn't, I want her here, yet...

I have to keep a hold, I'm breaking into glimmers, I'm frames on a reel, I'm getting on and off the tube every station and all stations look the same. Claudia is dancing with me, got to hold on, she can't see I'm just a little wisp of myself trying desperately to grab the whole.

My soulmate would never hurt me, my soulmate would never mark my flesh or give me pain, you wouldn't abuse me, would you, where am I? I'm too tired, hurting too much to dance. Feel like my body is about to sink into the ground beneath, just fall, fall away.

I have to fight, keep the presence, feel the beat, I smile nervously at Claudia, she's not looking at me strangely, no she's not, but I can't hold *onto myself. I'm a flicker, a shadow, a dimming light that's neither on nor off.*

Gem says something to me, I only half hear. And where is Claudia? We were dancing. Just keep dancing, over there in that space on the floor, alone, but stay alert, have to keep hold, stop falling. "Heads down, arms up, that's the way…"

I love this one, just wish I didn't hurt so much. I miss Ilona, but, then, I don't want to return to Cline. I don't know what I want, just that I don't want this pain, not the physical or the mental, have to sit down, feel like I'm about to collapse, eyes are heavy, so heavy.

Day One Hundred and Twelve

De Sade leaves me a confused little kaleidoscope of life. Every instance of contradiction and inconsistency has a consequential domino effect. The laughing child cannot be the same child as the child in front of de Sade when de Sade is threatening to kill, but, at the same time, the quiet alert child cannot be the same child when de Sade is jovial and wanting to play. The developing child becomes mulled and twisted, pulled and pushed, moulded this way, then that. Just when one mood of de Sade is dealt with, another is revealed, constantly maintaining unpredictability. The child develops, a prototype, a persona, to deal with each and every eventuality, not to mention the damage within. This is not a moment of confusion, but over a decade in a constant whirlpool, ever changing direction and tempo. A mass of coping strategies and visages develop, and keep developing, and growing and modifying beyond de Sade to new experiences, because the same prototypes have always dealt with these situations. Why would they stop now? My body is an office block with many departments, each with their own regulations and ethos. The problem lies in the question, Who am I and what do I want?

I am depressed, articulate, artistic, idealistic, determined, sensual, emotional, teasing, sexual, feminine. I want a nice house in the country, with a herb garden and a study, time to write, time to relax and a big strong lover, excitement, yet security.

I am angry, powerful, understanding, ethical, strong, rational, detached, cold, alert, resilient, asexual, protective, yet loving. Other than Colette, I want to provide every need, I want the impossible. I want justice. I want to free all the children locked in the castle. I want to fight every form of de Sade to the death. I want ultimate respect among all, and protection of the soul. I can live and fight alone, but, failing that, I want interesting conversation and a sensual woman.

I am romantic, artistic, lazy, relaxed, expressive, masculine. I want a green leather-bound desk, in a country house, or a squat, or even a cardboard box, I don't really mind. I want summer evenings and lashings of inspiration from the elements of life. My mate would be a sensual, sexy, flirty, interesting woman with some mystery or unpredictability about her.

I am playful, young and bored with de Sade. I want to go shopping. OK, OK, I'll play ball, the country house sounds cool, and how about lots of time and places to visit, chocolate, lots of that, and friends, socialise, just a few young women to hang with, flirt a bit with?

I am spiritual, young, sensual, feminine. I want the sun beating on my skin, the stars looking down at me at night, watching the dawn and the summer rain and relaxing with nature and life.

I am professional, logical, intelligent, feminist. I want to research full time, own a horse, settle with someone open, intelligent and sensual.

De Sade wins, for de Sade has created a place with no consensus, just many goldfish in a bowl all swimming in different directions, colliding with each other, calling out for different food. Some of the fish are no problem because they will take their needs within the confines of the others. Some fish are dichotomously opposed in fundamental areas. Sometimes we want too much from life. Colette and I wanted too much and ended up with what we wished for, everything. There is a greed. A greed not to leave any foods untasted, any sensations unfelt, any emotions unexpressed, any experience unknown. It is an irony: the greed is not driven out of the hedonism of de Sade, yet the result is the same. How can a lover be even at times all things? How can she be feminine, masculine, soft, tender, strong, gentle, bossy, sensual, womanly, manly, playful, sullen, secure, exciting, passionate, open, kind, dominant, curvy, solid, and the opposites continue, how can she be all things? Why should she be? How?

Full circle

We are now, and no longer retrospect. The story has caught up with itself. A few events occurred between New Year and now, a fling with a chick called Roxy, she tricked me, said she wanted to stay up and talk all night. Ilona returned, then departed for good. Shona had another party. The weeks were spent slowly putting de Sade to rest. Tying up loose ends and still tying loose ends, some ends boring practical things, some merely parting from de Sade and the research and I'm left with less than I had before, having neglected it all to take this journey with de Sade. There was a time in my life I had everything, a short time, but nonetheless a time. Holding you in my arms, your soft black curls against my neck, you were going to Oxford, I was starting out a career, we would do everything and anything, all things were possible. This was pure. Complete transcendence, clarity, passion, relaxation, peace, focus, love, life. I've tried and tried to think when and where and how it could all go wrong, just spin around so fast. It was the distance, I should have moved. It was the fear, yours, mine, ours. It was our de Sades. It was the stresses affecting us both from outside. As a child with de Sade, you learn that the good windows are rare in the dark castle, so good moments are constantly sought, so much so that, instead of stopping and melting into those moments, we seek more and more in fear of their disappearance. The so fragile ego of the worthless child focuses on one thing that makes her valuable; once she has achieved that thing, she is yet again worthless, thus the striving for achievement cannot stop. It becomes a serotonin hit, without the striving for the achievement the serotonin decreases and we crave more, and nothing else matters but getting more. The brain becomes satisfied to the detriment of all else, including the emotions. So what, if I'm starving, alone, in squalid conditions? I just need that next degree, then the next, then the next, then panic sets in on two levels. The first, I'm an underclass kid, I can't do this, I'm a fake, a fraud, I bluffed my way through this achievement. The second level of panic is what if I reach the end, where is there to go? Damn the system, it stops at professor, but I have to go beyond that, have to keep getting the ego hits. Night becomes day becomes night and there really are twenty-four hours in a day of which to use. We beat de Sade completely. There is no time for de Sade, no headspace left, no time to break down, no time to stop and feel. No time for us: by beating de Sade, he beat us, he lost, we lost, none won.

Day One Hundred and Thirteen

That evening the Bishop, his spirits in a great ferment, wishes to have Aline tormented, his rage against her has reached fever pitch.

Allow me to remind you, Aline is the Bishop's daughter, she is eighteen years old. The Bishop anally raped Aline at the age of ten. She has lived in fear and pain all her life. Other than hating her abuse and her life with the Bishop and the Duc, Aline is no different from any other eighteen-year-old woman. She is beautiful, has delicate childlike features, is petite with an upturned nose, concerned with her appearance, close to her sister and playful. De Sade scribes her as indolent and lazy. Well, she's every eighteen-year-old woman you know, whose preferences lie in chatting and dancing, watching television rather than tidying a room or completing that essay. Eighteen years old and the big bad world is all there to be explored. In the summer, getting a tan in

the park is more important than work. Meeting new exciting
people at parties is more important than sleep. But Aline is not in
the big bad world, she's not at a party, she's not in the park. Aline
is in the castle. The castle can be anywhere, a detached in the
country, a semi in suburbia, a terrace in the city. The castle could
be next door to you, next door but one, a street away, certainly in
your neighbourhood, very close. Aline is one of the eighteen-year-
olds you pass in the street, she is the pretty one, the plain one, the
blonde, the redhead, the brunette, the rich girl, the poor girl, she
is all and any of these.

"She makes her appearance naked."

Maybe while you are watching *Coronation Street* or eating pizza
with the kids.

[H]e has her shit and embuggers her, then without discharging, he
withdraws in a towering fury from that enchanting ass and injects
a rinse of boiling water into it, obliging her to squirt it out at once,
while it is still boiling hot, upon Therese's face.

Allow me to reiterate. Aline, our young eighteen-year-old woman,
who might live next door to you, has just been anally raped. Her
whole body is shaking with fear, she might be crying out, "*No,
stop.*" She might have stopped crying out years ago, stopped
wasting her empty words that give her no power. Tears might roll
down her face, though after so many years in fear, it is more likely
the silent tears roll down what is left of her soul. The water is
boiling hot, that is boiling. I don't think you understand. Pour the
kettle, freshly boiled, over your hand. This is what Aline has had
squirted into her anus – correction: her anus that has just been
raped. Did the water hurt your hand? Did it scar? Does it still hurt?
Now we're getting a slight understanding of a tenth of the pain
Aline is experiencing. Wait, she is in the castle, surrounded by
people, other people. She is being raped, degraded and other

people are witnessing this. She has nowhere to hide her shame. Will you go to the shopping centre and remove your clothes? Multiply the fear of thinking about that by a hundred, because this is happening to Aline and she's not merely naked: she's raped and humiliated. The horror, this is happening to her and she cannot stop it and these people cannot only see it happening, they can see she cannot stop it, what shame.

After that Messieurs hack off all the fingers and toes Aline has left, break both her arms and burn them with red hot pokers.

Hold your hands out in front of you. Go on, humour me. Look at your hands, really look at them. These are your hands, this is your body. Beautiful, isn't it? Now, one by one, imagine somebody twice your strength forcing down your hands and with a knife strong enough to cut through bone, removing each of your fingers. Stop fighting it. Imagine it. Your little finger on your left hand first, it's beautiful, it's cute and it is being forced down and you can see the blade begin to slice and the seeping blood and feel the agony and you are still feeling the agony when you can see the finger over there and the flood of blood coming from the stump. It is not your finger any more, it is over there, you no longer have a little finger, it is not attached to your body. It is not part of you. It is not beautiful or cute any more. Your hand is not beautiful. Your hand is no longer your hand, your hand is now missing a finger and the pain runs down your hand, through your arm, hitting your chest and head. You cannot breathe, your head is pounding and you want the pain to go away and it doesn't, it won't and you are terrified that this pain will never stop. You are trapped in a prison of pain and fear, you are trying to gain control of your breathing. Keep trying because the third finger of the left hand is coming off next. While all this is happening you can see the shadow of your abuser, you can smell his sweat, his breath, hear his breathing mock your pain. Worse still you can smell his sex upon your skin, don't forget the preceding rape, your stump where your finger was is in agony, but so is your chest, your head and your anus. You worry about the bleeding from your hand, and at the same time you don't know whether you are bleeding to death from your anus too. This is de Sade. This is reality. This happens. Not to all eighteen-year-olds. Not always at this degree, but it happens, in every city, a street near you, it happens. Are all you people that revere him as some kind of liberating hero aroused yet?

She is next flogged, beaten, and slapped, then the Bishop, still further aroused, cuts off one of her nipples, and discharges.

To sum up, here we have Aline. Aline is an eighteen-year-old girl, like your daughter, sister, niece, neighbour. Aline now has no teeth, fingers or toes, two broken arms, a scalded anus, no nipple, previously Aline was an abused but healthy, pretty eighteen-year-old. She is not taken to hospital, she is not hugged, she is not given a blanket to ease the shock and her dignity. She has no use of her arms, no fingers, toes, teeth, she's in severe pain, so she is beaten and slapped, just to make sure. Make sure of what? What did you do wrong, Aline? What was your crime? Oh, yes, of course: the Bishop was aroused. The Bishop's arousal is all Aline's fault. It must be her fault: she has been tried, found guilty and held responsible for it. He couldn't simply masturbate or tenderly make love to a woman who mutually loved him. That would simply be too passé. Love, maturation, tried that, that's last year's fashion.

Shrinking world

For weeks Neo had been telling me about some problems his cousin had been having with a man who had bled him dry for over a decade. His cousin met this guy at a church and they began some kind of relationship, which led to this guy's taking advantage of Neo's cousin, through emotional blackmail, intimidation, forgery and fraud. Neo's cousin was petrified and destitute, the total sum was somewhere between twenty and thirty thousand pounds over the decade. Neo, who hadn't seen his cousin for years, had been called in by the family to support his cousin emotionally and practically.

The day was no different from any other. We were in Neo's car and I said, "How's your cousin?"

"He's better since the solicitor's letter was sent to this guy, but, get this for a strange coincidence, where this guy lives, Bennett Street..."

"Bennett Street? You say Bennett Street?"

"Yes, anyway, the thing is—'

"Shit, man, I have a half-brother who lives there."

We're driving around a roundabout and, since we are both facing each other. I am not sure there was any attention to the road. Shock is written over both our faces.

"He's not named Luke?"

"Fuck, man, yeah, it's him." I am total shame. "You mean all this time you've been talking about your cousin going through this shit, it was my brother."

Now, my brother is my half-brother by blood. We were never brought up together, I hardly know him, haven't seen him for over two years. He lived with his paternal grandparents from three, along with my other half-brother. Their grandparents were no relation to me. I rarely saw my brothers as a child; in fact I saw my cousins more. I knew they were my brothers, yet it was but knowledge, my life was that of an only child. I didn't see them at all for about a decade, until I bumped into one of them in town about five years ago.

"Luke is your brother?"

"Yeah, Luke is my half-brother and Konrad's full brother."

"There was a loan taken out in Konrad's name too, at my cousin's address, but I never realised it was the same Konrad."

Now Konrad is my brother, although it is difficult trying to get out *of an only child's mindset. Konrad is all right. Luke on the other hand is creepy. We were on holiday once and there was a long winding path between the caravan site and the village. I was about ten and Luke would have been fourteen; for some reason I was alone with him. The path was isolated, the trees hung over it like curtains. Luke was walking slowly.*

"I could just rape you here," he said.

"Yes, you could," I agreed, running and hoping the end of the path was nigh. He never did rape me, but the point was, very easily he could have and, to say thus, he was thinking of doing so.

The world is too small, way too small. How could Neo, whom I met while researching de Sade only months before, end up with a cousin being damaged by my blood and his wife, also my very disowned and contaminated blood. The world is too small, too small, I say, I want to escape. I want to run away. I want to jump on the first train out of here and keep running, never stop running, but whatever I do, wherever I run to I cannot escape myself, my genetics, my experience.

Day One Hundred and Fourteen

When everyone has retired to bed for the night, the Bishop goes in search of his brother, they wake Desgranges and Duclos and the four of them take Aline down into the cellars; the Bishop embuggers her, the Duc embuggers her, they pronounce her the death sentence, and by means of excessive torments which last until daybreak, they execute it. Upon returning, they exchange words of unqualified praise for these two storytellers and advise their colleagues to undertake no serious projects without their help.

The killings begin. De Sade, you smelly old corpse, wake up. Are you writing about a murder here, or about a business plan? Are you dealing with humans or products? Pray tell, if we all rise up and kill all you de Sades can we turn to the judge and jury and state.

"I did not kill him: I merely undertook a serious project." All crime is subjective, a wrong is wrong only in the minds of those who wrong it. The abuse of several children over decades might be wrong enough for a few months' incarceration. The disposal of that abuser is worth a life sentence, even a death sentence in America. Designing a space shuttle might be a serious project, killing people is no project. We can all do it, it's not a competition, how many people can you kill? As many as stand in front of a firing gun or walk into a sharp knife. It isn't nuclear physics, it isn't big, it isn't clever, and nobody is impressed. We can all kill. We can't all hold someone. We can't say the right things all of the time. We can't all reassure. We can't take away someone's pain. We can't all understand their pain. We can't all face a dying person and show compassion. We can't all calmly stop the blood flow of somebody in an accident. We can't all answer the phone at 3 a.m. to a friend who needs to talk. We can't all deal with suicide. We can't all clean up incontinence with dignity. We can't all listen. Abuse is vandalising a person; children vandalise, but they vandalise *objects*, since even they have the basic sense to know that what hurts them hurts others. How difficult is empathy?

You de Sades run through every stratum, every level of society, you weren't all missing attachment figures and that basic emotional development. It isn't rocket science to figure out that, if pain hurts you, it also hurts others. So you can't relate to or remember being a child as you all have cognitive deficits. Let me make it easy for you. Say an average man is twelve stone and the child is four stone. This makes the man three times the weight of the child. The child is three foot, the man is six foot, so the man is twice the height of the child. Now you Mr Justice, Mr Politician, Mr Teacher, Mr Unemployed, Mr whichever de Sade you are, are under attack by a twelve-foot, thirty-six-stone being with ten times your power. Do you get it yet? Not so impressive now, is it?

When he is wrong, he is right. Whatever he says goes, he has ultimate power, not by doing anything special, not by doing anything difficult, he just does because that is the way it is, OK? His power is a joke now, isn't it? He can sit and do nothing, he still has that power. Not so impressive now, is it, de Sade? Can you use a dictionary? So can the child. Can you do long multiplication? So can the child. Can you read a map? So can the child. Can you understand a metaphor? So can the child. Can you understand that pain hurts? No? Well the child can. Can you understand differences in size? No? Well the child can. Can you understand differences in development? No? Again, the child can. It looks like the child is beating you hands down, de Sade.

Personally I blame your mothers. They should have explained that killing stops the heart, and is in fact irreversible. They should have explained that sexual hormones don't mature until young adulthood, and, until such development, bodies are not designed for sex, after which minds are still not designed for such until a few years later. They should have explained that, naturally, attraction occurs between two adults. They should have explained that no is not just a two-letter word. If you watch child pornography, the child is being abused; if you watch snuff the child is actually being killed. There, that wasn't difficult, was it? Do you remember abusing us, de Sade? Do you remember scaring us? Too bad, you forgot we would grow up. We are not a third your weight, half your height or a tenth your power any more. Be afraid, be very afraid.

Urban terrorist
I'm still looking for de Sade as part of the research. I didn't find him in the sadomasochistic scene, only his name misrepresented under the Trade Descriptions Act. A tip-off was left on the child-abuse message board of AOL. Apparently, the place is full of dubious chatrooms, not hidden away anywhere, available to all by a simple click on all created

rooms. I click, I see the list includes room names such as "Schoolgirls", "D4DS". I enter a room, any room with a suspicious name, and within seconds I receive instant messages offering pornography.

"What kind of pornography?" I ask.

"Any you want, young."

"How young?"

"Teenagers, children."

Got you! I copy, I save, I wait for another, copy that, save it. I send to Scotland Yard, then to the press, whether they will do anything I don't yet know. The rooms are still there, the usernames are still there. I am complete helplessness. I am living, watching, knowing the thousands upon thousands abused at the hands of de Sade. I am complete disempowerment. I am the guilt of a nation who knows yet does nothing. I am every child waiting to be rescued. I am their pain. I am the rescuer who never arrives. I am the colluder who is not stopping de Sade.

I cannot sit and do nothing. AOL closed the child-abuse board down, no doubt because we were uncovering the rooms where child pornography was being exchanged and because we mentioned Operation Ore in our posts too often. We're a core of urban terrorists; some take screenshots of the room lists, pass them on to the police, the FBI. There may never be an investigation but, we are mounting pressure. We are responsible for our own society, we are capable of asking our own questions, we can print our own pages. The press are not responsible for de Sade, the government are not responsible for de Sade. I am, you are, we all are. This urban terrorist means to fight with far more frightening weapons than violence. I will free the children through truth. De Sade relies on covertness, lies, descent, inconsistency. Watch de Sade's castle built upon the sand tumble down. Let the "heroes" fight among each other with fire. We are the generation de Sade thought would die, would lie down and give up, would stay in the corners of darkness and cry. We are alive, we are standing, we are fighting the fire with water. Take our tears, take our words, take our truths. De Sade taught us the skills, now *we are using them to come and collect our justice. What a fool, de Sade. De Sade can track down a victim within minutes. De Sade can infiltrate the victim's surroundings. De Sade can trigger every painful button in the victim's psyche. What has de Sade taught the victims to do? That is right, we can track down abusers in minutes. We can infiltrate their surroundings. We can trigger every painful button of their psyche. If we were so inclined of course.*

Day One Hundred and Fifteen

While Curval is sodomising him, Narcisse loses a pair of fingers.

De Sade, now don't lie. Narcisse did not lose his fingers. Really he didn't. This twelve-year-old boy might be frightened, he might be being raped, but he did not misplace his fingers. Tell the truth: Narcisse's fingers were taken from him. This child was violated. His tiny body has been penetrated with violence and his hand deformed with violence. If you are hard and big enough to harm a defenceless child at least be honest about it. Curval is raping, violating, hurting, injuring, damaging Narcisse.

[T]hen Marie is hailed into court, red-hot irons are thrust into her cunt and asshole, more irons are applied to six places upon her thighs, upon her clitoris, her tongue, upon her one remaining breast, and out come the remainder of her teeth.

Marie is one of the elders. She is fifty-eight years old. She is four years older than my mum, the woman I'd watch clean the hearth as a toddler, her beautiful, long, shining, black hair, her high cheekbones, her soft smile. The woman I would slobber down as she held me to her chest as we listened to *Listen with Mother* together. Do you remember that programme? Maybe you listened to it with your mum. That beautiful woman who met me at the school gates, held my hand across the road, gave me my first taste of lumpfish caviar, counted stairs with me, taught me about Karl Marx by the time I was six – this is my mum. My mum will be the same age as Marie in four years' time. I have aubergines salting in the kitchen – my mum taught me to salt aubergines. Have you ever tasted unsalted aubergine? Bitter as hell. I forgot once. If you have a mum, maybe she is the same age as Marie, maybe she is younger, maybe older.

It doesn't matter, though, does it? It is not happening to you or me or your mum or my mum, it is happening to Marie so it doesn't matter. When you read the words, you didn't close up inside because you could almost feel the pain, did you? Neither did I, much, because, it's not happening, only to Marie. There was a poker waved about at my mum. I don't know what was going on there. I mean we had a coal fire, so there was often a red-hot poker. I'd have nightmares about it, maybe threats were made, but I'd be lying if I said they definitely were, because I can't rightly remember. I remember that my mum was not able to walk for four days after a beating. I remember the damage to her back from a beating, can still see the huge black bruise on her slender back. I remember all her clothes and belongings being thrown into that fire and burned.

We sat and watched, frozen with fear, because we would get beaten if we moved. I wanted to move. I wanted to move over to my mum, because she was crying and I wanted to hold her, hug her while she cried. He laughed. I mean he burned everything she owned, which wasn't much, all her clothes, photographs, everything, then he ran outside, watched the smoke from the chimney and laughed. The odd thing is, even while he is outside laughing, I daren't move, daren't lock him out, daren't run off through the front door, daren't even go to my mum but a few feet away and hug her, absorb her tears.

This is all I have to say to you today. We are on this journey with de Sade, we've travelled one hundred and fifteen days, and I don't know if you have travelled, if you understand yet, but, we are not Marie, so it's OK.

Drawing away

Gem has returned from a holiday. She calls me, it takes me a few minutes to recognise her voice. She asks me what she's missed. I don't know what she's missed. I really don't. I'm not Neo. I came, I watched, I explored, I analysed and now I'm leaving. I'm not going to hold a conference, or make a big statement. I'm just going to steal away as silently as I appeared. I have the rest of de Sade's words to churn and then it's goodbye from me and goodbye from him. I had a life, before de Sade, I had a life, somewhere, not sure where it is or if it is still there, but I had one, somewhere. I'm a tourist. I'm a fraud. I don't get aroused by pain, not mine or others'. Flogging someone is easy to do, but it isn't a particular hobby of mine. I'd rather catch a film, have a conversation, sink into a sofa and lean my head on a lover, massage her feet, while we idle the evening away. That's right, I am Ms Boring Average. I like leather, it looks cool, it smells intoxicating. I like it to wear, not to hit with. I'm not a dominant: I'm a bluffer. Sure, I can hit, anyone can hit. I saw it once on television, I copied it, not out of desire, want or lust. I wanted to get into de Sade's head. I think the outfits are great, as great as anyone dressed up on a Saturday night. I don't like the public sex, I can flog with a real good aim, because I'm blocking out the sex and the smells by focusing. I don't like men's bodies in the flesh, don't really want to see a woman nude unless she is my lover. I can cope with female hormones that aren't my lover's but male sex – I cannot stand the stench. It makes me want to vomit. I am sorry. I am a fraud, I like dancing, Lash is cool, it has a dance floor, no public sex, no nudity, it's like any other club, with added entertainment. I don't like Scarlet, I don't like the Sphere. I never meant to mislead, I'm not a dominant. I accept all things consensual, but I did lie.

My desire lies in a boring, private, relaxed, ordinary, monogamous love. I have no desire for anything different. I find making love within a

loving relationship exciting every time. I'm easy about position, detail.
I'm so ordinary and sad. If a lover wants to be fucked in the missionary
position every night for the rest of my life, I'm fulfilled with that; if we
do other things that's cool too. I'm so much of a fraud, I wouldn't want
any lover of mine flogging somebody in a club, I wouldn't want her
being flogged. I wouldn't want her being touched. Crucify me for it, but
I don't think I would be comfortable with a lover of mine even going to
a fetish club. There, I said it. I am sorry.

You have been wonderful friends, everybody I have met has been a
beautiful person. I am sorry I have been a fraud. Slowly and quietly I am
slipping away from you. I didn't mean any harm and it shouldn't cause
any harm. I am the cub raised in captivity who has been taken into the
woods to decide. I can hear the call of the wild. I'm lying still, looking
and lingering at who I'm saying goodbye to. My heart is with my life,
my real life, my pre-de-Sade life. I'm sorry but this is who the reality is.

Day One Hundred and Sixteen

Durcet, as a woman, marries Invictus, who enacts a masculine role;
and as a man he takes Hyacinthe to be his wife; the ceremonies are
performed that evening and, by way of festivity, Durcet wishes to
torment Fanny, his feminine wife. Consequently, her arms are
burned, so are her thighs in six different places, two teeth are
extracted from her mouth, she is flogged; Hyacinthe, who loves
her and who is her husband thanks to the voluptuous
arrangements hitherto described, Hyacinthe, I say, is obliged to
shit into Fanny's mouth, and she to eat the turd.

Is anybody confused yet? Durcet is one of the "heroes", Invictus a
fucker, Hyacinthe one of the boys, Fanny is one of the girls.
Apparently Fanny is the only female. "Apparently" is the operative
word because men in white coats decide sex at birth and no checks
of chromosomes are routinely made. For the sake of today's
journey, the brutality will be ignored, as will the scat, not because

I've had enough of one and the other makes me vomit, but to concentrate on sex and gender.

De Sade is a hypocrite. He appears to see through the social construct of gender, yet maintains the demonisation of the female. Some interesting boundaries are broken. Is a person ever all a male or a female? Is a person ever all masculine or feminine? I don't think de Sade takes the concept far enough: there are still confines, there are still labels. There are still man, woman, masculine, feminine. There is still that tick-box dichotomous choice, male or female. It's a childlike perception. When I was a child if I played and "married" a male toy child, I was female; if the object of marriage was a female one, I was male, and the toys in the toy box change sex depending on who is living with whom in the cardboard box, which duplicates as a toy house. When little girls kissed me, they'd call me their boyfriend. I've grown up since then. Take away male, take away female, take away masculinity and femininity, remove labels of sexuality. I am a person. I possess different qualities. Society puts labels of masculine and feminine upon my qualities, not I. I don't accept these labels. I would never voice my qualities as masculine or feminine. I don't see the need for labels of male, female or other. Labels exist to direct sexuality.

Let's be honest about sexuality, I mean really honest. Take the labels, male, female, masculine, feminine, homosexual, heterosexual, bisexual, and just throw them in the trashcan. Bodies are bodies. Attraction is to a person, not a sex. Attraction is to a certain look, the warm feeling inside on seeing that particular person, a meeting of minds, the locking of eyes. The sex act is no different for females, males, females and males. Everything that can be done with a woman can be done with a man. We all have sexual needs and nerve endings. If life were just about sex, the act could be done with any. It is physically natural to either at varying times or all at once to want to explore, touch, taste, kiss, penetrate, be penetrated – and the list goes on. Society determines confines.

We fall in love with one label more than another because one it is easier. Society wants a decision. Do you want to be with men or do you want to be with women? "I do not recognise those labels" is not the answer society wants.

The second factor is attachment. If we go with the theory that there is indeed a critical period for attachment, it then follows there is a critical period where the child needs to attach to the social construction of both sexes either within two people or one person. I am naturally emotional and monogamous within sex. I have no deep emotions for XY males. There is a little mental block in my head that simply feels nothing deep, no capacity for attachment.

The third factor is experience, if an early traumatic sexual experience is associated with one label, then people with similar bodies, body smells will trigger the trauma, regardless of adult attraction. These are some of the factors that limit sexuality not sex per say. Bring the whole spectrum of sex into the picture and see how useless a label of sex and sexuality is. Intersex are often classed as disorders: Klinefelter's disorder, androgen insensitivity disorder and so forth. No sex is not a disorder. There still are no two sexes, only the labels male and female. Do you really know your chromosomal and hormonal pattern? Are you sure you are XX or XY? Not XXX, XXY, XYY? Sexuality is a useless label, chosen on the basis of looks. Would you have a sexual relationship with an intersex, a transex? Would you know if you were? We all have fantasies, meeting a gorgeous person and living happily ever after, or maybe just having mind-blowing sex. Be honest, because no one else can read your thoughts. Are you always your given sex in your fantasies? More to the point are your fantasies always sexed? Have you never fantasised about an intersex, as well as women, or men? Have you never been intersex, or asexual, just no label, no sex whatsoever?

Which label to put on?

I'm going for a shower while I leave you with those thoughts. Though I have a dilemma. The sun is shining, the day is warm. I might require minimal clothing. Do I remove the hair on my legs or leave it? What about the hair on my chest? Or that line of thick dark hair from my navel to my pubic Mohican? A man wouldn't have this problem: he could go out with all his hair and proudly show it off. I could leave it and grow my goatee and move my research over to gender, infiltrate transgender, or even intersex if I could really pull off infiltration. Later apologise for being a fraud, though I'd be a fraud only some of the time, depending on whether I wake with a female head, or a male head or a none head. Today my head is objecting to all the labels. Why can't I wear a dress with thick dark hair, or a suit with smooth skin and lipstick? Today I am not male, female, masculine or feminine. Today I have no concern with sex, I simply don't like men. I am the head that before Colette didn't do love or relationships.

Day One Hundred and Seventeen

I have to end this journey. Have to run the remaining four miles, I can't stop, can't eat, can't think of anything else, but my life I left behind, and what might be left of it ahead of me. I have to finish it and I have to finish it now, it is a compulsion, a drive I cannot, will not control, even if I have to take days from work I have to continue and complete this tale. I could kill de Sade. De Sade is already dead, and to kill his modern counterparts, oh trust me, I lust for it, but to do so would make me the same ilk as de Sade. I never want to become de Sade. I could wait until love comes along and walk away happily into the sunset. I will break this to you in no gentle terms. There are no happy endings. Colette and I could both die tomorrow. We will never be together again, even our contact will eventually peter out to a distant memory. We may have a series of flings, we may find life partners, we may die alone, we may even die in an asylum. There is no conclusion. There are no answers. I don't know why de Sade is. I don't know why people are abused. I don't know how to stop it. I don't know how to stop the effects. I don't know why a certain egg meets a certain sperm and produces a chain reaction. I don't even know if life exists or not. I don't know why you are even asking.

Colette and I both knew ignorance is bliss, yet, although I envied it, I never wish for it, for I know only too well that what you wish for you may get. That's right: when the journey ends, the road still looks the same. There is a little sign that says "Debris here" where de Sade stops walking, but you know the story, you know the plot, you take that walk, "The Pennine Way", "The Staffordshire Way", there is a little sign that signals the end, but it never ends, not really, the path doesn't suddenly change. The ground under your feet, the view ahead doesn't just transform. There are no conclusions, no limits. There is never an end, an end is merely a beginning. Don't ask me the questions. I don't know the answers. I will not write your ending. I will not even acknowledge an ending that doesn't exist. I know how to cry. I know how to hate. I know how to love. I know how to walk into a room and command a presence, but only if I want to. I know how to hold someone. I know how to flog. I know I can do anything I want to do, and nothing I don't want to do. I can walk about scruffy, I can walk around smart, I can walk about naked. I can own my space and know whether I can take some of yours or invite you into mine. I have a confidence, or maybe it's indifference, or maybe it was an indifference. I can pin a woman against a wall, or love her tenderly. I can be fucked like a strong bitch or sweetly submissive. I can fuck hard and deep, intense, yet loving, like a woman, like a man, like neither. I can lose myself in your body, thrusting, scrunching your hair like an animal, or slowly and tenderly. I can respond to your mood, my mood, our mood, blending my soul with another, blending my soul with the whole "collective conscience" without fear.

There is no conclusion, there are no answers, yet there is no mystery. I can feel wary, anxious, yet I am not afraid of de Sade. I am not afraid of anyone and day by day I am becoming less afraid of myself. I am and life is both my dream and my nightmare. De Sade is the bogeyman who exists. Am I de Sade's bogeyman? I am the crazy bitch, who no longer fears him around every corner, but went out to look for him around every corner. I didn't pull the duvet over my head: I rose from my bed and challenged him. I am in your face without any loud hair or statement clothes. I am in de Sade's face and I don't apologise. Go and find your own answers – I am not your entertainment.

No time to breathe

I have the Sunday papers, but I haven't read them. I can't recall when I last did, not properly, not cover to cover. Now I've bought them, they are part of my life, my desires, yet I haven't even looked at the headlines. I buy them, because I refuse to give up my life, give up my pleasures, yet I can't stop this journey, not now. I eat at the computer. I smoke at the computer. For one hundred and twenty-one days I have lived in this metre square, but, for the observational research. I have no idea whether I have retained my sanity. I have not stopped to read my words and look back on the miles covered with de Sade. I can't remember everywhere we have visited and I don't know where I am going. I think anyone who knows where they are going is living a life within limits. I am bound only by my own ethics. Imprisoned only by principles, beyond which I am free. Freer than the keys to the city. I own every city I visit, every step I walk, I see no ownership of land. Torture me, beat me, incarcerate me for it, but I will move as freely as I please throughout this earth. I would tear up passports in front of your faces, laugh at the monarch. I will not bow to your socially constructed hierarchy. No one person, no one race has claim over another. We are not superior, none of us. De Sade is not superior.

What have we done? We can never recover that innocence. Never retrieve the awkward coyness. Never reverse the clock. I don't want to be here. I want to be there. This place, this time, two years ago. Before I knew de Sade, when we had spoken, but not yet met. When I thought "Mistress" was the title for any single woman, and "flog" another word for "sell". You haven't done it, I've done it, all alone, without plan or reason. You talked, you informed, you educated, then you carried on as normal. I listened, I learned, then I went away and tore everything apart. I had to. I had to demystify it all, had to understand, had to demystify you, us. I couldn't just leave it, couldn't just honour our memory. All those firsts we never did, couldn't just leave them precious to us, buried with our love as you did. What have I done? Mocked the child within, mocked it all, and worse than anything mocked us. I don't even know the reason. We ended and there was just de Sade left, and he became a momentum. I just couldn't stop the momentum until the end, until I had destroyed everything. I didn't mean to destroy it. I didn't intend to. I didn't know what I was doing. I don't stop and think. I become a cog in a machine and just keep spinning. I enter a dimension and live it to the end. You opened a door, we were walking together, then you left me, I couldn't stop walking, I didn't know what else to do. You were there, in my castle, then you were gone. I looked for you, looked for you all over, looked in the door you opened. I was trying to find you, not destroy you, not destroy us, not mock us.

Day One Hundred and Eighteen

Then comes Zelmire, whose death is not far off; deep into her cunt runs a red hot poker, six wounds are inflicted upon her breasts, a dozen upon her thighs, needles are driven far into her navel, each friend bestows twenty strong blows upon her face. They forcibly remove four of her teeth, her eye is pricked, she is whipped, she is embuggered. While in the act of sodomizing her, Curval, her husband, gives her intelligence of her death, scheduled for the morrow; she declares she is not sorry to learn the tidings, for 'twill put a period to her sorrows.

Stop, stop, stop. It is not funny any more. What is wrong with you people? When you are next to another person, when you touch her, she is there, not a cell away from you. She is not a comic-book character a million miles away. When you look into her eyes, your minds are not a thought apart. When you hurt her, you feel her pain in your nervous system. Why don't you? Her body is beautiful. Why do you want to destroy it? I don't understand your lust. I don't understand your arousal at pain. Other than the odd, say, bite or scratch in a moment of animal passion, I don't understand your desire to injure, bruise, mark, damage, break, burn, bleed. Being hit, it hurts, it fucking hurts. It is not sexy. You like inflicting pain? Here, take this knife, inflict it upon yourself. There is a bus, jump under it, break your own bones. What the fuck is wrong with you people? Yes, you disgust me. I disgust me, because I could just take a gun and take every one of you out tomorrow. I disgust me, because I cannot accept you. I simply don't want to be a part of this society any more, never did. I want the impossible, I want a "get out of society free" card. I want to opt out, you suffocate me, you contaminate me. I can count on one hand those among you I like, I really like. I am sorry, I do not like you, that disgusts me, but it is the truth. If we had a world crisis, after the children, there are very few of you I would save. In fact I would watch you drop to your fate, knowing I might be able to reach you. I would be excited. Excited at the prospect we could start the whole thing over without you. Yet, in feeling this, I am just like you, so I fight it, I accept, I lie to myself. I don't know my head from my tail, my reality, my beliefs are clouded somewhere in my ideology. I'm a human, an imperfect one, a flawed one. I don't want to be a god. I don't want to make choices. Even so, I could so opt out, go away, far away, and live with none but myself, see none but myself.

Curval goes in search of the Duc that night when all is still and, accompanied by Desgranges and Duclos, those two champions take Zelmire down to the cellars where the most refined tortures are put to use upon her: they are all much more painful, more severe than employed upon Augustine, and the two men are still hard at work by the time breakfast arrives the following morning. That enchanting girl dies at the age of fifteen and two months. 'Twas she who could boast the most beautiful ass in the harem of little girls. And thus deprived of a wife, the President weds Hebe the next day.

No, no, no! Torture is never refined! You do not kill a fifteen-year-old girl and then say, "Oh well, she had the cutest arse out of them all." The little girls are not a harem: they are individuals. There is Augustine, bright and intelligent; Fanny, quiet and gentle; Sophie, beautiful; Colombe, bouncy; Hebe, a cheeky twelve-year-old; Rosette innocent; Michette playful; and Zelmire, sensitive. Zelmire, sweet, sensitive Zelmire, whom you have just killed, you bastards. Not Zelmire with the cute bum. Zelmire the sensitive fifteen-year-old girl, who probably liked to listen to music, read a novel, getting lost in the story, dream of her future, the future she no longer has. I have failed. I have failed.

The children are being slaughtered in the castle and I have not rescued them, not figured out a way to stop their deaths. I am eternal helplessness. What use is my life, if the years pass by, and within the castle souls are murdered and I can't save them, even one life. I sit here analysing de Sade. I spent a summer dancing away, flogging away, looking for de Sade, and all the time, every second or so, another Zelmire dies. Another sensitive soul is murdered. I am the world's guilt. Why am I here? I should be there, standing in front of the child, protecting those children. In every home where children are having souls murdered, in every park, every school, I should be stopping it. I am the sum of uselessness. I am complete stupidity, and what when those children grow up against their dead souls? What do I say? I am sorry, I didn't know how? I didn't know what to do? What do I answer when they ask, "You knew de Sade, you faced de Sade, you went through this, your soul was murdered, how could you not know, why did you not know?" Because I am useless, because although de Sade is not a bigger force than I, there is more of him, because I am one person, I can't split my body into every home, every street, every school, every courtroom. But I am not even in one place, am I, not even in front of one child, not protecting one? If I protect one child every hour, there are twenty-four hours in a day, three hundred and sixty-five days in a year, and I am sure I can survive ten years without sleep, I could save eighty-seven thousand six hundred souls. Why don't I? Why don't I stop this, end this journey and start now? Because I am a useless excuse for a life and I don't know how. I am sorry, I am not going to fall to my knees because I don't deserve your forgiveness.

The still night

What? You expect something to be happening? The story is now, the serpent has eaten her head. I have no tale, no offerings for you. Just tonight, this, still, clear cold night, myself in my oneness. I'd say you are welcome to join me, but I'd be lying. You have had my blood, my sweat, my tears, my soul, now you want my thoughts as they create? You want my longings, my conflicts? You want to feel the pain in my head? The stench of my hormones as I run towards the finishing post? You want to feel the speed of my heartbeat, the shallowness of my breath, share my cortisol and adrenalin? Take it, take it, it's killing me anyway. I sigh and turn from you a second, run a hand against my head to check my temperature isn't increasing to boiling point.

I've no idea what my plans are, it is too soon to make any. For the foreseeable future, aloneness, it is the most honest choice. Not that I tend to make choices, just do. I'm going to miss Neo, just a bit, mind.

He's a funny, sincere, safe, confidant and friend. Perhaps "miss" is the wrong word, but I will think of him now and again, wonder how he is and forget I can no longer spill out my thoughts to him. I have another "Matrix coat" that Ilona gave me. It is bigger than mine and not as soft. I will give Neo the spare "Matrix coat". I couldn't give it to him before, couldn't possibly have him by my side in a coat the same as mine. There is after all room for only one black-leather, dark-haired, shaded presence. I won't be returning, not because I don't want to or I can't, just because I simply don't. I enter a space, fill it, know it, and if I leave I never return. It's like never returning to lovers left, I suppose.

Day One Hundred and Nineteen

The journey is nearly over. You may laugh at de Sade, his stinky decomposed sinews, but remember: there are no winners. De Sade may be dead, but I smell of putrid festering too. I died a long time ago. We are quickly approaching the day when almost all will die in the castle, but the truth is they died the moment de Sade imprisoned them. We have generation upon generation of walking dead. How can we fear death when we are already dead? I am a mind and a body without a soul. That's not strictly true: I carry around my soul in the tiny coffin, willing her, just willing her to be alive. Alas, she is not. I spent years thinking she had fled my body, searched for her, until I had to accept she was deep within me, dead. All I can do is sit and smile weakly as I turn to de Sade and say, "You killed her, you murdered my soul."

The bastard just smiles weakly back. "I know," he says.

Well, that's OK, then, we have ascertained responsibility, that makes it all all right, doesn't it? Oh, for God's sake, what do you want me to do? For years I was going to go after them and kill them, but what would that have solved? So I would have become the abuser of my abusers, and be incarcerated for becoming de Sade, the thing I most detest. I will not stoop to him, and do you think, if I do, it will lessen my pain? Will it help the children in the castle? Lessen their pain? When I read headlines, "Battered wife jailed for killing husband", I feel nothing, I tell you, just emptiness, anger at her incarceration, but no pleasure at her act, no justice, no lessening of pain.

There is so much I haven't told, so much you don't understand, so many complexities, another one hundred and twenty-one days, more, maybe a lifetime, but it ends here. Whatever is not included in this tale will remain lost fragments in your understanding.

Tomorrow, Neo will come for our weekly yoga – "bendy stretchy", as he calls it. Tomorrow, this journey may well be finished. Tomorrow may be goodbye. This little cub can smell the call of the wild. I'd like to surmise I will sleep for a week, watch trashy television, catch up with the fashions in the shops, do nothing in particular – but I doubt it. I have eight hours a day that Colette was to fill. Eight hours when I once slept, relaxed, read, sat. What did I do? Waste it? I don't remember. Two years is a long time, and, after Colette, de Sade replaced her. What irony! I vaguely recall shopping. I don't mean rushing out for food, and rushing back to return to de Sade, but really shopping, just idling round the supermarket, just in case. When I'm not looking they sneak something new onto those shelves, something that has not before graced my taste buds. I mean, this used to be fun. Spending half an hour in the corner shop listening to the local trivia used to be fun. Sitting on the grassy embankment just *being* used to be fun. I'm afraid, afraid I have lost something fundamental within myself. Not an innocence, but a simple purity a basic appreciation, the substance of being.

I will find it again, surely it can't be irreversible, all this was an accident, I can't have lost myself in the process. If I let go I will find myself again, I am sure, just have to trust, trust and let go.

Changing
My back hurts, my head hurts, I feel as though I'd sat in this position

for one hundred and nineteen days nonstop. I get lost in the momentum and forget the aim. The aim was to get over you, work through us, and what happened? At least that's what I think the aim was. Oddly enough it's lonelier than ever without you now. Lonely yet at the same time I know you couldn't, we couldn't, fill that gap any more. I don't even know if our minds would meet any more. You left me somewhere over there and I just started walking in a different direction. I miss you, but I miss you as the space I was when you met me and I miss that space. I have changed, I have moved from over there to the end of this journey with de Sade. Do not misinterpret me, I, myself, me, I have changed, not I am another part of my spectrum, not I am a part of me I never knew existed, I, me, I can't speak for other angles to me, but I have changed. Oh, I am the woman who fell in love with you, still loves you, whom you fell in love with, I am that woman, but I have changed. My love for you hasn't changed, but my experience of the world, my understanding, my perspective has grown. It hasn't just grown, it has leaped out of all dimension; in fact I'm running myself to keep up with it. I now have stretch marks on my mind to match those on my arm from the growth spurt at twelve.

Day One Hundred and Twenty

The torturing was arranged for the orgy hour; as the friends sat at dessert, word was brought to them that everything was in readiness, they descended and found the cellars agreeably festooned and very properly furnished. Constance lay upon a kind of mausoleum, the four children decorated its corners. As their asses were still in excellent condition, Messieurs were able to take considerable pleasure in molesting them; then at last the heavier work was begun: while embuggering Giton, Curval himself opened Constance's belly and tore out the fruit, already well ripened and clearly of masculine sex; then the society continued, inflicting tortures upon those five victims. Their sufferings were long, cruel, and various.

Do you understand? Do you understand what has happened here? Do you understand? Constance has been tormented by her father, her uncle for months. She knew her fate of death long ago, not just her fate, but the fate of her child. Constance is not merely killed. She has had a man lunge his hands inside her body and rip out a healthy, now dead, foetus. This is man, taking control of woman, hegemony at its most afraid. This is the crux of misogyny. De Sade is afraid of woman's ability to dictate life, so damn afraid he has to destroy it. Destroy essence of woman. Constance has beautiful, dark, Roman features, bastards. Come near Colette, in fact any woman I know, and I will kill you. The cowards have ripped out her baby. They have stolen her young. They have undermined her whole strength as a female. Who is female if she does not turn on any who threaten her pack? They have destroyed her soul, undermined her alpha. It shouldn't be us and you, de Sade, but you made it so. You created me so. Your males are welcome as long as they live by our rules, de Sade. Your misogyny didn't make me hate you all. It did create a superiority that I simply cannot shake off my skin, though, de Sade. Your abuse coated me with an arrogance. Yes, I put females ahead of you. Your males can live alongside us in our society, but touch one, just dare touch us or our young, and I see or hear about it, and you will feel my wrath, de Sade.

You think it is funny to mess with our oestrogen, do you? Do you find it amusing to destroy the life universal woman creates? Do you think it is impressive to write about ripping our young from our flesh, to teach males to do this? Whatever you were afraid of, whatever you were jealous of, you need to be more afraid of the consequences of your fear. Most of your little males trust us, de Sade. You ripped the young from us, you beat our mothers, you murdered our souls. Stop this war now. If we can't get you de Sade, any male will do. Do you really want to turn this into a hormone sex war? You live in our society. These are the rules. You do not hurt our females. You do not touch our young. You do not mess with our bodies. You do not mock our power. You do not mock life. You do not murder our souls. You do not piss with us, ever. If you hurt one of us, we will take two of you. One hundred and twenty days later and you confirm my wrath. Now you rip our young from our bodies, and sit on a bookshelf so teenage boys can grow up and do the same. Either surrender and teach your males respect or recognise your impotence. Some of us are logical and politically correct, I am simply angry and brutally honest.

What are you trying to prove by ripping a foetus from Constance's womb – not unaided I might add, but with the help of the storytellers and Constance totally restrained? How tough is that, four people onto one pregnant woman who is completely tied down? It's like, when you rape people, you choose a smaller woman, restrain her from behind first, use a weapon. That's a really fair fight, that is. Almost as fair as the children half your height, a third your weight, whom you abuse. Well-matched, strong man, a real display of your power. You expect us to grow up and take you seriously? We were tiny when you abused us, we know how weak you are. Look at you run from me now, half of you won't hold my gaze. As for the rest, I only have to glare or show my teeth and you start quivering like babies.

In principle I think all are equal, but this is not my principle, this is not my ethics, this is my truth from deep within and, yes, it goes against all I fight for, all my principles, and, yes, it disgusts me. I possess this conflict, but so do you, de Sade, but you don't voice yours so honestly, you simply act on it. I will never hurt you; I will never tear out your young; for as long as I carry this conflict, I will be aware of it, so I never act upon it. Just don't declare war, de Sade, don't declare war.

Mask of sanity?

I admit it, I am still awake, but only because my fingers are typing on their own. It is only half past midnight. If I stop soon I can still acquire six hours' sleep. The night air is cold, frosty still, compared with the warmth of the day. The seasons are fast approaching spring, that deliciously schizophrenic phase. I feel naked, as though I've removed everything, admitted to all I detest, exposed my wrath, with little left. Maybe I am but a mask of sanity, beneath which a dark truth hides, though I voice the truth, though sometimes there are many truths. I can speak my truth. The truth for the anger within, the failed defender. I can't speak for my pain. I can't speak for my emotions. Herein the insanity lies. Now to bed, for tomorrow we will wake again.

There is no food in. I've foraged. A bit of chocolate, which has now been eaten, stick of garlic bread, a pack of rye bread so out of date it needs throwing. The fridge was defrosted at some point and fresh soya milk left out in the heat, not even thrown away afterwards. There are priorities beyond de Sade. It took me a long time to put this stone of weight on. It was no easy task. It's neglect, which I'm sure is illegal. I could present myself at a police station, accuse myself of neglect, but none would listen. I am mute. De Sade, he gets one hundred and twenty days of attention and he's dead. All the time, throughout my life, I'm mute. Somebody thought it would be clever to put sticky tape over my mouth at birth. I wanted to play, not sit there like some slab of stone while some de Sade droned on and mauled my dead body beneath. Did he ask my permission? No, nobody asked me. I'm really gonna choose getting mauled, sitting still, working, then spending every spare second writing. Hey, I loved the experience so much, I wanted to be taken back there. I missed one hundred and twenty-one days of my life. I couldn't move from my little den to a place unsafe. Instead, time just disappears before me.

When de Sade is dead, I have to get all that time back, and appreciate every last second, make it worthwhile, recognise how special it is, because, if he comes back tomorrow, he'll take it all away again, time and life.

Day One Hundred and Twenty-One

Upon the 1st Day of March, remarking that the snow have not yet melted, Messieurs decide to dispatch the rest of the subjects one by one. Messieurs devise new arrangements whereby to keep their bedchambers staffed, and agree to give a green ribbon to everyone whom they propose to take back with them to France; the green favor is bestowed, however, upon condition the recipient is willing to lend a hand with the destruction of the other victims. Nothing is said to the six women in the kitchen; Messieurs decide to do away with the three scullery maids, who are well worth toying over, but to spare the cooks, because of their considerable talents. And so a list is drawn up; 'tis found to date, the following creatures had already been sacrificed:

Wives: Aline, Adelaide, and Constance...3
Sultanas: Augustine, Michette, Rosette and Zelmire...4
Bardashes: Giton and Narcisse...2
Fuckers: one subaltern...1
Total...10

The new ménages are arranged:
The Duc takes unto himself, or under his protection:
Hercule, Duclos, one cook...4
Curval takes: Bum-Cleaver, Champville, one cook...4
Durcet takes: Invictus, Martaine, one cook...4
And the Bishop: Antinous, Desgranges, Julie...4
Total...16

Messieurs decide that, upon a given signal, and with the aid of the four fuckers and the four storytellers, but not the cooks whom they do not wish to employ for these purposes, they will seize all the others, making use of the most treacherous possible means and when their victims least expect it; they will lay hands upon all the others, I say, save for the three scullions, who will not be seized until later on; it is further decided that the upstairs chambers will be converted into four prisons, that the three subaltern fuckers, manacled, will be lodged in the strongest of these prisons; Fanny, Colombe, Sophie, and Hebe in the second; Celadon, Zelamir, Cupidon, Zephyr, Adonis, and Hyacinthe in the third; and the four elders in the fourth; that one subject will be dispatched every day; and that when the hour arrives to arrest the three scullions, they will be locked into whichever of the prisons happens to be empty.

These agreements once reached, Messieurs appoint each storyteller the warden of one prison. And whenever they please, Messieurs will amuse themselves with these victims, either in their prison or in one of the larger rooms, or in the Lordships' bedchambers, depending upon Messieurs' individual preference. And so, as we have just indicated, one subject is dispatched daily, in the following order:

On the 1st of March: Franchon.

On the 2nd: Louison.

On the 3rd: Therese.

On the 4th: Marie.

On the 5th: Fanny.

On the 6th and the 7th: Sophie and Celadon together, for they are lovers, and they perish nailed one to the other, as we have hitherto explained.

On the 8th: one subaltern fucker.

On the 9th: Hebe

On the 10th: another subaltern fucker.

On the 11th: Colombe.

On the 12th: the last of the subaltern fuckers.

On the 13th: Zelamir.

On the 14th: Cupidon.

On the 15th: Zephyr.
On the 16th: Adonis.
On the 17th: Hyacinthe.

On the morning of the 18th, Messieurs and their cohorts seize the three scullions, lock them in the prison formerly occupied by the elders, and dispatch one upon that day,
A second upon the 19th.
And the last upon the 20th.
Total…20

Four men and thirty dead. If de Sade makes up only 1 per cent of the population, but each de Sade murders ten souls, that is five million, nine thousand people in the United Kingdom alone potentially murdered by de Sade. Ten per cent of our population. They don't have the question on the census, "Was your soul murdered by de Sade?" so the research is rendered invalid, one in three, small sample, not representative, one in seven, small sample not representative. It's not a problem, it is irrelevant, other than to the few thousand who have participated in those various unrepresentative small samples. It can't be asked on a national census – ethics and sensitivity, you see, and I agree: how can I disagree with my own ethical standards? – but is there also the small factor that they are just too afraid to ask? Will no one stand up to de Sade? De Sade is your colleague, s/he is your neighbour, your hunting partner, your darts team, your best friend. De Sade is not the lonely old man in the corner whom everyone ignores. Are you afraid to ask, "Was your soul murdered by de Sade?" "Are you de Sade?" Whom do you fear more, de Sade or the souls murdered by him? We might be contagious if you stand next to us, de Sade might kill you too; if you stigmatise us, alienate us, help de Sade, your life will be pardoned, just like those who helped him to kill. Don't panic: if you can cook, you are saved, he didn't kill the

Jacqueline Phillips

cooks, he lies, I can cook.

The following recapitulation lists the inhabitants of the Chateau of Silling during that memorable winter:

Masters...4
Elders...4
Kitchen staff...6
Storytellers...4
Fuckers...8
Little boys...8
Wives...4
Little girls...8
Total...46

Whereof thirty were immolated and sixteen returned to Paris.

Final Assessment
Massacred prior to the 1st of March,
In the course of orgies...10
Massacred after the 1st of March...20
Survived and came back...16
Total...46

With regard to the tortures and deaths of the last twenty subjects, and life such as it was in the household until the day of departure, you will give details at your leisure and where you see fit, you will say, first of all, that thirteen of the sixteen survivors (three of whom were cooks) took all their meals together; sprinkle in whatever tortures you like.

Letting go

This is our last day with de Sade. You will read this tale, then toss the book aside, remember it for a while, then forget the strange tale with the crazy protagonists. Life will go on. This life less ordinary. Colette and I will read about each other in some column lost among a sea of black and white. We will pass you in the street, and you will look. You will see her dark curls against her strong Roman features and you will wonder. You might be reading these words on the tube and if you turn quickly enough see the curve form on the lips of the petite, illusive, leather-coated woman behind you. She will continue to look out of her tidy high-rise apartment, over the city, in the exact spot I looked out with her. I will continue to remember the view. You may be walking in the streets below as she looks out. I will continue to look out of my untidy, tiny, run-down house, in the exact spot she looked out with me. Does she remember the view? You may pass the streets I look out on. The daily grind will continue, nothing will change, and the illusive creatures we are, you will forget our existence, even as you face her, face me, talk to us, your mind won't whisper, "Colette", "the unnamed narrator". We will come into your lives, touch your lives and quietly sneak away again, and you still won't know. You will come into ours, sometimes save us in ways we can never repay, and we will never forget, and still you will never know.

This is an ordinary end to an ordinary tale about two ordinary people. We don't stand out from ordinary. It is pretty sunny outside now. An ordinary world beckons this cub. I turn and look at you. Maybe I'll wear jeans, or combats, a colour other than black, anything I haven't worn for one hundred and twenty-one days. Put back on my ordinary clothes and slip out into the ordinary afternoon. Complete with my ordinary black leather coat, and ordinary shades, and that look, you know the one, just a little look less ordinary.